Luke put his a̶

him.

'Kitty love, I want you to think of all that's gone in the past as "Yesterday's Road". Tomorrow or the next day you'll be branching out on another road—and who knows what you might eventually find at the end of it?'

Two days later, Kitty took a final walk to her familiar haunts and saw everything with a new clarity: the copse of beech trees, glowing warmly in the autumn sun; the sparkling water of the stream rustling over brown mottled pebbles; the straight line of stately poplars in the distance which had always fascinated her. Then she climbed to the top of the rise and gazed at the white road that snaked its way to the next village.

'Yesterday's Road,' she thought, her heart breaking.

The wind stung her skin and when she turned to go back to the farm to say her goodbyes, the tears running down her cheeks seemed to turn to ice.

YESTERDAY'S ROAD

Mary Minton

ARROW BOOKS

Arrow Books Limited
62-65 Chandos Place, London WC2N 4NW

An imprint of Century Hutchinson Limited

London Melbourne Sydney Auckland
Johannesburg and agencies throughout
the world

First published in Great Britain by Century 1986
Arrow edition 1987

Printed and bound in Great Britain by
Anchor Brendon Limited, Tiptree, Essex

ISBN 0 09 952760 X

To my dear husband Robert
with love and thanks for all his help and understanding

Acknowledgement

My grateful thanks to Mr John Cook, Head of Glass and Ceramics at Leicester Polytechnic, who so patiently explained the art of glass-blowing and allowed me to try my hand at it.

Yesterday's Road has been travelled; a new road is waiting to be explored.

Emmalina Fowkes

CHAPTER ONE

It was the end of the weekly market at Mealton and the stallholders were packing up. The residue of the day's wares was being swept from the stalls to the ground, adding to the litter of bruised fruit, broken eggs, vegetable leaves and broken pots.

Through this litter trudged a woman with a child clutched in her arms. Every now and then she stopped to enquire the whereabouts of Abel Leddenshaw, only to be told in each case that he was 'somewhere's around'.

Naptha flares were being extinguished one by one, the acrid smell catching at the woman's throat, the taste lingering on her tongue. She must find Mr Leddenshaw; she must hand over the child to him before he left for home, for she could travel no further.

Part of the area was now in darkness and she made a last desperate plea to a man who was packing the last of his jam and maslin pans on to a cart.

'*Please*, can you help me? I need to find Mr Leddenshaw, Abel Leddenshaw. It's terribly important!'

'Abel? Saw him a minute ago. Yes, there he is over there.' He pointed to where a stocky, middle-aged man was fastening the flap of his wagon.

The woman murmured her thanks and went over to him.

'Mr Leddenshaw?'

He turned. 'Aye, that's my name.'

'Thank God, I thought I was never going to find you.' There was a pause then, 'Margaret sent me.'

'Margaret?' Abel's voice held the sharpness of surprise.

1

'She worked for you when she was younger. So you remember her?'

'Remember her? She was like a daughter to us. What happened? My wife and I searched for her for months. Do you know her whereabouts?'

'I'm unable to say. But this is her child; she begs that you and your wife will take care of her, she's been badly treated.'

'Yes, yes, we'll look after the child, we'll be glad to, but I must know about Margaret. Where is she living?'

'A long ways from here, sir. It's taken us days to get here, travelling by cart and wagon. I've given Kitty a little laudanum to help her over this last part of the journey. She should sleep the rest of the way. Could you please take her, sir? My arms are numb.'

'Yes, of course.' Abel handled the child with the gentle care he would give to a sick or injured animal. 'You called her Kitty – how old is she?'

'Nearly seven. Normally she's a lively child, but ...' The woman's voice tailed off as though there was much she would like to tell but had orders not to divulge. She added urgently, 'Margaret did beg that you would give Kitty your name, so that she will be safe from ... from anyone enquiring about her.'

Abel agreed at once and was so concerned about the child it was some seconds before he realized the woman had gone. He called to her to wait, but she had been swallowed up in the blackness. What was he to do? He could make a bed for the little girl in the back of the wagon – there was plenty of straw, a blanket, sacks – but she was so feather-light there could be little flesh on her. The woman had said she needed attention – did she need the attention of a doctor? How ill was she?

The child was wrapped from head to foot in a shawl and her face in the darkness was just a pale blur. Abel felt her forehead, then put a finger to her temple and, finding her heartbeats regular, decided to go straight home. Harriet would care for the little mite, while it could take an hour to find a doctor.

Abel made as comfortable a bed as he could in the back of the wagon and laid his charge carefully on it. He would keep a constant eye on her during the journey. The laudanum would help to ease the discomfort of the rough roads. Not that he approved of the wholesale use of the stuff, for too much could

2

kill, but the woman had said she had given her just a little.

He went round to the front of the wagon and climbed on to the seat. Then, after sitting deep in thought for a moment, he touched the mare's rump with the tip of his whip and said softly, 'All right. Bess girl, get going, and take it easy – we've a child with bird-bones aboard.' He urged the mare into the stream of traffic leaving the ground.

Adding to the rumble of wheels on the hard-packed earth road was the jangling of harness, the coarse jests of traders, the barking of dogs as they darted amongst the feet of horses and cattle and the curses of the men driving them. There was a fretful wail of tired children, the bawdy shouting of whores …

Abel was glad when he had left the mêlée and started on the quieter roads for his half-hour's drive home.

This was the time of market day that he usually enjoyed, the quiet contemplation after the hustle and bustle, especially on a still night like this with the autumnal mist hovering over hollows and the only sounds the occasional hooting of an owl or bark of a fox. But tonight he was not only troubled about the child, but also her mother. If the little girl had been badly treated, what about Margaret herself?

Abel thought of the day when he had found Margaret at the annual hiring fair; a twelve-year-old clutching at her shabby dress, her eyes dilated with fear as a burly man – the worse for drink – kept offering more and more for her services. Abel had stepped quickly between them and recklessly raised the terms and Margaret had come to him.

How dear she had become to them, and how grieved he and Harriet had been when, at sixteen, she had fallen in love with a hired hand at a neighbouring farm. No, not fallen in love – she had become besotted with the handsome braggart, who had eventually talked her into running away and getting married. They *had* got married, it was the only thing they knew from the one letter Margaret had sent. It was postmarked Derby, but when Abel travelled there he found the couple gone – no one knew where – and from then on there had been silence.

Now they had her child – and she would be welcomed as her mother had been, loved as were their four sons.

The boys, all sturdy and boisterous, were away for the day helping the dilatory Whittakers with their late harvesting. Abel hoped he would have time to get the little girl settled and talk to Harriet before they returned.

The weather had been dry for weeks and some of the ruts made by heavy downpours of early summer rain were now rock-hard. Abel tried to avoid the deepest, but there were times when the wheels dropped into them, jolting the wagon.

When this happened the child was roused from her drugged sleep to be plunged once more into the nightmare world of pain. First there would be the creeping cold that paralysed limbs, then would come the agonizing heat as flesh was pinched to restore life to arms and legs. It was not the lovely heat of the furnaces ... Furnaces?

She could hear voices, a girl's voice, then a man's ... 'You're a bad girl, our Kitty, wicked, I hate you ...' Then a booming voice shouted, 'She'll have to be punished, to be taught she must obey ...'

There were bright colours under her eyelids – yellow, gold, orange and a lovely bubble of glass. All so beautiful, yet somehow linked with the pain. She began to whimper.

Mercifully, oblivion came again.

It was nearly midnight when Abel reached the farm. When he carried the child into the kitchen Harriet, who was busy at the fire, said over her shoulder, 'You're late this evening, Abel, your supper's spoiling.'

The next moment she was staring at the bundle in his arms. 'What? Who?'

He explained what had happened and she came hurrying over. 'Margaret's daughter? I can hardly believe it. How is she? Who brought her to you? No, tell me later, this poor little thing must be attended to.'

Harriet sat near the fire with the child on her lap and undid the shawl. Then she looked up at her husband, her eyes full of distress. 'Oh, Abel, she must have been starved, she's just skin and bone. I'll get her clothes off. Reach me one of the boys' shirts.'

When Kitty was undressed both husband and wife stared at her, appalled. Her arms and legs were like sticks and there were bruises all over her body. 'How could anyone do this to a child?' Harriet exclaimed. 'Margaret could not have been responsible,

4

she was much too gentle. It must have been that braggart of a husband of hers!'

Abel looked grim. 'If it was, he deserves to be hung, drawn and quartered and I should like to be the one to do it! I'll find out, Harriet, I promise you, and the one responsible will suffer.'

Kitty's wrists and ankles were bandaged and although the pieces of rag were clean they were bloodstained in parts. When the rags were removed, cries of horror came from Harriet.

'She's been tied hand and foot! Look at the wounds. No child, however naughty, deserves such treatment. Fetch me some warm water, Abel, and some ointment. I must get her to bed. I'll sit up with her tonight; then if she rouses, I'll try and get her to take some gruel.'

Some time later Kitty had a feeling of sinking into softness, warmth enveloped her. This time when she gave a little whimper it was one of pleasure.

When Harriet came downstairs she said, 'I think she'll recover quickly; already there's a difference in her, as though she knows she's being cared for. Poor little Kitty, there must be something tough about her for her to have survived what she has been through. Days of journeying, you say? From where, Abel?'

Abel had to admit he was unable to answer her, and knew this was only the first of many questions his wife would ask.

It was four days before Kitty reached a level of consciousness where she was able to take in her surroundings. Although she had no idea where or who she was, she had a feeling she was safe. The bed was soft, the covers soft. The small room had whitewashed walls, flowered curtains. When a woman came in and spoke her voice was soft too. She had a round face, a round body.

'Hello, Kitty love! You've been ill, but you're much better now. I'll bring you some breakfast – a lightly-boiled egg, fresh laid this morning.'

Kitty thought she had seen an egg, but she had no memory of tasting one. The woman smiled at her, then went out. Kitty looked around her again. Where could she be? She tried to draw herself up in the bed, but found she had no strength. The woman had called her Kitty, so that must be her name. Was the woman her mother?

5

When Harriet returned with a tray, Kitty asked her.

'No,' Harriet said, 'but you've come to live with us. Our name is Leddenshaw, we live on a farm. We have four sons. We knew your mother when she was a little girl; she lived with us then. I think for the time being you must call me Aunt Harriet and my husband Uncle Abel. You will meet our boys later. Now, let me see you eat a good breakfast!'

Kitty ate all the egg, which Harriet fed to her, and liked it. She remembered then that she had tasted an egg, but never had a whole one to herself. It was all very bewildering, but when she started to ask questions she fell asleep.

And that was how it was for several days – waking, being fed and then dropping off to sleep again. But there came a time when the sleep was not so deep, when she was aware of people coming into the room and of whispering voices. Once she made out four faces, and although they were hazy she felt sure they were all men. One of the men touched her cheek gently. 'Hurry up and get well, little Kitty, then I can show you all the animals.' She knew his name because Aunt Harriet had said, 'Come along, Luke, we must let Kitty sleep now.'

It was after this that Kitty became aware of sounds. She would know it was early morning by the clattering of pails, the shouts of men, hens clucking. The first time she heard the hens, she remembered that they were the ones to give eggs.

Then would come a lot of movement downstairs and she would know the men had come in for breakfast. There was much talking, laughter. When they left the house again, Kitty would try to picture them, but the only one she had firmly fixed in her mind was Luke. She thought he had blue eyes and thick fair hair.

From sitting in a chair while her bed was being made, Kitty progressed to her first visit downstairs. Harriet wrapped her in a blanket and carried her into the kitchen. 'There, now, Kitty, I'll put you beside the fire.'

As she was put in a high-backed chair with wooden arms, a wave of terror swept over Kitty; she struggled out of the chair and slid to the floor. 'No, no—'

'Kitty – oh, my love, what is it?' Harriet picked her up and cradled her. 'I won't sit you near the fire if you don't want me to.'

Harriet, noticing the scarred wrists, suddenly wondered if the chair was responsible for the child's fear. If she had been tied to a similar one? Harriet pushed it back and brought forward an old cane chair with a cushion. 'How's that?'

Kitty seemed to settle in it all right and a few minutes later Harriet said, 'I'm going outside for a few minutes, but I won't be long. You'll be all right now, won't you?'

After Harriet had gone Kitty looked around her. The floor was stone-flagged, with a bright handmade rug in front of the fireplace. The fire was roaring up the chimney.

In a sudden silence Kitty became aware of a gentle tick-tocking and when she glanced over her shoulder she realized the sound came from a big standing clock.

She found herself thinking of the rhyme: Hickory dickory dock, the mouse ran up the clock . . .

A mouse could run up this clock, but it could not have run up the tiny little clock that stood on the mantelpiece at . . . at where? A picture flashed into her mind of an empty grate, the ticking clock that had ticked in her head – then the momentary image was gone, leaving her full of fear again.

When Harriet came in, Abel was with her. She said to Kitty, 'This is your Uncle Abel who brought you to the farm.' Kitty's fear died, for she liked this man with the grey hair. She had met him before.

'Hello, Kitty,' he said gently. 'I'm glad to see you downstairs. You'll meet my three older sons later, but I want you to meet our youngest son Luke – he's here now and has a surprise for you.'

Then Luke was there and he did not have blue eyes as she had imagined, nor did he have fair hair. His eyes were a warm brown and his hair was the colour of the copper jug that belonged to . . . Belonged to who . . . ?

'Hello, Kitty!' Luke said. 'You'll soon be well enough to go with me around the farmyard. In the meantime I have a little present for you.' He held out a tiny kitten. 'She doesn't have a name yet, but perhaps you can give her one?'

The kitten was a golden colour, with a black nose and paws. Kitty held it to her, put it to her face, crooned over it. When she looked up there was a joyousness in her. 'I shall call her Punty.'

The three adults exchanged wondering glances. Harriet said, 'That's a strange name – why Punty?'

'Because of the lovely glass bubbles,' she answered promptly. But when Harriet tried to question her about the glass bubbles and Kitty frowned deeply in concentration, Abel said, 'We'll get to know another time, just enjoy your little kitten.'

Kitty, unfortunately, got so excited playing with the kitten she became feverish and had to go back to bed again, so it was not until two days later that she met the other three Leddenshaw boys.

When Harriet brought her downstairs she put her beside the fire, but no sooner had she gone into the larder than she heard a scuffling sound, and on looking out saw that Kitty had seated herself on a small stool in a corner, the kitten held close to her.

Harriet, studying her, felt a tug at her emotions. The child was so like her mother had looked the day Abel brought her from the hirings. The dark, widely-spaced eyes that looked too big for the elfin face. Margaret had never lost that elfin look, but then that had been a part of her appeal.

A strong gust of wind brought a wild pattering of rain on the window-panes. It had deluged all day. Abel was working in the barn, but the boys were outdoors and they would be soaked. Harriet piled some more logs on to the fire.

Ten minutes later the door burst open and four figures came hurtling in, jostling, laughing, joking. Kitty, watching them from her corner, saw that Luke's brothers were the blue-eyed, fair-haired ones, and that they were all taller. The tallest of the three called:

'Ma! We're home and we're all famished!'

Harriet came bustling in from the larder. 'And drenched! Get those wet things off and come to the fire. What a day!'

Coats were discarded, boots unlaced and kicked off. Chairs were drawn up to the fire and four pairs of stockinged feet were held out to the blaze. Soon clouds of steam were rising and the pungent smell of toasting wool mingled with the aroma of roasting meat.

Harriet came over to Kitty, took her by the hand and brought her to meet her three older sons.

'Andrew – James – Matthew – I want you to meet your little foster-sister Kitty.' They jumped up and then all three were smiling, welcoming her. Kitty, suddenly overcome with shyness, hid her face in Harriet's skirts.

Her shyness persisted until Abel came in and when during the meal he and the boys began to talk about the animals and the work they had been doing, she listened absorbed and felt somehow she had been a part of this family and this happiness for ever.

It was still raining the following morning, but a watery sun promised better weather later. Harriet gave Kitty little jobs to do to keep her occupied. She would get her to bring a big spoon from the kitchen table drawer, some apples from the larder to make apple dumplings. She sent her for the flour dredger and the net cover for the milk jug. Kitty was so long fetching the net cover Harriet went to the larder to see what she was doing and saw her fingering the glass beads round the edges of the milk-jug cover.

'Do you like the little beads?' Harriet enquired. 'They're like crystal tears, aren't they? Come and bring them to the window and hold them up to the light; then you'll see all sorts of lovely colours.'

Kitty seemed totally absorbed for a moment, then she put the net cover on the table and ran to her corner, where she sat on the stool with her back to Harriet.

Harriet, bewildered, waited a moment then went over to her. She bent down. 'Kitty love, what is it? Why did the beads upset you?'

The child shook her head and was silent. Harriet gathered her into her arms and held her close. Kitty's whole body was trembling as Harriet stroked the dark hair. Poor little mite! Would it be right to probe further? Yet if she was unable to find out what was wrong, there could be a repetition of this fear. So she must try, but she would do it gently.

'I love the little glass beads, Kitty, have done since I was small. You love Punty and you said you had called her that name because of the lovely glass bubbles. There's nothing to be afraid of.'

For a moment Kitty buried her face against Harriet's neck, then the trembling ceased and she raised her head. Holding out her left hand, she circled the scarred wrist with her right one.

The kitten suddenly began to mew at their feet and Kitty wriggled to be down. The next moment she was playing with it, happily trailing a paper ball on a piece of string which Luke had given her.

So, Harriet thought, glass definitely had something to do with the child being bound hand and foot ... and starved. In time, perhaps they would get to know the connection. For now she would let the matter rest.

Later that morning Luke came in to fetch Kitty to see the animals. Harriet had fashioned her a hooded cape from a blanket and Abel had managed to get her a pair of boots from a neighbour. Any shyness Kitty had felt towards Luke was now gone. She moved from one foot to the other in her excitement at getting out and gave in without a protest when Luke insisted the kitten be left behind for the time being.

When he held out a hand and said, 'Well, let's get going then,' she slipped her hand into his and smiled up at him. He chucked her gently under the chin. 'You're a pretty lass, Kitty, when you smile like that. You'll have all the lads after you when you grow up!'

Kitty was not quite sure what he meant, but she knew it must be something nice by the way Luke was smiling.

Harriet called when they were at the door; 'You'll have to carry her, Luke, the yard's a quagmire.' Luke made to pick up Kitty but she ran on ahead and, childlike, began stamping her feet in the mud.

Then she stopped as she saw a line of geese coming towards her, wings outspread. At first she thought them very amusing with their honking and hissing sounds, but when she realized the sounds were angry ones and directed at her she turned and ran back to Luke.

He swept her up, shooed the birds away then said, 'Be warned, Kitty – you can't treat all the animals on the farm like you do Punty. Geese are marvellous watchdogs but they'll attack a stranger.'

A loud bellowing came from a barn further along as Luke started to walk towards it. 'I'm going to let you see Albert the bull, but you must never, Kitty, *not ever*, go anywhere near him unless one of us is with you. Do you understand?'

She nodded. Then, putting her hand on his cheek, she turned his face towards her. 'Why mustn't I go near him?'

'Because he might get mad and charge you, break down his

door, trample on you.' Luke wondered if he had gone a little too far – if he had scared Kitty to death – but the only effect it had on her was her look of interest.

'Why would he do that if I showed him I liked him?'

'Because he's a bull.'

'Oh,' Kitty said, as if that answered all the questions.

The bellowing became louder. Luke opened the top half of the barn door and spoke soothingly to the animal, who was tossing his head about. 'It's all right, Albert, it's just Kitty who's with me. She's our foster-sister and lives with us.' The bellowing stopped as though the animal understood.

Kitty was upset about the bull having a ring through its nose. No wonder it cried, she said – Luke would cry if he had a ring through *his* nose! He agreed, but since he was getting a little out of his depth he suggested they go to see Andrew and James who were 'muck-raking' around the corner.

The two brothers, who were shovelling the muck from a big pile on to a cart, paused as Luke called and gave Kitty a cheery wave and a greeting. She had to know, of course, what they were doing and it was Andrew who explained that the cart would be taken to a field and spread over the ground. It was manure, he added, and it fertilized the soil. Luke, seeing Kitty's mind working and guessing she was puzzling over the word 'fertilized', told her quickly he was going to take her to see Matthew ploughing and his father tending the sheep. Then, raising his eyes skywards at his brothers, he moved away leaving Andrew and James chuckling.

They left the yard, walked through a spinney and came to the fields. There Kitty saw land being ploughed for the first time and was fascinated as to how the furrows could be so straight. To her questioning on this Luke said, 'It's practice, Kitty. Practice makes perfect. It's something you have to learn how to do.'

'Like making a bottle out of a bubble of glass,' she said.

Luke felt his heartbeats quicken. This could be another step forward if he handled it carefully.

'Yes, just like that, Kitty.' After a pause he added, speaking lightly, 'And can *you* make a bottle out of a bubble of glass?'

She gave her infectious little giggle. 'No, silly, only men can make them! But Grandma Perkins said—'

When she stopped and Luke saw the familiar deep frown of

concentration, he prompted, 'And what was it Grandma Perkins said?'

Kitty shook her head. 'I don't know. I don't know who she is.'

'Perhaps you'll remember later. Oh, look, there's Father, up there in the top field. Can you see him?'

Abel was walking among the sheep, his dog Shep close to his side. When Kitty first saw the dog she had wanted to pet him, but was told gently by Abel he was not to be fussed. She had not questioned this at the time, but now she asked Luke why she could not play with Shep.

'Because he's a working dog,' Luke explained, 'and working dogs have only one master and that master must *always* be obeyed.'

He felt Kitty tense in his arms, then she began to tremble. Luke felt distressed at bringing the fear back to her by his questioning. He told her he would take her to the woods, where perhaps they might see the squirrels. They did see some squirrels and Kitty, charmed by them, relaxed again.

When they got back home and Harriet asked how Luke had got on with Kitty, he smiled and said, 'I feel more exhausted than doing a day's haymaking. She's got a lively mind, interested in everything. I think she has the making of a farmer's wife!'

'Perhaps, but I feel there's something different about Kitty. Last month the vicar spoke of Miss Peverill as being artistic – she had fashioned a picture of coloured wools, making up the scene as she went along. Well, I think Kitty is artistic. To me an autumn leaf is just a leaf, but to Kitty it's a thing of great beauty. There was one flattened on the larder floor the other day, which I must have carried in on my foot. Kitty knelt down and traced a finger gently over the veins, then talked about the colours with such feeling and I was sure there were tears in her eyes.'

Luke nodded, his expression thoughtful. 'You could be right, Ma.' He told her what Kitty had said about a bottle being made from a bubble of glass and they talked about it, but came no nearer to guessing where she might have lived. Harriet said she thought it would be just as well to let things take their course, never to encourage the child to talk about the past if it distressed her.

Harriet's next experience of Kitty's artistic nature came when on the Saturday morning she took her to help decorate the church for harvest festival.

The sound of muted voices reached them before Harriet pushed open the door; many helpers were already there, including children. Kitty stopped and gripped Harriet's hand as her eyes, round with wonder and awe, took in parts of the church which were already decorated. She saw mounds of rosy apples and golden pears set between ferns and glossy green foliage; saw vines festooned around pillars, men carrying large pots of shrubs to the chancel; watched women handling bunches of grapes and branches of tiny yellow crab-apples. Then she moved forward as she saw the children kneeling on a bed of straw, sorting through corn and oats and fashioning them into small sheaves. She looked up enquiringly at Harriet and in a whisper asked if she could help.

Harriet took her to the children and introduced her and although they were shy with one another at first, Harriet saw later they were all whispering together and that Kitty was making sheaves with nimble fingers.

Harriet was busy helping the other women for a time and when she glanced round again to see if Kitty was all right, she was astonished to see the child decorating hoops with fruit and flowers to go on the window-sills.

'She's a very bright child,' one of the women said. 'When she gets over her illness, you must send her to school.' Harriet agreed.

That evening when the boys and Abel were home Kitty, her cheeks flushed with excitement, described every little detail of decoration both inside and outside the church, even to the small lych-gate which had been draped and twined with ivy and flowers.

She had never seen grapes before and spoke of them in a dreamy way as having 'mist on their skins'. Harriet looked at Abel and said in low tones with a note of pride, 'Kitty belongs to another world, not one of farming.'

But as the months went by Kitty showed a great aptitude for farming life. She was here, there and everywhere, collecting eggs – never breaking one – feeding the hens, turning the handle of the churn at butter-making. She learned how to knit, to darn, to sew on buttons. And she was always asking if she could make cakes. Once or twice Harriet had let her make scones.

Abel put his foot down about Kitty going to school. Not yet, he said, perhaps in a few months' time. What he feared was that the children would start asking her questions about her parents and could set Kitty back in that fearful world of pain. When he felt she was completely well, he would let her go. In the meantime they could give her some teaching themselves.

It was mainly Luke who taught her to read and write; he was the pivot around which Kitty's life revolved. She would sit in the evening with the kitten on her lap, repeating words, adding up two digit figures, always anxiously awaiting Luke's approval. When he scolded her for daydreaming she looked so unhappy he stopped scolding and encouraged her to learn by promising little treats: he would take her to market, take her up to the fields, take her to a neighbouring farm.

Kitty still retained her elfin look, but she had lost the awful skinniness of the starved body and no longer frowned in deep concentration as though trying to recall the past.

Then one day Luke took her to see the litter of piglets which had been born in the early hours. Kitty laughed at the way the tiny animals pushed and shoved each other to get at their mother to feed.

'They must be very hungry,' she said. 'How many boy piglets has Peggy had and how many girls?'

'Only one son and nine daughters! Think what a terrible life that boy is going to have with nine sisters!'

'I have four sisters,' Kitty said, as she gently scratched the sow's back with a piece of twig.

Luke, ignoring the rules he had made for himself, said, 'Oh, and what are their names?'

The frown of concentration was back. 'V-Vi-Violet and—' Kitty suddenly glanced at Luke, the fear back in her eyes, and dropping the twig she turned from him and ran.

It was Harriet who caught her as she was coming out of the dairy. 'Kitty, love, what's happened? Where're you going?'

Luke was there by then and he picked her up and held her close. 'It's all right, Kitty, I'm here. No one is going to harm you.' She leaned her head against his shoulder and sobbed.

It was some time before they could calm her and for the rest of the evening it was impossible to get a word out of her. Harriet tucked her up in bed early and for once let her have the kitten in her room.

At three o'clock that morning, the household was roused by Kitty screaming. When Harriet tried to pick her up out of bed the child fought, shouting, 'Don't hurt me, don't hurt me—'

Abel, this time, was the only one who could calm her, probably because in the recesses of her mind she remembered him as the person who had brought her to the farm. He sat with her until she fell asleep, then the family went downstairs to discuss the problem.

Abel said, 'The poor child will never be rid of her fears until we learn the truth. Tomorrow I'll start making enquiries. There's wagons coming in from the North, from the South; I'll start questioning drivers. Somebody, somewhere, might know the whereabouts of Margaret and her husband, who had four daughters, one of them called Violet ...'

CHAPTER TWO

For weeks Abel questioned people on carts, wagons, wagonettes and on horseback, begging for information on Kitty's family, but drew a blank. He was worried about the child, for Kitty's nightmare had made deep inroads into her emotions; she had withdrawn into herself and although carrying out allotted tasks, she did them in a mechanical way. She would hardly let the kitten out of her sight and clung more and more to Luke.

This worried Harriet. 'She's becoming too dependent on you, Luke. What's going to happen if your Uncle Jed's not out of bed soon and you have to go and help out? Your aunt says he's real poorly.'

Luke told her not to worry; he would explain to Kitty that it would not be for long, he would be back. But the time came when he did have to leave, and when her thin little arms tightened round his neck and her big dark eyes held a terrible misery, he felt an ache.

'It's all right, little love,' he said softly. 'I'll be back soon. Now be a good girl, look after Punty and help Aunt Harriet. She'll need extra help with me away.' Luke set her to the ground. 'Come to the gate and then you can wave to me.'

Kitty stood watching him until he was out of sight and Harriet, watching the solitary little figure and sensing that the child was crying inwardly, felt a lump come into her throat. What were they going to do about Kitty? If she went on in this way, she could fret herself into a decline.

Abel said, 'Be patient, Harriet. Just wait until Luke's back and can finish off the doll's cradle he's making for her. By then you'll have finished the doll to go in it. That'll perk Kitty up!'

When Luke did return a week later some of the misery went from Kitty's eyes, but she was still withdrawn and Harriet found herself longing for the moment when she would receive her gifts. Margaret had been almost delirious with happiness when she had been given her first doll.

Luke had spent hours on the cradle, carving the sides and hood, and although the doll Harriet had made was just a rag one, she had embroidered the face and dressed it with scraps coaxed from the village seamstress.

To the disappointment not only of Harriet but Abel and the boys, Kitty showed little interest in the presents given so lovingly. She thanked them politely and from time to time would rock the cradle with her foot, but made no attempt to nurse the doll as she nursed Punty.

'Why, Abel, why?' Harriet appealed to her husband on a tearful note. 'It's not natural. All little girls will cuddle a doll, even if it's just a stick with a piece of rag tied around it. What's happened to change Kitty? She was so happy for a time.'

Abel shook his head and told her they must put their faith in the Lord – only He knew the answer and no doubt He would let them know in His own good time.

The following day Harriet was further distressed to find the doll was no longer in the cot nor anywhere to be found. And despite the gentle coaxing of Harriet, Abel and Luke, Kitty maintained a stony silence.

The puzzle remained until the following morning when Andrew went to clean out the pigsties and found the doll soiled and trampled in a corner.

Harriet discussed this in a shocked whisper. What had happened to make such a warm, loving child as Kitty resort to such a thing? Had she been given a doll, lavished love on it then been deprived of it and in consequence hated all dolls? Abel said he thought this as good a guess as any, but added that it was not to be talked about any more. The whole thing must be forgotten and Kitty was not to be spoiled in view of what had happened. The more normally the family behaved towards her, the more quickly she would become part of the family.

This did work to a certain extent. Kitty began to talk to Harriet, mostly about the animals. The kitten had replaced the doll in the cot and enjoyed the gentle rocking movement. It

17

would lie contentedly on its back, paws over the coverlet, blinking, yawning and making little mewing sounds.

Harriet would laugh, declaring Punty to be the laziest little kitten she had ever known, but no smile ever touched Kitty's lips.

Then in February with the snow thick on the ground, the ewes began to drop their lambs. And it was when Abel came in with a motherless lamb that Kitty came to life. Harriet had put a box near the fire, saying the lamb would have to be hand-fed, and Kitty begged to be allowed to do it. Harriet, seeing the child's eagerness, her eyes alight with interest, agreed, but warned she would have to hold tightly on to the bottle as a lamb sucked strongly and could wrest the bottle from her.

For Kitty it was a game and she chuckled with delight when she found she had to hold on to the bottle with both hands to control it. Afterwards she hugged the lamb, making crooning noises to it. At bedtime she sang a little lullaby to it in a sweet treble voice, a lullaby Harriet had not heard before which tugged at her heartstrings.

Sleep my little lamb, do not stir,
See the fires shining bright.
All is warm, all is light,
Ssh, my little lamb, I have you tight.

The next morning Kitty begged to be allowed to go to the field where the ewes were lambing. 'I won't touch them,' she said, 'I promise.'

Abel, who had made her a pair of leather gaiters, said, 'All right – get dressed Kitty, but I warn you, you must stay well away from the sheep. Sometimes one will get on its back then can't get up. When this happens, one of us will turn her over on to her side; then she'll leap up and if you get a kick from her hooves she could hurt you badly.' Kitty promised faithfully she would not go near and after Harriet had tied a shawl around her under her cape Kitty went off, trotting happily at Luke's side, every now and then kicking at the snow with the toe of her boot, a joyousness in her.

The morning was clear and bright but with an icy, capricious wind sweeping up flurries of powdery snow, building up drifts. The morning was filled with sound – the plaintive baa-baaing of sheep, the shouts of men, the barking of Shep, the mournful lowing of cattle in the byres and the incessant squawking of hens.

Once they reached the fields Kitty began her questioning. Why had Uncle Abel said that lambs were dropping all over the place? Where were they dropping from? Andrew, who had come up, grinned at Luke and said, 'I'll leave you to answer that one!'

Luke, to avoid answering the question, directed Kitty's interest to where men were building a windbreaker of wattle and straw, explaining that when a lamb was born one of the men would carry it behind the windbreaker where the mother would follow and use it. Kitty was greatly interested in this and had started to ask more questions when Luke stopped suddenly, ordered Kitty to stay where she was, not to move a step, and went hurrying away.

He stopped a sheep who was bleating as though in pain and a moment later Kitty witnessed the process of a lamb being born.

She was awestruck when she saw small hooves appear first, then the head tucked between them as if the tiny animal was diving to earth. And finally she felt tearful when she watched the lamb tottering on its spindly legs. She wanted to run to it, hold it close, but dared not because of Abel's and Luke's instructions.

She was further amazed when she saw a second head appear and another lamb dropping to the ground. Luke, gathering up a lamb in each arm, carried them to the windbreaker and set them down behind it. Within seconds the mother had followed. Luke called to Kitty and she saw the mother cleaning her offspring then nursing them. Luke then drew her away, saying, 'That is what it means by being born, Kitty.'

For once she asked no questions. Nor did she chatter excitedly to Harriet about what she had seen when she was brought back to the house. For the rest of that day she was quiet and thoughtful, and spent a lot of time beside the motherless lamb.

The following day a second orphaned lamb was brought to the kitchen and Kitty, using a phrase of Harriet's, said quaintly, 'We're going to have our hands full, aren't we?'

Harriet laughed with relief, having felt that Kitty's experience of the day before might have sobered her, made her too adult for her age. But Kitty ran around doing first one job and then another, talking in between to both lambs and the kitten, telling them what a busy time it was.

Once the lambing season was over, Kitty settled down to her lessons in the evening, putting figures and letters on her piece of slate with a slate pencil that screeched, setting Harriet's teeth on edge as it had done when her boys came home from school with lessons to do. Harriet felt that Kitty was ready to go to school, but Abel did not agree and it was not until the woods were carpeted with bluebells and the fields golden with celandines that he allowed her to go.

Kitty had an eager, questing mind and learned quickly. Luke teased her one day, telling her she would probably end up being a schoolmarm. To this Kitty replied promptly, without looking up, 'Oh, no, when I grow up I'm going to go to Italy.'

The adults exchanged glances, then after a moment's silence Luke said, 'Why do you want to go there, Kitty? Italy is a long way away.'

She nodded. 'Yes, I know, it's across the sea. You have to go on a ship. I would like to go across the sea on a ship. I've seen them at the . . .' she struggled to find the word '. . . quay-side.'

They were all alert now and Harriet whispered to Abel, 'Which quay-side?' He raised his shoulders in a helpless gesture. Then suddenly, disregarding the orders that he himself had given about Kitty, he began to question her.

Who had told her about Italy? To this Kitty replied, 'Grandma Perkins,' but when he asked her who Grandma Perkins was, she put pencil and slate away and then came and stood in front of him. 'I don't know who she is, Uncle Abel.' Then she climbed on to his lap and laid her head against his shoulder.

Abel held her close, feeling deeply moved. It was only on odd occasions that Kitty came and sat on his lap and he always felt that the child was remembering, in some recesses of her mind, the night when the woman had brought her to him at the market – and knew that with Abel she had found safety.

He stroked her hair, rocked her to and fro and presently Kitty fell asleep. Harriet undressed her and carried her up to bed. When she came down, Abel and the boys were discussing the various ports where a ship to Italy could embark.

Matthew suggested it might be the London docks, but Abel said that Kitty did not have a Southern accent – in fact, it was a mixture of the Midlands and the North. No doubt in time they would get to know the rest of the story.

But months went by without Kitty giving any hint about anything more to do with her past life.

She was a tidy child, always putting away everything she had been working on, but one evening she went to bed without putting her slate in the cupboard. Harriet picked it up, expecting to find it wiped clean as always, and was surprised to see writing on it.

Then as she saw one word repeated all down the slate, she stood with heartbeats quickening.

The one word was MOTHER; it was something that had never been mentioned to Kitty. Harriet would have liked Kitty to call her Mother, but dared not suggest it in case there was a time when Margaret came to claim her. What had been going through the child's mind? Had the children at school been asking her about her parents? If so, what had Kitty replied? Was there a longing in her to know her own mother?

After Harriet had tossed the problem round in her mind, she decided that Kitty had a right to know she had been brought to them for the best of reasons: out of love. She would tell the child when the right opportunity came, whether Abel approved or not.

Abel, as it turned out, did approve and so Harriet told Kitty on the Saturday afternoon when the house was quiet. She told her about Margaret coming to live with them because her parents were dead – which was true; told her about her mother running away to get married, making this sound most romantic; then explained that when Kitty's parents had become poor – too poor to give her proper food and care – they had sent her to the farm to be looked after.

'Your parents did it because they loved you so much,' Harriet concluded gently.

During the explanation Kitty's expression had never changed. All she had shown was an interest, but when Harriet told her about being given into the care of Harriet and Abel because of love for her, a light came into her eyes and she asked at once if her mother would come for her some day.

21

Harriet said, 'Yes, I'm sure she will, Kitty, if she possibly can. Until then, I hope you'll be happy with us.'

'Oh, I am, Aunt Harriet.' She flung her arms around Harriet. 'Very happy, I love you all!'

*

Two years went by and although Kitty was mostly lively and energetic, there were times when Harriet would see her standing motionless at the field gate, staring into the distance as though watching for her mother. Then Harriet would suffer with her.

Kitty had made friends with the children from a neighbouring farm and at hay-time she romped with them, had rides on the hay-wagon. She would always be of slender build, but her skin was tanned now and she glowed with health. Luke teased her once, saying she looked like a gypsy. This pleased Kitty, who told him she would *like* to be a gypsy.

Harriet never turned the gypsies away; she always gave them food and in return one of the women would tell her fortune. She always assured Abel she never believed a scrap of what she had been told, but there were times when some of the forecasts came true and none more so than when she had been told there would be another child in the house, a girl. Harriet, who had always longed for a daughter, had hoped she would become pregnant. It had never occurred to her that it would be Margaret's child who would come into the house.

And on a blustery autumn day when leaves were drifting to the ground and Kitty came running in to announce excitedly that the gypsies were coming, Harriet found herself caught up in the excitement and went into the larder to fill a basket with food. Perhaps the old Romany woman who had foretold Kitty's coming to the house might be able to tell her about Margaret.

With Abel's permission, the gypsies camped in one of the lower fields. There were always tales of gypsies thieving, but they had never stolen anything from Abel or from the house. Abel respected them and they respected him.

Harriet sent Matthew with the basket of food, but refused to allow Kitty to go with him. 'Not yet,' she said. 'We must allow them to get settled. Perhaps tomorrow.' So Kitty had to control her impatience. All she could do was watch from a distance.

She was fascinated by the brightly painted wagons, but

22

disappointed by the drab clothes of the people. Harriet had told her a story once about a gypsy encampment and described all the colourful dresses of the women, the embroidered waistcoats of the men, the strings of beads the women and girls wore, the gold bracelets ...

And yet, as young as Kitty was, she recognized a difference in the gypsy women as compared with the homely farming women. She thought of it in her mind as queenly. Queens and princesses held their heads high. They were proud, Harriet said. Kitty raised her head.

She was in bed that night and on the verge of sleep when she heard the music. She sat up, listened for a few moments then, throwing back the bed-covers, she wriggled over the edge of the bed, dropped to the floor and went over to the window.

There she stood staring at the scene against the background of the woods, wide-eyed, utterly entranced.

By the blazing camp-fire a girl danced. A girl in a red dress with a swirling skirt, the gold bracelets on her arms glinting in the firelight. The people clapped to the strains of a fiddle – it was wild music like the music she had heard at a barn dance, yet it was different, it made little shivers go up and down Kitty's back. She wanted to be there with them.

Then a young man began to sing. He came to the girl and they sang and danced together. Kitty thought she had never seen anything more wonderful, more beautiful – it was so beautiful she wanted to cry.

Then she heard Harriet say gently behind her, 'Kitty love, you ought to be in bed.'

Kitty ran to her. 'Oh, Aunt Harriet, can I go to the gypsies? *I* want to dance and sing.'

'Not tonight.' Harriet picked her up and carried her back to bed. 'This is a special night for them; a young couple have been betrothed, in a few weeks they'll be married. You must go to sleep now, tomorrow I'll take you to the camp.'

Although the room was in darkness, Kitty could still see the bright scene vividly and although her gaze had centred mainly on the couple near the fire, she could now see under her eyelids other women colourfully dressed with many strings of beads about their necks, bracelets on their arms, big golden earrings. Some of the men too had worn earrings, dark-haired men with gold on their waistcoats, gleaming rings on their fingers.

The next morning when Kitty awoke and jumped out of bed to take another look at the camp, she wondered if she had dreamed the incident of the night before. A fire was burning but all was drab again – the men in dark clothes, the children in shabby dresses and the women with black shawls over their heads. A cold wind swept down from the top fields, sending dead leaves cartwheeling over the yard with dry whispers.

But late that morning when Harriet was getting ready to take her to the gypsies, Kitty was skipping about with excitement. 'Come along, Aunt Harriet, hurry! The gypsies might leave and I won't meet them.'

Harriet assured her they would be staying for at least a week before moving on, so she was to curb her impatience or she would be left behind. Kitty stood stiffly, not moving a muscle, then she began to giggle and Harriet laughed too.

'Go on with you!' she said. 'I'm ready now.'

Kitty had thought that all gypsies were dark-haired, but was surprised to find fair-haired adults and children too. Harriet was welcomed by the women, and Kitty was made welcome too after being introduced as her foster-daughter. Harriet was quietly pleased to see that the elderly Romany woman who had previously told her fortune was among the group.

Kitty was sent to play with the other children and all shyness was dissolved by the biscuits that she had brought to give to them.

Harriet talked with the women for a while, then as though by a prearranged signal she was invited into the elderly woman's wagon and motioned to take a seat.

It was spotless, colourful with ornaments, bright rugs pinned to the walls and equally bright rugs on the floor. The woman sitting upright, a dignified figure, said in a soft voice:

'You are troubled, my friend.'

Harriet nodded. 'Yes, it's about my foster-daughter.' She explained the circumstances, then said, her voice earnest, 'I do so want to know if Kitty's mother will come to claim her some day.'

'Yes, she will, but not for some time. You must not try to keep your foster-daughter. The child has a destiny to fulfil. She has a surging spirit, wanting to be free. Control her, but never stop her from being adventurous; never chastise her physically, this child has suffered.'

'Yes, I know. Her mother – Margaret – where is she? How is she, can you tell me? I long to know.'

'That knowledge is denied me. The child dominates. There will be two loves in her life. One of the men she will love is your son; she will be hurt by him.'

'Oh, no!' Harriet protested. 'Luke loves her, but as a sister. He is eight years older.'

The woman smiled. 'Age is no bar to love. You have other sons. Two of them will be courting before Christmas and both will be married the following Christmas.' There was a pause and when the Romany spoke again her expression was sombre. 'A great deal of trouble is brewing in other parts of the world. We will all be involved ...' She closed her eyes and when she remained silent, Harriet knew that the interview was over.

Harriet was not too displeased that two of her sons would be married by the following year, she wanted grandchildren, but she had hoped they would wait a few years before settling down.

Kitty, unaware that Harriet had gone quiet, prattled on about the life of the gypsies. 'They go *everywhere*!' she exclaimed, 'They've even been to London where the Queen lives and seen the palace where she lives, imagine!'

During the next few days Kitty kept running off to the gypsy encampment and it was not until Abel spoke sternly to her that she obeyed his order she was not to go without asking permission.

'The child is headstrong,' he said to Harriet. 'She must be kept on a tight rein, for her own benefit.' Harriet wanted to tell him what the Romany matriarch had told her, but thought it best to keep it to herself. Abel had no time for such prophecies.

At the beginning of the following year Andrew and James began courting and in the September had a double wedding. Kitty was bridesmaid to Andrew's bride Joan; she wore a pale blue cotton dress and a circlet of rosebuds on her dark hair. Her eyes were luminous with tears at the solemnity and beauty of the occasion and Harriet saw then that Kitty had the makings of a beautiful woman.

Both couples moved into cottages not too far from the farm, but had hardly had a chance to get settled in before news came that the English were at war with the Boers.

After that whenever people got together, the talk was all of war. Young men talked of volunteering to join the army and go to South Africa and fight, including all the Leddenshaw boys.

Harriet begged them to wait – the war could soon be over. Abel added his pleas to hers. It would be foolish of them to undertake a journey that could take many weeks and arrive only to find that the war had ended. Luke said if all men thought in this way, the British would be defeated. But they waited.

As the weeks went by, Kitty became familiar with the word 'defeat'. She remembered one incident because of the strange name, Nicholson's Nek, and another by Harriet's horror-stricken gasp as Abel read out, 'Buller's forces defeated at Colenso. A thousand men slaughtered.'

'A *thousand*,' Harriet had repeated in a whisper.

These defeats took place in the first and second months of the war. Then one day in December Abel came in with what he declared was brighter news: Lord Roberts had been appointed Commander-in-Chief in South Africa and Lord Kitchener Chief-of-Staff. 'Both excellent men,' Abel said. 'The situation will be different now.'

But in January there was more bad news: the Boers had attacked Ladysmith and at the battle of Spion Kop Buller had been repulsed with severe losses.

This set the boys talking again about joining up. After they had had their meal they changed, saying they were going to talk to friends at other farms. Harriet pleaded with them to make sure it *was* just talk; they were not to do anything drastic.

Kitty was aroused from sleep that night by movements coming from Abel's and Harriet's bedroom. Then, as she lay listening, she became aware of men shouting and of laughter. They began to sing, the discordant singing of men who had had too much to drink. When she realised what they were singing, she gave a shiver of fear:

'Goodbye, Dolly, I must leave you,
Though it breaks my heart to go ...'

Abel and Harriet had gone downstairs. Kitty got up and stood at the top of the stairs. Then as the door burst open and the boys stumbled in, still shouting and laughing, she went down step by slow step.

'Stop that noise, do you hear?' Abel commanded. 'Do you know what time it is?' As if to answer him, the grandfather clock struck two sonorous notes. There was a sudden silence. Kitty was in the kitchen by then.

The boys stood in a line; their eyes were glazed, their hair tousled, but they were still.

'What are you celebrating?' Harriet asked in a low voice.

Andrew, acting as spokesman, stepped forward. 'We've been to Leicester and joined up, Mother. We had to do it!'

'All four of you?' Harriet said in a strangled voice. There were sheepish nods, then Abel exploded.

'You had no right! Not all four of you, it's not fair to your mother.'

Luke asked quietly, 'Which one would you choose to stay behind, Father?'

Abel looked grey as he flung out his hands. 'I don't know, I just don't know, but I think we ought to have been consulted. How many more from around here have joined up?'

'Twenty-four – so far. There'll be more. We're needed. Don't you see, Father, if it was left to parents and wives, no man would go. The more recruits there are, the sooner the war will be over.'

Abel's shoulders sagged with defeat. Kitty crept out unnoticed, a tight knot of misery inside her, feeling if Luke went away her life would be ended.

The night before the men were due to leave, Luke took Kitty on his lap and tried to explain how important it was to fight for one's country. 'If I don't come back,' he said gently, 'you are not to grieve. I will have done my duty and been proud to do so. When you're older, you'll understand.'

Kitty, too choked to reply, sat with her head bowed. Luke raised her face to his. 'Kitty love, I want you to do something for me. I want you to look after your Aunt Harriet. She'll be grieving. When she's low, put your arms around her, give her a kiss and tell her you're sure we'll all come back safe and sound. Will you do that for me?'

Kitty promised and Luke laid his cheek to hers and told her that he would write and she must write to him. She felt then that her heart would break.

The next morning when the men were all assembled waiting to leave, there was a strange quiet among the people. There were no tears but their unhappiness was apparent by drawn faces, each not knowing whether son or husband would return.

When all the goodbyes had been said the men left, thirty-six of them, strong healthy men going into heaven knew what. They had reached the rise and turned to wave when Abel, a break in his voice, gave a cheer. It was taken up and then tears ran unchecked down the cheeks of both men and women.

Life after that for Kitty revolved around news of the war. Hopes would be raised when there was a small victory and dashed again with a subsequent defeat.

Andrew's wife Joan was a regular visitor to the farm, but James's wife came only occasionally. Kitty liked Joan; she chatted and had all sorts of little interesting bits of news to relate. But one day when she arrived she looked pale and after greeting Harriet, they talked in whispers for a few moments and then burst into tears. Kitty, with only one thought in her mind, tugged at Harriet's skirts and asked in an anguished voice if Luke had been hurt.

'Why no,' Harriet said in surprise, as she dabbed at her eyes. 'What made you think that? Oh, I see, it was because we were crying. We were crying because Joan is going to have a baby and Andrew won't be here when it's born. But we're happy otherwise.'

Kitty, relieved, said that she was happy about the baby too, then turned away. Luke was all right and that was the most important thing. Perhaps there would be a letter soon.

A week later the first letters arrived, one from each of the boys. Luke's was the longest. He described the camp they were in, where they were to do training before being sent abroad. There were volunteers from all walks of life, including those from wealthy classes. He had heard that 300 men from a London Club had volunteered, all crack rifle shots because of their hunting and grouse-shooting. He had also heard that many tough frontiersmen were joining up from Australia and Canada. So, he concluded, how could the British fail to win the war? God willing, they would all be home in time for harvesting.

A small slip of paper had been included for Kitty from Luke; 'Remember your promise, Kitty. I depend on you.' It was signed, 'With love from Luke.'

Kitty held it close to her. Her first letter! She would treasure it always.

A week ago harvesting time would have seemed years away, now this brought it much closer. She put her arms around Harriet and reaching up, kissed her on the cheek. Then she said softly, 'Don't worry, Aunt Harriet, they'll all be home soon, I know it.'

The next letters from the boys were posted at the docks before embarking for South Africa. They were cheerful letters, saying they had made a lot of friends and were looking forward to the voyage. They would write when they arrived.

Letters did come from the war zone, but they were few and far between. Luke's were the most honest; he said he thought they would want to know the truth. It was no use lying, there was no glory in war. He spoke of the slaughter, of the hardships not only of the British but of the Boer women and children who had to be uprooted from their homes. 'The four of us are still together, thank God,' he said, 'and we pray it will stay that way. Your letters are a joy to us, just to know that you are managing the farm. We long to be back. At the moment we are thinking of harvest when Joan's baby will be born. Andrew is cock-a-hoop at the thought of being a father. We all tease him and he laughs. Oh, yes, we can laugh. Without humour we'd be done for ...'

The only good thing that year at the farm was the safe delivery of a baby daughter to Joan. Harriet was full of a quiet joy. A granddaughter! The bad news was that terrible storms had destroyed the harvest and James had been wounded. 'Not seriously,' Luke wrote, 'but enough to put him out of action for a week or two. He's being well taken care of. He sends his love and tells you not to worry ...'

In the following January, Queen Victoria died and the whole country went into mourning. Harriet talked of nothing else for days.

On the day of the funeral she was getting ready to go to church for the special service when Kitty, who was waiting outside for her, came running in, calling, 'Aunt Harriet, the vicar's coming across the yard. Uncle Abel is with him.'

'The vicar?' Harriet thrust a pin into her hat. 'Why should he come here, he ought to be in church, he—' She stood motionless, feeling as though all the blood was draining from her body. There was only one reason the vicar would call on this day.

The two men came into the kitchen. Abel's weather-beaten face had taken on a pinched look. Coming over to his wife, he laid a hand on her shoulder and said gently, 'I'm afraid there's bad news, love.'

Harriet looked beyond her husband to the vicar and said in a voice devoid of emotion, 'One of our sons has been killed.'

At mention of the boys Kitty looked from Harriet to Abel in an agony of suspense, then she too turned her gaze on the clergyman.

With an expression full of compassion, he said quietly, 'I'm sorry to be the bearer of such sad news, Mrs Leddenshaw, but I'm afraid that three of your sons have been killed.'

Harriet repeated, '*Three?*' but no sound came.

Kitty, unable to bear the suspense any longer, asked, 'Is Luke—?' then stopped, realizing her selfishness.

The vicar put a hand on her head. 'Luke is the only one to be spared, Kitty.'

In the silence that followed Kitty was conscious of only one thing: Luke was safe. Then she saw the pain on the faces of Harriet and Abel and became aware then of the ponderous ticking of the grandfather clock. It grew louder and louder in her head until she thought it would burst.

Then Harriet was saying in a calm vice, 'Thank you for calling to tell us, Reverend. You must excuse us from church this morning. My husband and I must go and break the news to our two daughters-in-law.'

To Kitty she said, 'You go with the Reverend Marsh, my love. One of the family must represent us to pay our respects to our gracious Queen. God bless her!'

As Harriet and Abel left the house, the Reverend Marsh held out his hand to Kitty and said gently, 'Shall we go, my dear?'

CHAPTER THREE

When the war eventually ended there was great rejoicing in the towns and cities, but there was no rejoicing at the Leddenshaw farm, nor at other farms where sons and husbands had been lost. Kitty longed for only one thing, that Luke would come home for her fourteenth birthday. Abel and Harriet, not knowing her birth date, had set it on 20 September, the day Kitty had been brought to them. But Luke did not come home.

Harriet, who had aged ten years since the loss of her three sons, dared not hope that Luke would be spared to them. When his last letter had come there was still fighting going on. Anything could happen.

Six months after Kitty's fourteenth birthday, she was with Abel in the top field when she saw a stranger coming over the rise. He was stooped, limping, a scarecrow of a man. She pointed him out to Abel, saying, 'Poor man, he looks half-starved.'

Abel was staring. 'It can't be,' he whispered in a strangled voice. 'It can't be ...' He went forward slowly, with Kitty following.

The stranger stopped and waited for Abel to come to him. Then they were embracing one another, both weeping.

Kitty found herself repeating Abel's whispered words, 'It can't be ...' Tears welled up. What had happened to turn her lovely Luke into this scarecrow of a man? What would poor Aunt Harriet feel when she saw him? Kitty, wanting to prepare Harriet, was about to move away when Luke called to her, the familiar gentleness in his voice.

She ran to him, flung her arms around him, sobbing. 'Oh,

Luke, you're back, we've missed you so!'

'And I've missed you all too.' He stroked her hair. 'I'm a poor specimen now, but ...' He paused and when he spoke again his voice had strengthened. 'Just you wait! Give me a few weeks of all this lovely air and good food and I'll be back to what I was *and* helping to get in the harvest.'

Abel said gruffly, 'Well, come on, boy, let's get you a good hot meal. Kitty, run on and tell your Aunt Harriet that Luke's home.'

Kitty raced over the field, but slowed down when she reached the yard. Harriet was standing at the door, her hand over her eyes against the September sun.

'Who's the man, Kitty?'

Kitty swallowed hard. 'It's Luke, Aunt Harriet; he's poorly, but he'll soon be well again, we'll look after him. He said he—'

'Luke – are you sure?' Harriet's gaze went to the fields again, this time making a steeple of both hands to shade her eyes. Then she squared her shoulders in the way the boys used to laughingly call her 'schoolmarm' stance.

'Right,' Harriet said, 'that boy will need a good hot meal and a warm bed. I'll cook him a slice of gammon and some fried eggs – it's one of his favourites, Kitty. Put some bricks in the oven to warm. I've kept his bed aired, but he'll need some extra warmth for comfort.'

Harriet's voice quivered on the word 'comfort' and when Luke came in a few moments later she burst into tears. Wrapping her plump arms around him, she rocked him to and fro. 'Oh, my boy, thank God you've been spared.'

Then she held him away from her and dabbed at her eyes. 'But there, set you down and I'll cook you a meal. You'll feel better with food in you. Go by the fire.'

Abel pulled up two chairs and the men sat facing one another. In between laying the table Kitty kept glancing at Luke, trying to see some resemblance to the Luke she had known. But there was none. He had been so big, so strong. Now he was just skin and bone, his face gaunt with deep hollows at each side of his mouth. Even his hair was no longer copper-coloured.

Harriet and Abel talked about the farm, talked quickly as though afraid that Luke might want to speak about his war experiences and they were not ready to hear them.

Luke listened, asked a few questions, then after a while closed his eyes. He slept.

Harriet's hand flew to her mouth. She looked at her husband, pain in her eyes. 'Oh, Abel,' she whispered, 'will he ever be the same again?'

Abel shook his head, but made no reply.

When Luke did rouse he ate very little and afterwards, when he was nearly dropping off to sleep, Abel saw him up to bed. Luke slept the clock round. He still had a gaunt look, but the terrible lines of sheer exhaustion were gone. Harriet prepared him a bath and afterwards his hair was copper-coloured again.

Kitty, standing behind him, touched the curled ends at the nape of his neck. Luke turned his head, not with the ready smile of old, but a smile nevertheless.

'I bet you're glad I'm cleaned up a bit,' he said. 'You've certainly grown, Kitty – quite a young lady, and a pretty one at that. But then you always were pretty.'

Harriet teased him, said it was easy to see he was getting better, then she added quietly, 'Folks from all over were dropping in yesterday to see you, Luke. Some of them are coming this morning, but you don't have to see them if you don't want to.'

'I'll see them, Ma.' Luke's expression was sombre. 'We have to meet sometime, and the sooner I get back into the swim the better.'

Kitty wanted to be there when the visitors came, but Harriet found her jobs to do in the dairy and in the yard. Kitty resented being kept away from Luke, especially when she could see women neighbours coming with daughters who were older than she was, and knowing full well why the girls were there.

When she went in at midday for the meal and found Luke had gone to bed, exhausted, she complained bitterly to Abel:

'It's all Aunt Harriet's fault for letting all those people come. Luke should be resting, not having to deal with girls who're looking for a husband!'

'Now listen to me,' Harriet began with some heat, but was interrupted by her husband who held up a hand, telling her that he would handle the matter.

'So, Kitty, what is all this about girls wanting husbands?'

Abel had different voices for different occasions and although

Kitty knew he was speaking quietly, she also knew it was not his reasoning voice but his chastising one.

She tried to explain as carefully as she could that she had overheard some of the women talking the week before, and one of them had said that with so many young men being killed in the war, their marriageable daughters were going to have difficulty in finding husbands.

'And I thought,' she concluded, 'that these girls were just coming to find out if Luke was well enough for them to marry.'

'And if they were, Kitty, what right have you to complain? Luke is a man and quite capable of making up his own mind. He will marry one day, please God, and have children, but neither your Aunt Harriet nor I will attempt to tell him who he can or cannot marry.'

'I love Luke,' Kitty blurted out. 'I don't want him to get hurt, I want him to get well—'

'Kitty . . .' Abel's voice was gentle now. 'We all love him, but never make the mistake of wanting to possess him. Luke is his own man, he would never let us or anyone else smother him with affection. Do you understand?'

Kitty, feeling utterly miserable, nodded. 'He would never marry *me*,' she said, her voice breaking. 'I'm just a nobody.'

Abel and Harriet stared at one another, shocked, then Abel drew Kitty to him and held her close. 'Never say that, ever! We love you dearly, you're family.'

When Kitty still stood looking steeped in misery, Abel said, 'You know Mr Liker's dog Toby, the one with three legs?' Kitty nodded and Abel asked her if she knew how the dog had lost a leg.

'Yes,' she said. 'He saved Mr Liker's son from being gored by a bull and he got hurt himself.'

'And lost a leg, but Toby didn't sit down and feel sorry for himself. He trots all over the place – you said yourself how clever he was for managing to walk and run with only three legs. Toby once rounded up some lost sheep and brought them home, and another time tackled a fox trying to kill the chickens – and got hurt again. The fox slunk off. Toby doesn't think of himself as a nobody dog, neither do the Likers. They think he's a *somebody* dog. Do you understand, Kitty?'

Kitty made no reply, but the fact that she slipped her hand

into Abel's told him she did understand and accepted the lesson.

Luke's recovery was slow. Although he kept saying he was well enough to do some work, handling a spade for ten minutes had him breathless. Every day, after the midday meal, he would go upstairs to rest for an hour, then he would walk over the fields or through the woods.

Sometimes when Kitty came out of school she would see Luke waiting for her a short distance away. Then she would feel a lovely warmth inside knowing that he wanted her with him. Often they would walk in silence, Kitty having been told by Harriet that she was not to tire Luke with her chatter. She longed for him to talk about the war, sensing in her childish way that if he talked about his experiences he would not suffer as he did. There were times when he would become agitated and break out in a sweat, and this could happen on the coolest of days.

Always he would say, 'It will pass, Kitty, I'll be all right in a few minutes. It's just weakness.'

There came a day when he was forced to sit on a boulder by a stream to regain his strength. He was trembling and beads of perspiration gathered on his brow and lay on his upper lip. Kitty pulled her handkerchief from her pocket and wiped his face. Luke gave a feeble smile and teased her, saying he had decided now she ought to be a nurse.

Kitty knelt in front of him, then sitting back on her heels, she said, 'Luke, did you see your brothers being killed?'

His head came up and he regarded her in a startled way. 'Yes, I did, but I don't want to talk about it.' He got up and started to walk away, while Kitty stayed where she was. After a moment Luke stopped and looked back.

'You should talk about it,' she said. 'Aunt Harriet says it doesn't do any good to bottle things up. Perhaps if you talked to your father you would stop hurting inside.'

Luke came back and sat on the boulder. He cupped her face in his hands. 'Kitty love, you're so discerning, but I can't talk about what I saw in the war. It's too soon. The wounds inside me are still raw. They'll heal in time.' He drew his hands away from her face. 'But thanks for trying to help me. It's done me good, I'm beginning to feel better.'

He made no move and Kitty sat beside him, feeling the peace

of the countryside, the gentle gurgling of the stream, enjoying the sun's warmth that tempered the cool wind; savouring the touch of Luke's hands on her face . . . and wanting this moment to go on for ever.

Then suddenly the wind became boisterous, rippling through the grass, shaking the boughs of the trees. A dark cloud blotted out the sun and Kitty shivered as a fear rose in her. Was this an omen, was she to lose Luke? Oh, no, God, she prayed, please don't let Luke die.

Then for some reason Kitty knew her fear had nothing to do with Luke. It was something to do with her own life . . . something that had happened in the past. During the last few years there had been times when she would remember some small incident, but because pain was concerned with it she hastily forced it to the back of her mind and concentrated on what was happening at that particular time.

It had been easy to tell Luke to talk about the horrors he had witnessed, but she had no wish to relive the pain she had suffered. When she had first known about her mother and her reason for sending her to the farm she had longed to see her, had waited at the field gate every day, watching for her. But that longing was gone and she was happy at the farm, especially now that Luke was home again.

A big drop of rain splashed on to the back of her hand. Luke got up. 'Come along, Kitty, it looks as if it might storm.'

Oddly enough it was from that day that Luke quickly gained strength. By harvest time he was working in the fields all day. His skin had become a golden brown, his hair a burnished copper and Kitty was crazily in love with him.

She was turned fifteen when she started the monthly cycle. Harriet explained it, told her that she was now a woman. Kitty was very much aware of the swelling of her breasts and once when she imagined Luke touching them she experienced an emotion she had not known before. Conscious of this, she became shy with him.

Perhaps he was aware of it because he stopped teasing her – that is, until the evening they were going to the harvest dance. Although many families were still in mourning for sons and husbands lost in the war, Harriet decided she would make Kitty a white dress for the occasion. The dress was flounced, with a silk sash, and ribbons were twined in her long, thick, dark hair which Harriet had brushed until it was gleaming.

Kitty, flushed with excitement, came running downstairs wanting to know Luke's reaction. She was not disappointed.

'Well!' he exclaimed, holding her at arm's length, 'and who is this beautiful creature? Whoever she is, she's going to turn the lads' heads – *and* the men's too when she's a little older.'

Then he added softly, 'You really are beautiful, Kitty.'

'Will you give me a dance, Luke? There'll be lots of girls who'll need partners.'

'No matter how many girls are there, I shall dance with you, Kitty love. Save me three – no, four. Perhaps five if I can manage it. I do have duty dances to give.'

Kitty understood. It would be heaven to dance with Luke once, to have his arms around her.

It was a clear, starry night with a hoar frost silvering the grass and the branches of the trees and, as the barn where the dance was to be held was not far away, they decided to walk.

Kitty was wearing a big white shawl of Harriet's over her dress, but when excitement made her shiver, Luke was immediately full of concern that she might be cold.

'No,' she said, 'I'm lovely and warm, it was just coming away from the hot fire.'

She had hoped to walk with Luke, to go into the barn with him, but they had not gone far before they met up with neighbours and then the men walked together with the women following.

Judging by the buzz of chatter and the burst of laughter coming from the barn, many people were already there. Buggies and wagons were arriving all the while, greetings being exchanged between families. Kitty loved the atmosphere, the barny smell mingling with that of hay. There were trestle tables with all kinds of tempting food laid on snowy-white cloths; bowls of lemonade and one of punch for the men.

Matrons already seated on the wooden benches around the barn were exchanging gossip; children scrambled over the bales of hay, while most of the men stood around in groups. Two fiddlers were tuning up.

Harriet had taught Kitty to dance and Kitty was a very quick pupil; she could hardly wait to get on the floor. Although

Harriet had said that she herself would not be dancing, she took her husband's proffered arm for the 'Roger de Coverly' and Luke escorted Kitty.

After that it was a dream of an evening for Kitty. Luke kept his promise to have four dances with her, and in between she was never without partners. She had a vigorous polka with Luke, was swung off her feet in the 'Lancers' by a very attractive Leddenshaw cousin and waltzed sedately with Abel.

And to cap the joy of the evening Luke walked home with her, his arm across her shoulder – teasing her, telling her she had been 'belle of the ball'.

Kitty looked up at him, her eyes shining. 'Oh, Luke, it was wonderful! Everyone made me feel so . . . so grown-up. I felt like Cinderella!' She gave a tremulous laugh. 'Tomorrow I'll be sweeping in the ashes, cleaning the dairy.'

'And waiting for Prince Charming to bring the glass slipper,' Luke said softly. 'There would be no doubt about your slender foot being the right size.'

'*You* are my Prince Charming,' she said lightly.

'Hey, don't count on me!' he answered equally as lightly. 'I would probably lose the darn slipper on the way, or break it.'

Kitty's infectious giggle hung on the clear crisp air and Abel, who was walking in front with Harriet, called over his shoulder to know what the jest was about. Kitty replied, still laughing, 'Oh, it's all to do with Luke breaking the glass slipper.'

Abel, not quite grasping the meaning, raised his shoulders at his wife in a helpless way – and by then they were home.

Kitty lay wide awake in bed, reliving every incident of the evening – seeing Luke, tall and bronzed, smart in his Sunday suit and crisp white shirt, his copper-coloured hair visible wherever he went. She could see him edging politely away from mothers with a string of marriageable daughters, see him smiling at her from across the barn, coming towards her with outstretched hands, claiming a dance . . . It seemed impossible to be any happier than she had been that evening. She drifted into sleep . . .

Some time during the early hours she awoke from a nightmare, trembling and perspiring profusely. She had been trapped by a wall of glass slippers which one by one started to burst into fragments, the splinters piercing her skin. She could see herself, as though from a distance, horrified as blood streamed from her wounds.

She could hear voices calling, telling her she was all right, but it was impossible to find her way out of the encircling wall. Then, suddenly strong arms reached down and she was safe and held close.

Kitty aroused fully to find she was in Luke's arms.

'It's all right, Kitty,' he soothed. 'I have you.'

Harriet and Abel were there too, Harriet saying she would make a hot drink for obviously the poor child had had too much excitement for one night.

When Kitty had finished the hot milk, Luke laid her back on the pillows and smoothed the hair away from her brow, saying softly, 'You'll sleep now.'

She did, but when she woke at six o'clock she had a terrible feeling of premonition. She had been too happy: something bad was going to happen.

Late that afternoon, she was returning from taking the cows back to the field after milking when she saw Harriet and Abel going into the house with a thin, black-clad woman. Although Kitty was unable to see the woman's face, she sensed she was a stranger.

Kitty followed them into the house, but stopped outside the partly-opened door of the kitchen as she heard Harriet say in a tear-filled voice, 'But would it be right to uproot the child, Margaret, after all these years? She's made this her home. We all love her—'

'*I* love her,' the stranger replied, 'and I *am* her mother, she's my own flesh and blood. Please don't think, either of you, that I parted easily with Kitty ...'

Her *mother*? Kitty stood tense, her heartbeats quickening.

Then Abel was saying in stern tones, 'She'd been brutally treated when she was brought to us. You could have stopped it.'

'I couldn't, I couldn't! I was ill at the time, very ill; I had just had my seventh miscarriage. I knew nothing of what was going on until a neighbour told me – the same neighbour who brought Kitty to you.'

'Your *seventh* miscarriage?' Harriet said, distressed. 'God help you!'

'Arthur was not really a bad man underneath.' The woman

was pleading now. 'It was only when he had too much to drink that he lost his head. He *had* to drink. All the men did at the glassworks, it was the furnaces, the heat.'

Furnaces? Glassworks . . . memories began stirring vaguely in Kitty's mind.

'And now that my husband is dead,' the woman went on, 'I want Kitty back with me, with us – I have four other daughters.'

The name Violet sprang to Kitty's lips. And with it came fear. 'No!' she shouted, 'I don't want to go back, I won't!' and with that she turned and ran. She heard Abel calling to her to wait, but Kitty ran on and did not stop running until she reached the top field; there she dropped to the grass beneath a hedge, breathless and trembling, but determined she was not going to leave the farm.

'I won't, I won't!' she said aloud to a group of disinterested sheep. 'And no one can make me.'

Words, places, incidents, names were surfacing from the recesses of Kitty's mind, but because the name Violet had brought such fear she tried to stifle them by concentrating on the gentle crunching of the sheep cropping the grass. After a while, everything became jumbled together, leaving only one image clear. She could see herself running to the glassworks; then she had a joyful feeling.

Unfortunately, the joyful feeling could not be sustained. Her mother intruded – her mother who had given her away and now wanted her back.

It was Abel who found her, steeped in misery. He dropped down beside her and put his arm around her.

'We need to have a talk, Kitty love; you need to know the full story about your mother, not just a little snippet. You have to come and meet her, but before you do I'm going to try and explain what happened before you came to us.' Kitty put her hands over her ears, but Abel eased them gently away. 'It's no use trying to avoid the unpleasant things, Kitty; they are all a part of life, all a part of growing up.'

Kitty felt like protesting that she did not want to grow up, but instead she rested her head against the crook of Abel's arm.

And so Abel began the story of Kitty's earlier years.

'Your mother says you were a lovable, high-spirited child,

always running away to the glassworks where your parents both worked. The blowing of the glass fascinated you. You were forbidden the works because it could be dangerous with molten glass being handled. But in spite of many warnings, you still persisted in running away. Do you remember this, Kitty?'

When she made no answer, Abel went on, 'Your sister Violet was put in charge of you because of your parents having to work.'

At mention of her sister's name, Kitty tensed. She looked at Abel with pleading. 'Please, Uncle Abel, don't tell me any more. My sister hated me, she—'

Abel got up and drew Kitty to her feet. 'Come along, we'll go and see your mother.'

When they went into the kitchen the thin woman in black stood up; she had big dark eyes in a bloodless-looking face. When Kitty first went to school and children asked her about her parents, she told them they were dead simply because she was unable to put faces to them. Later, as she grew up, she knew a longing at times to meet her mother – never her father – but now that she was face to face with her she felt nothing, there was no recognition whatsoever.

Margaret said, in a strangled whisper, 'Oh, Kitty, how I've longed to see you!' She put her arms around her, but when Kitty stood unresponsive, she released her.

Harriet said gently, 'Give her time, Margaret, she has to get to know you. Abel and I will leave you to have a talk.'

Kitty felt a momentary panic at being left alone with her mother until Abel put a hand on her shoulder and gave her a reassuring nod. She sat on the stool at the opposite side of the fireplace.

Margaret talked in a quiet voice, telling Kitty about their life in the North of England and about Kitty's four sisters; she said that the twins Agnes and Mary, who were seventeen, and Ann who was eighteen, all worked in a factory, while Violet – three years older – was in service.

'Violet was unkind to you,' she said, a break in her voice. 'So was your father, although I do believe he thought it was for your own good. Violet is sorry for the way she behaved to you. Your father is dead. I want you with us, Kitty; we all want you to come home. And it is your duty. You've been well looked after by Abel and Harriet, grown into a lovely girl – very lovely – and I'm proud of you.'

Margaret's eyes suddenly filled with tears. 'Oh, Kitty, I'm saying all the wrong things! I'm talking about duty when I should be telling you that I love you. I've never stopped loving you, wanting to see you.'

'But I don't want to leave the farm,' Kitty protested, a desperate note in her voice. 'I love it here. I don't want to leave Aunt Harriet, Uncle Abel and ... and Luke.'

'I know exactly how you feel,' her mother said earnestly. 'I too loved the country, loved the farming life. Many times over the past years I've longed to be back. Harriet and Abel were the only parents I ever knew.'

Margaret was silent for a few moments, then she went on, 'I can't even offer you a life as comfortable as this, Kitty, but I do have the promise of a job for you. It's in a big house, where the cook is a friend of mine. You would have to start as scullery-maid, but I'm sure you could soon work your way up to a better position.'

For the first time Kitty showed some interest. A big house? Being a scullery-maid would be no worry; she scrubbed and cleaned here. But there was Luke ... How could she bear to leave him? Perhaps he would want her to stay, insist that she stayed. He was in town getting stores now and would not be back until evening. Kitty decided that if Luke wanted her to stay, then she would.

But to her disappointment, to her grief, he was all for her going with her mother.

'It's a great opportunity for you, Kitty. You'll meet more people, see a different way of life. I think you could make a place for yourself in the world. You're bright.'

'Won't you miss me?' she asked in a forlorn voice.

'Of course I will, the farm won't be the same without you, but we have to make sacrifices for those we love.' Luke's tenderness made Kitty want to cry. 'You won't lose us – Kitty, we'll write to you, tell you all that is going on. You can tell us all your news and if ever I get the chance to go North, I'll make sure I see you. That's a promise!'

Luke's promise seemed to make it inevitable she would be

leaving. Kitty made no further protest.

The next morning when Margaret said a little wistfully that she would like to visit certain places and walk along remembered paths of her younger days, Harriet insisted on Kitty accompanying her.

Kitty, whose mind was on one thing only – having to leave the farm – agreed without interest. Margaret made straight for the woods, saying it was where she had spent most of her free time.

It had been a long, hot summer and the fallen leaves were tinder-dry, making Kitty recall how Luke had once laughingly referred to walking over them as their 'Cinder Shuffle'.

Oh, Luke, Luke ...

Margaret said, speaking softly, 'It was in these woods that I first saw your father, Kitty. He was such a handsome man, so full of laughter and teasing. I wish you could have known him ... then ...' Her voice trailed off, as though uncertain what to say next, then in a forced brighter tone she added, 'I must show you my secret hiding place. It's on the other side of the woods.'

Kitty, whose mind was still on Luke, was only partially listening, but when they came out of the woods and her mother followed the stream for a short distance, then stopped and pointed to a clump of bushes saying, 'Well, there it is, my hideaway when I wanted to be alone!' she looked at the bushes and then at her mother with a mixture of surprise and bewilderment. This was her very own hideaway! No one knew about it, not even Luke. There was only a small opening, but once inside it was like a cave. 'Who told you about this?' she asked. 'It's *my* secret place!'

'It is?' Her mother's eyes went wide. 'Well, how strange. No one told me about it, I found it myself when I first came to the farm and wanted to be alone.' She gave a shaky laugh. 'It's almost as if you were aware of my presence. At least, I like to think so.' More soberly she added, 'Oh, Kitty, I do so want us to be friends.'

Although Kitty was not yet ready to concede any affection for her mother, she too thought it strange that out of all the clumps of bushes in the countryside she should choose this one for her hideout. She moved closer.

'Where else did you like to go?'

'To the top of the rise. It's such a lovely view.'

When they reached it they stood in silence. Below them stretched a patchwork of fields and copses, interspersed with farms and homesteads, with a long white road that twisted and curved to the next village.

Kitty, glancing at her mother, saw there were tears in her eyes. Margaret turned to her. 'Kitty, I think I should warn you that you'll find it very different where we live in the North. There are factories, smoke and streets of houses – small houses – but the people are friendly and warm-hearted, neighbour helping neighbour.'

'Who is Grandma Perkins?' Kitty asked suddenly.

'You remember her?' There was an eagerness in her mother's voice. 'She lived a few doors away and you often visited her; she was bedridden. Poor Gran Perkins, she's dead now. What else do you remember?'

Images were tumbling about in Kitty's mind. 'Her husband went to sea. He brought back a little glass ship with ropes like spun sugar. He brought it from ... Italy—'

'Well! Fancy you remembering that. You were mad about things made of glass, that's why you were always running off to the glassworks. But here – we're not going to talk about that, are we, not just yet? Oh, look, there's Abel waving to us.'

The images went on tumbling around in Kitty's mind. She would get flashes of colour, then would come a greyness ... and pain.

It was evening when she realized that the glassworks were connected with this pain. She looked at her wrists, then down at her ankles. At one time there had been scars on both wrists and ankles; now they were just faint marks. Once when she asked Harriet what they were, Harriet said that someone had tied her up in play and Kitty had struggled so hard to get free she had hurt herself. At the time she had accepted this, but now she knew that it was not quite the truth.

In bed that night she suffered a recurrence of the nightmare about the glass slippers. As before she was surrounded by them, and as before they were exploding and fragments were drawing blood on her skin. This time there were no gentle hands lifting her free, no soothing voices. She was being handled roughly; the voice was rough, a man's voice:

'You'll have to be taught a lesson, my girl, do as you're told.'

44

There was the sting of leather on her skin . . . a younger voice shouting, 'I hate you, our Kitty, you deserve it . . . If you're tied up you can't run away!'

It was her struggles in the nightmare to get free of the captive hands that brought Kitty to a trembling wakefulness. Her body was lathered in perspiration. And still images tumbled around in her head. Orange and yellow flames . . . a golden bubble . . . A dark shed, terror, pain . . . a girl taunting her . . . 'You're a bastard, did you know that? Dad hates you . . . So do I . . .'

For the rest of the night Kitty slipped into fitful dozes. The next morning at breakfast she made up her mind to ask her mother what had happened. Waiting until Harriet had gone outside on some chore, she said, 'My father beat me; was it because I'm a bastard?'

Margaret, who had been pleating the edges of a handkerchief, looked up startled. 'No, Kitty, you're not a bastard, who told you that?'

'I don't know. Whoever it was told me that my father beat me.'

Her mother became agitated. 'Only that once, Kitty. Before that he never raised a hand to you. You were disobedient and he said you had to be taught a lesson. But I didn't know anything about it until afterwards. I was ill in bed, very ill.'

'I was tied up, wasn't I, to a chair, in a dark shed?'

Margaret nodded, her eyes full of misery. 'For a week, if only I'd known! But that's all behind you. I think perhaps it's better if we *don't* talk about it, not now. Wait until you are older, then I'll tell you. After all, your father is dead; he can't harm you any more.'

'Why did Violet hate me?' Kitty persisted.

'Because she was put in charge of you. She resented it. Your other three sisters worked in a factory and Violet wanted to go to work too.' Margaret's lips tightened. 'But I was determined that at least one of my daughters would not be forced to go to work before she was ready. I was put to work at a very early age, sorting nails. I was so tiny I had to stand on a chair. I think I was about three years old.'

'*Three?*' Kitty said. Suddenly she wanted to get away. She jumped up and ran out – and went slap into Luke. He began to tease her, wanting to know where she was racing off to; then, realizing her distress, he put an arm about her shoulders and led her away. He walked her as far as the field gate, then turned her to face him. 'Now, Kitty love, what's the trouble?'

She felt so choked she was unable to answer, but Luke waited patiently. At last she was able to tell him, concluding with a desperate plea to be allowed to stay at the farm.

Luke lifted her on to a stile and took her hand in his.

'I think your mother's right, Kitty. You should try and put this unhappy experience behind you and start afresh.'

'I can't,' she wailed, 'I can't! I don't want to go with my mother, I won't. If I can't stay here, I'll run away, I'll go with the gypsies.'

'And take all your hurt and resentment with you,' Luke said gently. 'Resentment builds up into hatred and hatred festers, builds up in itself. I hated the Boers during the war, then I realized they were doing their duty just as we were. Your father punished you because you were disobedient. He obviously overstepped the mark, but as your mother says, he's dead now and one must forgive.'

'I don't want to go home,' Kitty moaned. 'I won't. I'd hate it.'

Luke drew his hands away. 'Very well, I'll speak to your Uncle Abel and Aunt Harriet. I'm sure they'll let you stay, but don't expect any respect from me, Kitty. I have no respect for anyone who's unable to forgive.'

Kitty wiped tears from the corners of her eyes and looked at Luke with dismay. How could he say such a thing to her, how could he be so cold with her?

Then she saw the compassion in his eyes and knew he was being cruel to be kind. 'I'll go home,' she said in a low voice.

Luke put his arms around her and held her to him.

'Kitty love, I want you to think of all that's gone in the past as "Yesterday's Road". Tomorrow or the next day you'll be branching out on another road – and who knows what you might eventually find at the end of it? You told me once that when you grew up you were going to Italy. It's obviously a dream of yours. Keep on wanting it – so often dreams do come true.'

Two days later, half an hour before Kitty was due to set out on the journey North with her mother, she took a final walk to her familiar haunts and saw everything with a new clarity: the copse of beech trees, glowing warmly in the autumn sun; the sparkling water of the stream rustling over brown mottled pebbles; the straight line of stately poplars in the distance which had always fascinated her. She walked the fields where the plaintive bleating of the sheep sounded as if they knew she was leaving . . . and saw for the first time a beauty in the swing of their heavy coats. Then she climbed to the top of the rise and gazed at the white road that snaked its way to the next village.

'Yesterday's Road,' she thought, her heart breaking.

The wind stung her skin and when she turned to go back to the farm to say her goodbyes, the tears running down her cheeks seemed to turn to ice.

CHAPTER FOUR

A neighbouring farmer who was going into Leicester was to take Kitty and her mother to the station, where they would catch a train to go North. Abel had insisted on them travelling by train and on paying their fares.

When the time came for the actual parting Kitty had difficulty in keeping her tears under control, especially when she saw the grief and pain in the eyes of Abel, Harriet and Luke. Each of them gave her a hug in turn. Abel told her they would always be there if she needed them; Harriet made her promise to write and Luke, holding her away from him, said softly, 'Dear Kitty, we shall miss you terribly, but we feel lucky we've had you with us so long. If ever I come North, I shall call and see you.'

'Oh, yes, please, Luke.'

He drew out a handkerchief and wiped away her tears. Then he smiled. 'I'm not going to say "be good". That would not be our Kitty! You're a rebel and a little fighter, and that will help you to fit into your new life.'

When they walked to the wagon he took her hand in his and after helping Margaret up on to the seat, he lifted Kitty up.

Her last view of them was standing in a line, Abel's grey hair lifting in the wind, Harriet twisting a corner of her big white apron and Luke standing with hand upraised in farewell, the sun glinting on his copper hair. Kitty waved then, choking back a sob, she sat up and looked straight ahead.

Margaret and the farmer made small talk, but Kitty was silent and it was not until they arrived in Leicester and drove to the station that her grief at parting was eased. She had never travelled by train before, never even been in a station and the hustle and bustle, the elegance of the people and the station itself imbued in her a feeling of adventure.

Porters were pushing laden trolleys of luggage, the station master with all his gold braid – a tall, haughty-looking man – was talking to a group of well-dressed people, who were equally haughty-looking. Then the train came – a big shiny black monster, belching forth steam and hissing like a dragon. Kitty felt a shiver of excitement running through her.

The farmer came on to the platform with them to help carry their luggage and all the bags of food Harriet had given them. Kitty was glad he was there because her mother was so agitated, asking two different porters if this was the train they had to get, in spite of Abel having given them a list of times and the changes they would have to make.

But at last they were settled in the carriage. The farmer waited, he too being greatly interested in the steam engine. Then the doors were being slammed and the train began to move, leaving with an important huffing and puffing and a shrill whistle. Margaret and Kitty waved to the farmer until he was out of sight; then Kitty flopped back in her seat. 'Isn't it exciting!' she said.

Margaret nodded, then closed her eyes. 'Calm down, Kitty, it will be a long and tiring journey. I wish we were home.'

It *was* a long and tiring journey. Margaret was exhausted by the time they arrived at their destination and even Kitty had to admit to feeling tired.

The afternoon was cold, with a feeling of greyness. Margaret said they would get a tram and after that it would not be too far to walk. Kitty struggled with the small bass hamper containing their clothes and two of the bags of food, while Margaret carried the rest. Once they were on the tram Kitty looked about her with interest, hoping to find landmarks she recognized, but no place was familiar to her. They travelled through a factory area with chimneys belching smoke which hung over the roof-tops.

It was not until they were off the tram and walking among a warren of streets with back-to-back houses, where a privy served five or six families, that remembrance began to surface. It was in one of these streets with refuse stinking in the gutters

49

that they lived. Kitty felt suddenly appalled. Was this to be her life from now on?

Margaret's feet were dragging and her face was colourless. Although Kitty remembered the streets, she could not recognize the one where they had lived. When she asked how much further they had to go, Margaret said in a whisper, 'It's the next one on the right. Number four.'

Before they reached number four a small wiry woman came out of a house nearby and greeted them with a warm smile. 'Back again then, Margaret, and your young Kitty with you! Come on in, I have the kettle on. I'll make you a nice cup of tea and get you something to eat. Here, let me take those bags, you look fair whacked out.'

The woman talked to Kitty as they went in the back way. 'I'm Jessica Perkins, Gran Perkins' daughter. Do you remember me, Kitty? You used to come to our house a lot. But then it was a long time ago, wasn't it? Eight years, is it?' They went through the scullery into the kitchen and Jessica took the hamper from her. 'Sit you down, the pair of you.' She pushed a big black kettle which was singing on the hob on to a glowing fire, saying it would soon be boiling.

There was a cosiness, a homeliness about the kitchen that reminded Kitty of the farmhouse. Tears stung at the back of her eyelids. There was a red plush cloth on the table, with a bobble fringe, and a matching piece round the mantelpiece. The lino was dark brown and well-worn, but a brightly coloured hand-made rag rug lay in front of the fireplace. The mantelpiece was packed with small ornaments and framed photographs, and looking at the photographs Kitty sat up and said, 'I do remember your mother. She used to show me a lovely little glass ship which your father had brought home from sea.'

Jessica paused in her bustling around to beam at Kitty. 'And do you know something? Mam left it for you. One of the last things she told me was to see you had the little ship when you came home. She said you always loved it. I'll get it for you later. The kettle's boiling, I'll make the tea.'

She spread a small white cloth over the red one, then carried in a plate of scones, some gingerbread and a pot of jam. 'I did a bit of baking, had a feeling you'd be home today! Come on, sit up and eat up. There's more if you want it.'

Jessica poured the tea, set the teapot down in the hearth and then said, 'I went in and laid the fire for you, Margaret. While you're eating, I'll go and put a match to it.'

Margaret, who looked ashen, got up. 'Harriet packed us some food, but I couldn't eat a thing on the journey. I think I might enjoy one of your scones, Jessica. No one makes scones like you.'

'Well, nice of you to say so. Help yourself to jam, I'll be back in a jiffy.'

By the time Jessica did return Margaret, who had eaten two scones and a piece of gingerbread, was beginning to get some of her colour back. Jessica chattered on about having been talking to this neighbour and that and how they were all interested in knowing that Kitty was home.

To Kitty she said, 'We're not rolling in money around here, love, but what we lack in wealth we have in friendliness. You'll get on all right, they're good people.'

When Margaret eventually said they must go, Jessica took Kitty aside and told her if there was anything they needed, *anything* at all, she was to let her know. Then she added to Margaret, 'Well! The fire should be burning up now – give you a bit of cheer.'

But when they did go home the fire was not big enough to chill off the room, nor the icy coldness that Kitty felt when she saw the poverty of her new home. A threadbare rug was the only covering on the floorboards, the only furniture a table with a scrubbed wooden top, four chairs and a stool. There wasn't even a single photograph, ornament or picture to give the room an identity. Margaret began apologizing for the conditions.

'I'm sorry, Kitty, there's so little comfort, but all the bits and pieces I had have gone to pay for food. It's been a struggle since your father died.'

'I thought you said my sisters are all working. Don't they give you some money?'

'Yes, they do.' Margaret stood twisting her hands together. 'And I work two days a week, sewing, but you see . . . well, the thing is, Kitty, I got into debt at one time and now I'm having to pay all that back – with interest. It keeps me poor.' Then she added quickly, 'But don't you worry, Kitty, I'll be all right when you start your job. Mrs Bramley, the cook, said she'd see you had some bits and pieces of leftovers to bring home on your day off, and I can ask for a pound advance on your wages. You will only get paid every six months, you see.'

Kitty said hesitantly, 'I do have a bit of money. Uncle Abel and Harriet and Luke all gave me something – to be used in an emergency.'

'No, no, you keep it, you never know what you might need. They gave *me* some money too. I put two blankets in pawn, I'll have to get them out before we go to bed. The trouble is there's bound to be fleas or bugs in them after being in the pawnshop.'

Kitty shuddered. She had heard about pawnshops from Harriet; they were places to be avoided.

'No,' she said, 'we'll buy some new ones. How much will they cost?'

They were distracted then by the arrival of the lamplighter who lit the gas-lamp outside the house. Margaret said, 'That reminds me, we haven't any oil in the lamp. Still, we can manage with the lamp outside. Let's sit down for a few minutes and get warm. We can go and see about the blankets later; the shop doesn't close until midnight.'

They sat down, both still wearing their coats. The fire burned fitfully, giving little heat. Her mother looked perished and when Kitty put the back of her hand to her own nose it felt like a piece of ice. She went out to the coal-shed . . . and found it empty. What was she to do? They must have warmth. She thought of the blankets that were needed. Just what bedclothes were there on the bed? Kitty came in and went upstairs, going unerringly into the room used by her parents when she had lived at home. There she stopped and stood motionless.

She had been appalled at the poverty she found on first coming to the house, but that was nothing to what she experienced now. Paper hung from the walls in damp strips; the double iron bedstead was rusted in parts, the sheet and pillow-cases that had once been white were now grey. One thin blanket and an equally thin bed-cover in a faded blue material were the only coverings.

There was not even a threadbare rug on the floor. A dress hung on a nail in the wall and on the floor, in a box, were a few pieces of clothing. Although the windows were closed a thin fog seeped in, bringing with it the smell and taste of soot. Kitty turned away and went into the bedroom she had once shared with her sisters, where they had slept head to tail in a double bed.

The bed was still there, but there was only a striped tick mattress on it and no bedclothes. Violet, she knew, was in service, but where did her other three sisters sleep now? They worked in a factory and must surely come home to sleep.

Kitty thought with longing of the farm, of digging her toes into the thick fleece of the sheepskin rug, of sinking into the feather bed and snuggling under the plump eiderdown. As she went downstairs, a feeling of despair swamped her.

Her mother was still sleeping. Kitty felt she wanted to shake her awake and shout, 'We must have warmth, what are you going to do about it?' But even as she thought this she knew her mother could do little about it; she was apathetic.

Kitty, remembering Jessica telling her that if there was anything they needed she had only to ask, decided that what she needed at that moment was advice.

Jessica eyed her gravely. 'Come on in, Kitty. I had a feeling you might be back. What's the trouble?'

Kitty came straight to the point. 'We need coal and blankets. I have some money – can you tell me how to get both? I want new blankets, not some from the pawnshop with fleas in them.'

Jessica nodded her approval. 'You've got your head screwed on the right way, young Kitty; I expect it's being brought up on a farm – they don't use pawnshops. Would you settle for a pair of second-hand blankets, nearly new, clean, from a good home? I know where I can get a pair. For coal and blankets I would need six shillings.'

When Kitty asked if that was enough, Jessica said grimly, 'It's all anyone around here expects to get and those who are selling are glad to get it to buy food. Wait here, I won't be long.'

The photographs on the mantelpiece caught Kitty's attention. There was one of Gran Perkins and her sailor husband, a strong-looking bearded man; Gran had been younger then. Memories of the old lady began to stir. Kitty looked at the door at the end of the fireplace wall, behind which were stairs that led to the bedrooms. Kitty could see herself clambering up the stairs and Gran Perkins calling from her bed, 'I'd know those little footsteps anywhere. Come on in, Kitty love, and tell me what you've been doing this morning.'

Gran had told marvellous stories of her husband's voyages and all the countries he had visited. She especially remembered Italy and a place called Venice where people travelled on canals in boats to get to their houses. That was when she had made up her mind to go to Italy when she was older.

Jessica came back with a bucket of coal in one hand and a pair of cream blankets under her arm. 'I'll get you some more coal in the morning. This will keep you going meantime. You want to build the fire up tonight and put some bricks in the oven to heat. The bed will need airing. Even if it's empty for one night, there's damp gets in with this weather.'

Jessica set down the bucket and put the blankets on the table. 'Sit down, Kitty, I think we'd better have a talk. Some folks might say it's not my business to tell you things, but I feel it's better you know now. It'll help you to cope.'

Kitty said, 'There's one thing I do want to know. Mother told me that Ann, Mary and Agnes worked in a factory. I expected they would come home to sleep, but there're no bedclothes on their bed.'

'They do work in a factory, but they live in. It's a small family business and they're well looked after. The factory's out at Dodspole and they would need to change horse trams twice, and then they have a mile to walk after that to get there. That's why they come home only on a Sunday; Violet comes then too.'

Jessica's lips tightened as she mentioned Violet's name and Kitty suddenly felt a quiver of fear run through her. It was the fear of the unknown, of not remembering all that had happened in the past, yet feeling there was something wicked about her eldest sister.

'It's Violet I mainly want to talk about,' Jessica went on. 'Your mother starves herself, gets into debt for her. And do you know why? To give her money for fripperies – yes, *fripperies*. It makes me mad.' Her voice was taut with anger.

'But why?' Kitty asked. 'Why should she buy these things for Violet when she's so poor?'

Jessica shook her head in a despairing way. 'Sometimes I feel she's blackmailing your mother. Do you know what blackmail is, Kitty?'

Kitty said not and Jessica, after explaining it, added, 'Mind you, I have no real proof, it's just what I feel. There has to be a reason why your mother does it.'

'It must be because she loves Violet the most,' Kitty said.

Jessica stared into the fire for a moment and was silent. Then she looked at Kitty. 'She doesn't, that's the whole point. I think she's afraid of her. You are the one who's special to your mother, Kitty.'

Kitty stared at her. 'I can't be, she gave me away.'

'No, not gave you away, *sent* you away for your own good. I know, for I was the one who brought you to Abel Leddenshaw. Your mother has been wanting you back all these years, Kitty, but she wouldn't do it until your father died. And even then she felt she was doing the wrong thing in bringing you here – to poverty.'

'I wanted to stay at the farm,' Kitty said in a low voice.

'I know.' Jessica spoke gently. 'But try and understand your mother. She longed to see you, she sacrificed herself by not coming for you sooner. Then one day she said to me in an anguished way, "I must see my Kitty before I die".'

Kitty felt an icy shiver go up and down her spine. 'I didn't know she was ill; at least, she doesn't look very well . . . but—'

'I think what your mother is suffering from mostly is loss of hope. She's had a terrible life with your father drinking and gambling, her losing all those babies, then your father dying and leaving her without money. Don't be too hard on her.' Jessica got up. 'We'd better go, your mother might be awake now and wondering where you are. But wait, just a minute.'

Jessica went upstairs and Kitty thought she had gone to get the glass ship, but she came down with a patchwork quilt. 'It belonged to my mam, it's been washed many times but there's still a bit of weight in it. I never offered it to your mother because I thought she would sell it or pawn it and give the money to Violet. You can tell her I gave it to *you*; she'll respect that.'

As they went out, Jessica stopped at the shed and collected some kindling for Kitty to start the fire the next morning. When they went into the house, Margaret was just getting up out of the chair.

'I fell asleep,' she said. Then she looked at the bucket, at the blankets and the quilt. 'What's this? I don't want charity!' Two spots of colour came to her cheeks.

Jessica said briskly, 'It's not charity. Kitty's paid for the coal and the blankets. I made her a gift of the quilt as a home-coming present. I'll see you both in the morning.'

When Jessica had gone and Kitty put some pieces of coal on the fire, Margaret protested that they could not afford to build up the fire like that. Kitty turned to her.

'Mother, I paid for the coal; I want to be warm, I want you to be warm. I want to heat some bricks to put in the bed too, the room's damp.'

Margaret sat down again and was silent. Kitty brought some pieces of chicken from the parcel of food Harriet had given them, then put the kettle on to make a cup of tea.

The silence continued and Kitty began to fret that she had upset her mother by going behind her back to seek Jessica's advice. Perhaps she would have been hurt under similar circumstances, she thought.

When the tea was made she carried the plate of chicken to her mother, like a peace offering. 'We can have it by the fire, I've cut it small; try and eat some, you've had hardly anything all day.'

Margaret ignored it, and ignored too the mug of tea that Kitty put on the stool beside the chair. When the silence lengthened, Kitty became angry.

'If you don't eat you'll die and if you do you might just as well have left me at the farm.'

Margaret looked up then, her expression vague. 'What?' She leaned forward. 'Kitty, I've been thinking. If you have a little money to spare, would you give some to Violet to get some stockings? The ones she's wearing have holes in them.'

The request was so unexpected Kitty stared at her. Then she said, 'Well, she'll have to darn them, won't she?'

'She has a sensitive skin,' Margaret cajoled. 'The darns hurt her.'

'I don't like wearing darned stockings,' Kitty said, 'but I have to. And if I can wear them, so can Violet.'

'You've turned hard, Kitty.' There was sorrow in her mother's voice. 'And I don't like to hear it.'

'No, I'm not hard. I'm just used to Aunt Harriet's ways. She was always saying that a person had to cut their coat according to the cloth.'

'That's easy if you have some cloth, but when you've got

nothing—' There was now a bitter note in her mother's voice.

'But, Mother – you must get money from Violet, and from Ann and Mary and Agnes. If you can't manage on that ...'

At this Margaret burst into tears. 'I'm in a mess, a terrible mess. Violet's always on to me to give her this and give her that and I'm in debt. Mr Giddon is pestering me to pay it off and I don't know which way to turn.'

Kitty went over and put her arms around her. 'Don't cry, please don't cry, we'll sort something out. It'll be all right.'

Kitty could hear herself speaking with Harriet's voice and she suddenly felt she had become an adult with all the weight of the world on her shoulders. A weight she did not want. She *wanted* to be back at the farm, to have Harriet fussing over her, seeing she was warmly wrapped up before going out into the cold; she wanted to be with Abel who always gave her such a feeling of security, and she longed for Luke, to have him tease – and care for her.

Kitty picked up the cup of tea. 'Have a drink, Mother, then something to eat; it will make you feel better.' To her relief, her mother drank some tea and ate some of the chicken and seemed a little brighter. But only for a while. Margaret began to try and work out how much money she owed. She thought if she gave Mr Giddon the money that Harriet and Abel had given her, it would keep him quiet for a while.

Kitty, knowing that Margaret had been given two golden sovereigns, felt alarmed. Just how much did she owe Mr Giddon? Margaret was vague about it. She thought it was about five pounds.

'Five pounds! Mother, how on earth can we ever get that paid back? How did you come to get into so much debt?'

Margaret held out her arm. 'How? I just don't know, it built up. The girls have to be clothed. Violet is a lady's maid, she has a position to keep up.'

'She's a *maid*, not a lady! That's where all your money goes to, isn't it? That's why you get into debt?'

'Who told you that?' A look of fear came into Margaret's eyes. 'Jessica, that's who – she never did like Violet. Violet is attractive, she could make a good marriage. I want her to get married. She must, she *must*!'

Her mother was so agitated that Kitty became alarmed again.

Her head began to ache, suddenly she felt dog-tired. She got up. 'I think we had better go to bed, Mother, we'll talk things over again tomorrow. Now I'll put the hot bricks in the bed to warm it up.'

The bricks warmed the parts of the bed where they had rested, but when Kitty moved her feet away from the warm patches it was like plunging them into icy water. Draughts seemed to be coming from everywhere. She curled up against her mother's back, but Margaret – who had little flesh on her – seemed to exude no warmth at all. Yet her mother was asleep in no time, while Kitty lay wide awake. Sounds of a cart rumbling by and the drunken singing of men were muted by the fog, which was almost a tangible thing hanging like a veil in the light of the street-lamp.

Money was something that Kitty had handled only on rare occasions, and then it was in pennies – gifts on her birthdays, at Christmas times. She had thought when she left the farm with a pound that she was rich, that it would last for ever. But now she had only fourteen shillings left after paying for the coal and the blankets. She had thought at first when her mother began to cry that she would give her the whole fourteen shillings, but Harriet's teachings told her that she must keep something back for an emergency.

She must talk to her sisters when they came on Sunday, especially Violet. But the thought of talking to Violet about anything had her shaking.

Kitty fell into a fitful doze. She heard the muffled striking of a clock nearby at ten, at eleven, then came the nightmare. First she was being dragged along a street by Violet, by her hair; then the thumping on her body started, the nipping of flesh between finger and thumb, with her sister screaming, 'I hate you. Hate you!'

Kitty awoke in a lather of perspiration, which quickly cooled, leaving her numbed and shivering. What would happen on Sunday? Fear of her sister swamped her and she began to understand something of her mother's apprehension.

Mercifully she fell into a deep sleep . . .

*

At the farm Kitty was always aroused by the rattle of milk-pails, the lowing of cattle, Shep barking, men shouting to one another. Here the sounds that roused her were the chattering of women in the street, the pitiful wailing of a baby, their next-door neighbour raking out the dead ashes of the fire. Then came a cry of 'Milk-O!' and Kitty got out of bed and dressed quickly. They had drunk tea without milk the night before and she had not enjoyed it.

She ran downstairs, took a penny from her purse, got a can for the milk out of the scullery and went out. The fog had cleared. A few doors away a group of women were laughing and joking with the sturdy milkman as he ladled the milk into can and jug.

All fell silent as Kitty came up, then the women were greeting her. She would be Maggie's girl, Kitty – nice to see her back. Their warmth and friendliness lifted Kitty's spirits.

'Cold, in't it, love?' one shawled-woman said. 'Cold enough to freeze the—' She paused and added with a grin, 'Cold enough to freeze the water butts.' There was general laughter at this and another woman said, 'You'll get used to us, Kitty love. Your mam all right?'

'Yes, thank you. I thought I would take her a cup of tea in bed.'

'Oooh, that'll be a treat for her! You look after your mam, girl, she's been right poorly lately.'

Kitty said she would and after she had had her can filled, she left them feeling that things might not be so bad after all. As Harriet would say, troubles always seem worse at night, they usually vanish with the light of day. And one of Abel's maxims was, 'There's no problem that cannot be solved.'

Kitty lit the fire, put the kettle on and when it boiled, took tea up to her mother. 'Oh, Kitty, how nice,' Margaret enthused. 'It was such a special treat to have a morning cup of tea in bed at the farm. Before then I don't remember when I had such a treat. I'll be working today, but I don't start until half-past eight. I'm at the Forsters' today; they have a big house and a big family, there's always mending to do and remaking of clothes to fit the younger children.'

Kitty asked if she got meals there and her mother said yes, but they were mean people; she added that she would like to get a job at the Earles' where Kitty would be starting work on the Monday.

'They're nice people, Kitty, and they feed their staff well. There's not a vacancy at the moment but my friend Mrs Bramley – she's the cook, I think I told you – will let me know if a post does become vacant.'

Kitty was pleased that her mother was in such a chatty mood and wondered if she had found a way of sorting out her money problem. She hoped so, for it would take a weight off her mind.

They had some of the bacon from the farm and Margaret said the smell of it cooking had her feeling ravenous. She was such a different person from that of the night before that it had Kitty puzzled. Finding a few pounds to pay debts was not something that would come easy in their position. Or was Margaret one of those people who could just shrug away problems, hoping they would solve themselves? It made Kitty realize how much a stranger her mother was to her.

When Margaret was ready to leave she said, 'Have a walk around town, Kitty, and call on Jessica; she said she would be pleased for you to drop in at any time. I'll be home just after four o'clock.'

Kitty said she would find plenty to do – she would buy some flour and bake some bread, perhaps make some scones. She refrained from adding that she would also scrub the floors and the table-top. It irked her to see the grime after the spotless conditions she had been living in at the farm.

Kitty realized when her mother had gone that she had forgotten to ask where the shops were, yet when she went out she turned left and knew instinctively she was going in the right direction. There were several children playing outside doors, all bare-footed. Kitty stopped to speak to them and scolded them gently to go in and get their boots on, otherwise they would catch their death of cold. A woman standing in one of the entries called, 'If you have any spare boots, we'd be glad of them, Kitty.' When the woman came forward, Kitty saw she was one of the group she had met that morning.

'I'm sorry,' Kitty said. 'I didn't realize.'

'You'll learn, love. Take care of the boots you've got, you mightn't have the chance of getting another pair.'

Hot colour rose to Kitty's cheeks as she walked on. It seemed she had a lot to learn.

What surprised Kitty was the fact that in spite of the air of poverty – paint peeling from door- and window-frames and filth in gutters- the majority of the windows were clean, doorsteps scrubbed. Several women further along the street eyed her with curiosity. Two of them said, 'Morning …' Kitty might have acknowledged their greetings had she not suddenly became aware of familiar landmarks. Ahead of her she saw the laundry where a girl had one been scalped by her long hair catching in the machinery. Kitty's heartbeats quickened. What a feeling of terror it had given her. Suddenly she knew why – Violet had once threatened her that if she didn't do as she was told she would take her inside the laundry and let the machine take off all her hair. Her mother had been very angry with Violet, telling her that if ever she threatened such a thing again she would have all *her* hair cut off. Violet had quietened after that.

Kitty, who had turned the corner of the street, stopped abruptly. In a hollow to the right of the long sloping road lay the glassworks with its tall and smaller cone-shaped chimneys. Remembrance came flooding back, happy memories and bad ones. Violet had other tortures than the threat of being scalped in the laundry.

Kitty could see herself running joyfully down the road, cutting through all the little streets and alleyways, running as fast as her long dress and skinny little legs would carry her. She would pause only for a moment when she reached the yard, then dart round sacks and crates, dodge the big hooves of the horses pulling the drays and go straight towards the furnace room, with its lovely heat and fiery red glow.

She remembered how a blob of glass would be picked up from the furnace on a blow iron and the iron rolled along the edge of a bench to shape the glass. There was a name for the bench … Kitty's mind became clouded. Was it then that the man blew down the iron to make a bubble? There was another one used … A punty rod! Yes, of course, that was why she had named the kitten Punty. But what was this one used for? A vague image came of a man sitting on a low wooden chair and rolling it over one of the long arms, but after that Kitty could only remember that she was never allowed to stay long enough to see the completed article. Violet would seize her not long after she had arrived and drag her away. But the thumping on her body and the agonizing nipping of flesh never started until they were well away from the yard. While they were in the yard her sister's fingers would be digging into her arm while Violet was exchanging smiles and words with some of the men.

Kitty walked determinedly across to the shops. She must forget it.

She was making for the grocer's when Jessica hailed her and came hurrying up. 'Both bound for the same place, I see. How are you this morning?' Kitty said that she was all right, and was aware of Jessica giving her a quick glance as they went into the shop together.

To Kitty's surprise Mr Shaw recognized her. 'Well, well, well – little Kitty Harvey!' He stood grinning at her. 'Eee, lass, I remember when you could just see over the top of the counter. Standing on tiptoe you were and you'd lisp, "Pleath, Mithter Thaw, I want a pennyworth of tea for me mam." He shook his head, still grinning. 'You never came without money to buy for *your* house, never had anything put on the slate, not as far back as I can remember. Even your dad's baccy was paid for on the spot – and him a gambling man.'

Kitty saw Jessica give him a warning glance and Mr Shaw coughed. 'Yes, well, this won't get me no business, will it? Now what can I get you this morning?'

She told him what she wanted and he talked about the town, remarking that she would be noticing a lot of changes after being away. 'And is your ma well?' he asked. 'Thought she looked a little peaked the last time she was in.'

Kitty thought it was like a story that Harriet had once read to her, where every little bit of conversation helped her to get to know the characters. She had not known that her mother had never been in debt when she was young, nor that her father had a principle of paying there and then for what he wanted, although being a gambling man.

How much more, she wondered, would she get to know about sister Violet when she came home on the Sunday, and her other sisters who had always been so quiet? They had never given any trouble that she could remember.

Other memories beginning to stir in Kitty's mind made her look at her scarred wrists. This brought such a feeling of panic to her, a dryness to her mouth, that she began talking to Jessica in a feverish way. 'If you can think of anything I'll be needing, will you tell me, Jessica? It's not being used to shopping, you see; I'm sure I'll forget something!'

Jessica laid a hand on her arm and nodded to the goods Mr Shaw had already brought. 'Take these for now,' she said quietly. 'If there's anything else you need, we can soon come back for it. Right now we'll go back home and have a cup of tea and a bit of gingerbread. How's that?'

Kitty managed a wan smile. 'It sounds lovely.'

CHAPTER FIVE

Kitty found herself waiting for Sunday to come, when she would meet her sisters. Margaret had told her that their day off could begin at any time from eleven o'clock to two o'clock, depending on what work there was to do. Kitty hoped that Violet would be the first to come so that she could get over her nervousness, find out how her eldest sister would treat her. But as it turned out, it was Ann, Mary and Agnes who arrived first, just after eleven o'clock.

Although there was a year between the sisters they could have been triplets – all the same height, all with pale faces and mousy-coloured hair. The only difference was in their eyes; Ann's blue, Mary's grey and Agnes's hazel. Kitty did not recognize them.

They were shy, but all seemed pleased to see her. Ann's cheeks flushed as she said, 'It's lovely to have you back with us, our Kitty, we missed you.' She turned to the other girls. 'Didn't we?'

Mary and Agnes nodded and Agnes came and hurriedly kissed Kitty, as though afraid to show emotion. Then Ann and Mary kissed her too.

'Well, come and sit down, all of you,' Margaret said, 'and you can tell Kitty about your jobs and she can tell you about the farm.'

Margaret had been on edge all morning; there was a nervous tic in her right eyelid and she kept glancing out of the window in an anxious way. Kitty guessed she was apprehensive because of Violet's intended visit.

Ann did most of the talking, telling Kitty about their work as machinists. There were ten machines in the room, they made shirts, it was terribly hot in summer with all of them in the small room, but it made for warmth in the winter. The woman in charge was very strict, but at the same time she saw that the girls had some decent food.

'It's not like some places,' Mary said, 'where you're starved. What was it like living on the farm, Kitty? Weren't you afraid of the horses ... and ... and things?'

Kitty said not and explained about the different kinds of animals and the work that had to be done on a farm. The girls listened absorbed, so absorbed they seemed not to hear when their mother said in an urgent whisper, 'Here is Violet.' But Kitty heard and broke off in mid-sentence, her heart thumping.

There was the click of the scullery door, then the door of the kitchen was pushed open and a soft voice said, 'Hello, it's me!'

Everyone's gaze turned towards the door and there was a sudden silence. When Violet walked in, Kitty drew in a quick breath, astonished that her eldest sister was not the thin-faced, cruel-looking girl of her nightmares but a tall, beautiful girl with deep gold hair and the tawny eyes of a cat.

Although Violet was wearing a simply-cut dark green coat and hat, there was an elegance about her. Kitty had thought her tall at first, then realized it was the erect way she held herself that gave an illusion of height. Her sister came straight towards her and said with a sweet smile, 'Why, Kitty, what a lovely girl you've grown into! Let me look at you.' Violet put her hands on her shoulders and held her at arm's length, studying her with head inclined.

Kitty, who had automatically stood up as Violet came in, plucked at her dress, uncomfortable that she should have been so wrong about her sister. Her nightmares must have been all a figment of her imagination.

Violet turned to her mother. 'Isn't she lovely, Mam? She has your eyes and dark hair, yet she's not really like you, is she? Nor does she take after Dad. Difficult to say who she *does* take after.'

Margaret turned away and spoke in a suddenly bright voice. 'Well – now that you're all here I'll put the meat pie that Kitty made into the oven. She made it last night, she's a good little cook. Made an apple pie too, with apples Harriet gave us.' Then she said to Agnes, 'Will you go and see if you can borrow a chair or a stool from Jessica? I meant to ask her earlier.'

When Agnes had gone, Violet drew up a stool and sat facing Kitty, her smile now apologetic. 'Oh, Kitty, I behaved dreadfully to you when you were younger. I do hope you've forgiven me. You were such a wilful child, you made me so terribly angry that I didn't really know what I was doing. I was frustrated, I wanted to go out and do a job and I couldn't because I had to look after you.'

'Yes,' Kitty said, 'Mother told me.' She felt wooden, sensing that under the sweetness and the soft voice there was malice. It had been there, like an undercurrent, when Violet had been speaking about Kitty not resembling her mother or her father, yet she could not wholly understand it.

Violet began talking about her job and how much her mistress depended on her. 'It's so rewarding,' she said. 'When she was ill two weeks ago I never left her side, and do you know what she gave me?' She drew from the pocket of her dress two tortoiseshell combs. 'Aren't they attractive? They came from Spain.'

She rubbed a finger over the gilt trim of one of the combs. 'There's little opportunity for me to wear them now, but there will be – oh, yes, there will be, in the future.' Her voice was lowered, and a sleepy cat-like look had come into her eyes.

When Margaret asked her if the new head gardener was still paying her attention Violet looked up, distaste in her expression.

'Oh, him! I had to tell the mistress about him; he was pestering me. He got the sack yesterday.'

Margaret said in surprise, 'But you told me you liked him, you told me he was serious about you, that you had been walking out with him on your evenings off.'

'I had, until I realized how uncouth he was. I'm not cut out to be the wife of a gardener. The master told me that.'

'Oh, Violet, don't get involved with Mr Underwood. He's, well ...'

'He's what, Mam?' There was an arrogant tilt now to Violet's head. 'You ought not to believe all the rumours you hear. Mr Underwood is a gentleman. The parlourmaid who was sacked lied about him. Her mother beat the truth out of her.'

Violet suddenly began to pull the pins from her hair; it was heavy hair that gleamed, but was arranged in a rather severe style with a bun at the back. With the pins out Violet coiled it loosely, pinned it higher at the back then pushed a comb in each side. 'How do I look? Don't you think I'm ten times more attractive than Mrs Underwood?'

When they all stared at her a slow smile spread over her face, then she was laughing. It had a silvery sound. 'Oh, if you could see your faces! Didn't you realize I was funning? Why don't you all laugh, enjoy yourselves?'

'*Laugh*?' Margaret echoed bitterly. 'What is there to laugh about? I'm poverty-stricken—'

'Didn't the Leddenshaws give you any money?' Violet's eyes had narrowed. 'You promised to get me some stockings.' She kicked off one of her lightweight shoes and held out a slender foot. 'Have you seen the holes?'

'Why don't you darn them?' Kitty said, feeling quite calm now that she had the measure of her sister.

Violet turned to her. 'I would, Kitty, if I didn't have such a sensitive skin.' She was all apologetic again, her smile full of sweetness. 'People who have tough skins just don't understand. It's agony for me to walk with darns in my stockings.'

'Well, you'll have to get married, won't you?' Margaret said, her voice sharp. 'Then your husband can buy you your stockings. Just don't expect me to buy you any. I haven't got two pennies to rub against one another.'

'All right, Mam ...' Violet was now smiling. 'I'll get a pair somehow.' She put on her shoe, then stood up. 'I promised to look in on old Mr Hendry – he likes young company. I'll be back in time for dinner.'

They all watched Violet leave, walking with an easy grace. Then Margaret jumped up looking suddenly alarmed. 'You don't think she would ask Mr Hendry for money for stockings, do you?'

'No, of course not,' Ann said. 'Sit down, Mam, and stop worrying about her.'

Margaret sat down, then got up again. 'I'm going after her. There'll be no one from this house to go begging.' She hurried out.

Mary sighed. 'I wouldn't put it past our Violet asking the old man for money. He thinks the sun shines from her, so do a lot more people. Let me warn you, Kitty, our Violet is capable of smiling into someone's face and stabbing that person in the back at the same time. I wish she would get married and go and live at the other side of the world. Every time she comes home she upsets Mam.'

'And we don't know what to do,' declared Agnes.

Neither did Kitty. This was a situation beyond her.

When Margaret came back she looked despondent. She said, 'Violet told me that of course she wouldn't ask Mr Hendry for money, but I have a feeling she'll wheedle some out of him one way or another.'

When Violet did return she wore a demure expression. Mr Hendry had been very kind, she said as she jingled some coins in her pocket.

Margaret said, shocked, 'You told me you wouldn't ask him for money.'

'And I didn't, Mother dear. I simply took off my shoes and held out my feet to his fire and he saw the holes in my stockings. I explained about my sensitive skin and he understood.' She jingled the coins in her pocket again. 'Mind you, he was not *over*-generous.'

'You should be ashamed of yourself, our Violet,' exclaimed Ann. 'I don't know how you could be so mean, taking money from a poor old man.'

Violet gave her an amiable smile. 'That "poor old man", as you call him, owns two streets of houses and four shops. If I thought he would die soon, I'd marry him.'

This statement was greeted by a shocked silence and Violet laughed in a joyful way. 'Oh, it's lovely to tease you lot, you never seem to realize when I'm funning. I wouldn't marry old Mr Hendry if he were the last man on earth. His breath stinks!' She shuddered.

Kitty could not understand this sister of hers at all. Had she been serious when she said she would marry Mr Hendry? Or had she been, as she said, making fun of them?

Several neighbours dropped in during the next hour, including Jessica. Violet was all softness and gentleness as she enquired about their children, the women's husbands. She said how lovely it was to be home and to see Kitty again. And she really sounded genuinely sincere.

One of the women said, 'You always had a bit of class about you, Violet love, but having this lady's-maid job has given you a bit of extra polish; you could pass for one of the upper crust any day.'

'Oh, thank you, how kind of you to say so.' Violet had put on her demure act again, Kitty thought, and with the thought she knew it *was* all acting with her sister. Jessica, judging by her disapproving glances, was the only one of the neighbours who seemed to realize this too.

When the other women had gone, Jessica said to Margaret, 'I was just thinking last night, there's an armchair in Mam's room you could have. The springs are down a little, but it's still comfortable.'

Kitty, noticing her mother's lips tighten and guessing she was about to refuse, said quickly, 'Oh, that would be nice! We can all help to carry it in.'

Ann, Mary and Agnes got up at once. Violet kicked off her shoes and held out her feet to the fire.

Getting the chair out of the bedroom and manoeuvring it down the narrow staircase called forth a lot of instructions and a lot of laughter. When at last they got it into Jessica's kitchen, Ann flopped into it and declared with a breathless laugh that no one was going to get her out of it for five minutes at least.

Kitty felt happier then than she had been since she arrived. If only she had just these three sisters – if only Violet *would* get married and go miles away!

When they finally got the chair into the house and Kitty insisted on her mother trying it, Margaret had to admit it was certainly more comfortable than sitting on one of the hard chairs. Jessica gave a small nod of satisfaction in Kitty's direction that the gift had been accepted.

Kitty longed to have some time alone with her younger sisters, feeling that from them she would get answers to the many questions she wanted to ask. She had thought of suggesting they went for a walk, but thought that Violet might want to come too.

As it happened an unexpected opportunity came when, after the meal was finished and the washing-up done, Violet announced she had to leave early; her mistress was going out to a special dinner and needed her help.

When Violet had gone, still all surface sweetness to Kitty and wishing her well in her new job, Margaret asked the girls if they would mind if she went upstairs and lay down for a while. They all urged her to go and Kitty guessed that her sisters were longing for a talk too.

With the fire made up, the darkening room giving an intimacy and with Kitty ensconced – at her sisters' suggestion – in the faded blue plush armchair, Ann said, 'And now, let's hear all that's been going on. What happened when Mam came to the farm? I bet it was a big surprise to you?'

Kitty told them that it was a very big surprise. She described her feelings, her reluctance to leave the farm, then after a pause said, 'There's one or two things I'd like to ask. First, what was Father like?'

The three girls exchanged quick glances, then there was silence.

When Kitty pleaded for an answer, Mary said, 'We were all afraid of him, Kitty. He was a big man, with a big voice, and he drank a lot.'

It seemed to Kitty that her sisters had all shrunk a little at the mention of their father.

Then Agnes said in a low voice, 'It wasn't that he ever hit us, but we always felt he would and when he did raise a hand he would half-kill us ... as he nearly did with you.'

Kitty's heart began an uncomfortable beating; she swallowed hard. 'What *did* happen? Mother told me part of it, but I know there's more.'

Again the girls exchanged glances and again there was a following silence, eventually broken by Mary. 'We don't like talking about it, it was so awful. Violet complained to Father that you were always disobeying her – running off to the glassworks – and she was at her wits' end to know what to do. Then Father warned you and you just sat there in your nightie smiling at him and telling him you liked going to the glassworks ...'

'And he flew into a terrible rage,' Ann said in a whisper, 'and took off his belt. Oh, Kitty, I'll never forget it, never forget the pitiful look on your face! You cried out only once. After that, big slow tears ran down your cheeks as he went on beating you. It was dreadful. Worse than if you had screamed.' All the colour had gone from Ann's face. 'Mam was very ill in bed, she knew nothing about it. I shouted to Agnes to go and get help, but Father caught hold of her and threw her in a corner, threatening that if any of us mentioned this to anyone he would kill the lot of us, Mam included.'

Kitty looked up. 'I was . . . in a . . . shed.' She began to tremble as she relived the pain.

Ann nodded. 'But we didn't know that then. Violet went with you and Father, but when she came back she wouldn't tell us where you were, except that you were all right. She looked scared. And even though she became sort of cocky during the next few days and kept telling us that you were all right, that Father had an old woman looking after you, still she never really lost that scared look.'

Kitty stared into space. 'He tied me to a chair . . . it was dark nearly all the time in the shed. He told Violet I was to have only bread and water until he said otherwise. I remember that. And I remember that I couldn't eat the bread; it was hard, it choked me and Violet wouldn't give me any water to wash it down. Not at first, not until I was burning hot, then she gave me some sips of water. After that I was icy cold. I was hot and cold . . . hot and cold . . .' Kitty's voice trailed off. She raised her head. 'How did you find me?'

'It was Jessica, she had followed Violet several times but Violet always managed to dodge her. Then one day Jessica—'

'Jessica just came right out with it,' Mary interrupted eagerly. 'She told our Violet that if she didn't tell her where you were, she would see she was put in prison. Our Violet broke down then and told her, but was in a state because she said Father had threatened to kill her if she let on to anyone.'

'When Jessica carried you in that evening . . .' Ann's voice broke. 'Oh, Kitty, it was awful, we couldn't believe it was you. You were just skin and bone, you were filthy, your wrists and ankles were all blood. Jessica took you home with her to nurse you.'

'What did Father have to say about that?' Kitty asked in a low voice.

'He raved and stormed, told Jessica to keep her nose out of his business and Jessica told him it would be police business if he didn't get out and leave you with her. He left, but before he went

71

he threatened that this wouldn't be the end of it.'

Kitty nodded slowly. 'So that was why Mother had Jessica take me to the farm.'

'Yes, she was terrified that Father would eventually kill you. She wasn't even out of bed then, and it set her back so much we all thought she was going to die.'

Kitty's head came up. 'Why did Father hate me so much?'

'Oh, it wasn't just you, he hated the three of us as well. He wanted sons. Violet was all right, she was the first – and a novelty. His beautiful little doll girl, who was able eventually to twist him round her little finger.' For the first time there was a bitter note in Ann's voice. 'When you were born, Kitty, and he realized it was yet another girl, he told Mother to keep the "brat" out of his sight. Then he got blind drunk and was out for two days. When he got over it he pulled Mam out of bed and told her to get back to work ... and she did, they had no money.'

Kitty looked from one to the other of her sisters. 'Yet, before he beat me and tied me up, I can't remember being afraid of him.'

'You weren't,' Mary said. 'I don't think you were afraid of anyone until that awful time. The men at the glassworks used to scold you and tell you to go home – afraid you'd get burned – but one of them said it was difficult to get really cross with you because you had such a lovely smile and winning ways.'

Kitty sighed. 'I don't think I have any winning ways now. I just feel old ... and sort of frumpish. Our Violet is so beautiful.'

'And wicked,' Agnes said. 'But do you know something, I think I can understand how she felt at not only being saddled with us to look after but you, our Kitty, from the time you were two days old.'

The talk after that became desultory. The lamplighter came, bringing a soft glow to the darkening room; coal shifted, sending dead ash plopping into the tin below. Many questions had been answered, but for Kitty one at least had remained unanswered. Why had Violet been blackmailing her mother? She longed to ask, but sensed that when Jessica mentioned it she hadn't intended this information to go any further.

Margaret came down looking more relaxed after her rest. They had tea and at six o'clock the girls prepared to leave. The ringing of the church bells nearby reminded Kitty of Sunday evenings at the farm. A wave of homesickness engulfed her. The farm, she felt, would always be home to her.

With the girls gone, Margaret began to prime Kitty about starting her new job the following morning. Kitty would be answerable to Mrs Bramley, who had the combined position of cook-housekeeper. She must speak only when spoken to and must never, *never* answer back. The work of scullery-maid was hard, different from the hard work on a farm. The Earles entertained quite a lot, so if twelve people were to sit down to dinner and eight courses were served, that would mean over a hundred plates alone to be washed. Add to that vegetable dishes, the cutlery, the cut crystal – a different wine with each course – plus the plates and cutlery of the staff ... and in some cases it could be one or two o'clock in the morning before getting to bed. Then up at six o'clock again.

When Kitty asked what other staff there would be, Margaret reeled them off: under-housemaid, housemaid, parlourmaid, two lady's maids – one for Mrs Earle and the other for the two eldest daughters. Then there was a nannie for the younger children. The male staff consisted of footman, coachman, gardener, Mr Earle's valet and the butler.

Margaret then described the house as being four-storeyed, one of eight in a row, but being on the corner the Earles' house occupied quite a large area of land. The house was in the Elton district and they would need to get a tram in the morning. They had to be there by seven o'clock, as Mrs Bramley wanted to have a word with Kitty before she started breakfast for the family.

'You're really very lucky to get with the Earles, Kitty; they're good people to work for,' her mother said. 'And lucky to get the job without an interview. It's just that Mrs Bramley had known me for some time and is sympathetic. She's hinted, although she hasn't said outright mind you, that if you worked well you might get the job of kitchen-maid in a month's time. The present girl will be leaving, her family are moving to Bradford. It would mean a rise of five pounds a year for you, Kitty!'

'Five pounds?'

Margaret nodded. 'And if you eventually rise to parlourmaid, which I feel sure you could do, your wages could be doubled.'

Kitty decided there and then she would give no cause for complaint, whatever the conditions.

They went to bed early, but Kitty found it impossible to sleep, her mind was full of all the incidents of the day. She puzzled over her sister Violet. Had she meant it when she said she would marry Mr Hendry if she thought he would die soon, or had she really been funning? She thought of her father whom Ann had described as being a big man with a big voice, and found it impossible to conjure up an image of him.

She relived what she thought of as the 'terror time' when she had been tied to a chair, then tried desperately to put it to the back of her mind. Otherwise it was always going to haunt her. Kitty still felt there were a lot of questions that remained unanswered.

Although Kitty was used to getting up in the dark in winter at the farm, she had always come down to a blazing fire. Here they came down to an empty grate and, because Margaret refused to have a fire lit when they were both going out, this meant they had to leave without a hot drink.

And to make it worse the morning was cold and wet, with sleet stinging cheeks. Factory hooters were going, calling people to work, as Kitty and her mother reached the main road where they would catch the horse-drawn tram.

Although the tram would stop anywhere to pick up or put down passengers, they walked to where several other people were waiting, Margaret saying it was a strain on the poor horses having to stop and start a lot of times. The clip-clopping of the horses' hooves could be heard before they loomed out of the murky gloom. There was such a dejected air about them that Kitty felt sorry for them.

There were no seats available inside or on the open top of the tram, but a man inside got up to give Margaret his seat and then stood, strap-hanging, his eyes closed. The passengers were mostly workmen and there was a mingled smell of oil and mustiness from damp clothes. Through the windows Kitty could see a stream of black-shawled women and dark-clad men making for the factories. There were a number of factories along this road and several hooters were going at the same time, all with different sounds. About half a mile further on factories gave way to shops, then to streets of small houses with tiny gardens in front. Here was the end of the line for the tram. The horses were steaming. The driver got down and put a nose-bag over each horse; Kitty felt better to see that they were being looked after.

'This way,' Margaret said, starting to cross the road. 'We go over the bridge past the park, then we're nearly there.'

The rain had mercifully eased. There were elegant looking gas-lamps on the bridge. Gold vines with leaves trailed round the black-painted posts. There were fields beneath the bridge and Margaret stopped to point out a big house where she had her sewing job. She said she would go there on her way back, there was a short cut.

When they finally reached Stratton Gardens where the Earles lived and Kitty saw the house, she was greatly impressed. The front entrance was on the corner with wide shallow steps shaped in a curve leading to a massive door. On either side of it were two lit wrought-iron lamps in the shape of torches. A number of the windows were lit too, bringing a feeling of warmth to Kitty. It would be interesting to live in a house like this, even if she did have to work hard.

Margaret took her by the arm and led her along by the side of the house, saying, 'We go down the area steps to the basement, it's round the back.' They went through a wicket gate that said, 'Tradesmen's Entrance. No dogs allowed', and into a large garden with a thick, high yew hedge. Kitty had no time to take in more than that the garden was beautifully laid out before her mother was leading the way down the basement steps.

Margaret's gentle knock brought a girl in a buff-coloured print dress to the door. She looked flustered and called to someone inside, 'I think it's the people you was expecting, Mrs Bramley, ma'am.'

A sharp voice replied, 'Well, bring them in, girl. Don't leave them standing out in this weather!'

Kitty's spirits drooped when she heard the sharp voice and when she saw the woman who belonged to it they drooped yet further. She had met four cooks when Abel took produce to some of the big houses in the district; all four had been buxom, pleasant. This woman was not only sharp-voiced, she was sharp of feature and rake-thin.

And yet there was a kindliness in the eyes of Mrs Bramley when she greeted Kitty. 'Well! So you are the youngest. If you're as good a worker as your ma was when she worked for me years ago, you'll do, girl. Sit you both down; there's tea in the pot, I'll pour you some and you can drink it while we talk. I don't have much time.'

Kitty wondered why her mother had made no mention of working for Mrs Bramley. All she had said was they were friends. Something else to add to the mystery.

Mrs Bramley, after ordering the girl who had opened the door to get on with her job, poured the tea and sat down. And while she was talking in a low voice to Margaret, Kitty looked around her.

The kitchen was as spotless as the one at the farm, only very much larger. There were massive ovens at either side of the grate where a fire glowed red. Then there were two more ovens on the same wall, which Kitty took to be gas ovens. Above these were shelves of pans – some shining copper ones and the others iron, well-blackened from the fire. There were three huge sinks with two taps in each. Why two? Kitty wondered. To fill the sinks more quickly?

'Well now, Kitty, I'll tell you your duties.' Kitty turned to face the cook, who repeated most of what Kitty had been told by her mother the night before. Then Mrs Bramley went on, 'We have family prayers only once a week here, on Sundays. Your mother tells me you can read and write and you know your Bible.'

'Yes, Mrs Bramley, ma'am.'

The woman folded her hands in her lap and a prim expression came over her face. 'I'm an educated woman meself and a God fearing-one, and I appreciate that you have some learning and religion. If you behave yourself and do all that's asked of you, there might be a bit of promotion for you. But we'll talk about that if the time comes.'

Mrs Bramley went on to say that Kitty would share a room with Ivy, the under-housemaid, the girl she had just met, and explained that dresses would be provided for her. Mrs Earle provided all the uniforms for staff and Kitty should consider herself very lucky in this respect, most staff having to provide their own, or having it bought and then the amount deducted from their wages.

Margaret interrupted tentatively to say that Kitty had good underwear and boots and stockings; Mrs Leddenshaw had seen to that. Mrs Bramley gave a nod of approval and then, after giving Kitty further instructions, concluded with, 'You are not, and I repeat *not*, to go upstairs into any part of the house – apart from your own room, and then you'll go by the back stairs – unless of course you are sent there for any reason, which I very much doubt, you being only a scullery-maid at the moment.'

The girl Ivy came back and Mrs Bramley ordered her to take Kitty up to their room, find a dress to fit her and warned them they were not to stay talking. When neither girl made a move she rapped out, 'Well, come on, get moving, there's work to be done – for both of you!'

Ivy scurried out, with Kitty hurriedly following. Ivy led the way up a narrow flight of steep wooden back stairs, pausing on the first landing to say, 'We're nothink, nothink at all! Treated like alimals, that's what. No, not even alimals, folks talk to dogs and cats but that snotty-faced lot down there—' she jerked a thumb over her shoulder, 'don't even look at folks like you and me. I thought when I got a lift up to under-housemaid they'd throw me a word now and then, but no, I'm still nothink!' Ivy started up the second flight, then paused on the second landing to ask Kitty her name.

When Kitty told her Ivy said, 'You aren't half pretty. I wish I looked like you. I like to bet when *Lady* Bettina leaves next month – she's the housemaid – you'll be offered her job. I don't mind, though,' she added frankly, 'I like you!'

They climbed the next two flights in silence, both needing their breath for the steep stairs.

The attic room they went into was not large but adequate. There were two iron bedsteads with a piece of matting between them, a cupboard for their clothes, a marble-topped washstand with a china basin and ewer, and a mirror above it with only a tiny crack at the corner. Kitty looked up at the window in the roof and Ivy said grimly, 'When it's pelting with rain, it drums on there and keeps you awake.'

'But the sun will come in too,' Kitty said.

Ivy turned and stared at her. 'My, but you're a rum 'un. I never thought of a thing like that!'

Kitty was able to take stock of Ivy for the first time, really take stock of her. She was rake-thin, with a pale pinched face, her nose red-tipped. A piece of dark hair – looking as if a chunk had been chopped off it – stuck out like a sore thumb from under her mob-cap. She was wearing a buff-coloured cotton dress with a white bibbed apron over it.

'The sun will come in too,' Ivy repeated. 'I like that. I'm a miserable sod. Sorry, I shouldn't use that word, I'd get a clout if cook or me mam heard me. But that's what I am. Always have been! Gran said I was like a skinned rabbit when I was born and that I bawled for nearly a year. Dad said he nearly drowned me one time. It might have been better if he had.'

'Oh, no,' Kitty said, 'you mustn't say such a thing, and you must never think of yourself as a nobody.' She told Ivy the story that Abel had told her about the three-legged dog and when she had finished a slow smile spread over Ivy's face.

'Hey, I like that, and I like you too. I think we'll get on fine. I'll just go and find you a dress to fit you; I think Meggie was about the same size as you. They're in the cupboard on the landing. Be getting your coat and dress off, we'll have to hurry.'

Ivy came back with a buff-coloured dress and a dark brown pinafore. The dress felt damp, but Kitty struggled into it and buttoned it up. She then lifted her bass hamper on to the bed, prepared to unpack, but Ivy told her to leave it for the time being as they must go. When Kitty stood hesitant Ivy said, mimicking the sharp tones of Mrs Bramley: 'Well, come on then, get moving, there's work to be done—'

Then both girls laughed together and Kitty felt happy, knowing she had found at least one friend at Stratton House.

CHAPTER SIX

The rest of the day was bewildering for Kitty. She was at the
constant beck and call of Mrs Bramley: 'Fetch that bowl, that
tin, that pan, wash up these few pieces of cutlery, get me the big
wooden spoon, fetch the cream from the larder, the spices . . .'.
It went on and on. Although she met all the staff at different
times she never sat down to a meal with them until supper-time,
and it was only then that they began to register with her, for she
was formally introduced to them all by Mrs Bramley.

'This is Kitty Harvey, the new scullery-maid,' she said.

Kitty wished she could still be known as Leddenshaw.

Only two of the staff acknowledged her. The footman gave
her a smile and surprisingly, the parlourmaid whom Ivy had
nicknamed *Lady* Bettina gave her a brief greeting. The rest did
not even look in her direction. And in fact Mr Walton, the
butler, a bespectacled stern-looking man, spoke only to Mrs
Bramley and then not at any length. Ivy gave Kitty a nudge and
pointed at her plate. Kitty had hardly touched the food, she felt
too tired to eat. She made an effort after Ivy had whispered that
Mrs Bramley liked to see plates cleared, to do justice to her
cooking.

Ivy helped her with clearing the tables and the washing-up,
but even with help Kitty felt she was working in her sleep. One
thing that was a godsend was having hot water on tap, which had
recently been installed. Ivy told her before that, great big pans
of water had to be boiled to fill the sinks. When the last cup and
saucer was put away and the tables laid for breakfast the next
morning, Mrs Bramley said with a kindly note in her voice, 'Off
to bed with you, Kitty. It's been a hard day for you, the first one

always is, but tomorrow will be better.'

Ivy went up with her, saying, 'Don't you believe it, every day's the same, bloody hard! And don't tell me to stop swearing! It does me good. Gets the mad out of me. That rotten lot sitting there, all hoity-toity as if they were God Almighty.'

Kitty stopped taking in what Ivy was saying once they reached the bedroom. She was hardly aware of getting undressed and climbing into bed and was lost in sleep the moment her head hit the pillow.

It seemed she had been asleep only minutes before Ivy was shaking her and telling her it was time to get up.

And so the day started. But Kitty came to discover that Ivy was wrong and Mrs Bramley right. That day *was* an improvement on the first, and by the fourth day she was watching the staff sitting round the table and listening intently to all the gossip, which was mostly about the Earle family.

She learned that Mrs Earle ailed a lot and that her husband had a mistress in the background (this was spoken of in low voices), that Lavinia (the second eldest daughter) was a wild one and would be getting into trouble soon if she was not careful. And there was news of a possible engagement between the eldest daughter, Thea, and a Mr Ballantyne. Cook said, a sudden dreaminess in her eyes, 'I hope they do get engaged, I hope they get married, it would be lovely to have a bit of romance in our lives.'

Mr Walton made no response to this, but he rustled the newspaper he was reading as though in disapproval. Then Bettina, obviously annoyed, looked at him in a defiant way.

'And what is wrong with romance, Mr Walton?'

He lowered his newspaper and gave her a cold stare over the top of his spectacles. 'Just keep your opinions to yourself, *if* you please.'

Bettina flushed and seemed about to retort, then obviously thinking better of it, took out her feelings on a piece of bread by slicing through it with a vicious cut.

All of this intrigued Kitty and she made a mental note of each item to relate in her letters to the farm. She had started one the day after she arrived home and added little bits each day, but had not done any more since moving into Stratton House. Perhaps tomorrow.

The person that Kitty was interested in most was Bettina. She was not pretty, but she had a look of belonging to a good-class family. She ate in a delicate way, cutting her food up small and chewing it carefully, as though she had been taught from being young to eat in this way. Kitty envied Bettina her grey alpaca dress, her frilly apron with the big bow and long strings and the little starched cap that sat on top of her thick brown hair. Yes, Kitty decided, she would be parlourmaid one day and bob curtsies to the family and to visitors who came.

On the Thursday morning there was some excitement. In the basement kitchen were two windows, both at ground level. From one you could see some of the trees in the back garden and from the other one, could catch a glimpse of carriages stopping outside the front door. On this morning it was a cart that attracted the staff; it contained wooden crates which were being lowered carefully, and the excitement started when Bettina came running down to the kitchen and imparted the news that the crates were from Italy. They were presents for Mr and Mrs Earle from Mrs Earle's nephew, Mr Tyler van Neilson. She had apparently overheard Thea and Lavinia discussing it.

The next minute Bettina was away again, apron strings flying, calling over her shoulder that she would let them know later what the crates contained.

Mrs Bramley began talking about Mr van Neilson. A lovely man, she said, and as handsome as they came. And there was no one more generous when he came to visit – had he not given her five golden sovereigns the last time he came, as well as praising her cooking to high heaven!

Although Kitty would not be involved in any way with the contents of the crates, she had the same feeling of excitement as when the travelling man came to the farm with his wares and she had waited in a breathless way for him to open his boxes, to display all manner of things – combs, mirrors, fancy shawls, aprons, pillow-cases … endless goods.

Half an hour later Bettina was back again to say that the most beautiful glass chandelier and all sorts of lovely glass vases and bowls had been unpacked. The chandelier would hold about a hundred candles.

Glass … vases and bowls … from Italy, the place of her childhood dreams. Kitty felt her stomach contract. If only she could see them . . . but that of course was impossible, that part of the house was out of bounds.

'Workmen will be coming soon to hang the chandelier,' Bettina said in a breathless way, 'and all the candles will be lit when Mr van Neilson comes on a visit.'

'Oh, so he's coming on a visit, is he?' said Mrs Bramley drily. 'And when will that be, Miss Know-it-all? I haven't been informed of any visit and I certainly should be, seeing that I am the one to do the cooking.'

'I was just coming to tell you, Cook,' said a quiet voice from behind them.

The gaze of all turned swiftly to the tall, fair-haired woman who was coming towards them. She walked erect, but had a fragile air about her.

Mrs Bramley for once was flustered. She hastily drew out a chair. 'Oh, do sit down, Mrs Earle, ma'am, ought you to be out of bed? I would have come up with the menu, as I've been doing this past week.'

'Yes, I know you would, Cook, but I decided it was time to get into a routine again. Lying in bed can become a habit, and I want to be up for when my nephew arrives, to enjoy his company to the full. It's such a joy to have him.'

'I'm sure it is, ma'am, a real pleasure. And when would you be expecting him?'

'Actually, it's this evening. We have just heard. But you are not to worry about preparing a meal. He will not be here until late, it could be eleven o'clock. He's coming from Italy and may not want anything – a cold collation would do very well.'

Mrs Bramley, suddenly realizing that three members of her staff were standing idle, rounded on them. 'Come along, you girls, get on with your jobs! Standing here gawping.' She turned to her mistress, 'Begging your pardon, ma'am, for the language, but you have to be at them all the time.'

Mrs Earle said, 'The dark-haired girl, she's the new girl, is she not?'

'Yes, she is, ma'am. Kitty Harvey, who's taken Meggie Tate's place, and she's shaping up very well, if I may say so, ma'am.'

'I should like to meet her, Cook.'

Mrs Bramley called Kitty over and she came, wiping her

hands on the corner of her sacking apron. She bobbed a curtsey, her first.

'Well done, Kitty. I remember now Cook mentioning you. You were living on a farm, is that right?'

Kitty glanced at Mrs Bramley before replying and got a quick nod.

'Yes, ma'am. With Mr and Mrs Leddenshaw, my foster-parents.'

Mrs Earle asked her if she missed living on a farm and Kitty said that she did, she missed the fresh country air and her foster-family – then, catching Mrs Bramley shaking her head at her, she added quickly, 'But of course it's nice to get back to my mother and sisters.'

'Indeed, yes. Well, Kitty, you seem to have been well-brought-up by both your families. You're a pretty girl, nicely spoken. I hope you will stay with us.' Mrs Earle then turned to Mrs Bramley and suggested they now discuss the menu for the day. Kitty withdrew and went back to her washing-up. She found herself trembling. She ought not to have mentioned missing the fresh country air; Mrs Earle might have thought she would be homesick for the farm and would want to go back. And as much as she would like to go back, she had to stay here, she needed the money; her mother had debts to pay.

When Mrs Earle had gone upstairs Mrs Bramley was in an expansive mood and chatted as Kitty fetched and carried for her.

'I'm glad Mr van Neilson is coming, he always does the mistress so much good. She dotes on him, he's her favourite nephew. He makes her laugh and he talks to her about his work. She is *very* interested in it.'

Kitty, becoming more and more intrigued, forgot all about the maxim of not speaking unless spoken to and asked what work he did.

'He deals with glass, makes it and experiments with it. Mrs Earle had one of the outhouses at the bottom of the garden turned into a laboratory for him.'

Made glass and . . . experimented with it. Kitty felt full of awe that she could be living – or would be living – in the same house as such a man. If only she could meet him, talk to him. But that was like crying for the moon.

'His name sounds foreign,' she said.

'It is. Mr van Neilson's father is Dutch, his mother Italian.' Mrs Bramley laughed. 'He's a strange mixture all round. Some of his ancestors were English and others French. How's that for a family tree?'

Although Kitty knew she would be stretching her luck by asking further questions about this very interesting man, she felt she just had to know what he looked like. 'Is he good-looking?' she asked.

'As handsome as they come,' Mrs Bramley declared. 'Tall, with thick dark hair, and strong looking. Mind you, he likes his own way, does Tyler. His father is a banker and expected his eldest son to come into the business, but he refused. It caused a lot of trouble. He left home and I don't even know whether he and his father are on speaking terms.'

Mrs Bramley began to whip up a sponge cake. 'He has lovely eyes like dark brown velvet, very expressive. The girl who gets him will be very lucky indeed, because he's a considerate man. Got a temper though, mind.'

Kitty began daydreaming, seeing herself working side by side with Tyler van Neilson, helping him with his experiments.

'The cake tin, Kitty.' Mrs Bramley's sharp command made Kitty jump. 'I've asked you twice to grease it.'

'Yes, Mrs Bramley, right away, ma'am.'

There was no more opportunity for daydreaming and Mrs Bramley's good humour had changed to ill-humour by midday. A message had been sent down to say that Mr Earle was detained and the lunch would have to be served an hour late.

'An hour!' Mrs Bramley exclaimed. 'Everything is about ready. What am I expected to do, stop it from cooking? I'm not a magician! I'll have to let it cook and then warm it up. It's their own fault if it's not straight out of the oven. No other cook would stand it, this is the fourth time this month it's happened. Been delayed, he said. I can guess who's delayed him – his lady-love, that's who!'

Mr Walton, who had just come in, said, 'What, at this time in the day?' To Kitty's surprise a wry smile of humour touched his lips.

To this Mrs Bramley snapped, 'The time of day for that sort of thing makes no matter to *some* men!' She began to ladle the cake mixture into the tin. Mr Walton remarked that he was surprised Mrs Bramley should be so full of ill-humour when the *charming* Mr van Neilson was due to come for a visit. Mrs Bramley, bristling, handed the cake tin to Kitty, ordered her to put it in the oven and to close the door gently; then she turned to face the butler, hands on hips.

'Let me tell you something, Mr Walton. Mr van Neilson *does* happen to be a favourite of mine, but I know his shortcomings. He's artistic with glass, but when things go wrong he gets into an ill-humour. I am artistic in the culinary arts and when my creative efforts are about to be ruined for lack of thought on the part of the master of the house, I get into an ill-humour too.'

Mrs Bramley walked to the table, picked up two spoons, laid them carefully side by side, then looked up, tight-lipped.

'But you, Mr Walton, having no creative ability in your job, would not understand this.'

Kitty, who was drying dishes and hoping she looked as if she was not listening in to this conversation, tensed at the last remark, expecting the butler to explode. He did square his shoulders, but when he spoke his voice was quite calm.

'You speak of yourself as an educated woman, Mrs Bramley, but if that were so you would understand the efficiency of technique that is required in my job. I consider myself to be an artist too in my work.'

With that he went to the pipe-rack, drew out a pipe and began to full it. Mrs Bramley said something like 'Humph!' and began giving Kitty orders for items that were required – *at once*. Kitty jumped to the orders.

When Ivy came in and Kitty told her in a whisper about the upset, saying she was sure that Mr Walton would never speak to Mrs Bramley again, Ivy dismissed this as being like a married couple having to blow off steam. 'It happens all the time,' she said. 'They'll make it up in bed tonight – or this afternoon.'

Kitty stared at her. 'You mean they're husband and wife?'

'Course not!' Ivy gave a sly wink. 'But I know what goes on if nobody else does. Mind you, I think they might have got churched if Mr Walton didn't already have a wife. Not that he's seen her for years.' Ivy grinned suddenly. 'Judging by your face, you're getting a bit of education as well. It's life, going on all the time!'

It's life ... Kitty could hear Harriet saying this when discussing some tragic happening with neighbours, a girl getting into trouble ... a man running off with someone else's wife ... a jilted girl drowning herself ... And Harriet would always conclude with, 'It's happening all the time, isn't it?' and there would be a great sadness in her voice.

Was it happening all the time? Did cooks usually sleep with butlers? It seemed all wrong, against all Harriet's teachings and Abel's too. Fornicating, as the vicar had once called it in one of his sermons, was also against all the church's teachings.

Kitty felt she was growing up much too quickly.

That afternoon when Mrs Bramley had gone to lie down, Bettina came into the kitchen and announced that the chandelier was up and it looked really beautiful. 'A shaft of sun shone on some of the crystal drops,' she enthused, 'and you should have seen all the marvellous colours in them: blue, green, orange – you can just imagine how the whole thing will sparkle when the candles are lit for Mr van Neilson's arrival.'

Bettina trailed a finger along the edge of the table, then looked up and said with a smile, 'I've decided to set my cap at him.'

'You?' Ivy exclaimed. 'You don't stand a chance. You're nothink, like me. And anyway, all he's interested in is his work, his experi-, experi- the things he does in the outhouse. You told me yourself that he's never shown any interest in Miss Thea or Miss Lavinia, and Miss Lavinia is a beauty.'

Bettina's head went up. 'But *not* his type. Mr van Neilson needs someone who's interested in his work, I heard him tell the mistress that. I also heard him tell her that he was thinking of setting up his own establishment and for that he would need a wife to run it.'

'And you think you could run his home,' Ivy sneered. 'You'd better think again. Mr van Neilson is class.'

'In case you don't know it, I have aristocratic blood in *me*.' Bettina had an arrogant look then.

'If you have, then you're a by-blow,' Ivy taunted.

In answer to this Bettina turned her back, jerked her bottom – sending the big bow bouncing – then walked towards the stairs calling over her shoulder. 'You can think what you like. When I marry Mr van Neilson, I'll have scum like you curtsying to me.'

'Stupid bitch!' Ivy called after her. 'Your mother was a

laundry-maid, seduced by the weak-chinned son of the house. And *he* was thought to be a by-blow of one of his father's mistresses!'

By this time Bettina was out of sight and Kitty said, distressed, 'Ivy, please don't say these things. I'm sure you only say them because you don't like Bettina.'

'I don't, I hate her! I can't stand folk who try to be better than they are. Not like you, Kitty . . .' The viciousness had gone from Ivy's voice as she made this last remark. 'You would never give yourself airs, I know it. Not even if you married into the gentry. And you could – you're pretty and you talk nice, sort of soft. But you watch out, don't let any of these fellows talk you into anything. They'll tell you all kinds of lies and make all sorts of promises to try and bed you.'

'Stop it!' Kitty cried. 'I don't like this kind of talk.'

'Well, you'd better get used to it!' Ivy retorted. 'You got to know how to dodge these fellers with ten hands.' Her expression suddenly softened. 'I don't want any harm to come to you, Kitty. You're the only friend I've ever had in me whole life.'

Kitty felt deeply moved. 'I'm glad to have you as a friend, Ivy. Didn't you have a special friend when you went to school?'

'I never went to school, never had no learning. What I know now is what Mrs Bramley learnt me. Me mam had dozens of kids, I hated them all. It was a real treat when I got me first job. This is me second and the best; I want to stay here.' Ivy suddenly grinned. 'So I got to keep me nose clean, haven't I?'

For the first time Kitty began to understand her sister Violet's hatred of her – the longing to go out to work, but instead being saddled with looking after her four younger sisters, and Kitty herself being wilful, disobedient.

When Mrs Bramley came down from her rest she was still in a bad humour and Kitty felt glad, sure now that Ivy had been wrong about Cook and Mr Walton sharing the same bed.

Kitty was set to peel shrimps, with Mrs Bramley saying that Mr van Neilson had taken a liking to seafoods the last time he was here, but she must prepare something else as well, in case there had been a rough crossing and seafood might be the last thing he wanted. She then went on to say how she used to send special little meals for him to the outhouse when he was working for long hours, and how much he had appreciated it.

'Not that I agree with a man spending days working like that,' she added. 'Shutting himself off from people. If he had a wife she would certainly complain.'

'Far better spend it there than in someone else's bed,' Ivy said, with one of her sly looks.

Mrs Bramley rounded on her. 'You watch your tongue, my girl, or you'll feel my hand around your ear.' She then turned to Kitty. 'And you get on with your work, standing there gawping.'

The kitchen staff had a bad hour, with Mrs Bramley continually complaining; then Mr Walton came in, said something to her in a quiet voice and almost at once the atmosphere changed.

'See what I mean,' whispered Ivy, 'all lovey-dovey again. Makes you sick, don't it?' Kitty moved away from her, not wanting to hear any more of Ivy's kind of talk. It made her uncomfortable.

When the elderly coachman, Mr Greenhill, was putting on his cape coat to go to the station to pick up the visitors he said, jerking his thumb in the direction of the stairs, 'My, but that's a right bonny chandelier thing in the hall, worth taking a look at it. Real bonny, it is.'

He had puffy cheeks and a red-veined nose and was normally a sullen man who had little to say. Ivy had once remarked that he was drunk most of the time, but he was sober enough now and Kitty quite liked him. His eyes had a twinkle in them.

Kitty said a little wistfully that she would like to see it, she would like to see it very much. Mrs Bramley reminded her, not unkindly, that the hall and everywhere beyond it in that part of the house was forbidden to her. Kitty nodded and said, Yes, she understood.

Mr Greenhill then began to coax Mrs Bramley to 'let the lassie take a little peek', pointing out that she need go only a short way up the stairs to see the lighted chandelier. Mrs Bramley hemmed and hawed then finally gave in, warning her that as soon as she had seen it she was to come down right away.

Kitty eagerly agreed and in a state of excitement at this special treat, smiled around at those of the staff who were in the kitchen. Then, rubbing the palms of her hands down her apron, she went tip-toeing across the kitchen and up the first few stairs. She paused, took a quick breath, then climbed the next few to a landing leading to a turn in the stairs. Once up the next five steps she stopped and looked up, then gave a gasp of pure delight as she saw the chandelier. Every candle in it was lit, some of the flames rising up straight, others flickering as though in a slight draught.

Kitty remembered seeing her first cut-glass beads that edged a muslin milk-jug cover at the farm and how entranced she had been as the sun caught the beads, making them dance and sparkle with colour. Prisms of light, Harriet had called them. Kitty had seen these prisms later in a dewdrop, and been overwhelmed at such beauty in a drop of water.

But that was nothing in comparison with this tier after tier of cut crystal pieces that kept changing with each flicker of a candle. How was it possible for a man to make such beauty? How had he released such magnificent colours – purples, emerald green, blue, yellow, orange . . . They were the colours of the rainbow, but so . . .

'Kitty! Come down.' The urgent whisper of Mrs Bramley brought Kitty from a fairy-tale world back to reality. She backed down one step, then went up it again for a final look.

'Kitty, do you hear me, *at once!*'

She turned and came down slowly. 'Like a sleep-walker,' Ivy said afterwards. 'If you could have seen your face, just as if you'd seen an angel. I don't know what you're all going on about, they're just lumps of glass.'

'Lumps of glass?' Kitty stared at her appalled. 'How can you say such a thing, Ivy? Every piece that makes up the chandelier has been hand-cut. I can't imagine how a man could create such beauty.'

'Listen to her!' Ivy exclaimed. 'She goes all daft when she talks about things like that and about things that grow. She talks about *beards* of moss, and the *pale wax candles* on the chestnut tree, and about beautiful *Tiger* lilies. Tigers are fierce alimals. Me uncle told me.' Ivy grinned affectionately at Kitty. 'They'll lock you up one of these days.'

'You'll both get more than locked up,' Mrs Bramley threatened, 'if you don't get on with some work. Kitty, get this table scrubbed down.'

Mr Greenhill said to Mrs Bramley, 'You and that Ivy ain't got no souls. Let the lassie dream for a bit. God knows there's little beauty down in this here place.'

Mrs Bramley reminded him grimly that they didn't work in the kitchen for beauty but to live and eat – and Kitty had best get a bucket and scrubbing brush and get scrubbing, or else ...

Kitty scrubbed but she was in another world, the beautiful world of Mr van Neilson who worked with glass. What an impressive name he had. Kitty liked the word 'impressive'. Luke often used it when describing a sunset, or when he went out at dawn after a heavy fall of snow and there was not a mark to be seen on the vast expanse of white. *Very* impressive, he would say.

Luke Leddenshaw was an impressive name too, Kitty thought, knowing she was feeling a little guilty at thinking so much about the coming visitor. She dipped the scrubbing brush into the water and began to scrub in earnest.

For the past few nights Kitty had been longing to get to bed, but this evening she lingered, finding small jobs to do so that she could wait up for the arrival of the visitor. Mrs Bramley was fussing about too, putting last-minute touches to the cold collation as well as the dish of seafood she had laid out. There were wafer-thin slices of beef rolled around spears of asparagus, slices of roast ham, game pie and liver pâté, the dishes being trimmed with sprigs of watercress, slices of cucumber and chives.

She stepped back and surveyed her work. 'There, that's ready if needed.' Then she looked around the immaculate kitchen, gave a nod of approval and Kitty, knowing she was going to tell her to get off to bed, hastily brought out the sewing basket and pointed to a tiny hole in her apron.

'Must darn this. Aunt Harriet was always saying that a stitch in time saves nine.'

'And she's right. Get it done, then, and you and Ivy can get to—' Mrs Bramley raised her head and stood listening, then she called to Mr Walton who was in the butler's pantry, 'That's the carriage coming, Mr Walton, if I'm not mistaken.'

He came out, slipping into his jacket. 'I heard it, Mrs Bramley.'

Bettina was already upstairs, waiting to take the guest's hat, coat and stick. Kitty moved carefully to where she could look out of the window that faced the front. She heard the crunch of wheels on the gravelled drive and her heartbeats quickened. Mr Walton went unhurriedly up the stairs, his back stiff, while Mrs Bramley looked about her and asked where Ivy was. 'Not upstairs, I hope!' she added. Ivy came out of the scullery.

'I'm here, Mrs Bramley. Been putting me dirty apron in the laundry basket.' She turned away, gave Kitty a wink and put a finger to her lips.

This had no meaning to Kitty and when she heard the carriage drawing nearer, she indicated the window to Ivy: they both moved closer. Mrs Bramley was standing listening at the foot of the stairs.

Although the front part of the house was lit by the lamps on either side of the front door, all that could be seen apart from the carriage wheels were two pairs of legs: one long pair and the shorter ones of George who had gone to collect the luggage.

Ivy now indicated that they move nearer to the stairs, but no sooner had she moved and Kitty was about to follow than Mrs Bramley ordered them both to bed. She waved a hand towards them, 'Off, off, it won't be all brightness and merriment in the morning, will it? No, it'll be droopy eyelids and yawns.'

'Brightness and merriment!' Ivy exclaimed as they trudged up the back stairs. 'That's a big laugh. It's all right for her, ain't it? She can stand and listen. I wanted to hear Mr van Thingummy's voice. I bet it's lovely and deep.'

So Ivy dreamed too, Kitty thought, but would never admit it if she tackled her with it. She asked, 'Ivy, what did you mean when you winked after you came out of the scullery and put a finger to your lips?'

'Because I didn't want you to blurt out who I was with in the scullery. And if you didn't know I ain't telling, so don't start asking questions.'

Kitty was puzzled. Who could have been in the scullery with Ivy, and why should she make such a secret of it? The answers to both questions eluded her and she put them to the back of her mind, longing to be in bed where she could do her own dreaming.

But it was not of the visitor that Kitty thought first when she got into bed. The hard bed seemed damp this evening, and although there was some weight in the bedclothes there was not the comfort of her bed at the farm, where she would be snug and warm, deep in the feather bed with the plump eiderdown covering her. And with thoughts of the farm it was Luke she began to dream about.

How many times had she imagined herself married to him, caring for him and their children! They were just dreams, but they were a part of her life. Every person must dream. Ivy had proved that *she* did and so had Mrs Bramley when she talked about a marriage between Miss Lavinia and Mr Ballantyne. There had been a dreaming in her eyes. And although Bettina had talked in a hard way about 'setting her cap' at Mr van Neilson, there must be a longing in her too – to be wanted, to be loved.

And with thoughts of Mr van Neilson, Kitty thought it strange how close she could feel to a man whom she had never met, nor was likely to. It was his work, of course, the beautiful glass. How clever he must be! Earlier, Bettina had mentioned an exquisite blue vase, all twists and spirals, saying that something like it must cost the earth. Bettina did recognize the beauty of the vase, but at the same time linked it with its worth in money. That was wrong. Kitty began to imagine herself working with Mr van Neilson in his laboratory, he asking her advice on one of his experiments, then stopping and looking deeply into her eyes . . .

Suddenly feeling terribly disloyal for having such thoughts, she tried to bring her mind back to Luke, but somehow he seemed so remote, a world away. What was happening to her? She loved Luke, shared his love of farming and she wanted to share that life with him . . .

Kitty drifted into sleep. But it was not of Luke she dreamed, but of a tall dark-haired stranger with eyes like black velvet, who was building up around them a wall of glass slippers which sparkled and showed all the glorious colours of the rainbow.

Her lovely trance-like state lasted after Ivy had called her at six o'clock, but once Kitty was out of bed and standing shivering as she washed in icy-cold water, their breaths a mist in the chill of the room, reality returned.

'Ooh,' she said, 'let's get down to the kitchen and get a bit of warmth from the oven.'

The day started like any other, but when in the afternoon

Kitty found herself for once completely alone in the kitchen, she wondered if she dare take another peep at the chandelier. Mrs Bramley was lying down, Bettina had an hour off to see some relative who was sick, Ivy had gone on an errand and the rest of the staff seemed to be busy with various tasks. She crept towards the stairs, went up three, stopped, continued with and with rapidly beating heart climbed up until she could see the chandelier.

The sky had been cloudy all morning and the chandelier, although still beautiful, lacked the sparkle of the night before. The house was as silent as though everyone had gone and Kitty, with a longing to see the vase Bettina had mentioned, wondered if she dare venture a little further.

With the recklessness of her younger days, when she gave no thought to the consequence of disregarding orders, she ran swiftly up the next few steps ...

And stood, overwhelmed by a feeling of awe. Never in her wildest dreams had she imagined such elegance. A massive golden rug covered nearly the whole of the hall, leaving only a border of dark honey wood, polished to a mirror brightness.

There were gilt tables, spindly-legged chairs with curved backs – their seats and backs covered with a rich blue brocade. At the window were floor-length velvet curtains in blue, with braided looped pelmets. Her gaze moved slowly round the tables, which carried ornaments and photographs, then as though for her benefit a sudden shaft of sunlight picked out a vase on a tall pedestal. Kitty gasped at the beauty.

Luke had once described a foreign bird he had seen in an aviary at one of the big houses where he called with produce.

'It was blue,' he said, 'but when it spread its wings and flew from one tree stump to another it looked as if molten moonbeams and sunbeams had been poured over its feathers. Never seen anything like it, Kitty.'

He had taken her with him once, hoping to show it to her, but the bird had gone, sold to another rare bird collector.

Kitty looked from left to right, glanced behind her and when there were no movements or sounds, she went carefully on tiptoe towards the vase.

Bettina had been right when she said it was all spirals and twists, but they were so intricately intertwined she marvelled at the expertise. She had put out a finger to touch it when a voice, deep but soft, said: 'If you are thinking of stealing it, you have made a wise choice.'

Kitty, horrified at being caught, turned swiftly to see a tall, well-dressed man coming down the wide staircase. Even if it had not been for the strange accent, she would have known by Mrs Bramley's description that it was Mr van Neilson.

Reaching the bottom of the stairs he said with an amused expression, 'I am not going to arrest you. Who are you, what is your name?'

Kitty's mouth was so dry she was unable to utter a word.

'Please tell me; you have no need to be afraid. I am interested in you. You appeared to like this vase.'

His smile was warm and it encouraged Kitty to give a quick nod.

'Ah,' he said, spreading his hands. 'How terrible, you have no tongue. You poor child!'

Kitty knew he was teasing her and she straightened. 'Yes, I have ... I love glass ...' She looked up at the chandelier. 'I saw it lit last night. It was just so, so beautiful.'

'And you wanted to take another look,' he said softly. 'I feel flattered, seeing that I fashioned both.'

Kitty started to back away, saying she must go, then she stopped and said on a desperate note of appeal, 'I've been forbidden to come upstairs. If anyone hears about it I shall be ... sacked on the spot.'

'Then you must go at once. Your secret is safe with me.'

With a gasp of thanks, Kitty fled.

It was not until much later when her trembling had stopped that she realized how lucky she had been. What other man in Mr van Neilson's position would have been so kind to her under those circumstances?

She wished, but thought it highly unlikely, that she would have an opportunity of thanking him properly.

But an hour later, when the storm broke over her, Kitty felt she hated him.

CHAPTER SEVEN

Kitty, who had been sorting through jars of preserves on the larder shelves to find the one required by Mrs Bramley, came out to find Cook waiting for her with hands on hips, her expression grim. Kitty was about to apologize for taking so long when Mrs Bramley said:

'And what, might I ask, were you doing upstairs this afternoon, *Miss Kitty Harvey? And*, talking to a guest. How dare you! How *dare* you?'

Kitty felt sick, So Mr van Neilson had broken his promise. She had trusted him.

'Well?' Mrs Bramley demanded. 'I'm waiting for an explanation.'

'It was the chandelier,' Kitty said in a low voice. 'I wanted to see it again.'

'The chandelier!' Mrs Bramley flung up her hands. 'Was seeing that more important than keeping a secure job? You must be mad, girl. The thing's just made of bits of glass.'

Kitty was surprised that like Ivy, Mrs Bramley could not see in the chandelier what she herself could see. Then a voice behind her said:

'The girl happens to find beauty in glass.' It was Mr Walton and he spoke quietly. Kitty had been aware of figures in the background, standing as motionless as a tableau, but had not realized who they were. The butler came forward. 'Not that I'm condoning the offence, Mrs Bramley. I am just giving a reason for the lapse.'

At this Bettina came forward, a vicious look on her face. 'The reason she gave about the chandelier is a lie! She knew Mr van

Neilson was there and made up to him; I saw her.'

Kitty felt a sweet flood of relief to know that Mr van Neilson had not betrayed her.

Mrs Bramley's tight-lipped expression was now directed at Bettina. 'It's stupid to say that Kitty was making eyes at our guest. She's not that kind of girl.'

'Don't be deceived by that wide-eyed innocent look,' Bettina retorted. 'I've watched her!'

Ivy suddenly came into the scene, springing at Bettina with her fingers curved into claws. 'You spying bitch!' Mrs Bramley caught hold of her and clouted her around the ears.

'We'll have none of that talk around here, girl!'

'She's called me scum,' Ivy yelled. 'She's scum! Kitty hasn't a wicked thought in her head – she's good through and through.'

Mr Walton said sternly, 'Ivy – Kitty – go to your room and wait there until I send for you.'

Ivy went storming out, muttering obscenities about Bettina under her breath. Kitty followed her, then stopped as Ivy turned at the foot of the stairs. 'If Mrs Bramley hadn't got hold of me, I'd have scratched that Bettina's eyes out. It's a good job she's leaving in a month's time, or she wouldn't have been safe from me.'

Kitty said, ' I doubt whether either of us will even be here tomorrow. It was nice of you to stick up for me, Ivy, but I'm sorry for being the one to get you into trouble.'

Ivy dismissed it; she was always in trouble.

They trudged up the four flights of stairs together and going into their room, sat on the edge of the bed. They sat in silence for a while and Kitty got colder and colder. Without comment they both stood up and Ivy, taking off the bed-cover, put it around their shoulders. As they sat down again, Kitty said in a disconsolate voice, 'I wish I could learn to do as I'm told. It's my mother who's going to suffer when I'm sacked. She needs my wages.'

Ivy suddenly straightened. 'I don't know what we're worriting about. We'll not get the sack; they can't do without us. They're short-handed as it is, with Clara sick and Meggie having died.'

Kitty turned her head quickly, 'Meggie ... died, who was she?'

'The scullery-maid – you took her place. She got a bad bellyache one afternoon and Mrs Bramley dosed her, but she got worse and worse and the doctor came. They took her to hospital and two hours later we heard she was dead.'

Kitty was as much shocked by Ivy's matter-of-fact attitude about death as she was on hearing of the loss of such a young life. 'How awful, how dreadful, to go so quickly.'

'Well, we all got to die sometime, ain't we? *Haven't* we?' she corrected herself. 'Here, tell me about this van Neilson. What's he look like, what did he say to you?'

'He was kind, very handsome. He promised he wouldn't tell anyone about me going upstairs and he didn't.' Kitty looked at Ivy as something suddenly occurred to her.

'Ivy, I'm not wearing one of – Meggie's dresses, am I?'

'You might be, on the other hand you might not. We've a pile of dresses and anyway, they would all have been in the laundry. You're not worriting about that, are you? It couldn't do you any harm.' Ivy laughed. 'She didn't have the plague. Come on, tell me more about our handsome guest.'

Kitty said there was no more to tell and Ivy then got irritable, wanting to know what that blasted Mr Walton was doing. It was time he let them know about their jobs, keeping them sitting up here freezing to death – which told Kitty that Ivy was not as confident about being kept on at the Earles' as she made out.

Both girls were numb and their teeth chattering by the time word was sent for them to come downstairs. Mr Walton and Mrs Bramley were alone when they went into the kitchen. After the chill of the bedroom, the heat reminded Kitty of the pleasure of going into the furnace room at the glassworks. Mr Walton eyed first one and then the other over the top of his spectacles before he spoke. He looked stern.

'Well, Mrs Bramley and I have talked this matter over very carefully and have decided to give you both another chance. But let me warn you that such disobedience from you, Harvey, and such appalling behaviour from you, Johnson, will not be tolerated a second time. It is only because your parents would be the main ones to suffer by your dismissal that we are giving you another chance. Is that understood?'

Both girls nodded, Kitty vigorously. Then Mr Walton said he

would leave them with Mrs Bramley who wanted to say a few words to them.

Cook had more than a few words to say, especially to Ivy whom she had caught giving a triumphant glance at Kitty.

'I know just what you're thinking, Ivy Johnson,' she exclaimed. 'You were thinking you couldn't be done without, but let me tell you – you would have gone, and gone this very night, if it hadn't been for Mr Walton, who's a very temperate-thinking man no matter what anyone might say otherwise.'

There was a lot more, about loyalty to the people you were working for, loyalty to staff. What you did affected a number of people, violence begat violence ... two wrongs didn't make a right ... jealousy was one of the mortal sins – in Mrs Bramley's opinion. Ivy might be jealous of Bettina, but Bettina did right to report Kitty. Not that she upheld Bettina's *real* reason for telling about Kitty's disobedience ...

By the time the lecture was concluded Ivy was as subdued as Kitty. And they remained subdued all the next day. Bettina was seldom around and Mrs Bramley had little to say to anyone. It was not until the early evening that the cook approached the subject of family prayers, which were to take place the following morning.

'Now listen to me, Kitty, and listen carefully because I'm not going to repeat myself. Prayers are held in the morning-room, with Mr Earle presiding. Mr Walton will lead the way, you will bring up the rear. You must carry your prayer book and keep your eyes on it, or on the floor; never once must you look at any member of the family, although I must admit it will be tempting.'

For a moment a smile touched Mrs Bramley's lips as she said how much she wanted to look at everyone during her first job and first morning prayers. Then soberly she added, 'Discipline and obedience are difficult things to learn when one is young, but prove valuable assets in future years. Take heed of my words and you both won't go far wrong.'

For once Ivy had no comeback to Kitty about the lecture, but she did say with a laugh when they were in bed, 'You can always take a peek at the family when they have their eyes closed during prayers.'

Kitty said she wouldn't dare take the risk in case a member of the family should have his or her eyes open, but Ivy explained that it was easy to have a glimpse from under lowered eyelids. Aching to see Mr van Neilson again, Kitty also wanted to see Mr Earle and the two daughters and knew she would need all her discipline to stop herself from looking.

Kitty and Ivy wore freshly laundered buff cotton dresses with the addition of tiny white collars for the occasion; Bettina wore lavender with white stripes, while Mrs Bramley was in her usual black.

At ten minutes to eight Mr Walton led the way upstairs and into the morning-room. Kitty kept her gaze on Ivy's feet – they were large feet. All she was aware of otherwise was the softness of the carpet, the hardness of oak flooring and the smell of polish. Then they were assembled in the room. Kitty concentrated on a green leaf in the carpet and was still staring at it when muted voices reached her. But when the family came in there was silence. It was agony not to look up, not to know if Mr van Neilson was there.

Mr Earle had a strong, clear voice. He bade them all good morning and began the prayers. Kitty took Ivy's advice and glanced from under lowered lids, but all she could see were three pairs of trousered legs and a number of skirts. The men would be Mr Earle and his valet, and . . . possibly Mr van Neilson. The women would be Mrs Earle – if she was well enough – the two daughters, the governess, the two lady's maids and perhaps the nursery-maid. The younger children were not there, probably too young to behave during prayers.

Then Mr Earle said he would read the lesson about the devils being cast out from the eighth chapter of Luke.

At mention of the name Luke, Kitty's head went up of its own volition and before she lowered it again quickly she had looked into the dark eyes, the *smiling* dark eyes of Mr van Neilson. Her heart was racing, not because of the look, but because she was terrified she had been *noticed* looking. She forced herself to concentrate on Mr Earle's voice.

'. . . And Jesus asked him, what is thy name? and he said, Legion, because many devils were entered into him.

'And they besought him that he would not command them to go out into the deep. And there was there an herd of many swine feeding on the mountain: and he besought him that he would suffer them to enter into them.

'Then went the devils out of the man, and entered into the swine: and the herd ran violently down a steep place into the lake and were choked.'

At this point Kitty stopped listening. How could Jesus put the evil spirits into the swine? They had not deserved such an awful death. Jesus did good deeds. God performed miracles. Why had He not just taken out the evil spirits and cast them straight into the lake so that the evil spirits would choke?

Kitty was still mulling over the problem and why Mr Earle had chosen this lesson when morning prayers ended. The family left first and Kitty forced herself to keep her gaze on her prayer book.

When they were back in the kitchen Kitty began to discuss the lesson with Ivy, saying that it was a terrible thing Jesus did. Ivy eyed her in astonishment. 'They were just alimals, what are you getting so upset about? They'd have been killed and eaten anyway.'

'But pigs are lovely animals,' Kitty said earnestly. 'You get to know them and they know you. And they're called *an*imals, not *al*imals.'

Mr Walton who had heard them, said in his stern voice, 'Harvey, do not question the motives of the Lord, otherwise you will be lost.'

'But ...' Kitty began, then stopped. Harriet was always saying much the same thing: 'Put your trust in the Lord.' Harriet had even accepted that it was God's will when her three sons were killed together in the Boer War.

'Yes, Mr Walton,' Kitty said, but still not understanding.

With breakfast over, the dishes washed and put away, Kitty was free to go home for the rest of the day. Mrs Bramley put up a little parcel of food for her, saying, 'Give that to your mother, Kitty, it'll help out a bit.'

Kitty thanked her, then said, 'And thank you, Mrs Bramley, for your kindness to me. I've made mistakes this first week, but I'll try not to make any more.'

'I know you will, Kitty, that's why you've kept your job. Give my regards to your mother and enjoy your day.'

Kitty had found out from Ivy that there was a short cut to the main road by going out of the wicket gate near the bottom of the garden. She was not bothered about short cuts – walking was something she had missed since coming North – but she was curious to see the outhouse where Mr van Neilson did his experiments. It was not visible as she walked down the path and she presumed it must be beyond the tall yew hedge. Kitty came to the wicket gate, which was a few yards from the opening in the hedge, paused for a moment consumed by curiosity, then raised the latch with a firm click and opened the gate. As she turned to close it a tall figure appeared from the opening in the hedge. It seemed that all the pulses in her body began to throb.

Tyler van Neilson gave her a brief bow. 'The little glass girl! I trust you did not get into any trouble yesterday?'

'I did, awful trouble; I nearly lost my job.' Kitty felt as breathless as if she had been running a long distance. She wanted to leave, but something held her there.

'I'm sorry, so terribly sorry.' His face was full of concern. 'I kept our secret.'

'I know, it was the ... one of the staff saw me.'

'And gave you away – how mean.'

'I deserved it, sir, I disobeyed orders.'

'Oh dear, if we did what we were told it would be such a dull world.' His eyes held a twinkle. 'Would you not agree, Miss—'

'Kitty Leddenshaw,' she said without thinking. And to keep the division between them she added, 'In my position I *must* obey. And now I must go, sir. Thank you for not telling about me.' Kitty hurried away.

Instead of feeling elated, excited at seeing the man she had dreamed about the night before, Kitty felt oddly upset. It was not that she had been disappointed in his appearance or manner – if anything, he was more attractive in the light of outdoors. His thick dark hair, she had noticed, had a slight curl to it, his eyes were most expressive and his clothes immaculate.

Instead of going to catch the tram Kitty kept on walking and as she walked she knew why she was upset. This man belonged to the world of glass – a world she would like to enter, he could tell her so much – but she was barred from sharing his knowledge by the rule of class. At that moment Kitty felt she belonged to the 'nothink' people whom Ivy felt so strongly about.

It was a long walk and she was feeling tired and dispirited, beginning to wonder what lay in the future for her. She had become interested in cooking, had been noting everything that Mrs Bramley did. Would she end up being a cook, never knowing romance, depending on her loving for sleeping with a butler?

Then Kitty remembered Tyler van Neilson saying he had kept their secret and although they were words he might have used to Ivy in a similar situation they were said with warmth, making her feel brighter. After all she was young, the whole world was before her. If she kept on working hard she might become a parlourmaid, perhaps eventually a lady's maid, then she would be in a world of beautiful things like the glass ornaments and lovely clothes.

Kitty laughed to herself as she could hear Ivy saying, 'I don't know what you're worrying about.'

It had worried her early that morning when she got up and thought about Violet being home for the day. Now she felt she could deal with Violet and anyone else who was going to be nasty. She would ignore her, as she had ignored Bettina when she had cast vicious looks at her once or twice that morning. As Luke had once said, if people say something unpleasant to you and you show you don't care, if you can smile, it takes the wind out of their sails.

It was in this mood that Kitty arrived home to find the back door leading into the scullery locked. Strange. She seemed to recollect that doors were never locked, had never been locked, not even overnight. She went to the kitchen window and peered in. There was no fire burning in the grate; the room looked cheerless, unlived in. Her mother was expecting her and her sisters, so surely she would have lit a fire under the circumstances. Kitty went back to the door and rapped on it. When this brought no response she stepped back and looked up at the bedroom window. Could her mother be ill? That could be the answer. She must go and ask Jessica.

To Kitty's astonishment she found Jessica's door locked too. What on earth was going on? She stood, puzzled. Come to think about it, there had been no one about when she walked along the street, no children playing or women gossiping; no curtains had been twitched aside. She thumped on the door with an urgency that brought a voice calling, 'I'm coming, I'm coming!'

Seconds later Kitty heard a tapping on the window and saw that it was her mother. Margaret shouted, 'I'm going to open the door, but you are not to come in.'

Mystified, Kitty waited. Bolts were withdrawn, the door opened a fraction and her mother said, 'Don't come any closer, Kitty. There's an epidemic sweeping the town. Strikes like lightning and has hit rich and poor alike. Jessica's gone down with it, she's very ill.'

'Then let me come in and help.' Kitty put her foot on the step, but Margaret closed the door quickly, shouting from behind it, 'You must go, go at once!'

Kitty began to feel annoyed. 'Mother, open the door, we can't talk through it. I promise to keep my distance, but I want to know what's happening.'

The door opened a fraction again. 'I'm asking you to go, Kitty, because you could carry the illness to Stratton House. Violet and some of the people in the house where she works have gone down with it. Agnes, Mary and Ann are ill, with some of the other girls who work with them. The lad who delivered the messages told me what was going on.'

'What sort of epidemic is it? What's caused it?'

'Nobody knows, they're just suggesting it might be the water. You start with sickness and diarrhoea, then you run up a temperature. Only one person has died of it so far, but then it's only just struck. Kitty, go now! The epidemic might reach Stratton House, it seems just to be around here and in the Sansome district.'

'I can't leave you! What if you become ill? There'll be no one to look after you.'

'Neighbour helps neighbour, Kitty. Oh, please go – and don't get on the tram, you might catch it from a passenger.' When Kitty stood, unwilling to leave, Margaret said, suddenly impatient, 'Kitty, if you become ill you would be one more to nurse. Be sensible. I can manage to look after Jessica. Now do as you're told – for once!'

'Well, all right ...' Remembering the parcel of food Mrs Bramley had given her, Kitty laid it on the step. Margaret took it, told her to thank the cook then closed and bolted the door, leaving Kitty feeling like one of the lepers in the Bible with people calling, 'Unclean ... Unclean ...'

She gave a last look at the window then walked away, thinking there had been so much she wanted to tell her mother. Now it would have to wait until next week – if then. How long would this epidemic last? Supposing her mother died? If she caught this sickness it *could* kill her; she had little stamina, she had proved this in her visit to the farm, when she had only to walk a short distance to need a rest.

Kitty was soon to discover that although she could walk for miles in the country without feeling tired, the long walk back to Stratton House in the smoke-laden air, after her earlier walk home, was making her feel tired. And by the time she was nearing Stratton House her feet were beginning to drag. She wondered what Mrs Bramley would say when she knew her reason for returning so soon, and suspected that if anyone went down with this mysterious illness later, she would be blamed for having carried the infection. Well, it was no use worrying about that now.

Kitty turned the next corner which had given her the first glimpse of the house a week ago, then stopped abruptly. A carriage stood outside the house and a man carrying a medical bag was going up the steps, a uniformed nurse on one side of him and a middle-aged woman wearing a red armband on the other. Kitty's heart began an uncomfortable thudding.

So . . . the epidemic had reached Stratton House.

All tiredness gone she began to run, and after racing down the area steps, through the laundry room and along the passage she came into the kitchen – to find utter chaos. Mrs Bramley was standing with her apron thrown over her face, wailing, 'It isn't my fault, I tell you! *My* cooking isn't responsible, the master had no right to blame me.'

Mr Walton was barking orders and staff were in and out of the larder, opening cupboards, getting out bowls and buckets – and all in each others' way. As Ivy came in he hailed her. 'Johnson! Fill some carafes with water and take them upstairs; put one in every bedroom.' Then catching sight of Kitty he said, 'What are you doing here, Harvey? I thought you'd gone home.'

'I did,' Kitty said, then explained about the epidemic. The apron came down from Mrs Bramley's face. 'Well! Thank heaven for that! Praise the Lord, it's not my fault at all.'

Mr Walton said sternly, 'I can see no reason for praising the

Lord who has brought this pestilence on the house! All the adults, apart from the mistress, are now down with it.' To Kitty he added, 'Harvey, go up to the nursery and see to the children; both Miss Pettifor and the nursemaid have had to take to their beds. Help in any way you can, wherever you can. Get an apron on, hurry, hurry!' Kitty whipped off her coat, fastened on an apron, asked where the nursery was and within seconds she was running up the stairs.

Before she reached the second landing she could hear a child screaming. She had learned that there were three children, Marguerite who was four, Robert aged three, and baby James only eighteen months. Kitty had wondered at the time if Mrs Earle was the second wife, as there was such a gap between the younger children and the older daughters.

The nursery door was open; Marguerite and Robert were standing in a circular playpen. It was Marguerite who was screaming. The baby, Kitty saw, was astonishingly asleep in his cot despite all the noise. She went over and picked up the fragile-looking little girl with the golden curls, holding her close and soothing her.

'It's all right, pet, Nanny will be with you soon. Now you be a good girl – your little brother is not crying and he is just a baby.'

Marguerite put her arms around Kitty's neck and laid her wet cheek against hers, the screaming dying to hiccuping sobs. 'Nanny took Rebecca away from me . . . and I . . . want her . . . I love her.' When Kitty said, 'Rebecca?' the little girl drew away and pointed to where a doll dressed in a brown velvet dress was perched on top of a tall chest.

Kitty stared at it, a feeling of revulsion swamping her. No, she thought, I can't touch it, I won't! But in the end it was Marguerite's pitiful pleas which made Kitty go to the doll, lift it with her fingertips and hand it to the child . . . who hugged it to her, sobs ceasing.

A woman's voice called weakly from a room leading off the nursery. 'Whoever is there, please help me, I'm dying!' Kitty put Marguerite back beside her brother; the little boy was staring at Kitty with puzzled eyes. She smiled and patted his head. 'Be a good boy, I'll be with you in a minute.'

As Kitty went into the room, the smell of vomit and excreta made her stomach heave for a moment, then she swallowed hard and went to the bed where a white-faced, middle-aged woman lay clutching the bedclothes.

'The doctor,' she whispered, 'I need a doctor.'

Kitty explained that he was in the house and no doubt would come to attend to her eventually, adding that in the meantime she would try to tidy up a little. But before she could start there came a moaning from what appeared to be a double-doored cupboard. When Kitty opened it she found a small room with a girl in a truckle bed, a girl whose eyes were full of fear as she gazed at the floor. Kitty knew why – she had missed the slop bucket and been sick on the linoleum. She told the girl quietly not to worry – she would clean everything up.

It took Kitty over half an hour to clean room, woman and girl, change the sheets and empty and scour out the slop buckets. She was busy changing the baby, who had just woken up, when Mrs Earle came in. She appeared to be the most unflustered of all those in the house. She thanked Kitty for looking after the children, said Mr Walton had told her she was caring for them, also Nanny and the nursemaid. She then asked Kitty to take the children downstairs, since someone from her sister's house was coming to collect them. 'My poor darlings,' she said, 'I cannot even embrace them in case I infect them. Their papa is very sick and so are my two elder daughters. I must go back to them.' Only a slight tremor in Mrs Earle's voice betrayed her worry.

She was at the door when she turned, 'Oh, Kitty, would you ask Mr Walton to see that Mr van Neilson is given some medicine when it arrives. My husband's valet is sick too – perhaps Mr Walton may be able to engage another manservant.'

Kitty promised. She dressed the children and took them downstairs, where she found two maids waiting to collect them. She then delivered Mrs Earle's message to Mr Walton, who said on a note of irritation that there was no chance of engaging any extra staff, he had already tried. Meanwhile the situation was getting desperate. George the footman, and the coachman were now laid up. He also told her that the volunteer nurse had had to be taken home, as she had become ill ten minutes after her arrival.

When the medicine was delivered and Kitty reminded Mr Walton about seeing that Mr van Neilson was given a dose, he told her she would have to take it up, which had Mrs Bramley protesting that it wasn't right for a young girl to go into a gentleman guest's bedroom – to which Mr Walton said, with temper controlled, then Mrs Bramley had better take it up herself, since there was no one else. Cook gave in, but warned Kitty she was to come right down again as soon as the dose had been given. Kitty made no promise, but laid medicine glass and a spoon on a tray.

Although she had done this quite calmly, she felt a tremor in her stomach when she tapped at the heavy oak door and went in. All she could see of the gentleman was his thick dark hair above the coverlet. She tip-toed over to him and when she saw he appeared to be asleep she wondered what to do. There was no unpleasant smell in the room and presumably he was not too ill. Then as he stirred, pushing the bed-cover away from his face, she noticed that his skin had the pale clamminess of sickness. She spoke his name and he opened his eyes. They looked feverish. He murmured something, gave a groan and closed his eyes again.

Kitty put the tray on the bedside table and said firmly, 'Mr van Neilson, sir, I've brought some medicine for you, doctor's orders.' He groaned again and heaved himself over, away from her, then began retching. Kitty looked around frantically for a slop bucket, but could see none. She opened a cupboard, found a chamber-pot and stood with it in her hand as her patient seemed to have settled again. Then she remembered the medicine and began to coax him.

'I don't like to disturb you, sir, but you really must take your medicine. You could get worse and then you would be a sorry sight, I promise you, a *very* sorry sight. I've seen some of the patients who are laid low with this illness.' When he still made no effort to sit up, she quoted the proverb about a stitch in time saving nine and then added, trying to sound bright:

'Well, sir, I think that one dose of medicine might save you nine days in bed.'

At this he heaved himself up and said weakly, 'You've won, little glass girl, let me get it over with.' He took it in one gulp, shuddered, then as he retched again he slid hastily down the bed and pulled the cover up to his nose. 'Go, please,' came his whisper.

Kitty stood hesitant. If he was sick he would make a terrible

107

mess of the silk coverlet or the carpet. She placed the chamber-pot by the bed, putting it down with a thump so that he would know it was there. Then, after telling him softly she would be back later, she left.

Outside the door she bumped into Bettina, who demanded to know what she was doing in Mr van Neilson's room. When Kitty explained she said haughtily that he was *her* responsibility, pointing out her priority in the house so far as status was concerned. She then told Kitty that if it was men she wanted to nurse, there were the footman and coachman who needed attention. Kitty forced herself to smile and say, 'Yes, of course, I'll see to them at once.'

And she did help Ivy to attend to both men. After that she went up to the nursery again to see to Miss Pettifor and Jean the nursemaid. Both were worse if anything and looked as if they were running temperatures. She laid cold compresses on their foreheads and emptied more slops. When she went downstairs the next time, Mr Walton told her that help was needed with Miss Thea and Miss Lavinia, Bettina seemed to have disappeared and Mrs Earle was showing signs of succumbing to the sickness.

Thea, the eldest daughter, dark-haired, with a quiet manner, thanked Kitty for her help, while Lavinia, auburn-haired and petulant, did nothing but complain. Why had she to be the one to suffer? She had an important invitation to a big party the following evening. A bout of sickness put an end to her complaints.

Kitty learned that the girls' lady's maid and their mother's maid, who both had the evening off the night before, had not returned. Thea thought this most unfortunate, but Kitty privately considered it to be a blessing in disguise. It was obvious they were too ill to return and two more patients to look after would have been a trial.

By late afternoon Kitty felt she had been running up and down stairs, emptying buckets, putting cold compresses on foreheads and cleaning up sick people for a week. She had wondered several times if Mr van Neilson was all right, but it was not until she and Ivy were made to sit down by Mrs Bramley for a few minutes in order to have a cup of tea and a bite to eat that she learned about Bettina.

'Told me she would have to go to bed,' said Mrs Bramley, 'but there didn't look to be much wrong with her to me. Been in bed now for . . .' she looked up at the wall clock, 'since one o'clock, it must have been.'

'One o'clock?' Kitty jumped up. 'What about Mr van Neilson? He should have had more medicine, it had to be given four times a day. He was inclined to be feverish when I saw him earlier. I must go up.' Without waiting for permission, she found his tray and left.

The bedroom was in darkness and Kitty took a box of lucifers from her pocket and lit one of the gas-jets. From the bed came low murmurings like a person in delirium. He was in a mess, the bed was in a mess. He would have to be washed and changed, and the sheets changed too. She must fetch Mr Walton.

But when Kitty went downstairs she found Ivy and Mrs Bramley trying to cope with Mr Walton, who had suddenly collapsed. 'Oh, my goodness!' Mrs Bramley wailed. 'What are we going to do, how are we going to get him to bed?'

'Drag him,' Ivy said in her practical way. 'You take one arm and I'll take the other.' Mrs Bramley protested: she had a bad back as it was, one pull and *she* would be in bed. Kitty offered to help, and so between them they dragged the butler across the kitchen and along the passage leading off to where Mr Walton had his own rooms. But once they had got him there Mrs Bramley came in, hurriedly telling them that once he was on the bed she would see to the rest.

Ivy gave Kitty a wink, and whispered, 'Terrified we'd get eddicated about – you know what!'

Kitty had decided she would have to ask Ivy to help her with Mr van Neilson, but this comment made her change her mind. She would have to manage on her own, somehow. It would be terrible to have Ivy treating the changing of Mr van Neilson as an adventure and relating it to someone else with sly winks.

When they were back in the kitchen, Kitty was just trying to think how she could get away without Ivy knowing where she was going when the bell from Mrs Earle's room rang. Ivy gave a deep sigh. 'Off again . . .'

Kitty waited for a few moments, then went upstairs. Her patient was quiet, but when she felt his forehead it was burning. Kitty was wondering how best to tackle her task when she remembered seeing Harriet roll one of the boys over in bed to change the sheets when he had a bout of bronchitis. That was it, she would do it in easy stages.

By the time Kitty had finished the job perspiration was trickling down her spine, not only because of the work involved but also because of her embarrassment at seeing a man naked. He must *never, ever* know!

He had roused several times while she was busy, but only to say a few unintelligible phrases. Now as she stood looking down at him he looked peaceful and his cheeks seemed less flushed. His thick dark lashes lay on his cheeks, reminding her of Luke when he was sleeping. Although Luke had copper-coloured hair, his lashes were dark brown ...

Luke – Kitty felt a sudden guilty pang. He had not crossed her mind for the past few days. Then as she thought of him knowing she had washed and changed this handsome man in the bed, her cheeks burned. She turned the gas-jet low and left. In another hour she would return.

CHAPTER EIGHT

At six o'clock when Ivy and Kitty were sat down to a meal which Mrs Bramley insisted they must have, Bettina walked in looking surprisingly fresh. They all stared at her. Mrs Bramley said, 'I thought you were supposed to be ill.'

'I was.' Bettina drew out a chair and sat down. 'But I feel much better now and find I'm hungry.'

Ivy accused her of having gone upstairs for a rest, then said, 'Good, ain't it? She takes it easy while Kitty and me are run off our feet.'

Bettina ignored this and helped herself to some cold meat. When Ivy started on her again, Mrs Bramley said sharply, 'What's done is done. What we have to think about now is someone being on duty all night to answer bells. None of us can go to bed until after midnight, so I'll have to draw up a list of shifts.'

It was eventually decided that Bettina would do the twelve to two duty, Ivy two till four and Kitty four till six. Mrs Bramley said she would have to sit up with Mr Walton since the poor man was 'proper poorly'.

Ivy said afterwards, 'Cook? Sit up? More likely she'll be sharing old Walton's bed.' Kitty made no reply to this; she wanted to tackle Bettina about neglecting Mr van Neilson, but did not intend to stir up more trouble, not while Mrs Bramley was there.

As it turned out, an opportunity came later when two bells rang, one from Mrs Earle's room and the other from the nursery.

Bettina got up, complaining bitterly that it was time they

found a cure for this epidemic, since she had not been engaged as a nursemaid. Kitty got up too and followed her, saying as they were about to go upstairs, 'Bettina, would you look in on Mr van Neilson? He's been quite ill while you were upstairs.'

Bettina turned to her, sneering, 'And I suppose *you* played little Miss Florence Nightingale! He refused to take his medicine when I saw him last; he deserved to be left alone. But yes, now I will attend the *gentleman*, if only to stop you giving yourself medals.'

Kitty did not see Bettina again that evening. Just before midnight Mrs Bramley sent Ivy and Kitty off to bed. Both girls dragged themselves up the stairs, Kitty wondering how she was going to get through the next day if the situation did not ease.

Kitty slept soundly, but when Ivy roused her at four o'clock she felt that the only break in the previous day had been a coming up and going downstairs.

And the only change in the routine of that morning was the visit of a younger doctor, who had brought with him some different medicine – hinting, although not stating positively, that the cause of the epidemic had been found.

Kitty longed to know how Mr van Neilson was, but dared not ask in case of seeming to show too much interest. But when she heard from Ivy later on that Bettina had collapsed and was quite genuinely ill, she went to Tyler's bedroom. Once there, she stood outside in an agony of embarrassment, wondering if he would remember she had washed and changed him the day before. Then she squared her shoulders, knocked on the door and went in.

Tyler was sitting propped up with pillows. He was unshaven, looked pale and when he spoke his voice was weak. 'Good morning, Nurse Leddenshaw, you've been neglecting me.'

He was so solemn Kitty wondered if he was still running a fever and had mistaken the role she played in the house.

She went over to the bed, explained about the new medicine and poured him a dose. He took it without protest, in one gulp. Kitty, concerned to see him so weak, said, 'Are you feeling a little better, sir?'

He rubbed the stubble on his chin. 'I would feel better if I could get rid of this.'

'I could shave you, sir,' she said earnestly. 'I shaved Uncle

Abel when he broke his right arm once. He was very pleased
with me.'

'Barber, as well as nurse?' He was still solemn. 'And a very
competent and caring one, if I may say so. I had no liking for the
other nurse who came to attend me. I missed you, missed your
gentle ministrations.'

Kitty noticed then a twinkle in his dark eyes and hot colour
rushed to her face. Had he remembered? Been aware of all she
had done the day before? She was about to turn away when he
caught hold of her hand and said quietly, 'I would be very
pleased if you could tidy me up. I'm most grateful for all that
you have done.'

Kitty felt herself trembling as she gathered up everything
necessary for shaving, and when she tucked the towel under his
chin she wished herself anywhere but in this bedroom.

Then Tyler said gently, 'I feel I'm taking advantage of your
good nature. Tomorrow I may be stronger and able to manage
the shaving myself.'

This pulled Kitty together. The teasing had been a natural
thing; he was a caring man, he had proved that. She told him she
thought he would feel much better if he was shaved and she
would like to do it, if he felt he could trust her.

'I trust you, Nurse Leddenshaw,' he said, and his teasing was
gentle.

She stropped the razor and he complimented her on her
expertise. Then she lathered him, taking care not to get any of
the soap up his nose, but when she was taking off the lather and
put a finger under his nose, tipping it up to get the lather from
his upper lip, he began to laugh.

'Oh, please, sir,' she said in alarm, 'you mustn't laugh, I could
cut you.'

'I would be proud of any scar inflicted by you,' he said softly.
'You are a very dear girl, Kitty Leddenshaw. Shall we
continue?'

It took all Kitty's will-power to complete the job without her
hand shaking. She felt he was capable of sponging his hands and
face, but she did this for him too, wanting to do it. And she even
combed and brushed his hair and he let her do that too, thanking
her gravely after she had finished and straightened the bed.

With the promise to come up later and see if he needed

anything, she left on silent feet, carrying the tray. Outside the door she stood for a moment, unable to believe what had happened. He had called her a very dear girl. With her exhaustion gone she hurried along the corridor, prepared to look after all the patients in the house if necessary, so long as she could serve Tyler van Neilson.

It looked at one time as if Kitty *was* going to have to attend to all the invalids. Ivy fainted. She came round quickly and said it was the first time in her life this had happened, but although she kept saying she would be all right, Mrs Bramley insisted on her going upstairs to lie down for a while. Then the nurse who was looking after Mr and Mrs Earle and Mr Earle's valet, came down to say she must have some rest; she had been snatching no more than minutes' relief at a time and was at the end of her tether. Mrs Bramley told her it was impossible to get help, the doctor had been unable to get anyone and Mr Walton had tried too.

The nurse then stated that *someone* would have to take over for a few hours, and Mrs Bramley glanced at Kitty with a comical look of despair on her face. Then she turned to the nurse whose eyes were almost closing, and told her to go to bed – they would do their best.

After the woman had gone, Cook looked at Kitty now with appeal.

'Do you think you could help out, love? You might not even be needed, but you have to be prepared.' As she spoke a bell on the wall tinkled and Mrs Bramley threw up her hands. 'Oh, Lord, it's the master's room.'

The way she spoke struck terror in Kitty's heart. All she had seen and heard of Mr Earle on the Sunday morning at prayers was a pair of trousered legs and a strong, rather harsh voice. Then she thought that at the worst he could only snap her head off and tell her to go.

'I'll do my best, Mrs Bramley,' she said, and left.

In answer to Kitty's timid knock a voice, barely weakened by illness, summoned her to enter. This room was sombre, furniture and furnishings dark in contrast to the other rooms with their elegance and lightness.

In a tester bed facing her sat a bearded man in a white nightshirt who was glaring at her. 'Who are you?' he demanded.

114

'What are you doing here?'

'I came to see if I could help, sir.'

'Well, I don't want you ...' He waved an arm, dismissing her. 'Send in my nurse!'

When Kitty explained that the nurse had desperately needed rest he roared, 'And I need to be attended to. Get her out of bed, at once!'

At this anger rose in Kitty. 'She would collapse, sir, so she would be of no use. Mrs Bramley has sent me – as a last resort, there is no one else, the rest of the staff are ill.'

'Then tell Mrs Bramley to phone and get *extra* staff. What is the woman thinking about?'

Kitty told him how Mr Walton and the doctor had tried, but so many people were ill, hospitals were full, doctors were run off their feet ...

'Get out!' he said. 'And wait there until I call you.' He was already throwing back the bed-covers when he called her back and told her to hand him his dressing-gown.

Kitty went out, fuming. *She* was nearly at the end of her tether and all she had received was abuse for offering to help. She could hear Mr Earle shouting and presumed he was speaking on the telephone; he was a long time and was getting more and more angry. Kitty thought that if it had not been for her mother needing her wages, she would have given in her notice and gone back to the farm. Then she thought of Tyler van Neilson and knew she would stay as long as there was a chance of seeing him.

When at last Mr Earle called her in, Kitty learned he had achieved what both the doctor and Mr Walton had failed to do; there was a nurse coming that evening and a manservant would be here the following day at midday. Still wearing his dressing-gown, Mr Earle got back into bed and sank back. Kitty asked if there was anything she could get him and he said, Yes, a drink of water. She poured it, put her arm around his shoulders and held the glass to his lips. He took a few sips, lay back again, closed his eyes then thanked her. Kitty was so surprised that she stood there a moment. 'I'll ring if I need you again,' he said in a quiet voice, and she went out.

Kitty felt she had learned something during the last few minutes – that although wealth could bring a person certain

115

things it could not bring everything. Here was the master of the house dependent on a poor little scullery-maid to give him a drink of water! She did not feel cock-a-hoop about this, but rather chastened. Her mother had said that neighbour helped neighbour; it would be a good thing, Kitty thought, if rich and poor alike could help one another.

She had to attend to Mrs Earle only once before the nurse came and the mistress was sweet with her and grateful for any help. 'What would we have done without you?' she said.

The room was beautiful, decorated in pastel colours. And Mrs Earle looked more fragile than ever in a flimsy nightdress and a bed-jacket all tucks and lace. When Kitty told her that another nurse would be coming later and that Mr Earle had arranged it, Mrs Earle's eyebrows went up and a faint smile touched her lips. 'My husband usually manages to get his own way,' she commented.

Each time Kitty looked in on Tyler he was sleepy and wanted nothing but his medicine. At bedtime he was humped under the bedclothes fast asleep; she tip-toed out.

The next morning, to her astonishment, he was up and dressed and telling her he would be down for breakfast; he felt famished. Then he laughed at her surprise and told her it was all due to her nursing. He added, his voice soft, 'Would you tell Cook that I shall be down for breakfast?'

'Oh, yes, yes, sir.' Kitty fled. And as she ran along the corridor she repeated to herself 'All due to your nursing ...' What wonderful words to treasure from this attractive and caring man. It was something to dream on.

But Kitty's dream was short-lived when she told Mrs Bramley about their guest wanting breakfast. 'I know what men's appetites are like after they've been poorly,' Cook complained. 'Eat like navvies, they do. I expect he'll want ham and eggs and kidneys and what-have-you.' She then ordered Ivy to go and lay the dining-room table and told her she would have to wait on Mr van Neilson.

Ivy reported later that their guest had eaten a 'hearty' breakfast, and he had actually spoken to her, not treated her like the rest as though she were invisible.

'Ah, well,' said Mrs Bramley, 'he's one on his own, isn't he? A rebel, won't take orders from nobody. He defied his father, who insisted on him going into banking. It's probably because he's a foreigner.'

'Well, I think he's a lovely feller,' Ivy declared, 'foreigner or not – and I might have lost me heart to him if he hadn't been bespoken.'

When Kitty repeated, 'Bespoken?' Ivy laughed. 'I mean *you*, you daft thing, you've been all mooney whenever you've been in his room.' Kitty, relieved that Mrs Bramley was not in hearing at that moment, decided she would have to be more careful in future.

But during the next few days she did not even catch a glimpse of Tyler. Sunday morning prayers were cancelled because of Mr Earle's indisposition. Kitty had hoped she might have time off to go and see if her mother was all right, but Mrs Bramley said it wouldn't be wise, the infection might still be lurking about. Whereat Kitty pictured a beast with bared fangs waiting to grab her.

By the Monday morning most of the invalids were beginning to recover.

Bettina came down, looking colourless, saying she was fed up with being stuck on the fourth floor on her own. An hour later Mr Walton appeared, looking as drained as the rest of the patients. The coachman and George the footman were still too weak to begin work.

Although Kitty and Ivy were still run off their feet, Kitty had a feeling of getting back to normality with Mr Walton once more in charge.

On the Wednesday morning an urgent message came for Tyler and Mr Walton said, 'This will have to be taken to Mr van Neilson at once. He's gone to Smirton's glassworks. I cannot telephone him because the instrument is out of order.' He looked at Cook over the top of his spectacles. 'I cannot imagine what you've been doing with it, Mrs Bramley, while I've been laid up.'

While Cook was protesting indignantly that she had never touched it, that she hated the wretched contraption, Kitty was in a state of eager anticipation that she might be asked to deliver the letter. Smirton's was not the glassworks near her home, but she had seen it, it was on the tram route.

Mr Walton followed Ivy's progress as she raced into the

117

kitchen, picked up several things – complaining that she would never get through half of what had to be done that morning – and ran back up the stairs. The butler then turned to Mrs Bramley and said, 'Harvey will have to go, there is no one else.'

Kitty, who was still not used to her surname of Harvey, was standing wondering who he meant when it dawned on her. She went forward; 'Yes, Mr Walton, sir—?'

He told her he was going to entrust her with an important letter, a *very* important letter which she was to take to Mr van Neilson, adding that it was to be placed in the gentleman's own hands, not left at the gate. Was that understood?

Kitty nodded vigorously. 'Oh, yes, sir, indeed sir, I shall guard it with my life. I know where Smirton's is.'

'Good.' He handed her two pennies to pay for the tram fare and while Kitty was putting on her hat and coat Mrs Bramley gave her strict instructions that she was to come back straight away: there was to be no loitering on the way, or at the glassworks. Kitty promised and left.

Excitement mounted in her as she ran towards the main road where she would catch the tram. Not only would she see Mr van Neilson again, but she might get right inside the glassworks, perhaps see some of the finished goods.

The tram seemed a long time in coming and when Kitty did get on, the horses seemed to be going so slowly she felt like getting off and running the rest of the way. What if he had left? Where would she find him?

It was a relief to her when they left the cleaner, fresher part of the district and came to where factory chimneys were belching out black smoke. When the tram stopped the next time and the driver seemed to be having a lengthy chat with someone, Kitty jumped off and began to run. When she turned the next corner she could see the gates of Smirton's at the end of the road.

Sometimes soot fell in pieces and Kitty prayed that none would settle on her face. If she tried to rub them off she would have smudges and if she let them stay she would feel a fool.

She arrived at the yard without any seeming mishap, to find the usual activity with drays leaving, sacks and crates lying about, men shouting and going in and out of the factory, but the furnace room was not immediately visible. When she stopped to ask a man how to find Mr van Neilson he directed her to an office, where a youth listened to her request without interest and held out a hand for the letter. Kitty drew back. 'No, this has to be given into Mr van Neilson's hand, and you'd better find him quick or your boss will know about it. This is an urgent message.' The youth gave her a sour look, but he did move.

A woman and an elderly man were sitting at adjoining desks; the woman looked up at Kitty and smiled. 'Mr van Neilson will come right away, he's that kind of man.'

Kitty felt a swift disappointment. If he came to her in the office there would be no chance of seeing inside the works; he would want to leave right away.

When Tyler did arrive Kitty's heart missed a beat. He looked so handsome, so imposing in his fawn suit, his dark hair gleaming. 'Why, Miss Leddenshaw,' he greeted her with the courtesy he might have extended to a countess. 'I understand you have a message for me?'

She gave him the envelope and stood uncertain whether or not to leave, but as she half turned away he told her to wait. When he had read the letter he put it back in the envelope and turned to a man who had come into the office. 'I have to return to Rome right away, Mr Cade. Urgent family business. But I shall come back and continue our discussion, perhaps in a month's time.'

An order was given to the youth to have a carriage brought round for Mr van Neilson and to bring his coat and hat.

Within minutes Tyler was leading Kitty to the waiting carriage, with her protesting she must go by tram.

'Why the tram?' he said. 'I want you to travel with me.'

Kitty stopped abruptly and looked up at him, her expression earnest. 'Mr van Neilson, sir, I am a scullery-maid. I would get into serious trouble if I were to arrive back in the carriage with you, both from Mr Watson and Mrs Bramley.'

He assured her quietly that she would not get into trouble, then he added with a teasing smile, 'To me you are a princess.'

A princess? Flowery words, but very pleasing nonetheless. She got into the carriage, feeling quite awed at sitting beside such an eminent man and wishing that her sister Violet could see her. He said nothing until the horse had been urged into a trot, then he asked Kitty to excuse him and took out the letter to read again. While he was doing so Kitty kept glancing back with a

119

feeling of disappointment that an opportunity of seeing inside the glassworks had been missed.

With the letter back in his pocket, Tyler sat back, his hands resting on a silver-knobbed cane. Then she began to be aware that he was watching her. But he made no comment until they arrived at Stratton House and he helped her out of the carriage.

'Kitty, when we first met I realized you were very much interested in glass. If circumstances had been different today, I could have shown you around the works. But I promise you this: when I do return I will arrange to give you a conducted tour.'

Kitty felt a sudden radiance, then it just as quickly faded. 'It sounds wonderful, sir,' she said in a low voice, 'but it's impossible. Neither Mr Walton nor Mrs Bramley would allow it.'

'Nothing is impossible.' He pulled out a handkerchief, said, 'Allow me,' and before Kitty could realize his intention, he was rubbing lightly on the end of her nose. 'A smut – ah, I've made it worse!'

It was Tyler's amused smile that brought a rush of tears – she must look a fool, a dirty-faced scullery-maid. She whispered, 'I must go,' and turned to run, but he caught her by the arm.

'Kitty, I've upset you, I'm sorry. I was smiling, but I was not making fun of you.' There was a great gentleness in his voice. 'You have a very nice little nose, a smut does not detract from it one small fraction. Please believe me.'

He sounded so sincere that she accepted it. Then, after thanking him for the ride in the carriage, she left. Before she reached the area steps she glanced back – he was still standing, looking in her direction. Kitty felt a tremor go through her. She had first thought of this very attractive man as someone who could give her an insight into the world of glass-making. Now she realized just how much she had been dreaming about him, seeing him as the Prince and herself as the Cinderella of the fairy story. Tyler raised his hand in a brief farewell, then turned to go up the wide curved steps to the imposing entrance. Kitty went slowly down the area steps. Mrs Bramley greeted her with, 'So you're back then. Did you find Mr van Neilson all right? What was the urgent message?'

Kitty, keeping her back to the cook, told her about him having to return home, adding that he would probably be letting her know this himself.

Tyler did so, and a beaming Cook informed her later that he had been generous with his tips as usual. She handed Kitty two golden sovereigns and Kitty looked up at her, wide-eyed. 'For me?'

'That's right, love, and you deserve it the way you slaved after him. But don't tell Bettina and Ivy, they didn't get so much. Keep it in your pocket for now, but when you have a minute find somewhere safe to put it.'

All Kitty could think about that day was the money, and how much it would mean to her mother. It would pay off her debts. One thing she was definite about, her sister Violet was not going to benefit from it!

The extra nurse and the temporary manservant had made life a little easier, but there were still plenty of jobs to be done, rooms not being used had been left undusted and there were carpets to brush. Although this was not Kitty's job, she helped. Ivy had helped her with the washing-up.

Then Clara, the housemaid who had been ill, returned and although she had little to say she was certainly a worker. Kitty hoped that she might have the chance of her day off on the Sunday. She asked Mrs Bramley, explaining that she had no idea if her mother had been ill, was still ill or anything. Cook said, 'No news is good news,' but offered to let her go on the Sunday after the washing-up was done, warning her she was not to go into the house if there was any illness. Kitty promised.

When she was ready to go, Mrs Bramley gave her a parcel of food to take home, then pressed some coppers into her hands, saying they were her 'perks'. To Kitty's puzzled query about 'perks', Cook said, 'They're your due, girl, we all have our perks, which is a little extra on top of our wages. Yours is bones. I've sold them for you. There's some cooks who keep this money, but I believe that fair is fair. Give my regards to your mother, and don't be too late back.'

Kitty felt elated. These pennies would add up in a month, she would save them. When she got home she would ask her mother what the girls above her got. They must get more. If she could rise to parlourmaid . . . perhaps lady's maid in time . . . Oh, this was wonderful. She would be able to give her mother more comfort, make it possible for her to have larger fires, get a thick hearth-rug . . .

When Kitty did arrive home she was delighted to find that her mother had escaped the sickness, that her sister Violet would not be coming – her mistress needed her – but that her other sisters would be home at any minute. They arrived before Kitty had had time to take off her hat and coat, looking like frail little ghosts. But they were smiling, pleased she had come and wanting to know all about her new job.

Margaret made tea and they sat round the fire, which was a blazing one for once, Kitty thinking how lovely it was to be without Violet dominating them all. They talked at first about the epidemic and the havoc it had caused with the majority of the people in the town struck down with it. Agnes said that all the girls in their factory had been ill, and also the couple who ran it. 'The place got to be like a cesspool,' she said.

'Oh, stop it,' Mary wailed, 'Let's talk about something else. Kitty, tell us about your job – what do you have to do, and what are the staff like?'

'Were they all ill?' Ann asked. 'And what about the family?'

Kitty told them briefly, then Margaret asked her how she got on with Mrs Bramley, and whether she got enough to eat.

'Oh, I get on fine with Mrs Bramley and I'm learning all about cooking. She's a *good* cook. Not that she cooked much when everyone was ill,' Kitty laughed. 'Ivy said she was spoiled rotten. Ivy's very funny. But where was I? Oh, yes, food. Once the invalids were getting better, Cook really made up for it. Do you know what we had yesterday? A *soufflé* . . . And do you know how many egg-whites went into it? *Twenty!*'

'Twenty?' the girls chorused.

Kitty gave a quick nod. 'I had to separate the whites from the yolks, then whisk the whites until it was stiff enough to . . . Guess what?'

When they all shook their heads Kitty said, 'Stiff enough to hold the weight of an egg. Imagine! My goodness, it was hard work; it took half an hour, but I did it. We didn't get very much of the *soufflé*, but what we had was absolutely mouth-watering. I think I want to be a cook – I'm not sure.'

Ann begged to hear about all the fancy food and Kitty, in her element, told them about cakes that took a pound and a half of butter, fourteen egges and a gill of brandy; about having fricassée of chicken, turbot pie, green melon in flummery, transparent pudding (which wasn't transparent at all) and went on with various soups ... then she stopped, suddenly realizing she was showing off to people who would be living on ordinary fare and – in the case of her mother at least – not much of it. So to make herself seem less important, Kitty told them about the mistakes she had made.

'Oh, yes, I made a lot of them! On the second day was the funniest. We in the kitchen were having muffins for tea and when they were toasted Mrs Bramley told me to "put them on the footman". Well, as you can imagine, I stood staring at her ... gawping, as she calls it, and she said, "Come on, girl, get on with it, put them on the footman." I stood looking at George and suddenly Cook began to laugh. She pulled up a brass stand with feet on it. Set it in the hearth in front of the fire and told me it was called a "footman" and was used to keep plates and toast and things like muffins warm.'

Kitty began to giggle and then they were all laughing, Margaret saying, 'Oh, Kitty, you're like a breath of fresh air! Tell us more.'

In a fit of recklessness, Margaret put more coal on the fire and Kitty talked then about Mr Earle and about him shouting down the telephone and managing to get extra help. Then she spoke of Tyler van Neilson and had Ann giggling helplessly as she described shaving him. Mary said, 'Oh, dear, weren't you worried about cutting him? I would have had ten fits if I'd had to do it!'

'Oh, he told me that any scars I gave him, he would consider an honour.' Kitty was silent for a moment, then said softly, 'He really is a lovely man.'

At this Margaret became alarmed. 'Kitty, listen to me! It was very nice of the gentleman to give you a generous tip for all you'd done, but don't get any ideas about him. I know you're young and he was probably treating you as a child, but when you grow up you might find one of the gentry expecting ... well, rewards for their generosity.'

When Kitty, puzzled, queried 'rewards' and Ann replied promptly, 'Kisses', Margaret tried to explain that men in Mr van Neilson's position did not marry into the servant class.

Kitty was silent for a few moments, then she looked up. 'I don't want to get married; I want to learn how to be a cook, or perhaps a lady's maid.'

'That's what you say now.' Her mother was still looking worried so Kitty, to take her mind off Tyler van Neilson, brought up the subject of 'perks', mentioning the pennies she had received from Mrs Bramley and asked what servants higher up the scale would receive.

Margaret said she knew that a cook got ten per cent from tradesmen for all food ordered, that the butler got a percentage on wine and spirits and she thought that an under-housemaid was given stubs of candles and shavings, but that was all she knew.

Ann said, 'I know that lady's maids get all their mistresses' castoff clothing, which they can either sell or remake. Our Violet must have plenty of money; her mistress is wealthy in her own right, I was told so. I think I would like to go into service.'

Kitty, wishing Ann had never mentioned lady's maid because it had brought her sister strongly to her mind, changed the subject yet again by telling them about Ivy and the funny things she said.

They were all in a happy, relaxed mood when the kitchen door leading from the scullery opened and a soft voice said, 'My, we are enjoying ourselves, aren't we?'

They all froze and in the ensuing silence Kitty could hear the faint rustling of Violet's skirt as she moved forward. Today she was wearing a saxe-blue dress with a matching coloured cape and hat and looked as elegant as the last time Kitty had seen her.

Margaret got up. 'Why, Violet, I thought you were not coming today. A boy brought a message.' Violet sat down in the chair vacated by her mother and they all waited while she pulled off each glove, finger by finger, straightened both and then looked up.

'My mistress told me I could have two hours off.' She looked from one to the other of the girls, then at her mother. 'How many of you escaped the epidemic?'

'Kitty did and so did I,' Margaret said. 'Agnes, Mary and Ann were ill and I understand that you were. You seem to have got over it very well.'

Violet raised a languid hand. 'I had a mild attack, but I thought I would make the most of it and have a rest. Why not? Staff were brought from their country house and I was well looked after.'

'Trust you!' Ann declared with spirit. 'There was our Kitty run off her feet, hardly had time for sleeping.'

'More fool her! She should have done as I did and had a rest.'

Agnes spoke up then. 'But our Kitty's not you, is she? She's not mean, she wouldn't lie abed knowing people were suffering and needing help.'

'Oh, dear, our little "Saint Katherine".' Violet sneered. She got up. 'Mother, come upstairs, I must talk to you.'

Margaret cast a frantic glance at Kitty and Kitty guessed what was in her sister's mind. She wanted money. Would her mother be strong enough to resist Violet's dominant ways?

Violet was already going up the stairs and Margaret made to follow, but Kitty caught her by the arm. 'Mother, if you give her those two sovereigns, I'll never give you any more money I get.'

For answer Margaret took the coins from her pocket and pressed them into Kitty's hand. 'Hold them for me, then I can honestly say I don't have any money!'

Neither Kitty nor her sisters said a word when their mother had gone upstairs. They listened to the murmur of voices above them, Kitty sitting up when Violet's voice became angry: 'You'll get it or else—' Quick footsteps were coming down the stairs, then Margaret was heard to say, 'And you needn't go to Mr Hendry, I've told him what you are!'

When Violet came into the room her expression was vicious. She glared at Kitty. 'You're responsible for this, you bitch, but I'll get even with you!' With that she swept out.

When Margaret came down she looked drained. 'I didn't give her anything, but I wish I had.'

Kitty and her sisters were unanimous in their condemnation of Violet receiving any money. 'Why should you give her any?' Ann demanded. 'She has plenty. If you have money to spare, we could all do with some!'

Margaret gave a weary sigh and asked them to let the subject drop, she had no wish to talk about it. She began to make preparations for tea. All the joy had gone from the visit and Kitty felt she would be glad when it was time to leave.

Her sisters left first and after they had gone Kitty handed the sovereigns back to her mother. 'I'm glad you didn't give them to Violet.'

'I only hope there won't be any repercussions.' Kitty was thinking that her mother's voice held fear when Margaret unexpectedly kissed her on the cheek and said, 'You'd better go too, love. It's inclined to be foggy. Thank Mrs Bramley for the food; it's most welcome. Look after yourself.'

A few minutes later Kitty was walking along the street, wondering what her mother had meant by repercussions. The fog, swirling in patches, deadened sounds and blurred the street-lamps. There was no one around. She turned the corner of the street and was about to cross the road when a figure loomed up and stopped in front of her. Kitty looked up, startled, and as the fog shifted found herself looking up into the smiling face of her sister Violet. A smile, Kitty thought, that held malice. Her heartbeats quickened.

'Hello, little Miss Goody-Two-Shoes, I thought you would be leaving about now. I have something to tell you.' There was a deceptively pleasant note to Violet's voice. 'You had no right to poke your nose into my business.'

'If you mean about Mother giving you money, then I have a right to protest, so have Agnes and Mary and Ann. We're earning it.'

'It's a pity you did protest, because now I'm going to tell you something that dear Mama did not want you to know.' The tone was still deceptively pleasant.

'All right then, tell me,' Kitty said. 'I have to get back to Stratton House.'

There was a pause before Violet said, her tone changing:

'*You*, little Miss Goody-Two-Shoes, are a bastard! How do you like that. Illegitimate! The daughter of an unknown father.'

Kitty felt a dryness come to her mouth. 'It's a lie,' she said. 'I believe you would say anything out of spite.'

'Not this time, little sister, not this time. It's truth. You'd better ask dear Mama the next time you see her.'

Kitty felt she wanted to be sick, but she stood her ground.

'Well, at least now I know you won't have the chance of blackmailing Mother again.'

'Oh, I know of other ways of making money.'

Kitty then pushed past her, saying she had to go for the tram. She forced herself to walk away, but when she turned the next corner she ran, not wanting to stop, not wanting to think ...

CHAPTER NINE

By the time Kitty arrived back at Stratton House she felt physically ill. It had been impossible *not* to think. Violet had once called her a bastard when she was young, but she had not known then what it meant. Now she did ... and knew what it was to be a bastard child. She had heard children at school calling the name at a little girl in the same class. Kitty had asked Harriet what it meant and when she explained had felt sorry for the girl. She had tried to make friends with her, but she would not accept friendship.

Kitty stood at the bottom of the area steps for a long time, not wanting to go into the kitchen and face questions from Mrs Bramley. How many people knew? Violet had implied that her mother had been with some unknown man. Who was he, where had she met him? Was it some man who had come to the glassworks? Perhaps, Kitty thought, this was where she got her love of glass. But then the man she had known as her father had had a job at the glassworks. She sat on the steps and covered her face with her hands. Did Harriet and Abel know, did Luke? Oh, no, not Luke, please God, not him!

Kitty would never have believed that grief, despair could be such painful things. Every part of her seemed to be aching, her stomach trembled. This terrible thing would be with her all her life. She suddenly became aware of voices, whispering voices, then someone giggled. Kitty sat up – it was Ivy.

There was an urgent murmur of, 'I've got to go, I *must*. See you tomorrow night.' Then came a quick patter of steps. Kitty was getting up when Ivy all but knocked her over.

'What you doing sitting on the steps? You'll get your death of cold.'

'I ... don't feel well,' which was the truth.

'I bet you've caught that infection. Come on, get inside.'

'It's not that sort of illness. It's just that I'm – well, aching in every bone in my body.'

'Growing pains,' Ivy said promptly and opening the door, pushed her inside. 'Go on, get into the warm!'

Mrs Bramley equally promptly confirmed Ivy's diagnosis; she had 'suffered terrible' from such pains when she was a girl. She ordered Ivy to get a hot brick from the oven, wrap it in a piece of flannel and take it up and put it in Kitty's bed. Cook then made Kitty a hot drink, which tasted spicy. 'This should do the trick, you should be as right as ninepence in the morning!'

Although Kitty knew she would have to pull herself together by the next morning, she submitted to the cosseting and in fact enjoyed it, feeling terribly sorry for herself. In bed she held the warm brick to her as she went over Violet's conversation, wishing now that she had gone back home and asked her mother if it was true ... and if it was, demanding to know who her real father was. She would have to wait a whole week, unless she might be able to get an evening off. She would ask Mrs Bramley when the time was right.

The next morning Kitty was surprised to find she had slept soundly, but when she got out of bed the enormity of her bastardy was like a weight on her shoulders.

'You all right this morning?' Ivy asked. 'You don't feel sick or anythink? If you do you should stay in bed – you ran around plenty when everyone else was ill.'

'I'm all right, really I am. It was perhaps the cold and the fog that made me ache last night.'

Mrs Bramley seemed relieved to see her in the kitchen and assured her that the 'growing pains' could disappear as quickly as they had come. There was no more cosseting, but Mr Walton did show some concern and asked if she was all right. Later Kitty heard him say to Cook, 'I've never seen Harvey look so peaky, I hope she's not sickening for something.' The 'growing pains' were not mentioned again and that was the end of it as far as Mrs Bramley was concerned, but the astute Ivy did not let go of it so easily.

'Something happened when you went home, didn't it?' she asked.

Kitty longed to unburden herself of her feeling of guilt, but much as she liked the girl she was afraid to tell her, knowing that Ivy was a born gossip. It would be all over the house in no time. She told her it was family business and something she was not able to talk about, which Ivy accepted.

That day Kitty learned something more about this girl who had a coarseness in her and a seeming indifference to death. Ivy helped her in every way she could and once rounded on Mrs Bramley in defence of Kitty when Cook chided her for daydreaming.

'Can't you see she's proper poorly! Nearly dropping on her feet she is, but struggling to do her work. You're always saying that folks ought to make allowances.'

Normally Ivy would have had a box on the ears for the way she had spoken, but Mrs Bramley looked across at Kitty and asked her if she felt ill. Kitty said she had felt ill the night before but was feeling better now; she apologized for not having paid attention to what Mrs Bramley had said.

But although Kitty did make an effort to try to put her problem to the back of her mind, it was always there and things got to the stage where she would find herself trembling for no reason. It was when she dropped a plate and it shattered into a dozen pieces and she burst into tears that Mrs Bramley began to question her. After making Kitty sit down she asked her what was wrong, her voice quiet but firm.

'I must know, Kitty. Is it anything to do with any of the staff? Has George – or anyone else – been upsetting you?'

Kitty wiped her eyes, took a quick breath and looked up. 'No, Mrs Bramley, it's family business. I think I could get it settled one way or another if I could go home and talk to my mother. It's something I *have* to know. If I could have even an hour off . . . ?'

There was a look of curiosity in Mrs Bramley's eyes, but she asked no more questions. 'Yes, you can Kitty. If you leave at four o'clock and come back at six to see to the dishes, that will do.' Kitty thanked her, relief flooding over her.

She went by tram, praying her mother would be in. There was no light on in the living-room, but usually her mother would sit by the fire depending for light from the street-lamp. There was a fire going, as Kitty could see when she passed the window, and Margaret was in.

She eyed her daughter in surprise. 'Why, Kitty, what brings you here? It's not Sunday.'

'No, I asked for time off to come, there's something I have to know. When I left here on Sunday, Violet was waiting for me at the end of the street. She told me I was a bastard. Is it true?'

Kitty had not realized what a shock her words would be to her mother until she seemed to crumple before her eyes. Margaret sank into a chair and covered her face. Kitty felt as though insects were crawling up and down her spine. Until that moment she had hoped, deep down, that her sister had lied. Now she knew it was the truth.

Suddenly, uncaring of her mother's feelings, she burst out, 'Why didn't you tell me? I had more right to know such a thing than our Violet. Who is my *real* father – an unknown man, I was told.'

Margaret lowered her hands and looked at her, dry-eyed.

'I can tell you only one thing, Kitty, you are *not* a bastard.'

Kitty felt as though someone had given her a hard punch, knocking the breath from her body, and it was some time before she was able to speak.

'Then why did Violet say such a thing? She knew I would ask you.'

'Violet knows only half-truths,' Margaret said in a low voice, 'and I'm unable to tell you the full truth. There's too much involved.'

Kitty sat on the stool and stared at her. 'She was blackmailing you. Why should she do that if the man I knew as my father *was* my real father?'

Margaret wrapped her arms around herself and rocked backwards and forwards. 'Please, Kitty, don't ask any more questions, *please*! I'm unable to answer them. Be satisfied that you are *not* illegitimate.'

Kitty felt a coldness seeping into her. 'I don't believe you. Your husband hated me, he knew I was a bastard, that's why he beat me and tied me up; that's why you had me sent to the farm, because you knew he would go on being cruel to me.'

'No, no, you've got it all wrong!' Margaret wailed. 'You have

131

to believe me that you are not illegitimate. I'll swear it on the Bible and I fear God's wrath. There may come a time when I can tell you the truth, Kitty, but it's not now. Please, oh, *please* accept it! I can't stand much more worry.'

In the light that filtered in from the street-lamp her mother looked old, shrunken. Kitty felt a sudden pity. Jessica had told her that Margaret had had a terrible life. She got up, went over and put her arms around her. 'All right, Mother, I won't ask any more questions. And I won't even give Violet the satisfaction of knowing that I've been terribly upset.'

'Thanks, Kitty.' Her mother's voice was barely a whisper. Kitty said she would not be able to stay very long, but would make a cup of tea, so she filled the kettle, stirred the fire and placed the kettle on the glowing coals, thinking how different it was from the previous Sunday when they had all been laughing and chatting. Now she felt there was just nothing she wanted to talk about. As she waited for the water to boil she put up a hand and gripped the edge of the mantelpiece, feeling that nothing would ever be the same again. Her finger-tips encountered something bulky and she picked it up. It was a letter. When she turned with it in her hand Margaret said, her voice without expression, 'It's from Harriet. There's one inside for you from Luke. It came a fortnight ago, but then you didn't come because of the epidemic and on Sunday I forgot to give it to you.'

Kitty stood gripping the envelope – a precious letter and her mother had forgotten to give it to her. One inside for her from Luke! Anger swamped her for a moment, then slowly receded. Being blackmailed would be a much more important thing to her mother than a letter from the farm.

She longed to read it, but wanted to be alone to savour every word, so told Margaret she would take it with her and bring back the one from Harriet on the Sunday; no doubt her mother would want to answer it.

When Kitty was ready to leave she said, 'I'll just pop in and see Jessica for a few minutes, then I'll have to get back.'

Margaret unexpectedly kissed Kitty on the cheek. 'Don't worry about what Violet told you, don't worry about anything she says – she's jealous of you.'

'Jealous? Of me? With her looks and her position . . .'

'Yes, Kitty, with all that.' Her mother sounded completely

drained. 'You'd better go or you'll be late getting back. Tell Jessica I'll look in on her later, or else in the morning.'

Kitty felt more bewildered than ever as she walked to Jessica's house. Her mother must be mistaken, there was nothing that Violet could be jealous about. The whole thing was mystifying. Would Jessica know the truth? Kitty made up her mind to ask, but as she went along the entry to the back she felt this would be disloyal to her mother.

Jessica, seeming as energetic as ever but looking a little paler than usual, was delighted to see her. She would have set her down to a meal had not Kitty explained she had only a short time to stay. Jessica asked Kitty how she had fared during the epidemic and after Kitty had described the problems briefly she had to listen to a discourse from Jessica about how she had been affected, how everyone else in the street had been affected, concluding by saying that she had heard earlier the water had been responsible and every drop now had to be boiled.

If Mrs Bramley knew this, she had made no mention of it. Kitty thought it would make a good talking point when she got back, so as to take Cook's mind off her visit home. She got up, saying she was sorry to rush away, but she must go.

Jessica suddenly jumped up. 'Just remembered something, hang on a minute!' She was up and down the stairs again in seconds, holding out a small wooden box: 'The little glass ship. I've kept forgetting to give it to you.'

Kitty took off the lid and looked at the delicate glass ship in its bed of cotton wool, with its ropes like spun sugar. She looked up. 'Oh, Jessica, I'll take great care of it!'

'I know you will,' Jessica said softly. 'Mam knew it too, that's why she left it for you.'

Kitty replaced the lid and put the box in her pocket as Jessica walked to the door with her. 'Take care of yourself, love.'

'And you ...'

As Kitty walked along the street, fingering the box in her pocket, her eyes suddenly filled with tears. A small gift from a dead woman that meant so much. She had loved Gran Perkins and the old lady had loved her. What were her mother's feelings towards her? She had kissed her this evening as if she really cared. Kitty wondered if she would ever know the truth about her birth.

When she reached Stratton House and went into the kitchen she produced the little glass ship at once. Ivy 'oohed' and 'aahed' over it, Mrs Bramley said it was very pretty and then asked in a casual tone how her mother was. The curiosity was back in her eyes.

'Oh, she's quite well.' Kitty spoke brightly. 'We got the little problem settled.' Then more soberly she added, 'I was told that the water was responsible for the epidemic, and that every drop has to be boiled.'

'So Mr Walton told me an hour ago!' Cook's voice was full of indignation. 'We should have been told this right way! We might all have died. The whole town could have died!' While she was going on about this drama, seeming to relish the fact that there was not enough space to bury people, Kitty put on her coarse apron and started on the dishes.

Ivy came to help her. 'So you got the trouble settled then, did you?' Her expression held curiosity too. 'Who did you say gave you the ship? Your gran?'

Kitty explained about Gran Perkins being part of her childhood and how she had told her about a lovely place called Venice and how she would like to go to Italy and ... Kitty was away dreaming again, until Ivy gave her a nudge and she found herself standing with a plate midway between the sink and the draining board.

'Eee, you're a daft one, Kitty Harvey, but I reckon you'll get where you want to go.' Ivy gave her an affectionate grin.

Mention of the name 'Harvey' made Kitty remember the letters she had to read and wonder how on earth she could have forgotten them. Still, there had been no chance – she would have to wait until she went to bed and read them by candle-light.

When they did go up to bed Ivy was intrigued that Kitty not only had a long letter from Harriet to read but also one from Luke – this one all for Kitty's own self. 'Will you read a bit to me?' Ivy asked, a wistful note in her voice.

Kitty kept Luke's letter to open last, not really wanting to read it aloud at all. Harriet wrote a very descriptive letter, relating all they had been doing; Ivy listened attentively as Kitty read it and said she would like to see all the 'alimals' and so on, but when Kitty unfolded Luke's letter she waited, almost with breath held. The candle flame flickered with the movement of the paper, then settled into a steady flame as Kitty began to read:

My very dear Kitty, I waited until I felt you would be settled into your new job before writing to you. We all miss you terribly here, the farm isn't the same without you. Shep still routs all over, searching for you. When Bess and the other cows come to the field gate, which you used to open, she always looks back at the house as though to say, where is our little Kitty? I think it is very nice to be remembered so well. There was a dance on Monday night in the Croft's barn and just everybody was asking after you. I think you must be vey pleased that you are so popular. They all send good wishes and hope you will be back among us soon. I know this is not possible, not yet, but someday you will be with us, or I shall come North to see you. I miss your lively chatter, your laughter, your roguish smile when you've played a trick on me. Take care of yourself, dear heart, write when you can,
Love from Luke.

Ivy was ecstatic over the letter. If only she had a feller like that, she said but Kitty was crying inside, the doubts about her birth with her once more. She folded the letter and put it in the envelope, then damping her finger she nipped the candle flame to extinguish it, the acrid smell vividly bringing back her bedroom at the farm. If only . . .

Ivy said, 'I wish George said nice things like your Luke. He's just out for a bit of rough and tumble, but I ain't having it. I like him, though!'

It took several seconds to register with Kitty that she was talking about George the footman. 'We'll talk tomorrow, Ivy,' she said. 'I'm nearly asleep. Good night.'

In the flickering lights under her eyelids Kitty could see the words 'dear heart', and she ached with longing to see Luke again. It was true she had been dreamy-eyed about Tyler van Neilson telling her she was a 'very dear girl', but dreaming about him was all it was; he was out of her reach, but Luke was a part of her life and always would be, just as Abel and Harriet would always seem her true parents and the farm her home.

And yet . . . doubts came into Kitty's mind. Last Sunday when she had been at home, she had felt quite close to her mother and Agnes, Mary and Ann and, although the house had little to offer in the way of comfort, she had thought about it as 'going home'. And again tonight. She worried about her mother, about her being in debt and whether she had enough to eat. Harriet once said that blood ties were strong, they kept families close and bound them together. Kitty might have thought this was true had it not been for Violet. She would never be close to her, not *ever*.

A sudden thought sent Kitty's heart pounding. Was this because they had different fathers? She was back once more on the treadmill, going over and over again everything her mother had said. It was finally exhaustion that made her sleep.

When Kitty came down the next morning, Mrs Bramley 'tut-tutted' at the dark circles under her eyes. 'I bet that Ivy has kept you awake half the night chattering; I'll have to have a word with her. Work suffers if you don't have your proper sleep. Get on with your chores, girl, and no daydreaming today!'

Kitty had no wish for anyone else to be blamed for her sleeplessness and hoped that Cook would forget the incident if she worked doubly hard that morning. As it happened, another incident put just about everything out of Mrs Bramley's mind. Word had come down that she and Mr Walton were to go to the drawing-room after breakfast.

'Both of us,' she said, looking worried.

At first when they left to go to the drawing-room there was a breathless feeling of waiting in the kitchen, then speculation began. George suggested the pair of them had been fiddling – Mr Walton the wine and Mrs Bramley the food. Bettina sniffed and said more likely it had been found out that they were sharing a bed. At this Clara remarked quietly that a butler and cook of their calibre were hard to come by and that a blind eye would certainly be turned in these circumstances, *if* what Bettina said was true, which she very much doubted. Bettina had opened her mouth to reply to this when Ivy, to Kitty's astonishment, rose in defence of the couple, saying that small minds like Bettina's could only think filthy things. Then she turned and gave Kitty a wink and a grin.

When Bettina tried again to have her say, the coachman said they should all 'shut their faces' until Cook and Mr Walton came back.

When Mr Walton and Mrs Bramley did return to the kitchen, everyone suddenly found a job to do. Mr Walton said, 'You can all stop what you are doing for a minute, we have something to tell you.' Both were solemn-faced. 'This weekend ...' he paused, 'we will be leaving here – all of us.'

'All of us?' came a bewildered echo.

A smile suddenly trembled on Mrs Bramley's lips and she looked up at the butler. 'Go on, tell them, don't keep them in suspense!'

Mr Walton smiled. 'Actually, we will be packing up to go to the master and mistress's country house for the hunting. Other years only some of the staff have accompanied them there but Mrs Earle feels that all are in need of some good country air after the epidemic.'

Mrs Bramley added, 'We have a lot to do, plenty of packing, many things will have to be taken as the house at Mealton is larger than this. We'll be leaving next Tuesday morning.'

Mealton? Kitty felt her heart had stopped beating. Dare she ask if it was the same Mealton? 'Mrs Bramley, ma'm, is the house near Leicester?'

'Yes, it is. All those of you who can get home will be allowed a short visit on Sunday, but it *will* be short. Now ...' she clapped her hands, 'back to work!'

Kitty looked at Ivy, wide-eyed. 'I can't believe it! That's where I lived, at the farm. I'll see Luke!' Mrs Bramley shouted at them to stop chattering or they would be left behind. This had the desired effect, but Kitty felt all the time as though a magician had waved a wand over her and put her in a trance.

There was great activity during the next two days, crates being packed with china, silver, linen and food. All the beautiful glass was packed and the chandelier. 'To show off to their friends,' Ivy said.

From her Kitty learned that Bettina would not be going to Mealton. She was going home, so it would not be worth while taking her all that way only to leave in two weeks' time. Another parlourmaid would be hired.

On the Saturday morning after the breakfast dishes had been washed and cleared away, Mrs Bramley – who had been upstairs – came down and called Kitty to tell her that the mistress wanted to see her.

Cook's face was flushed and a tremor of fear ran through Kitty. What had she done wrong? If it was something awful she would not be allowed to go to Mealton and could even get the sack.

Mrs Bramley said, 'There's no need to look as if you'd broken a piece of the best china. It could be good news. There's talk of promoting you to under-housemaid!'

'Under-housemaid?' Kitty exclaimed. 'But that's what Ivy is.'

'Yes ... well– she might be promoted to housemaid. But you're not to say anything to her, do you hear? Not yet. Nothing's settled. I might say I'm not too pleased that I might be losing you. You're a good worker, Kitty, one of the best I've ever had. At the same time I don't want to deny you promotion.'

Mrs Bramley went to a cupboard, brought out a bundle and handed it to Kitty. 'Mrs Earle wants to see you in uniform.'

There was a grey alpaca dress, a white cap and apron. Cook told her to go into the larder and change; it would save time.

Kitty, shivering with a mixture of excitement and cold, changed quickly, unable to believe her luck. Not that she had the promotion yet, but ... When she came back into the kitchen Mrs Bramley eyed her critically, said she looked very presentable but thought it might be better if her hair was pinned up. She untied the ribbon holding Kitty's hair back, took hairpins from a small vase on the mantelpiece and while she rolled and pinned, told Kitty the reason for the suggested promotion.

'The mistress said you behaved splendidly during the epidemic and everyone else you attended agreed. Even the master spoke of you as one of the most capable girls he had ever met. Which, I might say, was very high praise coming from him!' She thrust in another pin. 'And I couldn't but agree with that. There, let me look at you.' She turned Kitty to face her. 'Yes, it's an improvement and makes you look older. Keep your hands behind your back. They'll get less chapped once you've stopped having them in so much hot water. Keep rubbing in the fat I gave you, every night. Now, let's go up.'

When they reached the drawing-room Mrs Bramley adjusted Kitty's cap, told her to remember to curtsy and knocked. To the call of 'Enter!' they went in.

Kitty, whose stomach had been trembling with nerves, suddenly became calm, knowing that getting the job could depend on her behaviour. Her gaze went to Mrs Earle, who was sitting in a high-backed brocaded chair looking like a queen, her hair beautifully done, her blue silk dress and pearls giving her great elegance.

When they stood before her Kitty curtsied, and after that lowered her gaze. 'Look at me, Kitty.' There was a smile in Mrs Earle's voice. 'You don't have to be afraid. You curtsy beautifully and you look very nice in your uniform. Cook, I know, will have told you of the suggested promotion. You are young, but you carry yourself well, you speak well and your manners are good. Your mother has been informed and I want you to have a talk with her tomorrow; she will explain certain things to you. I want her permission for you to go with us to our country house.'

Permission? Was it likely her mother would refuse, since there would be extra money? Although Kitty tried to convince herself that Margaret would agree to the promotion, there was nevertheless a small doubt niggling in her mind.

'That will be all then, Kitty. Thank you, Cook.'

When they left the drawing-room Kitty said in a beseeching tone, 'Mrs Bramley, ma'am, can you think of any reason why my mother would not give her permission?'

'Yes, I can, Kitty, but that is something you must discuss with her. Come along now, there's a lot to do and you'll have to get changed.'

When they returned to the kitchen Ivy was grinning all over her face. She winked at Kitty. 'All settled then?' Mrs Bramley snapped that No, it wasn't settled, and ordered her to get on with her work.

It was not actually until bedtime that the girls got a chance of talking, then Ivy said, 'You could've knocked me down with a feather when I knew. Housemaid, eh? Mind you, although I shout my mouth off sometimes down here, I know how to behave meself upstairs. I go all soft like and say, 'Yes, ma'am; no, ma'am; yes, sir; no sir; three bags full, sir! Why, what's the matter with you? You look as if you'd lost a sovereign and found a penny!'

Kitty told her worriedly about having to get her mother's

permission, but Ivy dismissed this as a foregone conclusion. Who would refuse the extra money involved? Not *her* mam and she was sure that Kitty's mam wouldn't either.

Kitty began to feel more hopeful after this. Her mother would certainly be glad of the extra money. It was probably a rule of the upper-class household that such permission had to be given. And with this resolved, she felt again her earlier excitement and could hardly wait for Sunday to come.

CHAPTER TEN

Kitty kept breaking into a run on her way home the following afternoon. Mrs Bramley had let her leave earlier than usual and she was anxious to get there before her sister Violet arrived, not wanting to give her the chance of gloating if her mother refused to allow her to go to Mealton.

She arrived breathless to find her mother sitting over a low fire. Margaret looked up. 'Why, hello, Kitty, you're early.' She looked worried. 'I have the kettle nearly boiling; I'll make a cup of tea, get your coat off.'

Kitty told her she had not long to stay . . . and waited. But Margaret said nothing until the tea was made and poured. She took a sip, then eyed her over the rim of the cup. 'I'm not altogether happy about this promotion, or the move to Mealton, Kitty.'

'Why, Mother, why? I can't see what you have against it. It will mean more money for you and I'll be able to see everyone at the farm. What's wrong with that?'

'Several things, but in the first place money isn't everything. Yes, I know I'm in debt, but I still hold that there are things much more important, such as keeping yourself out of trouble.'

When Kitty gave a despairing groan and asked what trouble, Margaret put down her cup and leaned forward. 'I'll tell you. When they go to Mealton there are house guests, they have parties and some of the young men go wild. Your duties as under-housemaid will take you upstairs to clean, to dust, make beds. You'll lay fires in bedrooms, light them – and there are young men who think every pretty servant welcomes their attentions.'

'Oh, Mother, I can take care of myself, stop worrying. If there was any trouble I have only to speak to Mrs Bramley and she'll tell Mr Walton, who will know how to deal with it.'

'But sometimes it's too late,' Margaret said bitterly, 'and the damage is done.'

The fear was back with Kitty again about her birth. Was this what had happened to her mother, had *she* been speaking half-truths when they had discussed it earlier? She said quietly, 'I think the girls who get in this kind of trouble are afraid to protest. I wouldn't be afraid, I'd scream the house down.'

'And what would you do if the man said he hadn't touched you? They would believe *him*. You would get the sack.'

'Mother, the only reason I would get the sack is because I was careless and broke something valuable. I want this promotion; I'm lucky, very lucky to have this chance. I want to get on, I want to rise to the position of lady's maid. Now, it's up to you.'

After a silence Margaret gave a deep sigh and looked up. 'Very well, Kitty, I only hope I won't live to regret it. And I'll say only one more thing. Don't let this promotion go to your head, don't get too big for your boots and think you can conquer the world, like I did. You need friends in life, not enemies.'

Her mother's words made a deep impression on Kitty. She kept going over them as she walked back to Stratton House. Judging by Margaret's remarks it was as though she had been in service and been approached by wild young men ... and yet earlier there had been no hint from her of this life, or from Harriet. Kitty was beginning to find her mother's world more and more of a mystery.

When Kitty arrived back at Stratton House there was no more time for speculation. Everyone was running around, for there had been a sudden change in plans. Instead of leaving on the Tuesday, the staff were now leaving the next morning. They were to travel by train. The family had already left to stay with friends and would be travelling later in the week.

When Kitty ventured to ask why there had been a change, Mrs Bramley threw up her hands. 'I don't know, why should *you* know? Nobody tells me anything! There's dust sheets to be put over all the furniture. Don't stand there, girl, this kitchen has to be bottomed before we leave.'

Kitty was scrubbing until midnight; she went to bed at one-thirty and was up again at five, but she felt bright with excitement. It was later when she was in the train that tiredness hit her and the others. Their chatter trailed off.

A hamper of food had been packed to sustain them on the journey and to drink there was cold tea or beer. Kitty enjoyed that part of it, because it reminded her of the times when she took baskets of food and beer to the men during hay-making time. She thought with pleasure of the surprise they would all get at the farm when they knew she would be coming to see them. She must write a letter when they got settled in at Mealton. She could see Luke, his whole face alight, lifting her off her feet and swinging her around ... 'dear heart' ...

With this came the thought of Tyler van Neilson who had told her she was 'a very dear girl', and Kitty felt suddenly sad that she might not see him for a long time and that even when she did, he might not remember her. He could at this very moment be telling a servant in his father's house that she was a 'very dear girl'. She closed her eyes, not wanting this attractive man to have any place in her heart. It was Luke she loved, always would.

The whole party was weary by the time they arrived at Leicester, with Mrs Bramley moaning that now they had a carriage drive that would 'shake her up'. All she wanted was to lie down somewhere for an hour – or less, ten minutes would do!

Kitty was just the opposite. Once she was in the carriage she sat on the edge of the seat, especially when they reached the country roads, hoping to see familiar landmarks, but this was impossible in the dark. There were the lighted windows of homesteads, of farms, big houses, but none she recognized. She knew she would recognize the Leddenshaw farm and was hoping they would pass it on their way to the Earles' house. If there was not too great a distance between, perhaps she would be able to slip over to the farm for an hour in an evening.

Her eyes were getting strained watching and when they passed a mill, she realized with a feeling of disappointment they were on a different road from the one she was familiar with. She sat back in the seat, bone-weary now and, like Mrs Bramley, wanting somewhere to lie down.

It was when the carriage slowed and they drove between a stone-pillared entrance that they all came to life again. They passed under a tunnel of trees and came out in parkland where the house was outlined against the skyline. There seemed to be dozens of chimneys – tall, twisted ones – and dozens of windows, but only two in the downstairs rooms were lit.

'Isn't it big?' Ivy said, a note of awe in her voice. 'It's a proper country mansion, isn't it?' To which Mrs Bramley asked tartly what else she expected.

The carriage wheels crunched over the gravel drive, and came to a stop outside a porticoed door. Then the door opened, spilling a warm glow on to the gravel, and a man and a woman came out with two young girls and a youth. The man, whose name was Dunn, introduced his family, explaining to Mr Walton that he and his wife were caretakers and their daughters and son would be part of the staff: kitchen-maids and boot-boy.

Mrs Dunn – a big, pleasant-faced woman – and Mrs Bramley seemed to take to one another right away, for within seconds they were chatting about the journey and the house. Mr Dunn and Mr Walton walked ahead, while the two girls and their brother stayed behind to help the coachman with the luggage.

In the normal way they would have gone in by the servants' entrance but, possibly because the family were not here yet, they went in by the front door. And when Kitty saw the staircase in the spacious hall she was the one to be awed. 'Oh, Ivy, look!' she breathed. The staircase of white marble had wide, shallow steps with balusters of carved animals – strange creatures, tall and thin, sitting on their haunches – while the banisters were carved with tiny animals.

'Isn't it beautiful, Ivy?'

Ivy sniffed. 'Bloody cold, I'd say! It could do with a bit of carpeting on the stairs.' Kitty gave her a quick nudge as Mrs Bramley turned her head and glared at them.

They moved towards the back of the hall, but not before Kitty had taken in marble columns with standing figures on them, two holding lamps at the top of the stairs: one man, one woman. She would have liked to linger, but Ivy was pulling her forward. They went along two passages and came out into a massive kitchen, with a stone fireplace big enough to roast an ox. 'Cor!' Ivy exclaimed. 'What a size, it's big enough to hold a ball.'

A cold meal had been prepared for them, but most seemed too tired to do justice to it. Mrs Bramley . . . who kept stifling yawns, said at last that she really must be excused and it was time the girls got to bed too, for they would have to be up early the next morning.

Ivy and Kitty, as before, shared an attic bedroom, but here there was a little more luxury, with plump eiderdowns on the bed and three thick hand-made rugs on the floor. And, instead of having a window in the roof, there was a long one at floor level through which, Kitty said, she would be able to survey her surroundings and try to find out where the farm lay. But that was for another day. Right now it was time for bed.

At first when she tried to settle, she could hear the sound of the train wheels drumming in her head – clackety-clack, dockety-do – then she found herself enveloped in steam and carried away into the sky.

She thought it was the shrill whistle of the engine that had aroused her, but found it was the ringing of the alarm clock. She groaned. So soon?

From the moment of getting up from breakfast, Kitty and Ivy were on the run. There were fires to be laid, in what Ivy described as a hundred bedrooms but which Kitty estimated were nearer thirty, and beds to be made up. Mrs Dunn helped them with this and told them that another older daughter would be helping too when the family arrived. There were corridors and carpets to be swept, furniture dusted – statues too, which seemed to be all over the place. Kitty and Ivy stood giggling over a marble figure of a man wearing only a fig-leaf, Ivy declaring she would like to see what was under it. 'You're terrible, Ivy!' she was chided by Kitty. 'And if you don't stop swearing like you were five minutes ago, you'll never keep your job.' Ivy, sobering, said she was quite right, from now on she would be ladylike. She mimicked the cultured tones of the 'gentry', which kept Kitty laughing.

But the laughter soon died with the constant running up and down stairs. Tommy, the boot-boy, carried up buckets of coal; although thin, he was suprisingly strong. When Kitty asked him where all the marble had come from he said from a place called Athens – the elderly Mr Earle had spent a year there and had it shipped home.

When Mrs Bramley went for her rest that afternoon Kitty and Ivy slipped away up to their room, Ivy as anxious as Kitty to know if the farm could be seen. They knelt down to look out of the window and below them could see kitchen gardens and greenhouses. Beyond this lay a patchwork of fields, interspersed with spinneys, cottages and farms where cattle grazed.

Kitty searched, looking for a landmark of six cedar trees, but after a while began to shake her head. Then suddenly she gave a whoop of joy, 'There it is, Ivy, over there! To the right, you can just see the end of the house and two of the trees. It must be three or four miles away, but that's nothing, I could get there in an evening. You must come with me one time.'

Although Kitty had expected it would be some time before she would be able to go to the farm, she was surprised when two mornings later she was told by Mrs Bramley she could have the afternoon off to go and visit her foster-parents. Ivy could have time off the following afternoon, both girls had worked like Trojans, she was pleased with them.

Kitty could hardly contain her excitement and when she set out for the farm with warnings from Mrs Bramley not to stay too late, she felt she wanted to run and shout as she crossed the first field. The late October sunshine had little warmth in it, but there was a feeling of summer to Kitty, with the clarity, the clear blue sky and fleecy white clouds – something that seemed rare in the smoke-laden atmosphere of the Northern town.

When she opened a gate, sheep who were huddled together scattered; cows stood looking at her with mournful eyes as they chewed on their cud.

'Hello, you lovely "alimals"!' she called, laughing as she thought of Ivy's word. She rode back on the gate, then thought that she was wasting time and ran to make up for the delay.

When she neared a cottage a woman came out, sleeves rolled above her elbows. 'Morning!' she called. Kitty greeted her and paused to ask how far it was to the Leddenshaw farm. The woman squinted into the distance. 'About a couple of miles, perhaps more.' She turned and eyed Kitty, then she smiled. 'You'll be their girl. Went up North, didn't you?'

'That's right. I'm working at the Earles'. I've come with them for the hunting.'

'Oh, good people to work for, the Earles, they don't come no better. My man works for them. Are you coming in for a bit?'

Kitty thanked her but said No, she must go – some other time

146

perhaps. She cut across fields, through spinneys, through farmyards where dogs barked, bringing out a woman or a man to see who was coming. Kitty, wanting no more stops waved and shouted, 'I'm on my way to the Leddenshaws...' and she would get a wave back.

When she neared the farm she stopped abruptly, her heart beginning a slow pounding as she saw the stocky figure of Abel. He was standing, hat tipped back, watching a hawk swooping down to seize some prey. Kitty began to run, calling, 'Uncle Abel, Uncle Abel...'

He turned and his astonishment made her want to laugh and cry.

'Kitty! Why, Kitty girl, what are you doing here?'

He came hurrying towards her, then his strong arms were around her holding her close and there was a break in his voice as he said, 'I can't believe it.' He held her away from him. 'What's happened?' He looked beyond her. 'Is your mother with you?'

'No...' Kitty told him quickly where she had come from and Abel scolded her gently, saying she should have written and told them. Kitty told him it wou!d have spoiled the surprise.

'Surprise?' he echoed. 'Just wait till Harriet and Luke see you. Harriet's in the kitchen, Luke is up in the field. Come on—'

Harriet had seen them and was running towards them as they came up. Then she and Kitty were hugging and laughing and crying together. And, of course, Harriet wanted to know why she was here.

Abel said he would tell Luke but Kitty said No, No, she would go to him, she wanted to surprise him. Harriet told her to go now and bring Luke back with her, while she would put the kettle on.

Kitty ran, scattering hens, laughing at their squawking and calling, 'Sorry, I'm in a hurry!'

When she reached the gate of the top field she stopped. Luke, like his father, was standing in the middle of the field but he was looking towards the farm, where swallows were gathering in groups on the eaves of the house and outbuildings, ready for their big migration. Kitty always found something sad about their departure, as though the birds were leaving the summer to die alone.

Kitty opened the gate, closed it and walked towards Luke,

emotion threatening to swamp her. How dearly familiar his straight figure, his copper-coloured hair glinting in the thin sunlight. She was quite close to him before he became aware of her. For a moment there was silence, then it all happened as she had imagined it – his whole face lighting up with pleasure as he came to her and picking her up, swung her round and round.

'Kitty Leddenshaw! I don't believe it. Where have you sprung from?' Like his father he looked beyond her as he put her down, and seeing no one held her away from him. 'Let me look at you. I swear you've grown three inches, and more pretty than ever. Oh, Kitty,' he held her to him, 'how we've all missed you!'

'And I all of you,' she said softly.

There was a moment when Kitty was aware of the lovely closeness there had always been between Luke and herself, then he was saying, 'Well, let's hear all the news. I expect Mother will be wanting to know it too. And Dad!'

They went back to the farm hand-in-hand, with Kitty talking all the way, knowing that everything would have to be repeated but wanting Luke to be the first to know about so many things that had happened. But only the nice things at the moment, the things that would make Luke laugh. He had such a warm, deep laugh.

When they reached the yard Shep came rushing up, barking, his feathery tail threshing, a joyousness in him as he ran in circles in front of Kitty. Luke said, 'He remembers you! He still searches barns for you.' Kitty caught Shep and fondled his ears, disregarding Abel's earlier orders not to make a fuss of him. Shep suddenly went racing ahead and Kitty and Luke followed, with Kitty feeling a lovely golden glow. She was home. When they went into the kitchen she called, 'We're here, I've brought Luke straight ba—' she stopped as a small dark-haired girl got up out of a chair. 'Hello,' the girl said shyly.

Harriet introduced them. This was Louise Chater, she had come to look after her grandmother who was ill – did Kitty remember the old lady? She lived in the first cottage past the Trevor farm. Harriet seemed to be talking in an over-bright way and Kitty could not understand why until she saw the dark-haired girl smiling at Luke. To Kitty, there was an intimacy in the smile. What of Luke?

Abel pulled out a chair. 'Come on, Kitty girl, sit down – and

you too, Louise – there's a cup of tea on the way, I can hear it.'
The lid of the kettle in the fire was rattling merrily away and
Harriet went to it to rinse the teapot. Kitty felt a sudden chill in
the warm room. Abel's voice too had seemed a shade over-
hearty.

With the tea made, Harriet brought a cake from the larder.
'It's a coconut cake, Kitty, one of your favourites. I must have
known you were coming!' Kitty, feeling she must do something,
got up to pour the tea and when Harriet protested that she was
not here to work, it was her afternoon off, she said, 'It's not work
when you're at home. It's a pleasure!'

Following a small silence Harriet passed the cake round,
saying to Louise as she took a piece, 'I still can't believe that
Kitty's here. She's been such a miss.'

'Yes, I know.' Louise smiled at Kitty. 'I feel I know you so
well, I've heard such a lot about you. Do you like working for the
Earles?'

'Yes, I do.' Kitty made an effort to pull herself together, to
forget her resentment, otherwise this visit was going to be
spoiled. She explained about the family coming for the hunting,
then Harriet began to question her about her work and she and
Abel and Luke were all delighted to know Kitty had been
promoted to under-housemaid. Kitty explained it had all come
about because of the epidemic and told them about Mr van
Neilson, and how she had shaved him. Harriet 'tut-tutted' that
she had been alone with the gentleman in his room, but when
Kitty went on to describe how she had tilted his nose to get the
lather from his upper lip, Harriet as well as the others burst into
laughter.

'Oh, Kitty, you're quite a girl!' Luke exclaimed, wiping his
eyes. 'You're so adaptable, so resolute. I can see you eventually
marrying into the nobility.'

The misery was back with Kitty again, a tight knot inside her.
She had told Luke once when she was about ten years old that
she was going to marry him and he had laughed and said, 'Then
hurry and grow up.'

Abel and Luke got up then, Abel saying there were chores to
be done but they would be back soon. Louise got up too, she
must also go. She thanked Harriet for the tea and cake, told
Kitty she hoped they would meet again soon and left with the

men. Harriet cut Kitty another piece of cake.

'A nice girl, Louise, very gentle yet most capable, lovely with children. She and Luke played together when *they* were children; she's Luke's age, although you'd never believe it.'

'No, you wouldn't.' Kitty crumbled a piece of cake between her fingers, guessing what Harriet was trying to tell her. Her misery deepened.

'What's wrong, love?' Harriet spoke softly.

Kitty shook her head, unable to answer for the lump in her throat. Harriet came round the table, drew out a chair next to her and sat down. 'You must tell me what's troubling you, Kitty. Is someone unkind to you at the Earles' place?'

'No ...' Kitty swallowed hard. 'It's just that I – expected to come back and find nothing changed, but it has.'

Harriet laid a hand gently over hers. 'Nothing has changed here, love, it's you who have changed. You're growing up, you're meeting a different class of people, seeing a totally different way of life.'

Kitty looked up, her eyes brimming with tears. 'I might have changed, I don't know, I only know that I hurt just the same.'

'It's Luke, isn't it?' Harriet spoke with sorrow. 'He's always meant a great deal to you, Kitty, and he loves you, but he's a man, love. Although you're growing up, you have a long way to go before you reach ... well – marriageable age.'

'And Luke wants to marry Louise, is that it?' Kitty said in a low voice.

'He hasn't said so, but they do get on well together. Oh, Kitty, I don't want you to be unhappy. You know how much we all love you; you're part of the family, always will be, we want to know everything that you do. I don't think there's a day goes by but your name doesn't crop up. You like your job, you've had quick promotion and other promotions could come, but if there's anything you don't like, or anyone upsets you, you must tell us.'

Harriet suddenly drew back. 'No, that's wrong, I was forgetting about your own mother for the moment, she is your real family. You must tell *her*. How is Margaret? How do you get on with your sisters?'

Kitty longed to tell Harriet what Violet had called her, but in spite of thinking of the Leddenshaws as her real family she knew it would be unfair to burden them with these problems. She talked about Violet, how beautiful she was and how she had become a lady's maid. She spoke of her other three sisters and said how alike they all were, it was difficult to tell them apart. Then Kitty suddenly thought that really they were not so alike, and she told Harriet this in a wondering kind of way.

'They *are* different. They all admit to being terrified of ... Father, when they were younger, but Agnes I feel would have her say now. Ann could get angry, but Mary is quiet. I find myself wanting to see them again.'

Harriet queried, 'But not Violet?'

Kitty said No, but not wanting to enlarge on it she talked about Jessica, then about Ivy and her funny words and ways, and by the time Luke returned she had recovered from the awful desolation she had first felt when seeing Louise.

Abel came in as Luke was talking about Louise's family, but Kitty was not listening; she was sitting frozen, staring at the doll in Abel's hand. He laid it on the chair, saying that young Frances must have left it in the barn and he would take it over later; Frances would never go to bed without it. Frances was the child of Abel and Harriet's widowed daughter-in-law.

Harriet talked about making a meal, but Kitty said she would be unable to stay; she would have to get back, it was just an afternoon off.

'Oh, so soon!' Harriet wailed. 'How quickly the time has gone. When will you be able to come again, Kitty?'

She said she had no idea, perhaps not for some time, for the family would be arriving at the weekend and Mrs Bramley had been hinting at guests coming with them.

'Well, if you must go,' Luke said, regret in his voice, 'I'll walk with you over to the Earles' place.' He picked up the doll, which was dressed in a brown woollen dress and bonnet. 'I can drop this in to Frances on the way.'

'No!' Kitty exclaimed, staring at the doll. 'There's no need for you to come with me, I know the way. It's all right, have your supper.'

'What's the matter, Kitty?' Luke asked, bewildered.

Harriet took the doll from him and laid it on another chair, saying quietly, 'Kitty won't want to be delayed and you would be if you called at the cottage. She has only been given the afternoon off.' To Kitty she said, 'Luke will go with you. It was all right coming in the daylight, but you could lose your way back in the dark.' She drew Kitty to her, held her close for a moment then patted her arm. 'Come and see us when you can, love.'

Abel kissed her. 'If you know in advance when you're likely to have time off, Kitty girl, let us know and either Luke or I can pick you up in the trap. Off you go now.'

Luke, still looking bewildered, held out his hand to Kitty. She put hers into it and they left.

When they had gone, Harriet turned to her husband. 'Oh, Abel, what is it about a doll that terrifies Kitty? What happened in the past? Supposing she ever has children, how will she behave? She might have a little girl, who could never own a doll. It's terrible, if only we knew!'

Abel shook his head. 'I don't know, Harriet, I just don't know, I wish we did.' He paused, then added, 'What happened between you and Kitty after Luke and I went out? She was different when we came back, subdued, and that's not Kitty.'

Harriet told him about their talk and Abel stood, thoughtful. 'So – that's it, is it? Well, Kitty's young, many girls have thought themselves to be in love at her age. She'll meet other people and forget him. That's not the worst of our worries, it's the doll that's bothersome.'

Luke was worried about Kitty when they came out. Although she was known among the people in the area as a 'little tough 'un' there was a sensitivity, a delicate mechanism in her, like the silver watch belonging to his mother which he had once taken apart to find out what had gone wrong.

Knowing now that it was the doll which had upset her, Luke could have kicked himself for not remembering what had happened to the one his mother had made for her when Kitty first came to the farm. Why had she discarded it, put it in the pigsty where it had been trampled and dirtied? The family had often discussed this, but reached no conclusion.

When he started in the direction of the top field, she stopped and withdrew her hand. 'We're going the wrong way, the Earles' house is over there.'

'We're going by the road, that's the way I'll come in the trap on your next afternoon or evening off. It's only a short way further. And it saves going through all the fields and spinneys, opening and closing gates.'

She had moved away from him and he sensed there was something more than the doll troubling her. He glanced at her, but away from the lighted house and with his eyes not yet adjusted to the darkness, her face was just a pale oval blur.

'What's wrong, Kitty?' he asked gently. She told him nothing was wrong and started to walk ahead, but he caught her arm and turned her to face him. 'You've never found the need to lie to me before, Kitty, why now?'

'Are you going to marry Louise?' Although she had raised her head in an almost defiant gesture, there was a veiled anguish in her voice. It hurt him.

'What made you ask such a thing?' It was difficult to keep his tone as casual as he had intended. 'Louise is a friend, I've known her a long time. I like her, I like her very much, but I had not been thinking about her in terms of marriage.' That at least was true.

'She's in love with you – and don't say she isn't, because I know she is.'

'I wasn't aware of it, Kitty,' he said quietly, 'but I don't see why this should upset you. Louise will be here no more than a few weeks. Once her grandmother is well again, she'll be going back home. I may not see her for years.' He tilted her chin and smiled. 'Satisfied?'

Her eyes looked huge, anguished. 'I love you, Luke, and I thought you loved me. You called me "dear heart" in your letter.' Her voice broke.

'Oh, Kitty . . .' Luke put his arms around her. 'Come and sit down, we must have a talk.' He led her to the sawing bench and when they were seated he said, 'You are dear to me, always have been, we all love you.'

'You love me as a brother, is that it?' A small sob escaped her.

'It's more than that, Kitty, it's a very special love, but you're young.'

'That's what they all tell me! Do you have to be old to feel pain, heartache?'

'No, I felt pain and heartache when I was thirteen, over a girl. She came to stay with an aunt for the summer and she helped with the haymaking. I was really love-sick – I couldn't eat, couldn't sleep, my work suffered. Dad told me he would belt me if I didn't pull myself together. I couldn't, but he didn't belt me, he talked to me – told me that when the girl left I would fall for someone else. I didn't believe him. But you know, Kitty, he was right. A girl called Helen replaced the girl of the hay-making time and I was just as besotted with her. That's how it is with adolescence. It can be an enduring love and some couples stay together for the rest of their lives, but so often it's off with the old love, on with the new.'

Kitty made no answer and for once Luke felt at a loss what to say next.

It was the time of day, time of year when a great silence settles over the land – animals bedded, hens roosting – a time when Luke enjoyed a solitary walk. A soft throaty clucking from the barn behind them disturbed the silence, seemed magnified, then all was quiet again.

And it was then that Luke became aware that Kitty was crying silently with a hopelessness that pulled at him. 'Oh, Kitty—' He put an arm around her, bringing her head to rest against his shoulder. 'What I feel for you is an enduring love, very different from the days of my boyhood. But I'm so much older than you, I've been through a war. Sometimes I feel vey old, as though I'd lived for ever. You are on the threshold of a whole new world, you have years ahead of you; they're so precious, believe me. I want you to be happy.'

Suddenly it was enough for Kitty that Luke did have a special love for her. She felt sure now that he would not rush into marriage. He was obviously still suffering from the horrors of war, just as Harriet and Abel were still grieving over the tragic loss of their three sons. 'Time heals all wounds,' the vicar had told them. Perhaps in time Luke would forget all the horrors that he had witnessed and would then want to get married, want a home of his own and children. By then she would be grown up. Plenty of much older men married girls of sixteen. And Luke was not old, he was only eight years older – or was it nine?

'Oh, Luke, please wait for me,' she begged silently.

She gave a hiccuping sob and looked up at him. 'I'm all right now, we had better go.' They walked up to the top of the rise, then Kitty stopped. Although there was no moon it was lighter here. Ahead of them, below the slope, snaked the white road that she always associated with the 'Yesterday's Road' that Luke had talked about. There were other roads waiting for her, he had said.

'Race you!' she cried, and they went helter-skelter down the slope. At the bottom, Luke caught her and swung her off her feet. 'This is my lovely Kitty. Never change, *please*!'

'I won't, I promise.' He took her by the hand and laughing they set out to walk to the Earles' house.

CHAPTER ELEVEN

The morning following Kitty's visit to the farm, Mr Walton announced at breakfast that the Earle family would be arriving early that afternoon, bringing with them eight guests. Mrs Bramley flung up her hands. Wasn't it typical of the gentry, to give only a few hours' notice? Didn't they realize all the work that had to be done? They seemed to think that everyone working for them had ten pairs of hands.

'Not that I mind the extra cooking,' she announced to all and sundry, which surprised Kitty, seeing the fuss she had made the morning Tyler van Neilson wanted a cooked breakfast, while the majority of people in the house were still ill.

'No, I don't mind the cooking at all. I prefer catering for large numbers, it stretches my artistry. Oh, yes,' she informed Mrs Dunn, 'there is an artistry, a creativity in cooking that would beat any of the old masters with their dreary paintings!'

Mrs Bramley helped herself to a second piece of toast then, realizing that Kitty and Ivy were still at the table, she demanded to know what they thought they were doing, sitting there gawping? There were fires to be lit, warming-pans to be taken over sheets – some of them might want to lie down after their long journey – there was dusting to be done and not a speck was to be found anywhere, or else ...

From then on Kitty and Ivy were constantly on the run, up and down stairs. As the fires were not burning up very quickly they had to keep coming down to the kitchen to get hot coals to put in the warming-pans. Even though there was very little dust to be seen, they went over every piece of furniture, with Mrs Dunn's eldest daughter helping them in the final stages. In the evening Elsie was going to act as parlourmaid with Clara.

Extra temporary staff had been engaged for when the family arrived and they had to be rounded up. There were only six or seven, all of whom would be living out, but when they were all in the kitchen together, it seemed to be overflowing with people.

'It's as though a regiment had invaded the place!' Ivy complained, 'with old Walton acting as the general and Bramley the sergeant-major.'

Actually Kitty was enjoying all the hustle and bustle; it was exciting having visitors. Since her visit to the farm she had felt strangely happy, possibly because of having been with those she loved the most, especially Luke. Although they had laughed together on their way back Luke had talked to her quietly about life in general, the struggle at times to exist, the satisfaction of achieving something, even if it was just being able to get the harvest in on time. He had talked about planting, watching seedlings grow, and she had known it was not only about plants he was speaking but about people ... about her ... he had watched her growing, developing and in his quiet way wanted what was best for her.

Kitty was upstairs when family and guests arrived and it was in the kitchen later that she heard all the details from Ivy.

'Cor, they're a rum lot! Two weak-kneed looking fellers with high, la-di-da voices, two horsey-faced girls with braying laughs, a married couple, an elderly colonel-type feller and a woman who looks like a dowager duchess – all furs, a muff the size of a pillow and eyeing everyone through them kind of spectacles on a stick!'

'They're called lorgnettes,' Mrs Bramley informed her, 'and the lady you mention belongs to an old but impoverished noble family. She has a title, but likes to travel incognito and is known by the name of Mrs Helder. So just you treat her with respect, my girl!'

There came a time in the kitchen when every bell from upstairs seemed to be ringing at once. When only Kitty was available, Mrs Bramley despatched her to the 'duchess's' room, with a warning to remember her 'Ps and Qs'.

Kitty took a quick breath before going into the room, but still felt nervous when she saw a tall, austere-looking woman with grey hair eyeing her through the lorgnettes. But when she spoke her voice was soft, her expression gentle.

'What is your name, my dear?'

'Kitty Leddenshaw, ma'am. No, sorry, ma'am, it's Harvey.' Colour rushed to Kitty's face and she was glad that at least she had not slipped up with her curtsy.

'You have a stepfather, I presume, is that it?' Mrs Helder smiled in an encouraging way.

'No, ma'am, I had foster-parents, I lived with them for eight years.'

'I see. Well, Kitty, I want you to do something for me. At this time of day I like a cup of tea. I have brought my own, it's special. I want you to make it for me and bring it up; I shall give you directions how to make it.'

Kitty was not only given a casket of tea, but three small boxes; she had to put a pinch from all three into the teapot one minute after the tea had been infused.

'Finicky folks,' Mrs Bramley said with a sniff. 'It's a pity she hasn't something else better to do with her time!'

When Kitty took up the tray, she found that Mrs Helder had brought her own cup and saucer too; they were so delicate Kitty was almost afraid of handling them. When the tea was poured, Mrs Helder took a sip, smiled and pronounced it perfect. She then said she would like Kitty to make her tea at seven o'clock every morning and also at this hour of the day.

Kitty hesitated, not knowing whose toes she might be treading on. She said, 'I'm willing to do it, Mrs Helder, more than willing, but I will have to ask Mrs Bramley's permission first.'

Mrs Helder said she would arrange this and although she still spoke softly, Kitty got the impression she was a woman who could get her own way.

There was no opportunity for Kitty to mention Mrs Helder's request, for no sooner had she returned to the kitchen than an urgent ringing of one of the bells had Mrs Bramley despatching her to the 'Green Room', occupied by an 'honourable'. 'But just call him sir,' Cook called after her.

The young man who had summoned her had a receding chin, a long thin nose and pale blue eyes. He threw a jacket at her, told her a button was loose and asked for it to be attended to at once.

Kitty took it to the kitchen, secured the button and took the jacket back right away. She laid it on a chair then waited, thinking there might be other orders. He glared at her.

'All right! Hang it up, do you expect *me* to do it?'

Kitty tried to accept that she was less than nothing to this type of person, but it was not easy. She fled with her cheeks burning, thinking she might have been better off staying in the kitchen. Then she thought of all the washing-up, which Mrs Dunn's younger daughters would be dealing with, and decided that not all people were like the man she had just dealt with. Take Mrs Helder. Kitty liked her and hoped she would be allowed to serve her and make her tea.

Mrs Bramley raised no objection to her doing this task and Kitty was happy again.

She and Ivy shared their experiences at bedtime, Ivy's main complaint being that one of the horsey-faced girls had had her upstairs five or six times that evening, wanting only two pieces of coal at a time put on the fire. 'She could have picked up the tongs and put them on herself,' she declared.

Kitty said, teasing, 'If you had the wealth and she was the servant, what would you have done?'

Ivy grinned. 'The same as her.'

Mrs Bramley's 'artistry' was not stretched to the full until the Sunday evening and when Kitty saw the display waiting to be taken into the dining-room, she half wished she was back in the kitchen once more. The arrangements, the use of certain dishes intrigued her. There was a three-tiered gold and blue stand which was a pyramid of colour with dark red sugared plums, purple grapes, rosy-cheeked apples, yellow-skinned pears all garlanded with trails of greenery.

Mrs Bramley, whose brother was a lighthouse keeper, had also fashioned a 'lighthouse' cake, covered in chocolate and studded with halved almonds to represent stones. A jelly concoction had a deep base shaded from pale to emerald green, on top of which stood six gold columns draped with diagonal jelly ribbons in rose pink. Then in a hollow square, its walls intricately mosaiced with tiny pieces of carrots, turnips and potatoes, nestled a pair of garnished grouse. A wheel with spokes of prawns had the spaces between them filled with crushed spinach. There were many intriguing-looking dishes which Kitty did not have time to examine, but she had to agree that Mrs Bramley was certainly an artist.

Although it was not Kitty's place to serve in the dining-room, she kept on so much about how she would like to see the table set and all the guests that Mrs Bramley eventually relented and gave her a dish to take in. Having to keep her gaze averted and take the dish straight to the sideboard, all Kitty was aware of at first were the voices: everyone seemed to be talking at once, with one voice louder than the rest which she took to be the Colonel.

Even when she turned to leave, the only person she really noticed was Mrs Earle who was sitting at the lower end of the table, her white dress and fragile air giving her an ethereal look.

Later Kitty was able to link up faces with some of the colours: Thea Earle in dark blue, her sister Lavinia in yellow satin and Mrs Helder in black velvet, a dignified figure whose sole adornment was a single string of pearls.

Kitty thanked Mrs Bramley for giving her the opportunity of going into the dining-room and said her arrangements and the food looked beautiful; which pleased the cook, who remarked that she had slaved to get the right impression.

The following morning the younger ones went riding before breakfast. Kitty and Ivy watched them from an upstairs window, Ivy saying viciously that she hoped the bitch who had her running up and down stairs to put coal on the fire the night before would fall off and break her neck. In the next breath she said she was looking forward to seeing the Hunt leave on the following Monday, adding that Mrs Bramley had told her it was a sight to behold.

Kitty agreed it was, but she hated the fox being chased. On the farm they had to be killed because of them killing chickens – just biting their heads off – and worrying and maiming the sheep. But then the foxes were killed quickly. She wished that no animals had to be killed.

Ivy had no qualms about this; she said she liked a bit of meat herself and anyway, what difference was there between killing animals and slaughtering men who went to war? Which Kitty had to admit was true when she thought of the three lively sons of Abel and Harriet who were killed in battle. She gave a small shiver. 'Come on, or we'll be dreaming of slaughter tonight.'

Kitty had not thought deeply about Tyler van Neilson for some time, but that night it was about him she dreamt. They were walking along the road which she and Luke had walked the evening before, but in the dream she and Tyler were silent. At the end of the road was a big glass bubble in blue and silver. When they reached it Tyler took her hand and, still without speaking, they walked into the bubble. They were in a ballroom with a mirrored floor. They danced around the floor, but although she kept glancing down she could see no reflection in the mirror. After a while they went out of the other side of the bubble and found themselves in a strange place where there were canals with gondolas on them and in the lagoon she saw a large version of the little glass sailing ship which Gran Perkins had left for her. The water turned out to be glass and they walked over it and boarded the ship; then the sails were unfurled and they sailed away, without an exchange of words between them.

When Kitty awoke from the dream, she found herself trembling. What could it mean? Although they had danced, neither of them had been happy. There had been nothing, no feelings at all. Was this some omen? Harriet was a great believer in omens. Was Tyler unhappy? Had there been trouble with his family?

Kitty dismissed it. It was just a dream, come about because she had thought about him that morning and he was connected in her mind with beautiful glass.

But all that day the dream was at the back of her mind, worrying her, and when Ivy asked what was wrong she told her what she had dreamt.

Ivy was impressed. 'Fancy you doing all those things when you're asleep! I never dream, not often anyway, I can only remember once. It was when me brother was killed in the war and I was just little. And when I saw me mam crying I knew what had happened, because I'd seen Dickie in a dream. He was sailing away on a ship and he was waving to me.'

Kitty felt an icy shiver go up and down her spine. 'Oh, Ivy, I wish you had never told me, now I'll be thinking that Mr van Neilson is dead.'

''Course not! It could mean anything, he could—' Ivy stopped and eyed her with curiosity. 'I believe you really like that feller. You were a bit daft about him when he was here, weren't you?'

'I ... liked him, he was kind to me.'

'Well, you forget him, he's not for folks like you and me. You stick with your nice Luke. You never did get finished telling me what happened on your afternoon off at the farm.'

Kitty found herself talking in a feverish way about Luke, enlarging on the smallest incident, wanting to get the thought of Tyler being dead out of her mind, but it persisted with her for odd moments during the next two days until she heard Mrs Bramley saying to Mr Walton, 'Yes, the mistress was telling me that Mr van Neilson is back in England and talking about coming for the hunting. He must have finished his business very quickly, mustn't he? But then he's a man who doesn't seem to waste time. Not that he'll have anywhere here to carry out his experiments.'

To this Mr Walton replied that knowing van Neilson he might have a colleague or a friend somewhere in the vicinity who was in the same business.

Kitty's heartbeats had quickened when the conversation started, now she had a feeling of elation. Tyler van Neilson coming to this house! He had promised to give her a conducted tour of Smirton's glassworks. Were there any glassworks in Leicester? Coming on Monday ... It seemed ages away. Kitty wanted to rush and tell Ivy, but restrained herself; she would tell her the news casually when she had a chance.

But trying to speak normally did not deceive Ivy. 'You're all excited, your eyes are sparkling. You're daft, Kitty Harvey, daft – you'll land yourself in trouble. Now, I'm telling you!'

Kitty shook her head. 'No, Ivy, I won't get myself into trouble, not the kind you mean. I want to get on in the world. I want more money so I can help my mother.'

'Now I know you are daft, touched ...' Ivy put a forefinger to her temple. 'A loony! What did your mam do for you? She gave you away, didn't she?'

'No – she sent me to foster-parents so that I wouldn't come to any harm, but that's something I don't want to talk about.'

'All right, all right, but just don't have anything to do with that van Neilson, that's all!'

The conversation with Ivy made Kitty simmer down, but it did not stop her from thinking about Tyler. If he was as kind, as nice to her as he had been when he was ill, she might pluck up courage to tell him about her dream and he might be able to suggest a solution to it. Not, of course, that she would tell him that *he* was the man in her dream.

As it turned out, it was not Tyler who was the first to hear about the dream, but Mrs Helder. When Kitty took up her afternoon tea the old lady said, 'And what are you daydreaming about, my dear? I would have thought there was little to dream about in the busy life you lead.'

Kitty, unaware that her mind had been wandering, was embarrassed. She apologized and asked if she should pour the tea. Mrs Helder said later, for the moment she would like to share her pleasure. 'You are not too young to be in love and I am a very romantic person!'

'I was thinking about a dream I had, ma'am,' Kitty blurted out, 'but it was just a dream and ... may I pour the tea for you now, ma'am?'

Mrs Helder gave Kitty her encouraging smile. 'Do tell me about your dream; I think they have great significance.'

'You do, ma'am? Aunt Harriet does – she's my foster-mother – but Uncle Abel thinks it's foolish to put an interpretation on them.'

'I am on the side of your Aunt Harriet. There have been men who have interpreted dreams from biblical days. Please tell me about it, my dear.'

Kitty ran her tongue over her lower lip. She longed to talk about it, to know the interpretation of her dream, but apart from being away from the kitchen too long, she was worried that she was overstepping her position by holding a conversation with such a woman.

However to Mrs Helder's prompting she talked, omitting the name of the young man.

Mrs Helder eyed her thoughtfully for some time when she had finished, then said, 'A most unusual experience, Kitty. Why the glass ball? Can you account for it?'

Kitty said, oh, yes, she had a great love of glass and told her about her parents working at the glassworks and how she had so often run to the works to watch the men blowing the glass. She went on to tell about Grandma Perkins having left her the little glass ship.

'Ah, said the old lady, 'now something is beginning to form.

163

This young man in your dream – do you know him?'

'Yes, but—' Kitty was becoming agitated, feeling she was getting in too deep. 'Mrs Helder, ma'am, I'm afraid I must go, servants are not to ... well, I ought not to be talking to you – a guest – I'll get into trouble.'

Mrs Helder leaned forward in her chair. 'We shall talk about this again, Kitty. You are a very unusual girl, and I want to think over your dream. I shall give orders that when I ring for attention, I want *you* to come; I shall find out the most convenient times. Run along for now, my dear. We shall talk some time this evening.'

To Kitty's relief she had not been missed, but when later in the day a tight-lipped Mrs Bramley told her she wanted to have a word with her, she knew that Cook had been approached.

'So what's this about Mrs Helder?' she demanded. 'What's going on between you? According to what I can make out, you've been talking to her and now she wants you to attend to her whenever she rings.'

Kitty, remembering Ivy once saying that if you ever do anything wrong, try to look innocent, made a pretence of surprise.

'Nothing's going on between us, ma'am. She's talked to me, about her tea and that sort of thing. I think actually she's a little bit lonely.'

This last remark surprised Kitty, then she thought that Mrs Helder could be lonely. She seemed to spend most of the time in her room.

'Well ...' Mrs Bramley conceded in a grudging tone, 'she *could* be lonely, but if she sends for you you're not to stay too long, do you hear?'

'Yes, ma'am,' Kitty answered demurely, feeling a surge of excitement. This evening she might get to know what her dream meant.

At eight-thirty Mrs Helder's bell rang. Kitty, her heart beginning a fast beating, straightened her cap, smoothed her hands over her frilly apron and went up. Mrs Helder, in dark grey this evening but looking as dignified as ever, smiled and motioned her to sit in a chair opposite her own. Kitty sat on the edge and folded her hands in her lap, alive with anticipation, sure now for some reason that her dream did not have anything to do with death.

'Now then, Kitty. I've thought over your dream very carefully and have come to various conclusions. The first is that this young man you know is in a higher position than yourself. I feel you are in love with him, but at the same time you think of him as being completely unattainable.'

Kitty eyed her in astonishment. How could she possibly know such a thing? It was not as if she had been in Stratton House when Tyler was there. Mrs Helder went on to ask if Kitty would like to know how she had come to that conclusion and she nodded.

'It was the mirrored floor, my dear, and the fact that you were unable to see the reflections of this young man and yourself in it. It means that you could not accept the differences in status that is between you. The fact that you were dancing together shows that you are happy when you see him. Now, about the glass bubble. This was large, so ... glass, as you said, plays a big part in your thoughts.'

'Yes, that's true,' Kitty said in an awed voice.

'And the little glass ship you were given is a symbol of a dreaming to travel on a ship. Where is it you want to go?'

'To Italy, ma'am, to Venice.'

'You certainly *are* an unusual girl. Your dream is all wrapped up in this young man and your ambition to travel; with the water being made of glass too, and the fact that you were able to walk to the ship, tells me that some day you may have your dream realized.'

'You think so, ma'am?' Kitty was now wide-eyed with astonishment not only at the interpretation of the dream, but at the prophecy that she would realize her ambition. She would have liked to stay all evening and listen to the interesting old lady, but she got up.

'Thank you, ma'am, thank you very much for interpreting my dream. I think you are very clever. I mustn't take any more of your time. Thank you, ma'am, thank you!' She bobbed a curtsy and made to leave.

'Kitty, I have all the time in the world. I am chaperoning the two young ladies, the Misses Weston, who are cousins. Their only interest is horses and the only excursions they have made so far have been to the stables.'

There was such a wealth of sadness in the old lady's voice that Kitty realized for the first time that belonging to a noble family and having a title did not necessarily bring happiness.

'And Kitty, if you are asked why you were so long, tell Mrs Bramley that I was talking about horses – also tell her that I would like you to read to me for half an hour this evening, if you can be spared. There is something going round in my mind which I should like to discuss with you. This is our little conspiracy, just between the two of us. You *can* read?'

There was a glimmer of mischief in the old lady's eyes and Kitty smiled and bobbed another curtsy. 'Yes, ma'am. Yes, I can read, and write.'

Kitty left with a feeling that another road was opening up for her; she had no idea in what way, but she felt a shivery feeling of excitement.

Mrs Bramley accepted the request from Mrs Helder, with a 'Humph!' She supposed it was all right so long as she did not expect Kitty to read to her during the day when they were exceptionally busy.

Kitty went up at nine o'clock and Mrs Helder motioned her to the chair. Without preamble she began: 'Now, Kitty, I thought if you had ambitions to go to Italy you ought to know the language, or at least a smattering of it. I am fluent in several languages, but Italian is my favourite. Would you like me to give you some lessons?'

Kitty was so overwhelmed by the offer that she was unable to speak and Mrs Helder, perhaps taking her silence for refusal, said, 'Even if you do not get to Italy, the language could be useful in some other way. In commerce. Positions are now becoming available for young ladies in offices as secretaries, interpreters ...'

'Oh, ma'am, I didn't reply because I *couldn't*. I was so taken aback at your offer. I think it's wonderful, generous of you, and yes, I would be very pleased to learn another language.'

Mrs Helder talked about the language, the beauty of it, the rhythm, and having written down several simple phrases for Kitty she spoke them then asked her to repeat them. She was a dedicated teacher, who would not let a word go until it was pronounced as correctly as Kitty could manage. 'Good, good,' she kept saying, 'you have an ear for the language.'

When Kitty left she felt she was walking on air. What an opportunity! What other girl would get such an offer? How lucky she was. She repeated the phrase, '*Buon giorno, Signore,*' and imagined herself saying it to Tyler van Neilson. Then immediately she sobered; she would do no such thing, it would be stepping out of her class. She *had* stepped out of her class by accepting Mrs Helder's offer, but then if she had refused where else would she get another chance? Also, Mrs Helder would be disappointed. Kitty had been aware of a difference in the old lady that evening, a lightness of spirit. She likened it to the time when she had started at Stratton House and everything had been of new interest, a challenge. Yes, that was it, Mrs Helder saw it as a challenge to teach a servant girl a language.

Kitty went slowly down the stairs to the kitchen. Well, she would not disappoint her teacher; there would be plenty of time for going over the phrases in her mind when she was polishing, dusting, making beds.

The only thing that worried Kitty a little was having to lie about the project, but Mrs Helder had said it was a conspiracy between them and conspiracy it would have to remain. So, when Mrs Bramley demanded to know what book Kitty had to read, she twisted the reading aspect a fraction and told her in a casual way that Mrs Helder was interested in a place called Venice, adding that it sounded very nice.

Mrs Bramley's reply to this was that she didn't believe in stuffing the heads of young girls with talk of places they were never likely to see. Kitty made no reply.

Ivy knew about Kitty having been asked to read to Mrs Helder and was full of awe that Kitty could read and write. She couldn't do either, she said, but she could sign her name – Mrs Bramley had taught her how to do that.

For two days Kitty's footsteps were light. There was not only the fact of looking forward to possibly seeing Tyler on the following Monday, but there were also the lessons to look forward to. Mrs Helder would greet Kitty with a new phrase when she brought the morning tea, translate it and ask Kitty to greet her with it when she came up in the afternoon. In the evenings, Mrs Helder started on the basics of the grammar.

On the third morning, Kitty was dusting one of the bedrooms when a voice said from the doorway, 'Hello, Kitty.' She turned swiftly to find Lavinia, the Earles' second-eldest daughter, smiling at her. Kitty bobbed a curtsy, then waited.

Lavinia stood a moment, closed the door then came forward slowly. 'Kitty – I want you to do something for me.'

'Yes, Miss Lavinia.'

'I want you to deliver a letter to the Grange the next time you have an afternoon off and visit your foster-parents.' Kitty was silent, knowing this was an unusual request. 'The Grange is on your way. The letter is to be delivered personally to a young man.'

Kitty fingered her apron. 'Well, I don't know, Miss Lavinia. I would have to ask permission to call at the Grange.'

'No! No one is to know about it. My parents have forbidden me to see the young man.'

'Oh, in that case, miss ...' Kitty was alarmed. Doing such a thing could lose her her job. When she pointed this out, Lavinia cajoled at first and when Kitty remained firm she spoke sharply.

'I think you *will* do as I ask, Kitty. You see – I know ... your secret!'

The shock had Kitty's hand going to her throat, her immediate reaction being to think of her bastardy. How could Lavinia know such a thing? She stood staring at this attractive girl with the auburn hair who had been described by Mrs Bramley as being wild, a rebel.

'How did you know, miss?' she asked in a whisper.

'I heard you both as I was passing Mrs Helder's door the past two evenings. And for heaven's sake, don't look as if I were going to denounce you as being a murderess. There is nothing wrong in being taught a language, but I don't think that Walton and Bramley would be very pleased at the deception. You were, I understand, supposed to be reading to the old lady?'

Her relief at knowing it was to do with the language lessons was so great that Kitty felt she wanted to laugh.

'I'm sorry to have to do this to you, Kitty, but it's important to me that this ... gentleman has the letter. You see, we're in love. My parents' objection to him is his position; he's a gamekeeper,' Lavinia raised her shoulders in a gesture of despair. 'I swear if I don't eventually get their consent to marry him, I shall run away with him!'

Kitty, agitated, plucked at the frill of her apron. 'Oh, please, miss, don't do it, please don't! There'll be nothing but unhappiness.'

'What do you know about it?'

'My mother married a gamekeeper, but then ...' Kitty paused, 'I think in their case it was poverty that defeated them.'

'Money has nothing to do with it,' Lavinia retorted. 'We are on the same mental level – the gentleman is quiet, intelligent and well-read. I have no money of my own, but that makes no difference to him. The trouble is that he refuses to marry me until I have my parents' consent. Kitty, you *must* do this for me – if not, you know the consequences!'

In spite of the threat there was no underlying viciousness in Lavinia's words, not like there had been in Violet's voice when she was threatening, but still Kitty resisted, pointing out that she had no idea when she was likely to get an afternoon off as Mrs Bramley had told her this would be when it was convenient.

But it seemed this was no obstacle to Lavinia. The letter was written, she drew it from her skirt pocket saying, 'The gentleman concerned has a cottage in the woods.' Lavinia described man and cottage, and explained that he was usually there between three and four in the afternoon. She then concluded, 'No one else will know about the conspiracy between Mrs Helder and yourself.'

'But if *you* heard us talking, miss,' Kitty blurted out, 'then other people could.'

'I doubt it.' Lavinia grinned suddenly. 'I just happen to be a born eavesdropper. When I hear busy voices behind closed doors, I have to listen.' She handed the letter to Kitty. 'Take great care of it.'

Kitty put it down the neck of her dress, feeling as if it would burn her skin. All joy had gone. There was the feeling of guilt not only at having the Italian lessons but at having to deliver the letter. And also, the uncertainty of her birth had returned to worry her. She made up her mind to cancel the lessons – it was not worth the risk that Mrs Bramley might get to know about it and then she would lose her job.

But by the time she was due to take up Mrs Helder's pot of tea all the excitement, all the anticipation of learning a foreign

169

language returned and she greeted the old lady with, 'Buon giorno, Signora!'

Mrs Helder gave a nod of approval. 'Your accent is good, Kitty. Come along, let us "talk" even if it is just for a few minutes.'

Kitty had put the letter in the pocket of a dress that Harriet had made her. She wanted to be rid of it and hoped she would not have to hold on to it for a long time. Then, right out of the blue the following afternoon Mrs Bramley said, 'Kitty, you'd better take the afternoon off while you have the chance. The family and four of our guests are dining out this evening. If you're back by seven o'clock, it'll be all right. Off you go!'

Kitty felt breathless even before she ran upstairs to change. She was glad there had been no time to write and let Abel and Harriet know she was coming. Abel and Luke had intended to pick her up on her next visit to the farm and in that case it would certainly have been awkward – in fact, impossible – to have delivered the letter to the Grange.

Ivy was waiting for her when she came down, ready to leave. 'You're off then, Kitty. Perhaps one of these days we might manage to get an afternoon off together; then you can take me with you to the farm.' The wistful note was in Ivy's voice and Kitty felt mean for not having ever mentioned spending an afternoon off together. 'We must try and arrange it,' she said. 'Perhaps next time.'

There was no sun this time and a cool wind stirred the topmost branches of the thinning trees. Kitty would have preferred to cross the fields but she took the road, knowing where the turning led off to the Grange. It was one of the big houses where Luke delivered produce, but never at this time of day. Kitty only prayed that she would not see any of the servants from the house – she had met some of them when she had gone with Luke or Abel.

Although Luke had said it was not much longer going by the road it seemed to Kitty to be twice as far, possibly because of her worry at getting rid of the letter safely. Once she had taken the turning that led to the Grange, she branched off into the woods ... And immediately felt soothed. It was like a sanctuary, the only sounds the faint rustle of fallen leaves underfoot and the scurry of an animal in the undergrowth. Not a bird sang. Kitty came out of the wood into a field where cattle were grazing and, crossing to the trees opposite, opened the small wicket gate. It creaked and a cow gave a mournful bellow.

'It's all right,' she said. 'Sorry to disturb you!'

Kitty felt a little brighter after this. After all, once she had delivered the letter she was free to enjoy the rest of the time. And when at last she came across the stone-built cottage, her heartbeats did not even quicken. She approached it from the side; there was no garden in front, but there was a kitchen garden at the back, she could smell thyme.

The paint had a faded, weathered look, but the window panes were gleaming. She knocked on the door, thought at first there was no one at home but then the door was opened by a tall, fair-haired man who eyed her questioningly. Her heartbeats did quicken a little then as she handed him the letter, saying she had been asked to deliver it.

He took it, stood looking at it for a moment then asked if she would come in while he read it. She hesitated, feeling she would be getting more involved, especially if he asked her to take an answer. And this is just what he did do. He pulled out a chair and asked her to take a seat.

Kitty sat on the edge. Why, oh, why, had she not just put the letter in the letter-box? There could be a to-ing and fro-ing of notes.

She only had time to notice that the furniture was all dark oak and the room lacked a woman's touch when there was a sharp rat-a-tat on the door, followed by a voice calling, 'Are you at home, Edwards?'

Kitty tensed. Who could this be?

The gamekeeper got up, opened the door and Kitty rose slowly to her feet, unable to believe her eyes.

Mr van Neilson ... Her mouth went dry. Of all people!

CHAPTER TWELVE

When Tyler van Neilson walked into the room Kitty was not yet over the shock of seeing him so unexpectedly and she stood tense, a pulse throbbing in her temple. Why should he have come here, had he seen her and followed her? She realized this was not so when he stopped abruptly, his surprise evident. 'Why – hello – what are you ...?'

The gamekeeper explained, indicating Kitty: 'The young lady came to deliver a letter, sir. I'm afraid I don't know her name.'

'I do.' Tyler came forward smiling. 'The young lady and I have met before. How are you, Miss Leddenshaw?'

'Quite well, thank you, sir.' She plucked at a darned finger tip on her glove. Should she go, or should she wait for a reply? Miss Lavinia had not mentioned this. The gamekeeper settled things by asking Tyler's permission to pen a brief reply to the letter; this was given.

Tyler drew out a chair and asked Kitty to be seated. He pulled up another, sat facing her and began to chat, as though chatting to a servant was a commonplace thing. How extraordinary it was to meet her, he said – it was only the night before that he had been thinking about her. Was she still with the Earles? Yes, of course she was, it was obvious she was here with them for the hunting. Was she enjoying the change of living in the country?

Kitty found herself suddenly calm, which had so often happened at awkward moments in the past. She explained about having lived with her foster-parents at a farm in the vicinity for eight years and Tyler showed surprise once more.

'Well – how interesting!' He asked whether she was on her

way there, or was returning to the Earles' house, and when Kitty told him the farm, he offered to drive her there. Kitty thanked him but refused, speaking firmly; it was not far, she enjoyed the walk.

'The letter is ready, miss,' the gamekeeper said as he handed her the envelope. Kitty was immediately on her feet. She was not sure whether it was correct to bid Tyler van Neilson good-day, but she did so. The gamekeeper walked to the door with her and said in a low voice, 'My thanks to you, miss. There'll be no more correspondence.'

Kitty felt relieved and walked quickly away. But she had not gone far before she heard quick footsteps behind her and Tyler van Neilson caught up with her. 'Allow me to walk with you, Miss Leddenshaw, I shall be glad to stretch my legs. I can see Mr Edwards later.'

She did not want him walking with her, but she waited until they were well away from the cottage before she made a protest. Then she stopped.

'Mr van Neilson, sir, it's very kind of you to offer to walk with me, but I would rather you didn't, if you don't mind. If someone should see us together and report to Mr Walton or Mrs Bramley, I could get the sack. I'm not even supposed to be at the cottage; I only came to deliver a letter.'

'And hazarding a guess, I would say it was from Lavinia. Oh, yes, I know about the little affair. Edwards told me, he's a worried man. I believe his affection for the girl to be sincere and that he would marry her if the circumstances were different, but he feels that even if they had her parents' consent, there would be a great risk of the marriage not succeeding. I'm afraid I must agree with him.'

Although Kitty had been pleading with Lavinia that morning not to run away with her lover, she was now on her mettle at Tyler's remark.

'Why shouldn't it succeed – surely if—' Kitty stopped, realizing she was really overstepping the mark by attempting to argue with this man.

'If what?' Tyler prompted.

'Oh, nothing, sir. It's not important.'

He gave an exasperated sigh. 'Either you have something to say or you haven't. And don't make the excuse that you cannot tell me because I am a "gentleman", as you once put it, and you are only a servant. You have as much right to an opinion as anyone else.'

'I'm not allowed an opinion in the kitchen,' she said stiffly.

'But you are *not* in the kitchen! Tell me what you were going to say.'

Kitty realized she was seeing the rebel side of Tyler van Neilson which Mrs Bramley had mentioned, a man impatient with set standards.

'Well – I was going to say there would be a good chance of a happy marriage if the couple were truly in love and if the husband had a regular job.' The moment Kitty had said this she wanted to withdraw it, remembering the misery of her mother's marriage. But then ... her father had drunk, gambled. She added, 'That is, if the man is a steady person.'

'But what happens if the man is without work? If Edwards and Lavinia elope, which Lavinia wants, he would be without references. And if he was unable to get another job, how would they live? If a couple suffer poverty, romance flies out of the window.'

'Not if they are in love, sir, *truly* in love,' Kitty persisted.

Tyler gave a wry smile. 'I forgot for the moment that you are a dreamer, Kitty. Not that I would want you to change, but in a case like this common sense must prevail.' He put a hand under her elbow and led her away. Kitty wanted to resist, but not only had she felt a tremor at his touch – but she wanted very much to know his views.

'Lavinia has been cosseted from birth,' he continued. 'She's lived in luxurious surroundings, worn beautiful clothes; she enjoys a social life, thrives on flattery and enjoys good food. She once said that if she was ever penniless, she would steal to get food.'

'But if ...' Kitty began, but was brought to a stop by Tyler raising his hand and asking her to let him finish.

'Lavinia is a warm-hearted girl, capable of love; she likes children, but if those children were starving, too weak to cry, she would not know how to cope.'

Kitty's head went up. 'I think you are wrong there, sir. I was once told by Aunt Harriet about a wealthy girl who married a farmer's son. *They* ran away to get married. They suffered hardships, their crops failed, their animals became sick. She scrubbed floors in big houses to get food for her husband and children. They prospered eventually because their love meant everything to them. And I think that Lavinia has this strength.'

It was the longest speech Kitty could ever remember making and she flushed when she saw Tyler regarding her with some amusement.

She was furious, but managed to say in a low voice, 'You can mock me, sir, but I still think that true love will conquer all.'

'I was not mocking you, Kitty.' He spoke gently, his expression sober now. 'I have the greatest admiration for your beliefs. I can only trust you will prove to be right. Although I still doubt that Edwards would agree to running away with Lavinia – he's too sensible for that.'

'Aunt Harriet also said that where love is concerned *common sense* flies out of the window.'

Tyler began to laugh; he laughed heartily, throwing back his head. 'Oh, Kitty, I do enjoy your company, you are so refreshing. I should like to meet your foster-family some time.'

The last thing Kitty wanted was for anyone she knew to see them together, much less Abel and Harriet – or Luke. They had come out of the trees and were crossing the field to the gate that led into the next wood. When they came to it she said, 'If you don't mind, sir, I would rather go the rest of the way on my own. Should my foster-father meet us on the road by some chance, I think he would be upset at seeing me accompanied by a . . . by a man in your position.'

'I should think he would be pleased to know you were with a . . . gentleman,' he teased.

'Uncle Abel is a great believer in people knowing their places and keeping to them. My uncle is a wonderful man and my aunt is a wonderful woman; I would not like to upset them.'

They had reached the gate now and Tyler turned to face her, his expression sober again. 'Nor I. I understand what you mean. But your comments make me want more than ever to meet them. Perhaps one day.'

Tyler opened the gate for Kitty to go through, then closing it he stood with his gloved hands on the top bar. 'You know, Kitty, you've brought something into my life that I needed; to be able to see the other person's point of view. I'm an impatient man, I get irritable with conventions. If I had had my way I would have marched up to the farm with you, introduced myself and expected to be made welcome. You've made me see that this would have been wrong.'

He stood waiting, as though unwilling to leave. Then he reached out a hand and lightly touched her cheek. 'You are such a strange mixture, Kitty, a delightful mixture. One moment you are so full of innocence and the next so worldly-wise.'

Kitty felt confused at the emotions this aroused in her. She felt she wanted to comfort him, yet without really knowing why; she stood motionless, feeling she ought to go yet held there by his need for her. Or what seemed a need. She thanked him for walking this far with her and he said it was a pleasure. And still they stood, until Kitty took a step back.

'I must go, sir.'

'Yes, of course.' He took off his hat. 'I shall see you on Monday when I come for the Hunt. Until then I shall be staying at the Grange. When we do meet again, Kitty, perhaps we can settle some more problems of the world.' Although there was a teasing note again in his voice, there was a sadness in his eyes.

'Yes, sir,' she said, then turned and walked away. When she glanced back he was still standing at the gate, his thick dark hair uncovered, reminding her of the evening when he had brought her back from the glassworks in the carriage. She had wondered then what was in his thoughts and now she wondered about him again.

He had sounded so lonely. Yet a man in his position must have plenty of friends? And he had his business, the glass-making, his experiments. How could a person be lonely with so much? He had talked about poverty as if he had experienced it. When he left home, rejecting his father's wish for him to go into banking, had he been poor then?

There were so many thoughts going round and round in Kitty's head that she was not aware how far she had walked until the farm came into view. She looked for Abel and Luke in the fields but there was no one in sight. Nor was there any activity in the yard, which was unusual – there was always one farm-hand at least, doing jobs. In fact, the only sound was the throaty clucking of hens and when that suddenly stopped there was an uncanny silence. It was the silence that comes before a storm, but there were no storm clouds, nor was the air heavy.

It was not until Kitty was going along the passage towards the kitchen that she heard voices – the muted voices of women, a sound that can be heard in time of trouble. Kitty's mouth went dry. Something had happened.

When she pushed open the kitchen door Harriet and three other women who were sitting round the fire looked up. Harriet, although dry-eyed, looked pale and distraught. 'Why, Kitty,' she said, 'we weren't expecting you.'

One of the women shook her head. 'You've come at a bad time, love.'

Harriet came over to Kitty and put an arm around her. 'It's my brother Will and his wife, they've . . .' there was a tremor in her voice, 'they've both been killed.'

'Killed?' Kitty stared at her, shocked. 'How, what happened?'

The three women, who were neighbours, all began talking at once, no doubt wanting to save Harriet from telling what must have been told several times already, and Kitty made out that the couple had been driving in the trap when the horse bolted, the trap overturned and Will and Ada both were thrown against a drystone wall. A man who had been walking along the road at the time and seen it happen said they must have been killed instantly.

Harriet concluded, 'I suppose we should be thankful for that small mercy. Abel and Luke have gone over to see what they can do. They won't be back until late. Sit down, Kitty, I'll make you a cup of tea.'

Kitty said she would make it. She made quite a lot of tea that afternoon; other people having heard the news dropped in to offer sympathy and help, all shocked by the tragedy – Will and Ada had been popular figures in the district. Kitty grieved for Harriet, who had been very close to her brother.

When the last of the visitors had gone, Kitty said, 'I could stay a little longer with you, Aunt Harriet, until Uncle Abel or Luke get back. I don't think Mrs Bramley would be cross with me, under the circumstances.'

Harriet said she would be all right; her daughter-in-law was coming to spend the night with her and also Louise would be coming to stay for a few hours.

Louise? Kitty felt a small stab of jealousy. Although Luke had assured her that he was not in love with the girl and Kitty believed him, she had a feeling of being shut out. She wanted to stay, wanted to be there when Luke returned. Yet knew that even if it was possible, the only subject to be discussed would be the tragedy. And what did she want to talk about? She could not tell him about Lavinia, nor did she want to talk about Tyler van Neilson.

Harriet asked her how she was getting on with the Earles, but when Kitty started to tell her she realized that Harriet's mind was not on what she was saying, which was understandable. And at six o'clock when Louise arrived, Kitty said she thought she ought to go.

Harriet wanted to get someone to walk with her but Kitty said No, she would be all right, she might even meet Abel or Luke on their way back. When Kitty left she felt choked, being upset not only for Harriet, but also for herself as she felt she had been pushed out by Louise.

As she set out along the road she found herself straining for signs of Luke or Abel, but the only people she met were a family who bid her good evening, she had no idea who they were. When she reached the road that led to the Grange, she stopped a moment. The lights from the house were visible through the trees but the house itself was lost in the darkness.

Kitty walked on. The road back seemed long. When she arrived at the Earles' she found that the news of the tragedy was already known and Mrs Bramley was full of it. What a dreadful thing, what exactly had happened? Had they suffered before they died, or was their death instant? Kitty told her shortly, 'Instant', and turned to take off her hat and coat. But Mrs Bramley persisted: it would be a big funeral, they were well-known not only in Mealton but in Leicester. If Kitty wanted to go and be with her Aunt Harriet when the men were at the funeral, she thought it could be arranged. Then she went on talking about tragedies which had happened in the district and spoke of a niece she had lost, dabbing at her eyes with a corner of her apron – lovely girl, she had never got over her death.

At this Ivy made the tart remark that she couldn't understand why people bawled when other people died. If heaven was as wonderful as the church made out, those left should be overjoyed for them.

Mrs Bramley declared her to be a heathen and prophesied that she would end up in the fires of hell. The argument might have gone on had not Mr Walton intervened, saying the subject ought to be dropped because Kitty was involved in the tragedy and must be upset.

Kitty cast him a grateful glance, liking Mr Walton more and more.

Her next worry was about getting the letter from Mr Edwards to Lavinia, but when she went upstairs at nine o'clock with Mrs Helder's drink Lavinia was waiting for her. She held out her hand, and almost snatched the letter in her impatience. Tearing open the envelope, she brought out a small sheet of paper, read it, turned it over on to the other side then looked at Kitty. 'Is this all?'

'That's all I was given, miss.'

Lavinia stared at her, stricken. 'I don't believe it! He's told me our meetings must end. We were to be married . . . He can't do this. I love him, he loves me. I—' She stopped and now eyed Kitty with a baleful expression. 'What did you say to him?'

'Nothing, miss, I simply handed the letter over. He asked me to wait and said he would write a reply. That's it.'

Lavinia put her hand to her brow with a dramatic gesture. 'Oh, God, what am I going to do? I'll die if I don't see him. I'll kill myself!'

Kitty said, before she could stop herself, 'I wouldn't do that, miss, the gentleman might change his mind.'

Lavinia looked at her in faint astonishment, then began to laugh. 'Well – out of the mouth of babes – I hope you're right, Kitty.' Then she added, all laughter gone, 'I'm going to marry him, he *won't* throw me over! I just can't live without him. Next time you go to your foster-parents, I shall give you another letter. Every time I leave this house I am being spied upon.'

Kitty wanted to say she would rather not deliver the letter, but said instead that she must take Mrs Helder her milk. She moved away and knocked on the door.

Mrs Helder also knew about the tragedy and sympathized with Kitty. She said, 'I'm quite sure you will not feel like having an Italian lesson this evening, Kitty. What I've done is to write a few phrases for you to go over when you feel like it. There is no hurry, you have all the time in the world. If you can manage it, you ought to have an early night. Is that possible?'

Kitty said she was not sure, but she would try, and after thanking Mrs Helder for being so understanding she left.

She had a choked feeling again and wished she were somewhere else. If only she could get on a boat and sail away! She hated the underhandedness of delivering letters for Lavinia against the master and mistress's wishes, hated Mrs Bramley for making so much drama out of tragedy. She ached for Harriet, felt sorry for Tyler van Neilson who had seemed so lonely, whom she felt needed comfort, and sorry for herself because of Louise being at the farm to comfort Luke when he returned.

Kitty hoped she might be able to get to bed before Ivy, but she was denied this. They went up together, Ivy complaining about how at times she felt she could strangle 'old Bramley'. 'Thinks she's God Almighty, she does!'

When they were in the bedroom, Ivy said, 'All right then, now tell me what you were doing in Greencot Woods this afternoon?'

Kitty, who had started to undress, turned quickly. 'How did you know I was there. Who told you?'

'A little bird,' Ivy grinned. 'You never know who sees you, do you? Who did you go to meet – it wasn't that van Neilson feller, was it? I heard he's staying at the Grange.'

'No,' Kitty said sharply, 'I did not go to *meet* Mr van Neilson, nor anyone else.' Which was true.

'Then what were you doing there?'

'Why don't you ask your little bird?' Kitty retorted.

'Oh, now you're mad at me. I was just curious, that's all. I didn't mean to upset you, honest I didn't, Kitty. I wouldn't do anything to hurt *you*! You're me only friend.'

'It's all right, Ivy, it's been an upsetting day.' Kitty paused, unbuttoned her dress, then asked, 'Who was it that saw me?'

'George, but he wasn't spying on you. He had to deliver a parcel to the Grange for the master and saw you going into the woods. He wasn't spying on you, I promise. He said he thought you probably went that way to go to your foster-parents' farm. It was me who was joking with you about van Neilson. He's coming here on Monday, did you know?' Kitty said she had heard so and after pulling her nightdress over her head got into bed, saying she felt she could sleep the clock round; when Ivy started talking about Mrs Bramley again, she pretended to be asleep.

It was Mrs Helder who lifted Kitty from her gloom during the next two days, by talking to her about the countries she had visited. Kitty felt she was there: Greece, with its beautiful islands, its incredibly blue sky and sea, the shimmering heat; the wide shallow steps where one travelled on donkeys, the tall columns, the peasants so contented with their lot; the small fishing boats with their brightly coloured sails, the houses that rose tier by tier on the hillsides with pink and blue and green roofs, the whole seemingly garlanded with flowers.

Then there was Spain with the flamenco dancers, the swirl of flounced silk skirts, the quick clicking of heels and castanets, the haunting songs that hung on the night air under a sky of indigo velvet, where stars seemed so low one felt one could reach out and touch them. And in bed at night, the whisper of the waves as they ebbed and flowed over sand and pebbles, almost a song in itself.

And Paris – her husband had loved Paris, she said, and they had spent many happy hours there. She described all the famous places in such detail Kitty was enthralled.

'Ah yes, we travelled to so many wonderful places and I was much loved,' the old lady said softly. 'My husband and I had a beautiful marriage, adoring one another. I was bereft when he died; I still miss him dreadfully.'

In the soft glow of the lamp Kitty caught a glint of tears in Mrs Helder's eyes, and thought how wonderful it must be to have loved and have been loved so much. There was silence for a few moments, then Mrs Helder suddenly sat up and smiled.

'Oh dear, I'm getting much too sentimental! That is what happens when one gets older, Kitty, one lives on memories.'

'They're such beautiful memories, ma'am,' Kitty said softly. 'Thank you for letting me share them.'

'It's a pleasure to share them with you, Kitty. You have a feeling for beautiful things, beautiful places. I hope you have the chance of enjoying them some day.'

The following morning Kitty was busy dusting a bedroom and dreaming a little – thinking about Greece and Spain and trying to imagine hot sun and blue skies and sea, instead of the grey view from the window – when Ivy came rushing in, all excited.

'Hey up, Kitty! You have a visitor, guess who? Your Luke.'

Luke? Kitty felt a momentary terror, knowing it must be something terribly important to bring him to the house. 'What is it?' she exclaimed. 'What's wrong, what's happened?'

'Nothing, nothing else, he was just worried about you, asked old Bramley's permission to have a quick word with you and she invited him in ... and is she taken with him! I don't wonder either, what a lovely feller! That van Neilson is a good-looker but your Luke – well, he has something extra, I dunno what it is. He glows, sort of, with kindness. You know what I mean. I'd give me right arm for him to notice *me*!'

Kitty, who had straightened her mob-cap, took off her big apron, rolled it up, carried it to the door and then asked, 'Do I look all right?'

''Course you do, go on! Here, give me your pinny.'

Kitty tried not to run along the corridor, but it was difficult not to do so. Luke worried about her! The thought gave her a lovely warm feeling; Louise was no longer important in her mind.

She smoothed her dress before she went down the stairs. When she took the bend in the staircase she paused, seeing Luke standing at the far side of the fireplace smiling as he talked to Mrs Bramley. A small tremor went through her. 'Your Luke,' Ivy had said to her. Kitty seemed to see him through different eyes away from his home environment. Although not quite as tall as Tyler van Neilson, nor so well-dressed, he had a bearing. He stood straight, had a strength yet was listening now in an absorbed way as Mrs Bramley was telling him how much they thought of her. 'A lovely girl, Kitty, one of the best. So willing. Never answers back, she'll go far.'

Kitty hurried down the last few stairs and Mrs Bramley turned.

'Look who's here to see you, Kitty! Your brother was worried about you. Go and sit over there in the corner, but don't be too long, will you?' There was no demand this time, it was more an appeal to Luke.

Ivy had come down and was standing on the stairs, but Mrs

182

Bramley ordered her back to her work. Luke smiled. 'I've come at an awkward time, Kitty, but I had to see you.' They sat down near the window. 'I was very late in getting back last night. Mother told me you'd been and she was worried about you – said she should have broken the news about Will and Ada more gently.'

'It was a shock,' Kitty said, 'a terrible shock, but I was all right. I was worried about Aunt Harriet. I wanted to stay but ... Louise came and Mary was coming later to stay, so I—'

'As long as you're all right, Kitty.' Luke put a hand over hers. 'I didn't like you walking back alone.'

How dark with concern his eyes were. 'I was all right, Luke, really I was. How is Aunt Harriet?'

'A little better. Accepting it as God's will. You know Mother.' Luke's smile held a great sadness. 'She has great faith, great strength.'

They talked about his uncle and aunt's farm, about the three sons and two daughters who would take over, then Luke got up to leave, saying in a low, conspiratorial voice, 'Mustn't outstay my welcome, there may be another time when I want to come and see you.'

When Luke called goodbye to Mrs Bramley and thanked her for allowing him to see Kitty, she said, 'It's nice to have met you, Mr Leddenshaw, good to know you're so concerned about your sister – some brothers don't bother.'

Hearing Luke described as her brother gave Kitty a jolt. Was that how he saw himself? Felt he must take care of his little sister? Kitty did not want this to be their relationship. She wanted to be loved by him in an adult way. As she walked to the door with him, he talked about the funeral on the Tuesday and said that as she would be busy with the Hunt being on the Monday she was not to think of coming to his uncle's farm to be with his mother – there would be plenty of other women there. Kitty felt rejected and hurt until Luke added softly, 'I would rather you came when it's all over, Kitty, and we are a little bit back to normal. Take care of yourself, love. It was good to see you.'

She wanted to watch him walking away, but Mrs Bramley called to say that Mrs Helder's bell was ringing.

It was an odd time for Mrs Helder to summon her and when

Kitty went up she found out why. The old lady was lying on the floor, her face full of pain. 'I tripped over the rug, Kitty,' she whispered. 'I seem to have hurt my back.'

'Oh, ma'am, don't try to move. I must get help, you'll need the doctor.' Then Kitty, remembering Harriet's teaching about caring for people who had been hurt, brought a quilt from the bed and tucked it carefully around her. 'There now, ma'am, I'll be back as soon as possible. *Please* don't move!' She ran out and raced downstairs.

Mr Walton said he would telephone the doctor at once and then inform the mistress of the accident. Mrs Bramley suggested that Kitty make a pot of Mrs Helder's special tea and added that she would put a small flask of brandy on the tray: a teaspoonful was excellent for shock.

When Kitty took the tea up, Mrs Earle was there. Kitty mentioned the brandy then said, addressing her mistress, 'Ma'am, Mrs Helder would need to be raised to drink the tea, do you think it wise to—' Covered in confusion at her own effrontery, Kitty apologised: 'I'm sorry, ma'am, very sorry, it's not my place to—'

'It's a very sensible idea, Kitty. I think we ought to wait until the doctor arrives. We would not want to do any more damage, would we?'

Mrs Earle's gentle smile helped to put Kitty at her ease again and Mrs Helder said, 'What a gem this girl is, I could do with her as my companion!'

A few minutes later the doctor arrived, Mrs Bramley with him. Kitty bobbed a curtsy and left, then went back to the bedroom she had been dusting when Luke arrived. She worried over Mrs Helder, and realized how fond she had become of her during the short time she had known the old lady.

When she had completed the dusting of the bedrooms she went downstairs to find Mrs Bramley complaining to Mr Walton.

'I like Mrs Helder, like her very much, she's a real lady, but I see no reason why she can't have a nurse full-time. I know the doctor said it wouldn't be necessary, but it means that Kitty will have to keep popping in and out. The girl has other jobs to do and anyway, *I* give orders to my staff, *not* a guest.'

'Mrs Bramley – our guest is a special friend of the mistress and if Mrs Earle has agreed that Harvey helps with our invalid, then – so be it.'

Mrs Bramley said, 'Humph!' and banged down a bowl. Then noticing Kitty, she called her over. 'There'll be a nurse coming morning and evening to attend to Mrs Helder, but you'll have to keep popping in to see her. Don't you stay long, do you hear, there's other work to be done. It isn't as if she's broken her back, just pulled a muscle. And there's her dratted bell now. Remember what I told you!'

When Kitty went into the room Mrs Helder, who was in bed, flat on her back, turned her head and said, '*Buon giorno, Kitty!*' In spite of traces of pain on the old lady's face, Kitty saw a twinkle in her eyes.

'*Buon giorno, Signora.*' With the morning greeting over, Kitty asked her in Italian how she was keeping, '*Come stai oggi, Signora?*'

'I'm feeling very well,' Mrs Helder smiled. 'You are doing very well, Kitty, and I am feeling much better. What is the saying? It's an ill wind ... With my having to lie here, we shall be able to spend a little more time together. Oh, I know you have other duties, but a few minutes every now and then with a few phrases spoken ... we shall have you fluent in no time.'

Although Kitty was sensible enough to know a language could not be learned in a few snatches of conversation over a few weeks, she was eager to learn and determined to get to know as much as possible.

When Ivy eventually was told about it – Kitty making her promise faithfully not to tell anyone else – she looked completely mystified. 'What do you want to learn that for?' she asked. 'To be one of the la-di-da lot?'

'No, to be a glass-blower!' Kitty chuckled at Ivy's expression. 'It's a long story, but just let's say I have a love of beautiful glass.'

'But what's glass got to do with learning Italian?' Ivy asked, looking more mystified than ever.

Kitty became serious. 'I think it's all to do with fate, Ivy. It was fate that my mother brought me from the farm, that I found a job with the Earles and met Mr van Neilson. Fate that I met Mrs Helder, who is teaching me a language.'

Ivy shook her head. 'I just don't get it. Sounds crazy to me.'

185

'It all started when I was a little girl and an old lady talked to me about Italy, about a wonderful place called Venice, and showed me a tiny little ship made of glass. It set me dreaming; I wanted to go to Italy. I have a feeling that the fates are working for me and I might get there somehow, I don't quite know how.'

'Neither do I.' Ivy gave her an affectionate grin, 'I always thought you were a bit of a loony.'

'If being a loony means dreaming, then I'm glad I'm a loony,' Kitty said softly. 'You should try being one too, Ivy. It gets you over the bad patches.'

'All I want,' said Ivy, a wistful note in her voice, 'is a nice feller, a little house and kids. If that's what you call dreaming, then I'm a loony too.' Ivy laughed suddenly. 'Come on, race you to get into bed!'

A few minutes later Kitty was between the icy sheets wondering if Ivy was right and she was expecting too much. As she turned over on to her side and drew her legs up into the comfort of her white flannelette nightdress, she found herself wondering how to translate into Italian a phrase Harriet had once used ... 'without dreams we are lost ...'

CHAPTER THIRTEEN

The excitement of the first Hunt of the season began the moment the house was astir. Although Kitty had seen the Hunt many times, this one was different because of being involved and the fact that Mr van Neilson would be riding over with the people from the Grange. That evening he would be staying with the Earles, a bed had been prepared for him.

The morning was perfect, clear and frosty with a thin sun sparkling the hoar frost on trees and hedges. Later the frost disappeared and the thin layer of ice on pools dissolved.

Although normally family and guests breakfasted at different times, all those who would be riding were down by eight o'clock. Ivy said you couldn't hear yourself speak for the noisy talk of horses.

Kitty loved horses, although the only ones whose backs she had been on were the working horses at the farm, and then she had been a child and had ridden in front of Abel or one of the boys.

There was constant movement in the house, with a kind of ordered chaos in the kitchen where preparations were being made to entertain extra guests when the Hunt returned. Kitty, who was on call with the rest of the servants for various bedrooms, was told by Ivy that Lavinia wanted her, urgently. The hem of her riding skirt needed a few stitches. Kitty hoped this was not just an excuse to hand her another letter to take to Mr Edwards, but as it turned out this was just what it was. 'I had to see you to hand over this,' Lavinia said, holding out an envelope. 'I want you to get it to Mr Edwards as soon as possible. You'll be going to the farm, won't you? Haven't there been some deaths in the family?'

Kitty said, yes, to the deaths but told her she doubted she would be visiting the farm soon, adding, 'It's very difficult, Miss Lavinia, for me to deliver letters. I was seen the last time by—'

'I don't care *who* sees you, make some excuse! You must take this,' Lavinia thrust the envelope at her, 'and deliver it as soon as possible.'

Kitty, knowing she had no choice, took it and pushed it down the neck of her dress as she had done on the previous occasion.

Lavinia then ordered Kitty to help her to dress, saying the wretched maid whom she shared with her sister had a snivelling cold.

'I can't stand the girl near me at the best of times. I think I shall ask for you to be my personal maid, Kitty. You are a capable girl, everyone says so.'

Kitty felt alarmed. Much as she would love to be a lady's personal maid she did not want to be involved with Lavinia, who would make a slave of her in her demands to deliver letters to her lover, plaguing the poor man. Not only that, she would lose contact with Mrs Helder. She would have to refuse the position.

Kitty helped Lavinia on with her breeches. Although she had known that women, when hunting, wore breeches under their wrap-around black skirts she had never actually seen a pair being worn. Lavinia, who was a little on the plump side, was so tightly corseted that her waist looked as if a man's hand could span it. The black riding-habit became her auburn hair and creamy skin and when she was booted and wore her bowler-hat with its trimming of black veil, she looked attractive and elegant. Lavinia dismissed her, reminding her of the letter, but this time speaking in a more gentle tone of voice.

When Kitty left the room she heard the excited whimpering of dogs and, stopping at a landing window, saw eighteen pairs of hounds being released from a wagon. With tongues lolling, tails thrashing ecstatically, they ran in all directions. Kitty smiled – the hounds were such a lovely part of the scene.

Before long the morning was filled with sounds, not only the chatter of riders who were beginning to arrive for the Meet but from the people from cottage, farm and village to watch the

Hunt leave. There was always a big crowd gathered at the first Hunt of the season. Many of the people, including children, followed on foot, wanting to be in at the kill. Kitty shuddered; this was something she had never stayed to watch.

Kitty and Ivy had been promised by Mrs Bramley that they could watch the proceedings from one of the windows, but before then Ivy came hurrying up to her and gave her a nudge. 'Hey, the folks from the Grange have just arrived. Let's nip upstairs and see if we can spot your "van-thingummy" feller. We'll not be missed for a minute.'

Kitty's heart was racing as they ran up to a first-floor landing window. Ivy had never seen a Hunt before and in spite of always making disparaging remarks about the gentry, she was full of awe at the scene below them, the hunting pink of the men making a bright splash of colour among the sombre tones of other gentlemen riders and the black-habited women. Man-servants were moving among them with trays of stirrup cup. All was movement: dogs, horses, people.

Ivy suddenly exclaimed, 'Hey! There's your feller, over there by the big tree talking to Miss Thea and her feller.'

Kitty felt a tug at her emotions as she saw Tyler on a magnificent dark-dappled grey of about seventeen hands, man and beast complementing one another.

Then Mr Earle, who was master of the Hunt came riding up to them and said something which made Tyler laugh.

Ivy said, 'Oh, he's beautiful, in't he? Your feller I mean – real beautiful. I like your Luke better, mind you, but this van Tyler is something to dream about – in't he?'

A moment later Tyler was the centre of a group of women, admiring women. Kitty did not feel jealous – not like she had done when seeing Louise and Luke together – but she knew regret that a man such as Tyler van Neilson was out of her reach; there was so much he could tell her about glass-making.

The two girls went back downstairs in case they were needed, but they were told to go up to the second floor to get the best view and to hurry – the Hunt would soon be leaving. Mrs Dunn's two younger daughters went with them.

They were none too soon, for the riders were assembling ready to leave, the Master of the Hunt in the lead. About a hundred people were now gathered in the background.

Excitement was mounting and even from behind a closed window one was conscious of it. Kitty's mouth felt dry, as it always did at such a moment.

She still marvelled how the women managed to ride sidesaddle and look at ease with one leg round what seemed a large knob in the saddle. They sat erect, their small waists emphasized by the wide draping of their ankle-length skirts.

The sounding of the horn signalled the start and the horses moved away with Mr Earle leading. The horses trotted until they reached the open field, then they broke into a canter, with the hounds baying their excitement. It really was a magnificent sight, Kitty thought, as she followed Tyler's horse, so easily recognizable amongst the light and dark chestnuts and the duns.

There was a fence to take and the horses were urged forward. When they soared over the fence, muscles rippling, Kitty was near to tears at so much beauty.

The girls waited until the riders were out of sight, then they dispersed to do their respective jobs, with Kitty deciding to look in on Mrs Helder first.

Mrs Helder, who was lying on a sofa which had been drawn up to the window, did not greet Kitty in Italian as usual. She asked if she had enjoyed seeing the Hunt leaving and although she spoke brightly, Kitty detected an underlying forlorn note, which made her wonder if Mrs Helder had been reliving the days when her husband was alive.

'How are you feeling now, ma'am? I'm sorry I was only able to stay a few minutes earlier on. There was so much to do.'

'Yes, of course, I understand. I'm feeling a great deal better this morning, thank you. I walked a few steps, but nurse thinks I ought to rest for two more days. I hate this inactivity but ... Have you time for a lesson, Kitty?'

Kitty thought there was now a pleading in the old lady's voice and realized she was lonely. Kitty told her it was impossible at the moment, but perhaps later. Then she said, 'Is there anything I can do for you, ma'am? Plump up your pillows, get you a hot drink, bring you a book?'

To her consternation she saw a sudden glint of tears in Mrs Helder's eyes. 'Oh, ma'am, what is it, is your back worse? Have you taken your medicine?'

'Yes, I have.' Mrs Helder managed a smile. 'You might be

surprised to know that my tears are because I feel the warmth of being cared for. You are such a kind person, Kitty. If only my circumstances were different, but there ...' Mrs Helder made an effort to put on a bright smile. 'I am all right now. You run along, perhaps I'll see you later.'

Kitty nodded. 'Oh, yes, ma'am, definitely.'

Mrs Helder was on Kitty's mind as she went into one of the bedrooms to tidy it and make up the fire. It looked as if a hurricane had hit it, with clothes strewn everywhere. She hung up the clothes, recalling Mrs Bramley telling her that neither of the girls the old lady was chaperoning had looked in to see her, not even for a moment. Cook had also told her that Mrs Helder had no proper home, that everything had to be sold when her husband died to pay his debts.

'A lovely man,' Mrs Bramley said, 'but a gambler like all the men in his family.' Then she added that Mrs Helder stayed with various relatives until someone asked her to chaperone a daughter, or daughters. Kitty thought it must be awful not to have a home you could call your own. Although the farm would always be her true home, she knew she would be pleased to see her mother and sisters – that is, apart from Violet. Kitty wondered if Violet was still coaxing men to give her money for stockings.

When Kitty went downstairs again to the kitchen Mrs Bramley gave her a smile, it was an abstracted smile, but Kitty suddenly thought that since coming to live with the Earles it was like having a third home. She spoke to Mrs Bramley about the old lady, telling her she seemed to be a little better this morning and Cook said, tipping some flour into a basin, 'She thinks the world of you, Kitty, in fact she did say if she had a house of her own and could afford it, she would like you to be a companion to her.'

Kitty was dreamily thinking how wonderful it would be to have such a job when Mrs Bramley said, as she added a basinful of currants to the flour. 'Not that I'm going to lose you, my girl! You're doing very well here, thank you. The mistress speaks most highly of you and so does Miss Lavinia, who usually doesn't have a good word to say about anyone or anything.'

Mention of Lavinia brought the letter forcibly back to Kitty's mind. She wanted to be rid of it. She hesitated a moment, then

191

asked a little tentatively if it would be possible to pay a quick visit to the farm that afternoon, pointing out that she would like to see Aunt Harriet who had taken the tragedy very badly.

This brought a sharp retort from Mrs Bramley, asking Kitty if she realized what she was wanting? This was Hunt day – had she any idea what it entailed? The riders would be back at four, the womenfolk would be exhausted and muddy, there would be baths to prepare, riding skirts to be sponged, a hundred and one jobs to be done. Kitty would have to have time off when it was convenient and that would certainly not be for the next few days, not with extra guests in the house.

Kitty came to realize that evening how foolish she had been to suggest having time off to visit the farm. She, with the other servants, had never seemed to stop running, the extra guests being more demanding than those already settled in.

Kitty thought once of Tyler van Neilson, but if he was in the house she had not set eyes on him. She had managed to visit Mrs Helder three times – once just a quick look in to see how she was, the other times to take up her midday meal and later her afternoon tea. And even then her visits had been short.

Eighteen people sat down for dinner that evening, but although Kitty was allowed to carry some dishes to the dining-room they were taken from her at the door by Mr Walton or George. It was Ivy who passed her the information that although 'Kitty's feller' was in the house, he was not in the dining-room.

At nine-o'clock when Kitty took Mrs Helder her bedtime drink, she was surprised to find the room in darkness; only minutes ago the bell had rung to let her know she was ready for her nightcap. Kitty paused in the doorway and called, 'Mrs Helder, ma'am – are you all right?'

'Yes, Kitty, just one moment and Mr van Neilson will put on a light.'

Mr van Neilson? Kitty all but dropped the tray. What on earth was he doing in Mrs Helder's room and with the light off?

A match was struck, a gas-jet lit and then a red-shaded lamp. When Kitty walked forward she found Tyler smiling broadly at her. 'If you must know, Kitty, Mrs Helder and I were discussing the stars!'

Mrs Helder, who was propped up in bed, gave a happy,

spontaneous laugh. 'Mr van Neilson and I are old friends and share a love of astronomy. He tells me, Kitty, that you looked after him when he was ill. He was very impressed with your nursing, and I'm not surprised at that.'

Kitty was glad she was away from the brighter light of the gas-jet so as to hide her blushes; she only prayed that Tyler had not mentioned how she had washed and changed him. She put the tray on the bedside table and handed Mrs Helder her herb-flavoured milk drink, saying she hoped it would be to her liking. Mrs Helder took a sip, pronounced it perfect then said, 'We shall be having another discussion on the heavens later in the week, Kitty. Perhaps you would like to join us?'

Tyler's unexpected presence had unnerved Kitty and she was aware of sounding stilted when she said she thought it would be impossible. She asked if there was anything else Mrs Helder needed and was told with a puzzled look that there was nothing else at the moment. Kitty turned to leave and Tyler opened the door for her. He smiled but made no comment.

Once Kitty was outside she felt furious with herself for the way she had behaved. Mrs Helder had shown her nothing but kindness and she had acted like an ill-mannered skivvy, and why? There was nothing she would like better than knowing more about the stars. Luke was always saying what a vast subject it was.

It was not until much later that Kitty found a reason for the way she had acted. Alone with either one of them she had felt at ease, but seeing them both together, both from a world so different to her own, she had been conscious of her position. Being educated, they would no doubt be able to discuss astronomy on a high level, while her teachings from Abel and Luke had been a simple pointing out of the Pole Star, the Great Bear and Orion.

Then it occurred to Kitty that she had readily accepted lessons from Mrs Helder on Italian, which was not a usual subject for a girl in her position. Confused, she was glad that Mrs Helder did not call her again that evening.

At ten o'clock Mr Earle, with Thea and Lavinia and all the younger guests, left to go to a party at a house about two miles away. Lively chatter and bursts of laughter filled the night air as they climbed into carriages. Mrs Bramley remarked with a sniff –

that the lot of them would be *falling* out of carriages in the early hours. A wild crowd this lot were, it could be five or six when they returned.

It was four o'clock when they returned, noisier than when they had left. Kitty wondered if Tyler van Neilson was with them. When the shouting and some singing continued, Ivy exclaimed, 'It's all right for them, in't it, they can sleep the rest of the day, but us lot have to be up at six!'

Kitty learned later from Ivy that Tyler had come in for breakfast looking as if he had had a good night's sleep. He had talked about ordering a carriage and going to visit someone.

The nurse had been taking up Mrs Helder's breakfast and it was not until eleven o'clock that Kitty was summoned by the old lady. On her way up she met Lavinia who wanted to know if Kitty would be delivering the letter that day. She was in a peignoir edged with swansdown, looked bleary-eyed and kept pushing her fingers through her dishevelled hair. When Kitty explained that she would have to wait until she had time off, Lavinia said, 'You'll have time off today, it's the funeral. You'll be going to the farm to keep your foster-mother company while the men go to the funeral . . . won't you?'

The funeral? Kitty stared at her, appalled. How could she have forgotten it? Two people lay dead and all she had been thinking about was Tyler van Neilson, Mrs Helder and astronomy, and how this affected her life. It was awful, terrible – she would never forgive herself. She told Lavinia she would not be going to the farm – her Aunt Harriet would be going to her brother's farm and that was in a different direction from the Grange. And before Lavinia could say anything else she murmured that she had to see Mrs Helder and hurried away.

Kitty's heart was thumping. This wretched letter – it was plaguing her, hanging like a millstone around her neck.

In this distraught state Kitty reached Mrs Helder's room. She found the old lady up and dressed, sitting in a high-backed chair. 'Ah, Kitty, there you are. You will see a transformation in me, all pain gone. Isn't it wonderful?' There was a pause and Mrs Helder's smile died. 'What's wrong, Kitty? What's troubling you?'

Kitty was about to say there was nothing, when she remembered how irritated Tyler had been when she had made a similar remark. 'It's several things, ma'am, but no doubt they will sort themselves out.'

'It might be easier to sort them out with a little help,' Mrs Helder said gently.

The immediate problem to Kitty was the letter and although in the normal way she would never have mentioned such a thing, tension made her blurt out. 'I have an errand to do, ma'am, which is important to the person involved, but which could upset other people if I carried it out.'

'A question of torn loyalties, is it, Kitty? That *is* a problem. And I'm afraid it is something only you can solve.'

'Yes, ma'am, thank you for listening. You rang for me. Is it a drink you want?'

'No.' Mrs Helder eyed Kitty thoughtfully. 'I was thinking of going for a drive this afternoon; there is a carriage at my disposal. I did wonder if you decided to deliver your – package, if I might take you there.'

'Oh, no, ma'am, you see – the place is ... well, secret.'

'And it would remain your secret, Kitty. I would simply put you down near where you wanted to be. No questions would be asked. I would speak to Mrs Earle suggesting you came with me for company. You can mention this to Mrs Bramley.'

The offer was certainly tempting to Kitty. She would get rid of the letter and she would tell Mr Edwards she did not want to deliver any more. He seemed a reasonable man and if *he* explained it to Lavinia ...

'Thank you, ma'am, I'd be pleased if it could be arranged.'

Mrs Helder assured her it would be and Kitty went back to the kitchen to tell Mrs Bramley of the suggestion, expecting her to be annoyed. But instead Cook said, 'Well, it'll do the old lady good. I only hope she won't keep you out all the afternoon, there's jobs to be done!'

Ivy, when told about the outing said, 'Heavens! It'll rain frogs tomorrow, old Bramley letting you go! That woman who likes the funny tea has certainly taken a liking to you, she might leave you something in her will.' When Kitty told her that Mrs Helder had no money and no home, Ivy said, 'Well, would you believe it? Poor old soul. My mam and dad are no angels and the house is like a pigsty always, but I'd feel awful if it wasn't there to go home to.'

Which gave Kitty a little more insight into Ivy's character.

Driving with Mrs Helder would have been a treat for Kitty had it not been for the letter. The coachman had tucked a fur rug round each of them then enquired where 'Madam' wanted to go. Mrs Helder had already asked Kitty the nearest spot to put her down and Kitty had named a part of the road that could not be connected with the Grange. It would mean her running all the way to the cottage and back, even though Mrs Helder had told her she was prepared to wait.

The day was crisp and sunny and Mrs Helder talked about the countryside, about the drives she and her husband had taken and Kitty guessed it was to try and take her mind from the errand. Then Mrs Helder said, 'Kitty, there is something I'm going to put to you, a proposal for the future. Mr van Neilson has been left a house up in the North by his godmother. He has asked me if I would take charge, when the time comes. I agreed on condition I could have you to come with me as my companion. What do you think? Would you be willing?'

When Mrs Bramley had mentioned such a thing Kitty had thought of it as an impossible dream, but now the dream had acquired reality she could hardly speak for excitement. Companion to Mrs Helder? In Tyler van Neilson's house!

She turned to the old lady. 'Oh, ma'am, it would be wonderful, I can hardly believe it. It's like having a fairy godmother.'

'To me too, Kitty,' Mrs Helder said quietly. 'I've felt like a rudderless ship since my husband died, but now I have a course to follow, something to look forward to. It will not be for some time – there are some formalities to be completed – perhaps two to three months.'

'Oh, any time, ma'am, any time! My errand seems less of a burden now.'

Mrs Helder patted her hand. 'I'm glad, Kitty. I think it might not be wise to mention it until all is settled. You know the old saying, many a slip between cup and lip. But whatever happens, Kitty, I want you to look upon me as a friend.'

'Thank you, ma'am.' Kitty was unable to say any more.

She asked to be put down at the edge of a wood from where the Grange could not be seen. Once out of the carriage Kitty began to run, the layers of fallen leaves for many, many years softening her footsteps. If Mr Edwards was not in she would push the letter under the door, but she prayed he would be; she wanted to talk to him, tell him how she hated having to bring the letters.

When at last she reached the cottage she was breathless and stood for a moment before knocking. When she did knock the door-latch lifted so quickly it was as though the gamekeeper had been waiting for her. The next moment Kitty was staring at Tyler van Neilson.

'You've brought another letter,' he said. 'I'm sorry, Kitty, you're too late. Mr Edwards has gone away.'

'Gone away?' She felt stupid. 'You mean with Miss Lavinia?'

'No, he's gone alone. He left a note for me and one for Lavinia. He said he felt trapped, he had to leave. It's just as well for your sake, Kitty, Lavinia was getting you too involved in the affair.'

'She'll kill herself,' Kitty said. 'She threatened to before.'

'Not Lavinia, she's a survivor. Are you coming in for a moment?'

'No, Mrs Helder is waiting for me in the carriage. She knows nothing about the letter, only that I had an errand to do.'

Tyler told her he was sure that Mrs Helder would know of the affair, since most people knew about it; it was Lavinia who had her head in the sand. When Kitty stood looking at the letter in her hand, Tyler said, 'I'll break the news to her, you can return the letter later. And don't worry, Kitty, Lavinia will get over it.'

The result of Lavinia's knowing was that she came down to the kitchen at nine o'clock that night, quite drunk and demanding to see Kitty who was the only friend she had in the world! Kitty was grabbed by the hand and might have been dragged upstairs had not Mrs Bramley stepped between them and ordered Kitty to find Mr Walton.

Mr Walton came in before Kitty had a chance to take a step. Grasping the scene at once he took over from Mrs Bramley, talking softly to Lavinia, telling her he was going to take her back to her room and get her maid to see her into bed.

Lavinia refused to move. 'I want Kitty,' she demanded. 'She ... she'sh my friend, she under – understands me—'

'Yes,' said Mr Walton, 'you can see her later when you are in bed. She'll bring you up a nice cup of warm cocoa.'

Lavinia peered at Mr Walton. 'Are you my – my father?'

Mr Walton permitted himself a slight smile. 'I feel I am at this moment, Miss Lavinia. Now come along with me. Yes, yes, I insist.'

He propelled her towards the staircase and finally, with the help of George, managed to get her upstairs.

'*Well!*' declared Mrs Bramley. 'And that's a right how-do-you-do and no mistake. That's what happens when young rich girls get their own way when they're young. Spoiled to death, thought she could have any man she wanted. Got poor Mr Edwards to leave that nice cottage and a good job – could have been a job for life.' She turned to Kitty. 'But why she should claim you as a friend, I can't imagine. You've not had much to do with her apart from stitching the hem of her skirt yesterday afternoon.'

'And helping to look after her during the epidemic,' Ivy put in quickly. 'And anyway, Mr Edwards is as much to blame as Miss Lavinia, he's not a lad.'

'No, that's true enough, he must be all of thirty. Well, I'm sure he'll get another job somewhere, even if he doesn't get references from the Grange and, Miss Lavinia'll get over it and find another man to hang on to. Probably at the weekend. There's a big do on at Greenacres and we'll all be going – yes, staff as well as family. There's a ball on the Saturday night, and as there's about eighty bedrooms and most of them will be occupied, we'll have our work cut out.'

'Eighty?' Ivy echoed. 'Heavens above. We'll never find our way to clean them!'

The weekend party was all Ivy could talk about when she and Kitty went to bed, but all Kitty wanted to think about was the chance to be with Mrs Helder in Tyler van Neilson's house. What a wonderful opportunity it was. Would he be carrying out his experiments there? Would he let her see him working? If only he would!

'As for that upstart Lavinia,' Ivy was saying, 'she certainly got her come-uppance. I wish a few more fellers would walk out on her, then she'd know what for.'

Poor Lavinia, Kitty thought. If she really loved Mr Edwards, she must be suffering now, not knowing if she would ever see him again.

Kitty felt a sudden pang, realizing that when they left this house to go North her visits to the farm would end and she would not be seeing Luke. Not even having the chance to work for Tyler van Neilson could recompense her for that. It seemed to Kitty then that Harriet was right when she said once that life was a mixture of sorrows and pleasure.

CHAPTER FOURTEEN

The following afternoon the doctor arrived unexpectedly. He was taken to Miss Lavinia's room and was there half an hour. When he left Lavinia went with him, looking red-eyed. Speculation was rife. She must have made herself ill with the drink she had had the night before. But if so, why had she gone with the doctor? She could have been treated at home.

The speculation came to an end when Mrs Earle informed Mr Walton that her daughter had gone into a private nursing home with suspected appendix trouble.

'And we all know what that means, don't we?' sneered Ivy. 'The rich young lady's complaint. When she comes back we'll be told she's had her appendix removed, only we'll know it's something else that's been removed, won't we?'

Mrs Bramley boxed her ears and told her to watch her tongue, or else ... This did not stop Ivy from retorting, 'It's the truth and we all know it. She got herself into trouble and that's why her gamekeeper lover did a bunk, scared as a chased rabbit – don't think much of him!'

Mrs Bramley warned her that if she didn't get on with her job and shut up she'd soon know about it, which did stop Ivy's tirade, but she complained to Kitty later that they must think all folks were green – she'd guessed what was wrong with the snotty-nosed Lavinia two weeks before.

To Kitty's query as to what *was* wrong with Lavinia, Ivy gave a derisive laugh. 'Hey, where were you dug up? She's having a baby, of course.'

Before Kitty could protest that this could not be true, Ivy went on about her own mother trying to get rid of her ninth child. 'She didn't succeed, but the baby came at seven months – and lived. A skinny thing, just like a doll it was, that would have gone into a pint pot. Me Gran made it a tiny bonnet and shawl.'

A tiny bonnet and shawl? They conjured up vague memories in Kitty's mind, something to do with her childhood. 'Bonnet and shawl,' she repeated to herself. Suddenly her skin began to crawl and she pushed whatever it was to the back of her mind again. She found she was trembling and said quickly, 'What day is it we're leaving to go to this house for the weekend party?' and Ivy looked at her blankly for a moment before saying she thought it would be Thursday.

The preparations to go to Greenacres diverted attention from Lavinia and excitement mounted as the time drew near to leave. Even Kitty, who had been left disturbed by the stirring of her memories, was caught up in it.

The weekend at the eighty-bedroom country mansion was an eye-opener to Kitty in more ways than one. She was over-awed by the magnificence of the building and furnishings, the richness of dress, the pageantry of the ball on the Saturday evening, but taken aback by the knowledge that married couples, singly, shared the bedrooms of other husbands and other wives, and that young men spent the night in the bedrooms of unmarried girls.

'Oh, that's a regular going on!' Ivy declared. 'They're so bored with nothink to do, they have to have something to do to liven things up a bit.'

It was from Ivy too that Kitty learned that some girls liked other girls better than young men, and some young men liked other young men better than girls. This was something Kitty found impossible to understand, nor did she think she wanted to. When she mentioned it, Ivy said, 'That's daft; if you want to be eddicated, you have to know all about the bad things as well as the good, otherwise you'd never appreciate the good ones, would you?'

Kitty thought later she was probably right, because during the next month she looked forward so much to the times that she spent with Mrs Helder, learning Italian, going for visits to the farm, being with Luke and going over the short conversations there had been with Tyler van Neilson about going to his house with Mrs Helder. 'It's not large, Kitty,' he had said, 'but there is extensive land and I'm having a laboratory built.' Then he added with a smile, 'I promise you this, when it is built you shall have a try at blowing a glass bottle or a bowl.'

Kitty felt then as though she was bathed in sunshine. She had thanked him, breathlessly wondering what beautiful thing was going to happen to her next.

Ten days ago Tyler had gone to London and, according to Mrs Helder, he would be going from there up North to supervise the work on the laboratory. Then yesterday Mr Walton had announced that they would all be returning to Stratton House at the weekend, since Mr and Mrs Earle wanted to be home in good time to make preparations for Christmas. Lavinia would be home by then too. Apparently, since she had come out of the nursing home she had been staying with an aunt – a dragon of a woman, Mrs Bramley informed them.

There was only one reason why Kitty would be sorry to be leaving this house, there would be no more visits to the farm. She hoped she would be able to see them all before they left. She *must* see them! When she asked Mrs Bramley if this could be arranged, she was told it would be fitted in somehow.

Two afternoons later Kitty went to the farm to say goodbye. She had not mentioned the possibility of changing her job, not knowing for sure if it would happen, but now she knew it must be told.

'It's not certain even yet, Aunt Harriet,' she said, 'but I think I will be going as companion to Mrs Helder. She'll be driving over tomorrow to see you, to assure you I'll be in good hands.'

Harriet was silent for a few moments and then she looked up, her expression grave. 'I don't think you'll be able to take up this position, Kitty – not because of its unsuitability, but because your mother isn't well and Violet wants you home to look after her. I had a letter this morning.'

To Kitty it was as though a big beautiful bubble had burst, destroying all her hopes, her dreams. 'Why me?' she asked at last, feeling numb.

'Violet, it seems, has become boss, she's giving the orders. She wants to stay on at her job and she wants your other sisters to keep on with theirs.'

'She hates me,' Kitty said, 'she always has.' She sat, her hands on her lap, palms upturned. 'I was so happy, so looking forward to this new job. It must be written in my hand that I'm only to be allowed a little bit of happiness, then that's the end of it.'

'Oh no, love, don't say that.' Harriet came over and took Kitty's hand in hers. 'You're young, you have a whole life ahead of you. When your mother is better, you can probably still have the job, but if not there'll be others. Mrs Bramley will give you a good reference – you're very well liked, I was told so.'

Kitty felt a terrible bleakness inside her as she looked at Harriet appealingly. 'I wanted this job, Aunt Harriet, so very much.' Her voice broke.

'Oh, Kitty, Kitty,' Harriet gathered her in her arms. 'There are many worse things to weep for. Dry your eyes, love, I'll make some tea.'

Kitty had pulled herself together by the time Abel and Luke came in and although they seemed to realize there was something wrong, no remark was made until Luke suggested he and Kitty take a walk across the fields. When she told him of the change in her plan he was sympathetic, but pointed out gently that most people had family duties to perform and that it had fallen to her, being the youngest, to take care of her mother.

They had climbed to the top field, as they always did on her visits to the farm. The day was cold, the wind cutting; her cheeks stung. Luke drew Kitty over into the shelter of the hedge and standing her with her back to it, shielded her with his body. Putting his fist under her chin, he tilted her face to his.

'Don't let me down, Kitty,' he said softly. 'I've drawn my courage from you.'

Her eyes went wide. 'From me? I have no courage.'

'Oh yes you have, you're a little fighter. You were near death's door when Father brought you to the farm all those years ago; your body and your mind were bruised, but you fought all the way and got well. You've not only been an example of what courage can do, but a great joy to all of us. We all love you very much.'

Kitty searched his face, trying to read his mind. Did he love her the way she loved him? It was such a beautiful face – strong, his expression at the moment grave. Had *he* ever wanted his life to be different? Had he dreamed, did he dream now?

When she asked him, he said, 'I did dream once, Kitty. I wanted to go to Australia, sheepfarming. I had two cousins out

203

there. I thought about it a lot and I think I might have gone had it not been for the Boer trouble. All the young men, including the four of us, were excited at the thought of war. What adventure to join up and cross the seas to South Africa! I didn't realize until I had crossed the seas how selfish I'd been. And I realized it more than ever when I was the only one to return home. One of us should have remained at home and being the youngest, I should have been the one.'

'And I being the youngest in my family, should be the one to look after my mother,' Kitty said, a hopelessness in her voice.

'Sacrifices have to be made, Kitty,' he said gently. 'I am satisfied now with the life I have, but you can go on dreaming. Many changes could come your way.'

Kitty told him then about the job which had been offered to her and Luke said after a moment's silence, 'Do you have a choice, Kitty?'

She shook her head. 'No, I shall go home.'

'If you didn't, you would regret it, Kitty.' She agreed.

The parting with Abel and Harriet was a tearful one, but when Luke walked her back to the Earles' he made her laugh by recalling the time Kitty had brought Ivy to the farm for the afternoon – how she had been so taken with the 'alimals' and laughed so much when she managed to milk a cow that she fell off the stool.

Kitty was still smiling when they reached the house. Luke took her by the shoulders and said softly, 'Well, Kitty, another parting, but how sweet it is when we meet again! Perhaps it won't be too long. I'll write to you and I know that Mother will too. Take care of yourself.'

He kissed her gently – it was a brotherly kiss, not at all the sort Kitty wanted. When they parted she felt choked and waited a few moments before going into the house, hating to tell Mrs Bramley she would be leaving.

But Mrs Bramley already knew, as there had been a letter from Jessica explaining the situation. 'I've spoken to the mistress,' Cook said, 'and she's arranging for you to leave in the morning, by train. She's told me that if you want to come back at any time, there'll be a job for you.'

Cook went on discussing Kitty's mother, saying she got the impression from the letter that although Margaret was quite ill, she could recover with care and attention. 'And I know you'll take good care of her, Kitty love. We'll miss you, we'll all miss you very much.'

Ivy was very upset when she knew. 'You just got to come back, Kitty, otherwise I'll have to try and tame that moggy that's been hanging around; I gotta have something to love.'

The 'moggy' was a wild cat which came for scraps of food, but if anyone approached it went streaking away. Kitty wailed, 'Oh, Ivy, don't make it worse, I don't want to leave!'

The person Kitty most dreaded telling the news to was Mrs Helder, but to her surprise it was the old lady who gave her hope. 'Something tells me, Kitty, that we shall go together to Mr van Neilson's house. You might possibly find your mother greatly improved when you arrive. She will have been fretting to see you, and even knowing that you are coming will do her the world of good. I have an Italian and English language book I shall give you. Study it when you can, and look forward to the time when we can resume the lessons.' When Mrs Helder gave Kitty the book, she also pressed a sovereign into her hand, saying, 'It's just a small gift, my dear, for all you've done for me; you've given me a new zest for life! God go with you.'

For the rest of the evening the kitchen was like a morgue, with everyone telling Kitty what a miss she was going to be. And when the time for parting came the next morning, it was as tearful as the parting at the farm. Mrs Earle had left Kitty a sovereign, Mr Walton added five shillings to it and Mrs Bramley handed her a parcel of food. George travelled with her in the carriage to Leicester station and saw that she had the company of a family travelling North. Although Kitty had felt at first that she would have preferred to travel alone, she realized the lively chatter of the three children and their parents helped to shorten the journey. Even so, she was weary by the time she arrived. She took a tram home and found Jessica in the kitchen. Jessica put her arms around her, said, 'Hello, love!' and Kitty burst into tears.

'I'm sorry, Jessica, it's all been such an upheaval, it was so unexpected. How is Mother? What does the doctor say?'

'That she is worn out – too many miscarriages, too little food and overworked. She's sleeping at the moment, we'll go up later. In the meantime, let me get you a cup of tea.'

Over the tea Kitty asked how bad her mother really was and Jessica told her she was a very sick woman indeed – that was why she had written to Mrs Bramley to make sure she would let Kitty leave right away.

'She wanted to see you, Kitty, talked of nothing else. That is, when she had the strength to talk. She said there was something you had to know.'

'I know what it is,' Kitty said, a bitterness in her voice. 'She wants to tell me I'm illegitimate. Our Violet has called me a bastard often enough.'

There was the sound of coughing from above them and Jessica looked up. 'She's awake, we'd better go up. I wanted her to have a bed down here but she wouldn't, said she needed some privacy for when you came. I've kept a fire on.'

Although Kitty had been prepared to see a change in her mother, she was shocked at seeing the child-size face, dark eyes sunken in their sockets, the skin sallow against the pillows. She went over and kissed her mother and tried to force some brightness into her voice. 'Well, we'll soon have you up, Mother, now I'm here to look after you. I'll have to bully you.'

'It's good to see you, Kitty ...' Margaret's voice was little more than a whisper. 'I was praying you would come before I died.'

The fire burning in the grate had taken the chill off the room, but at her mother's words Kitty felt as though an icy blast had swept through it. 'Now what kind of talk is that?' she asked. 'As Mrs Bramley would say, you're good for another fifty years at least!'

Margaret's head moved restlessly on the pillows. 'No, Kitty, I know I'm dying and there's something you must know before I go. And I want Jessica to be witness to my words. There are some ...' Margaret paused to get her breath, 'some papers that will ... that will tell you the truth of your birth. You have a right to know.'

A coughing bout racked Margaret's frail frame. She pressed a piece of rag to her colourless lips and Kitty saw with distress that it was stained with blood. She looked at Jessica and asked if she should fetch the doctor, but Margaret whispered, 'It would be no use. Listen, Kitty ...' She tried to raise her head, but sank back exhausted. Her eyes closed.

Jessica motioned to Kitty to follow her out of the room and they went downstairs. 'It was no use staying; she would only get agitated. We'll give her ten minutes or so and then go up again.'

Kitty asked, 'Do you know the truth of my birth, Jessica? What are the papers that Mother talked about?'

'I have no idea, Kitty. I only know there was a time when your mother left your father for a while, taking the children with her.'

'And I can guess the rest,' Kitty said in a flat voice. 'She met some other man and I was the result.'

'I don't think so, Kitty. I don't know. I know nothing about any papers, but there is something I must warn you about and that's your Violet's attitude. She already has your mother dead and has decided that she'll keep on the house and that you and Mary, Agnes and Ann will hand over your wages to her.'

Kitty protested vehemently at this. 'Never! I would never give our Violet a penny and she can't make me.'

Jessica looked troubled. 'I'm not sure of the law, Kitty. She's the eldest and could appoint herself as the guardian of you all.'

'If our Violet was appointed as our guardian, then I'd run away and hide, go with gypsies. I would *not* give her a penny!' No more was said on the subject. Later Kitty took some soup up to her mother, but Margaret could only manage about three spoonsful then was exhausted again.

Kitty drew up a chair to the bed, prepared to wait until her mother had recovered. At first she felt a bit ghoulish, like someone waiting for a relative to die so as to inherit some money. But then, this was a totally different situation. Her mother wanted her to have the papers. But where could these papers be? There was no wardrobe, no chest of drawers, no cupboard in the room – just a bed, a chair and a cardboard box that held her mother's clothes. In the box? When her mother appeared to have drifted into sleep Kitty searched it, but there was nothing in the box but some well-worn and well-darned underclothes. Kitty went back to her chair, then was up again, remembering the other bedroom across the small landing.

But there was not even anything to search here. The only item in the room was the iron bedstead with a rusty spring. Kitty went downstairs and asked Jessica if she could think of any place in the house where the papers might be. Jessica tapped bricks around the fireplace, thinking there might be a loose one with a cavity, they searched the cupboard in the scullery, tapped bricks there, but drew a blank. Jessica then said the more she thought about it, the more she felt sure the papers were *somewhere* upstairs. 'Your mother was determined to stay up there, Kitty, and this could be the reason.'

'But *where* upstairs?' Kitty wailed. 'There's nowhere else they could be. Not unless – how about under the mattress or in the pillow-case?'

Jessica shook her head. 'No, I changed the pillow case yesterday and I turned the mattress to try and ease out the lumps. There was nothing. But . . .' Jessica suddenly eyed Kitty thoughtfully, 'there is one place, it's just occurred to me. I had an aunt who used to keep her bits and pieces in the bed post. It was a brass bedstead, like your mother's, the posts are hollow.' They both got up and then both sat down again, Jessica saying, 'We can't go rushing up and start screwing off knobs!'

'No, of course not, but when Mother's awake again I'll ask her if that is where the papers are. After all, she *wants* me to have them.'

But when they next went upstairs it appeared that Margaret had slipped into a coma. Jessica went to see the doctor and he came back with her. After examining the patient, he shook his head. 'She could live a few more days but on the other hand she could go during the night. It would be best if you sit up with her.' He patted Kitty's shoulder. 'I'm sorry, my dear. Let me know when it happens and I'll let you have a death certificate.'

Kitty shuddered at the word 'death'. How terribly final it sounded. She felt an ache as she thought of her mother's tragic life. Perhaps the only happiness she had really known was when she lived at the farm. All the miscarriages, the childbearing, the hard drinking of the man she married – Kitty could no longer think of him as her father – must have disillusioned her. And yet her mother had said that when her husband was not drinking he was a kind man.

Jessica brought up another chair and she and Kitty settled themselves for an all-night vigil, each with a blanket round their shoulders which Jessica had brought from her own home. Jessica said, 'Two o'clock is the testing time, the body is at its lowest ebb then; if your mother survives that crisis she could live another day.' After a pause she added, 'I'm wondering if we should look for the papers.'

'No,' Kitty said quickly. 'I feel somehow it would be like robbing the ... Let's wait.'

Time dragged and Kitty found the room eerie with the firelight and the flickering candle-flame making grotesque shadows on the wall. Sometimes her mother's eyelids would flutter and Kitty would think she was regaining consciousness, but then there would be a stillness again. Her mother had the pallor of death and once or twice Kitty drew in a breath, sure she had stopped breathing, but then she saw the faint pulse beating in Margaret's temple.

Two o'clock came and went, then three and four without signs of any change and Jessica suggested they take turns at cat-napping. Kitty's surface-sleeping took her to the farm, to the days before the Boer War and after; brought her home when her mother came for her and then to the Earles, and Tyler van Neilson was in her semi-dreaming when Jessica nudged her awake. 'Kitty – your mother seems to be rousing.'

Margaret's eyes were open, her gaze on Kitty as one finger lifted, beckoning her to come closer. The words were just a breath and Kitty had to put her ear close to her mother's mouth. 'Get the ... papers ... now. Don't want ... Violet to – have them. Get them, now ...' The hand moved upwards, then was pointing at the right column of the bed. 'In ... there ...'

She closed her eyes. Jessica got up at once and began to unscrew the knob. Kitty's heart was thumping painfully. When the knob was off Jessica peered inside the column, then looked up and shook her head. She tried the other three, but there was nothing. Her mother's lips were moving again. 'Have you ... got ... them ...? You – must ... *now* ...'

'Yes, I will, I will, I promise.'

There was a faint sigh, the sound of a rattle in Margaret's throat, another sigh, gentle, long-drawn-out, then she was still.

Jessica said gently, 'She's gone, Kitty.'

Kitty's emotions at that moment were a mixture of grief at her mother's death and a regret that she might never know the truth.

'Your Violet must have found the papers,' Jessica said, in an angry whisper. 'I feel sure they *had* been there. We'll tackle her when she comes; she and the girls said they would be here about half-past ten. In the meantime there are things to be done. It must be about eight o'clock. I'll go to the doctor's to get the certificate and call at the undertaker's on the way back. Your mother paid into a burial club and never missed a payment, so you don't have to worry about the cost of the funeral. I'll get Mrs Dawson to help lay her out.'

'No,' Kitty said, 'I would like to help you. I feel I must.'

'Very well, love. I'll bring some fresh sheets and a nightdress for your mam. She'll have to be washed, so get a kettle on the fire. I won't be long.'

Kitty felt herself trembling when she was alone with her mother's body. Harriet had laid out many people in the neighbourhood of the farm, but it was Kitty's first experience and she wondered if she could do it without making a fool of herself. She would have to let them know at the farm, for Margaret had been like a daughter to them. Would any one of them be able to come for the funeral? It was such a long way. Jessica had pulled the sheet over Margaret's face, but Kitty felt she could see her mother looking at her, wanting her to have the papers. Had Violet taken them?

Jessica was back quite quickly. Kitty had a bowl of warm water ready. She found it a harrowing task washing and handling the bird-bone figure with the weight of a child. When it was done it seemed to Kitty that her mother's expression had changed from one of pain to one of serenity and it was then the tears came. Jessica consoled her, saying they should be thankful she had found peace at last.

While they waited for the undertaker to come, Kitty spoke of her fear of Violet having found the papers.

'I feel sure that the man I knew as my father was not my father, and it was someone from the upper classes; if Violet knew this, she could blackmail him.'

Jessica glanced at her quickly and asked why she should presume such a thing. If there had been another man in her mother's life, it could have been someone she knew at the glassworks. Kitty said she doubted that and gave her reasons.

'There was a part of her life my mother never mentioned. She spoke of Mrs Bramley as being a friend of hers, but did not mention that she had worked for her. Mrs Bramley told me, said

Mother was a real hard worker. When was this? When she ran away from her husband? Oh, Jessica, if only I could know the truth!'

Jessica looked grim. 'I promise you this, if your Violet has taken them I'll get them from her. I'll threaten her with theft, I'll think of something!'

After the undertaker had been there was a constant stream of neighbours calling, but Jessica told each one to call later as they were expecting the girls home and there was some business to discuss.

Violet arrived first, at ten o'clock. She was dressed all in black and looked beautiful – yet hateful to Kitty.

'How could you come all in black?' Kitty exclaimed. 'Mother *has* died, but how do you think she would have felt had she seen you? You're evil, our Violet!'

Violet's eyes widened in surprise. 'I don't know what you are talking about. I'm wearing black in respect for my mistress's brother who has died.'

'A black band would have been enough,' Jessica snapped. 'You're not one of their family. You're a nasty piece of work, Violet.'

'Oh, dear, what a to-do!' Violet drew off her gloves, finger by finger. 'I think I must remind you, *dear* Jessica, now that Mother is dead I am in control here, and if I do not want you in the house you will go. Is that understood?'

'No, Violet, you will not get rid of me, not until your mother's will is read.'

Kitty glanced at Jessica, not sure whether this was something she had made up on the spur of the moment. Violet was watching Jessica with narrowed eyes. 'What will?' she demanded.

'The one your mother gave to me. No doubt you would have expected it to be with the papers you stole from your mother's room.'

'What papers?' Violet's surprise seemed to Kitty to be quite genuine. 'I know of no papers. What are you talking about?'

Jessica gave Kitty a quick puzzled glance, but said to Violet, 'Your surprise doesn't fool me – you have them, I know you do – but then they are not so important as the will.'

Violet, who could remain calm under most circumstances,

211

was now showing signs of losing control. Her eyes were flashing fire. 'If there is a will, then I as the eldest have a right to see it and handle it.'

'Oh, no, Violet, you are quite wrong. Your mother gave it to me. She made me her . . . executrix – I think that is the correct term.'

Through tight lips, Violet said that if no one had any objections she would like to see her mother, and went storming out of the room.

Kitty looked at Jessica and whispered, 'Is there a will?'

'A tiny one that means nothing,' Jessica whispered back, 'but it's left your ladyship worried. That will really give her something to think about.'

Violet was not long upstairs and when she came down she was no calmer. She had started to go on about the will again, demanding to see it, when Agnes and Mary and Ann arrived. Mary, with tear-filled eyes, said they knew when they saw the drawn blinds that their mother was dead. Ann, catching sight of Violet, wanted to know why she was wearing mourning. 'What's going on?' she asked. 'And you, our Kitty, when did you come? How long has Mother been dead?'

'Since eight o'clock,' Jessica replied. 'Your mother asked for Kitty to come home. I knew that you four would be coming anyway, so there was no need to send anyone with a message.'

Violet said, 'What I want to know is where are some papers belonging to my mother, and I also want to see the will she made.'

'Will?' Agnes said. 'Why should she make a will? She hadn't a penny to her name. And what are these papers you're talking about?'

'That's what I want to know. I've been accused of *stealing* them.'

They all looked blank and declared they had not seen any papers. But this did not satisfy Violet. She insisted that one of the three had taken them and she would make sure they were returned, even if it meant taking someone to court. 'And speaking of courts,' she added, 'I, being the eldest, will be taking over the house and all four of you will be answerable to me from now on. And you will hand over every penny of your wages to me.'

This caused something of an uproar and Jessica had to remind them that their mother was lying dead upstairs. Although things were conducted a little more quietly after that, Agnes, Mary and Ann were determined that Violet was not going to take charge of them, Ann concluding with the news that Freddie Beston had asked her to marry him a while ago and now she was going to agree to do so. She and Freddie would take over the house, or rent another one, and the girls could stay with them during their time off.

'Oh no, you don't!' Violet said, all quietness once more forgotten. 'I know the law, I've spoken to a solicitor about it. I *am* your legal guardian.'

Kitty jumped up. 'I can tell you now you'll never be mine.'

'*You* more than anyone, our Kitty, will be under my thumb,' Violet retorted, her tone vicious. 'I think you've forgotten you're a bastard and bastards have no rights.'

At this Ann stepped forward and said quietly: 'Kitty is not the bastard in this family. You are one, our Violet, and so are the three of us. Kitty is the only legitimate child.'

The silence at this was so complete that Kitty was sure they must all hear the slow pounding of her heart.

CHAPTER FIFTEEN

After Ann's dramatic statement Kitty's gaze went slowly from one to the other, needing desperately for someone to say it was true. But they were all standing woodenly. Then Violet suddenly gave a derisive laugh and declared the whole thing to be a load of rubbish. She turned to Ann.

'I don't know why you said such a stupid thing. Of course our Kitty is the bastard. Have your forgotten the time that Mother left Dad? What did she do? Dumped us all on Aunt Bertha and disappeared.'

'No, I haven't forgotten,' Ann said quietly.

'Then perhaps you'll also remember that she came back for us six months later, to take us home. And ... that seven months after this our Kitty was born. She was passed off as a premature baby, but I can tell you now there was nothing premature about her – she went her full time.'

'I wouldn't know about that,' Ann said. 'I only know that Kitty was Mam's only legitimate child, whether you want to believe it or not.'

'Oh, honestly ...' Violet gave a despairing sigh, 'how stupid can you get? Hasn't it occurred to you that Mother was living with some man? She was having an affair. *An - affair!*'

'She wasn't, she married him.'

Kitty had not been aware until then that a silence can vibrate. It was in her ears, her head. She looked at Jessica, but Jessica raised her shoulders in a helpless gesture. Then Mary's voice tremulously broke the silence.

'You mean that Mam ... committed bigamy?'

'No, Mary, it was the other way around. It was Dad who

214

committed the bigamy. When he married Mam, he already had a wife.'

'Oh, God,' Agnes said, 'then we *are* all—'

Violet jumped up. 'I don't believe it, our Ann's making it up.'

'Making it up?' Ann exclaimed. 'Do you think I'm enjoying admitting I'm illegitimate? Do you think it's something I like inflicting on Mary and Agnes? I don't care about you, our Violet, you deserve all that's coming to you, but I do care about our Kitty. She certainly has a right to know the truth after the way Dad behaved to her. He all but killed her.' Ann turned to Mary and Agnes. 'I hope you'll agree that what I did was the right thing.'

The two girls avoided her gaze and were silent.

Violet, who now looked pale and shaken, demanded to see the proof, said she would not believe it until she did. Ann told her there was proof, but Kitty would be the one to see it; the letters were hers, her mother had left them for her.

'Then why did you take them?' Jessica asked. 'You had no right.'

'No, I know, but I felt sure if Violet got her hands on them they would never have seen the light of day. I saw Mam putting them into the bedpost the last time we were here. Then I realized that Violet was following me upstairs. I wasn't sure whether she had seen or not, but before we left that evening I slipped upstairs and took them.'

Ann brought a rolled packet from her bag and handed it to Kitty.

'Here you are, no one has seen it but me.'

'For the moment!' Violet snapped. She began pulling on her gloves. 'I want to find out about my rights in regard to the four of you. And about the will. I shall speak to that solicitor again and ask him about it.'

'Our boss has a solicitor,' Ann retorted, 'and I'm sure he'll give *us* advice.'

Violet looked each one of them up and down in turn, contempt in her expression. 'Don't think you'll get away with anything. I'll beat you every time. The whole lot of you put together haven't the brains of a flea!'

She went out then, closing the door with barely a sound, which somehow made more impact than if she had slammed it.

Mary began to cry, tears running slowly down her cheeks. 'I don't want to live, I feel shamed to the soul.'

'Nonsense!' Jessica spoke briskly. 'Kitty has survived having been branded by Violet as a bastard and she's had promotion in her job. She's loved by many people and respected by the people she works for.'

Ann, calmer now, said, 'I told Freddie about us, but he said it made no difference to him, that children could not be blamed for what their parents had done.' Her head went up. 'I have no regrets at what I did, and if you two have any sense neither will you. The truth had to be told and you know it.'

Mary dried her tears but looked unhappy. So did Agnes; she asked about the will, why *should* her mother make one when she had nothing?

Jessica explained that it was no more than a piece of paper on which their mother had written that any money she had was to be shared among the five of them.

Agnes was looking thoughtful. 'Mam had nothing, but what about the man she married, Kitty's father? Does he have money?'

Kitty, who had been staring at the package in her hand, looked up. 'Does he, Ann? If so, tell them.'

'No, that's up to you. But I will say one thing: it's a beautiful love story. I only wish your father was mine too.' Her voice broke. She whispered that she was going up to see their mother now and asked if Agnes and Mary were coming with her. The three of them went upstairs.

Jessica came over and put a hand gently on Kitty's shoulders. 'Take the letters to my house to read, you'll have peace there. Neighbours will be dropping in here all morning. The fire's laid – put a match to it.'

Kitty thanked her; one part of her longing to read them but the other part feeling reluctance, not knowing what she would find.

In Jessica's house Kitty put a match to the kindling and when the flames were beginning to lick round the pieces of coal, took two envelopes from the larger one and studied them. One was marked 'Richard's Letters' and the other said: 'For my daughter Kitty, to be read after my death.' Kitty gave a little shiver, feeling that it was like receiving messages from the grave. For a moment she wished she had left things as they were, then she began to feel a stir of emotion; she would be reading letters that had been written by her very own father. She decided to read her mother's letter first.

The heading on the letter said: 'For my dear daughter Kitty, who was the only one of my children to be conceived out of true love.' This brought tears to Kitty's eyes and she sat a moment before brushing them away.

There were three pages written in beautiful copper-plate writing. Her mother began by saying that she never had any intention of falling in love in this way, it just happened. She had met Richard Tierne one evening on her way home from the glassworks, when she had fallen on the icy road and he had picked her up ...

... He was quality, Kitty, well-dressed, beautifully spoken, yet in spite of our difference in class he was so kind, so gentle. He even offered to see me home, but naturally I refused. After thanking him I left.

I had not expected to see him again, but to my surprise he was waiting for me the following evening at the top of the slope. He wanted to know if I had suffered in any way from my fall. I told him no, and because I felt disturbed by the way seeing this stranger again affected me I thanked him once more for his kindness and hurried away. A minute later he caught up with me and begged to speak to me for a few moments, saying he had not been able to get me out of his mind.

As you can imagine, I was astonished at this. I was a working woman, wrapped in a black shawl, pale and under-nourished at the time. I explained I was married, had four daughters and that my husband would be very angry if he saw us together.

Richard was full of apologies, said he understood and promised not to pester me again.

The awful part of it was that I could not get him out of my mind, his face was before me in my waking hours and in my dreams. I think his main attraction for me was his eyes – they were lovely dark eyes, so expressive, you have inherited them, Kitty. Yes, I know I have dark eyes too but his were different, they had depth, a warmth, a caring – and if I may be so bold as to say so – a passion. I went on dreaming about him, yet knowing it was wrong.

Then one day something happened that put him right out of my thoughts. I had an anonymous letter telling me that Arthur had married me bigamously. His wife had been alive at the time and still was, although she did not want anything to do with him, ever.

You can imagine my shock. It meant that my four daughters were illegitimate. Arthur denied the accusation at first, then admitted it, telling me I would not have agreed to run away with him unless he had promised marriage. How right he was! He tried to tell me he wanted me because he loved me so much, but I had learned by then that love to Arthur meant no more than lust. I left him, but I shall leave Jessica to tell you that part of it. I'm exhausted. I can't write any more. I shall try and tell you later what happened when I met Richard again . . .

Kitty ached to know the rest of the story, but knew she would have to talk to Jessica first.

There was no time that day. Neighbours and people Margaret had known at the glassworks came to pay their respects. News travels fast in a close community. Although Agnes, Mary and Ann stayed later than usual, there was no opportunity for private discussion about her mother's papers. Mary, who was still upset, said she didn't want to know about them anyway. Agnes said she did and would call the following evening.

The undertaker and his assistant dismantled the rusted iron bedstead in the spare bedroom and laid Margaret out there, but although it left the other bed free for Kitty she did not want to sleep in it, nor did she want to leave her mother on her own so as to stay overnight with Jessica, which had been offered. In the end Jessica said, 'All right then, I'll come and stay with you.'

And so over their cup of cocoa that evening, Kitty told Jessica about the contents of the letter.

Jessica was silent for a while, then she looked up. 'I must tell you right away, Kitty, that I knew nothing about the bigamy and although I knew about Richard Tierne I didn't know they had married. What she did tell me she begged me not to repeat to anyone.'

'So what happened after she left my – after she left Arthur Harvey?'

Jessica gave a deep sigh. 'She came to me one evening greatly distressed to tell me she was leaving him. I knew there had been a big row, I had heard Arthur shouting earlier when I passed the house. I thought she was leaving him because he had struck her, there was a bruise under her right eye. Mind you, this was unusual. Although she once confessed bitterly to me that sleeping with Arthur was like an animal mating, he was seldom violent towards her.

'Anyway, she told me she was going to take the children to their godmother who lived in Yorkshire. Bertha was a spinster who loved the girls; apparently she was only too pleased to have them to stay and when your mother wrote about this she also told me she had found a job as under-housemaid at a big house on the moors. Mrs Bramley was cook there at the time.'

Kitty looked up quickly. 'So that was where Mother met her. I wonder how much she told Mrs Bramley of what had happened.'

'Very little, I should imagine. Your mother kept things to herself. I didn't even know she had met Richard Tierne unexpectedly on the moors until she came back again to live with Arthur and that was six months later. She never mentioned him in the few letters I had from her.'

Kitty looked at her, puzzled. 'Why did she come back? We know now she was married to Richard Tierne . . . ?'

'She told me it was a necessity. She was in a terribly depressed state. Bertha had died, so there was no one to look after the children and your mother obviously had no money, because she said the only alternative would have been the poor-house and she wouldn't allow her daughters to suffer that indignity. Arthur took her back, welcomed her in fact – after all he had had no one to look after him.'

'He must have known I wasn't his child,' Kitty said, 'and that was why he hated me. Did *you* accept I was a premature baby, Jessica?'

'At first, yes, most people did, thinking that your mother's pregnancy was because of the reconciliation – *if* you can call it that. You were a small baby. It was only later, when I would catch your mother in unguarded moments looking at you with a world of love in her eyes, that I began to suspect. She had never looked at the other girls in quite that way.'

Tears blinded Kitty and she said in a broken voice, 'And I always thought she hated me because she gave me away.'

They sat in silence for a while. Then, when Kitty had her tears under control, she picked up the rest of her mother's letter and read it aloud:

On my afternoons off from my job I used to walk on the moors, and one afternoon who should I meet but Richard Tierne. How ordinary that must sound – I met Richard Tierne – but Kitty, it was as though the world had exploded into light. We stood staring at one another, then he held out his hands to me and said softly, 'This has to be fate.'

I thought so too. What else could it be? I came to work in a house on the moors, Richard had suddenly decided to visit friends and we both went for a walk at the same time, took the same path ...

How we talked that afternoon. When I told Richard the reason why I was working in Yorkshire, he said at once we must get married. I laughed at the idiocy, then told him it was impossible. But Richard thought anything was possible. We met after that for every moment I could get away, and I knew for the first time in my life the meaning of love between a man and a woman. Richard kept begging me to marry him and in the end I gave in. I handed in my notice to Mrs Bramley, simply saying I had to leave because of domestic problems. It was not until much later that I told her a part of my life. She was a good friend to me.

Richard rented a cottage on the moors, said we would have a three-week honeymoon and then go and collect the children. He had a house in town where we would live.

We walked on the moors, raced each other, laughed, talked and loved. Oh, Kitty, I wish you could have seen the roguish light in his eyes when he was teasing me, he was a great tease. But he had a very serious side to him too, yet whatever mood he was in we were gloriously happy. Later I was to wonder if the gods had decided we were too happy.

Our honeymoon extended to five weeks, neither of us wanting anything or anyone to intrude into our Eden.

Richard talked about his life. He told me how his parents had been in a boating accident and how they were both drowned. Although someone had rescued him he had been ill a long time, and it had left him with a weak chest. An aunt had brought him up and cosseted him. 'Smothered me with care and kindness,' he said. He told me he was not a wealthy man, but he could live comfortably on the money his parents and an uncle had willed to him.

One day we walked further than usual and a storm blew up. It deluged down, and by the time we got back to the cottage we were soaked to the skin, Richard shivering uncontrollably. By the evening he was feverish. I ran to a nearby farm to ask if someone could go for a doctor. The doctor was attending another patient miles away and it was four o'clock in the morning when he came. He did what he could, but it was too late.

I won't go into all the harrowing details, Kitty, I can only say I was ill with shock for a week. The only address in Richard's possession was the name of a solicitor in London. He was contacted and from him I learned that Richard's estate would pass to a first cousin who lived in New York. I didn't even query it, my grief was too intense. I didn't know at that time I was pregnant. When I did know, I took what money there was in the cottage – Richard had been generous with my housekeeping allowance – and I went to Bertha. She was not well, had not been well for some time but had not complained.

Two weeks later Bertha was dead. I just couldn't believe it. Her brother and wife came to take over the house and we had to leave. As Jessica would tell you, I came back to Arthur. I knew I could have gone to Abel and Harriet, but I felt they had done enough for me, more than enough. I had hurt them terribly when I ran away with Arthur. They had given me a home and love when I was a workhouse orphan. Yes, Kitty, I was brought up in an orphanage. I have no idea of my background.

You must have thought when I sent you to Harriet and

Abel that I didn't want you. I can tell you now that it was like tearing off a limb. I longed to see you, it was a constant ache. You were a child born of true love, Kitty. It was when I felt I had not long to live myself that I knew I had to see your dear face, have you with me if only for a while. And when you did come to live with me, I couldn't tell you just how much I loved you. Forgive me for that, Kitty.

I want you to read your father's letters so you will get to know him. He was such a sensitive man, attractive, of slender build. If I am honest, I think he lacked the strength that would make a woman depend on him in a difficult situation, but he was such a dear person, so loving, so caring. I hope I shall meet him when I leave this world.

God bless you, my dear, dear, daughter.

Your loving mother

Kitty was weeping before she had finished the letter, so was Jessica. Later Kitty said, 'If only she had talked about my father, she could have told me so much. How terrible that such a beautiful love could end in such a tragic way.'

Jessica got up, wiping her eyes. 'Read your father's letters,' she said gently. 'I'll go to bed and leave you – these are yours alone, not for others' ears.'

The fire had died down to a glimmer and in the creeping chill of the room Kitty began to feel unnerved. It was the silence, the knowledge that her mother was lying dead upstairs. It was not that the dead could do anyone any harm; it was more the mystery of death, the unknown. She gave a little shiver and took a letter from the envelope. Her mother had written on the top of it: 'Your father's first letter to me but not given to me until after we were married.'

Why is it, dear stranger, that when I picked you up from the icy road this evening, I should be so attracted to you? It was almost as if we had met in another life and were renewing our acquaintance. Were you aware of this, I wonder? There was a puzzlement in your lovely dark eyes. You were so light, a gentle leaf, trembling. Even when we stood apart I was aware of vibrations, passing from you to me. Would I have felt this had we not met in some other life? I was reluctant to let you go, but was forced to when I saw the fear in your eyes that we should be seen together by your husband. I pray we *shall* meet again, in circumstances in which we might be able to discuss this strange phenomenon.

I am your devoted slave,

Richard Tierne

Aware of vibrations in the sudden silence that morning, Kitty could understand how there could be vibrations between people who were attracted to one another. This was something, she realized now, that she had felt when she first met Tyler van Neilson.

Kitty brought out a second letter. This was written after her parents had been married a month.

My darling, I watched you this morning from the bedroom window as you stood listening to the bird-song. Your head was tipped back, your lovely dark hair a cloud round you. You were a part of the morning, a sprite. Dewdrops sparkled on the grass, and a single one was a jewel in a cobweb. You closed your eyes and there was a joyousness about you. It reminded me of one of the exquisite porcelain figures that my father used to fashion. It was his dearest wish that I followed in his footsteps, but alas I have not, and never have had, a creative bone in my body.

On reading this piece Kitty sat up. His father – *her* grandfather – a designer of beautiful porcelain figures? Was it from this unknown man that she had inherited her love of glass? If only her mother had talked to her before she died. Now she read the last part of the letter.

Dear heart, do you remember how I came down into the garden and, sweeping you into my arms, carried you back to our bed, which was still warm from our bodies, which are as one, and proved that the act of love can be as beautiful in the early morning sunshine as at night, with the romance of a room filled with moonlight. This memory will remain with me until the end of time.

Until the end of time ... Tears blurred Kitty's eyes. Were her parents now united? Or were they in limbo, destined never to meet again?

There was a poem at the end of the letter, written by someone called Lord Lytton:

A two-fold existence
I am where thou art.
Hark, hear in the distance
The beat of my heart.

Kitty stared at the now dead ashes in the grate and found herself thinking ... ashes to ashes, dust to dust. Then a faint glow appeared in the grate and from it a tiny flame spurted. It burned steadily and Kitty felt a beautiful warmth spreading through her. There must be an afterlife, this was a sign! True love like that could never die. She put the letter back in the envelope, knowing she could not read another one that evening.

Jessica was up first the next morning and when she came back after getting the milk from the milk cart, she brought in with her a gold and white kitten.

'It was mewing on the step,' she said. 'I've asked around, but no one seems to know who it belongs to. Poor little thing, I'll give it a saucer of milk.'

Kitty took it from her and put her cheek to the soft fur.

'It's like Punty, the kitten I had at the farm; it was the first animal I ever owned. I loved it so.' She put her little finger in the kitten's mouth and it sucked avidly. 'Ah, it is hungry, bless it.'

Jessica brought the milk and they sat watching the kitten lapping it up. When it had finished it licked the drops of milk from its whiskers and yawned hugely, showing a little pink tongue. Then, coming over to Kitty, the kitten looked up at her with such appeal that she said smiling, 'You know how to get attention, don't you?' and picking it up, she cradled it and began crooning the lullaby she had sung to the motherless lambs ... and to Punty so many years before.

Jessica said in surprise, 'Well! My mam taught you that lullaby. Do you remember the time? She made you a little doll and dressed it in a christening robe, and a bonnet and shawl. You said it was your baby and you wanted it to be christened. I forget what name you wanted it called. Christabel! That was it – wasn't it?'

Kitty's skin was crawling again. 'I don't remember.' She was still a few moments then, getting up, she laid the kitten on Jessica's lap and said she thought the fire was hot enough to do some toast.

She cut two slices of bread, speared one on the toasting fork and knelt down on the hearth-rug, conscious of Jessica being still too and watching her. Not wanting to answer any questions, Kitty said, 'I'll have to let Aunt Harriet and Uncle Abel know about Mother. They may not be able to come to the funeral, it's so far away, but I must give them the opportunity. How much will it cost to send a telegram?'

'Possibly a shilling, it depends on the number of words. You could send a letter for a penny.'

Kitty told her that it would have to be a telegram. She would write one out after breakfast and take it to the post office.

Suddenly there came the pungent smell of burned toast. With a despairing cry Kitty took the bread from the fork and jumping up, fetched a knife and began scraping off the burnt parts. Jessica came up and took bread and knife from her. 'Kitty, I don't know what it is that's upset you, but it's obviously something that happened when you were a child. What is it?'

'I don't know and I don't want to know, please don't ask me!'

'I must.' Jessica spoke sharply. 'If you keep it buried inside you, it could affect your future life.'

Kitty said in a piteous voice, *'Please, please*, Jessica, don't go on about it, not now! Perhaps later, when the funeral is over.'

'All right, love. I'll finish the toast, you write out your telegram.'

Kitty wrote in a shaky hand: 'Mother died yesterday. Funeral Wednesday. Love, Kitty.'

A reply came more quickly than Kitty would have thought possible. It said: 'Arriving Tuesday evening. Love, Uncle Abel.' When Kitty repeated the message, Jessica said she would make up a bed for him at her house.

Although Kitty was pleased to be seeing Abel, she could not help feeling a small twinge of disappointment that Luke would not be coming too. And yet, reason told her it would be difficult for both men to be away from the farm at the same time. And expensive as far as fares were concerned.

It was an emotional moment for all three of them when Abel arrived. He had not seen Jessica since the night she had brought Kitty to him at the Mealton weekly market. 'And thank God you did,' he said. 'We shall be eternally grateful to you for Kitty. She, like her mother, brought so much joy to our lives.'

Abel wept openly when he came down after paying his respects to Margaret. 'That poor girl, what she must have suffered at the hands of that Arthur Harvey. The man was a rogue for enticing her away from us. The only good thing I can say in his favour, if good it was, is that he did marry her.'

Jessica and Kitty exchanged glances, then Kitty said, 'Uncle Abel, there's something I must tell you. I'm sure Mother would want you all to know.'

When the story was told Abel looked drawn, his one thought centering on the bigamy committed and the agony of mind that Margaret must have suffered. Kitty then reminded him gently of the brief but happy marriage she had had with Richard, but Abel said, 'What was that, only a few weeks of her life? The rest was misery.'

Kitty thought. No, her mother had her memories of those weeks and they must have helped to sustain her.

Jessica then brought up the subject of Violet's claim of guardianship over the girls and her demand that they hand over their wages to her. Abel dismissed this as far as the older girls were concerned, but admitted he did not know how Kitty stood with regard to the law. 'But in any case,' he added, 'as we were foster-parents to Kitty for ten years, I think that would stand us in good stead. Kitty will travel back with me when I leave.'

This dismayed Kitty. As much as she loved them all, she wanted a different life from that of the farm. Already she had tasted another world and now that her mother was dead, there was an opportunity to go with Mrs Helder to Tyler van Neilson's house. But this was something she felt she could not discuss at that moment.

The funeral, the following morning, was at ten o'clock. Kitty went up at nine o'clock to say goodbye to her mother. In the dimmed room the waxen face had an ethereal beauty, a serenity that Kitty had not seen while her mother was alive. She shed no tears; her parents were together in their love.

Agnes did not come, as she had said, to read the letter. She arrived with Mary and Ann an hour before the cortège was to leave, Ann saying they had only two hours off from their work and would like to discuss the future with Violet. But Violet did not arrive until the hearse was at the door. Jessica said under her breath, 'Trust Violet to make an entrance!' Black became her and although Kitty knew she would never like her sister, she had to admire the dignified way she held herself. When she was introduced to Abel, she thanked him in a soft voice for taking such good care of Kitty. He said it had been a pleasure and Kitty had a feeling from the way he was looking at Violet that he was much impressed by her.

The five girls were to travel in the one carriage. Abel wanted, out of respect for Margaret, to walk behind with three men from the glassworks. Waiting to follow them was a surprising number of people, mostly women, but several men who were unemployed. Margaret had been well-liked.

When she came out of the house, Kitty felt a terrible bleakness at seeing the black horses, their black plumes and the hearse draped with black. The only brightness was in the bunches of Michaelmas daisies and the yellow button chrysanthemums that lay on the coffin.

Jessica had provided food for them to have when they came back from the cemetery. She had boiled a ham, made cakes and left two neighbours in charge who would have kettles boiled to make tea when they returned. It was a bitterly cold morning and Kitty hoped they could get all the mourners into Jessica's kitchen. They would need a hot drink after standing in the sleet-laden air at the graveside.

With time limited for Violet as well as her other sisters, Kitty suggested when they returned from the cemetery that they should go into her mother's house and discuss the future. Abel came with them.

The four girls, who were all prepared to do battle with Violet, had the wind taken out of their sails when she announced that as she was thinking of getting married – to a titled gentleman – it might be a good idea if Ann did get married too and could provide a home for her sisters when they had time off.

They all exchanged quick glances, then Ann asked Violet who

she was marrying. 'You wouldn't know him,' Violet's voice held a sadness. 'And, as Mother has just died, our wedding will have to be quiet. We shall probably be living abroad.' She tucked an escaped tendril of her golden hair behind her ear, smoothed it, then began to draw on her gloves. In a casual tone she said, 'Oh, by the way, Jessica spoke about Mother's will. I would like to know the contents before I leave, and I must leave quite soon.'

Kitty explained that it was merely to say that any money her mother might have left would have to be shared among them, but as there had been only coppers in her purse . . . She shrugged her shoulders.

For a split second Violet's eyes narrowed, then her expression was once more one of decorum as she asked about her mother's legal husband. 'Was he a man of – some substance?'

'He's dead.' Kitty could not keep a sharpness out of her voice. 'His estate went to a first cousin in New York.'

Now Violet's eyes widened in surprise. 'His estate? And he did not provide for Mother?'

'They were married only a few weeks.' It was Ann who answered. 'And I don't suppose he expected to die so suddenly. If there had been money, you would have had your share. Satisfied?'

'Of course.' Violet held out her hand to Abel. 'I'm sorry, but I really must go, Mr Leddenshaw. It's been nice meeting you, I'm sorry it was not under happier circumstances.'

'I am too.' Abel bowed slightly over her hand and Kitty thought despairingly, 'Oh, Abel, Abel, how could you be taken in by her?'

He watched her leave and when she had gone he rubbed a finger over his chin, looked thoughtfully from one to the other and said, 'She's a wily one, that sister of yours, she'll need to be watched.' Kitty felt a great relief.

Ann said, 'I wouldn't trust her as far as I could throw her, and I don't believe she's marrying any *titled gentleman* – she simply said it to impress. She's a liar, our Violet, always has been. There's something in her mind; I would like to know what it is.'

As none of them could offer any suggestions as to what this might be they went back to Jessica's and later, when the girls were preparing to leave, Ann told Kitty that she would let her know when she and Freddie were getting married; she would also let her know if they had any more trouble from Violet.

It was evening when Kitty made up her mind she must tell Abel she did not want to go back to the farm with him. It had to be done, she would wait until he came into the kitchen. At that moment he was in the scullery with Jessica mending a hinge on the cupboard door. They had been talking in low voices for some time.

Abel came back into the kitchen alone. Before Kitty could say anything, he began, 'Kitty I have something to say to you.' Drawing up a chair opposite to her, he sat studying her for a few moments, his expression solemn. Then he leaned forward, his large strong hands clasped on his knees. 'I've been talking to Jessica. She seems to think I'm being unfair to you by wanting you to come back to the farm.' Kitty's hopes soared. She waited. 'I know about this position you've been offered by this van Neilson fellow; Mrs Helder called to see us.'

'She did?'

Abel nodded. 'Mrs Earle came with her. She wanted to assure us you would be in good hands, should there be a chance of you taking the position. Harriet was agreeable, she thought it was an excellent opportunity for you, but I was against the idea.'

'But why, Uncle Abel? It's a chance in a million, I would never get such an opportunity again.'

'Yes, I know, Kitty. I was against it because of Mrs Helder saying she wanted you as a companion, but was hoping to teach you several languages, to teach you deportment – and I was afraid you would be absorbed into a different world that might change you.' Abel smiled sadly. 'I realize now I was terribly wrong; you would never change, Kitty.'

'Never, Uncle Abel,' Kitty said softly. 'I love you all too much for that.' She paused. 'And you will let me go with Mrs Helder?'

Abel nodded. 'Go to Stratton House. Mrs Earle will arrange everything with Mrs Bramley.' Jessica came in then and Abel got up. 'It's getting late. I'll go now and let you two get to bed. We'll have to be up early in the morning.'

Jessica went to see Abel into her house, saying she would not be long. Meanwhile Kitty, who had hoped to read some more of her father's letters, drew a sheet of paper from the envelope. It was creased, as though it had been crumpled up and then straightened. It was not a letter but scribblings of poetry, probably something her father had been trying to compose.

> I'll buy you a bonnet with roses on it
> And ribbons to tie up your hair—

This had a line crossed through it and there was the beginning of another verse.

> I'll buy you a gown of forget-me-not blue—

This line was followed by the words grew ... due ... hew ... A third attempt was:

> Do you know how much I care,
> Without you no day could start—

This too had a line through it and so had many other attempts. Then in capital letters Kitty read: DEAR HEART, I AM IN DESPAIR! WHY CAN I NOT EXPRESS MY LOVE IN VERSE AS THE POETS DO?

Kitty thought it must be wonderful to have a man love you so much he would go to all this trouble to express himself in words. How wonderful it would have been if she had seen her father only once, just to know if he liked her.

In spite of knowing about this beautiful love between her parents, and despite getting her wish to be companion to Mrs Helder, Kitty felt a sudden chill of apprehension ... And knew it had nothing to do with her parents but with her sister Violet. She was like a canker eating away into one's peace of mind.

Was there something underhand in her mind? Would she perhaps start probing in an effort to find out about Richard Tierne, and what his estate entailed? Could she cause trouble?

CHAPTER SIXTEEN

Kitty went to Stratton House the following morning with all manner of doubts plaguing her. Would the job as companion to Mrs Helder still be available? Tyler van Neilson could have changed his plans. All sorts of things could have happened. Who would have imagined when she left over a week ago to nurse her mother that Margaret would now be dead and buried! And if Tyler's plans had been changed, would Mrs Bramley be willing to have her back? It was all very well to say they would always find a job for her, but if hers had been filled ...

Mrs Bramley welcomed her back. No, the position had not been filled, they had heard about her mother's death. Kitty could fill in during the next two weeks anyway; there was plenty to do, guests were expected tomorrow and would be staying until after Christmas.

Kitty was wondering what would happen to her after the next two weeks were up when Mrs Bramley added, 'It would have been nice for you to be here for the festivities, but according to Mrs Helder you'll be spending Christmas at Mr van Neilson's house.'

Kitty's spirits lifted. It was going to be all right. They had not forgotten her.

Mrs Bramley asked Kitty about her mother – had she suffered much; and how many people had there been at the funeral; how many had walked behind the hearse – this being, she declared, a measure of respect for the dead. After Kitty had answered these questions Cook became brisk, 'Well, come along, girl, get changed and then go upstairs and help Ivy with the beds. There's plenty of work to be done!'

Ivy came out of a bedroom as Kitty went along the landing. A broad grin split her face. 'You're back! I aren't half glad, I've missed you, hasn't been the same without you.' She sobered suddenly. 'Sorry to hear about your Mam. Sudden, wasn't it?' Ivy picked up some clean linen from a pile on a table and took Kitty by the arm. 'Come on, we can talk while we make up the beds.'

While they stripped the bed in the next room, Ivy complained about Mrs Bramley. 'Been on the warpath, this week, accused me of wasting time. *Me*, wasting time! Cor – I've been doing the work of ten ... three anyway!'

Ivy unfolded a sheet, shook it out, threw one end across the bed for Kitty to catch and said, 'One afternoon when Clara had a bellyache, I had to make that funny tea for your Mrs Helder. Ain't she a lovely woman? Thinks the world of you, I could tell. I'm sure she was missing you too.'

When Kitty said she had not been sure whether Mrs Helder would have gone back with the girls she was chaperoning, Ivy snorted.

'Girls? Bitches I calls them. Good riddance, I say!' She unfolded another sheet. 'I heard that the mistress asked Mrs H. to come and stay here. I also heard that the old lady has royal blood in her, I don't know who from, Walton was telling old Ma Bramley. "Ain't it a shame," he says, "that Mrs H. has no home of her own, a nice lady like that. Lost all their money, they did. It wouldn't make any difference to us who has nothink, but to gentry like her ..."'

Kitty interrupted the flow to ask if Mrs Helder had mentioned a date for leaving, adding that Mrs Bramley thought it could be before Christmas. This had Ivy in the doldrums. She had been looking forward to the two of them being on duty together; it was the only fun there would be. In the next breath she said, her expression hopeful, that perhaps she could find a job in a house near van Neilson's.

Kitty smiled. 'That would be lovely, Ivy, we'll have to try and find you one.'

Later when Mrs Helder's bell rang and Kitty went up, the old lady held out her hands to her and said softly, 'How are you, my dear, you must have had a very harrowing time. I was so sorry to hear about your mother.'

Kitty found herself stupidly apologizing for not having had the chance to study any Italian. Mrs Helder soothed her – of course not, she had not expected it. Perhaps they would resume the lessons in the New Year. There might not be an opportunity before Christmas, there were so many plans to make.

As it turned out, any spare time Kitty had – which was very little – was spent with the dressmaker Mrs Helder had engaged to make her some clothes – as befitting her future position as companion.

There was to be only one black dress, Mrs Helder not holding with long terms of mourning, especially for young people. There were grey dresses for mornings, blouses and skirts for afternoons, dresses for evenings – simple styles, but in Kitty's eyes most attractive. As well as dresses there were two coats: one warm dark grey wool for every day, with a big shawl collar and a grey velvet hat; the other was in purple in a thick soft material, with a fur collar and a purple velvet hat to go with it. As well as these items there were boots and shoes and underwear, Mrs Helder saying that more clothes could be added later. Kitty was overwhelmed at what she already had and asked Mrs Helder if it was really necessary for more. As it was, she would be handing over her wages for years to come to pay for them.

At this, Mrs Helder set her mind at rest by saying that Mr van Neilson was paying for everything. He provided uniforms for all staff and considered all that had been provided for Kitty as uniform.

As the days flew by Kitty became more and more excited, not only because of seeing Tyler van Neilson again, but also the hope that he would carry out his promise to let her fashion an article of glass.

When the date was settled for leaving, Kitty asked if it was possible to have perhaps a couple of hours off to say goodbye to her three sisters and Jessica. Mrs Bramley told her she could go on the Sunday afternoon.

It seemed strange to Kitty to be going home and not to see her mother. How little she really knew of her; it was through her father's letters she was getting to know more. It seemed he was seeing into her secret soul, knowing her need to be wanted, her desperate need to be loved. But he was also aware of the need for humour too. There were lighter touches in several letters. At the

233

end of one she had read the night before was a poem that had made Kitty smile.

> If you become a nun, dear,
> A friar I shall be,
> In any cell you run, dear,
> Pray look behind for me.

How wonderful it would have been, Kitty thought, if her father had not died and they had made a life together, just the three of them. No, that was selfish. Her mother had the other girls to think about. And if she had lived with her parents, she would never have known Harriet and Abel or Luke. Although recently she had begun to feel closer to her mother, no one could take the place of her foster-family. No girl could have a more loving or caring home.

In the letter that had come that morning, in answer to hers telling them about the move, were notes from all three. Luke had concluded his by saying, 'Yesterday, when I was working in the top field I felt as though you were there, Kitty. I could hear you chattering away, teasing me, laughing. Although the miles separate us, you will always be in our hearts. Let us know how you like your new home. Love, Luke.'

Yes, it would be yet another home. Would she be like some nannies who spent most of their lives in other people's houses, seldom having a home of their own ... or a husband and children?

Oh heavens, Kitty smiled wryly. She was thinking as though she were sixty instead of sixteen! She had a whole life ahead of her. And Luke loved her.

When Kitty arrived home she found Jessica in the kitchen, trying to stir the dead-looking fire into some life. 'Oh, hello, Kitty.' She sounded worried. 'Ann's here, but Mary and Agnes are poorly.'

At the sound of footsteps overhead, Kitty looked towards the ceiling. 'Is that Ann? What's she doing upstairs?'

Jessica sighed and put the poker back in the hearth. 'Violet was here earlier, trying to stir up trouble. Here's Ann coming down now, she'll tell you about it.'

Ann greeted her. 'I'm glad you've come, Kitty. No doubt

Jessica's told you about our Violet. She says she has proof that Dad's wife was dead when he married Mam.'

'I don't believe it. Mother said she was alive at the time and I'd rather believe her than our Violet. What proof did she offer?'

Ann sighed. 'She had a letter; she wouldn't let me read it, because she said we wouldn't let *her* read Mam's letter. She told me she had found it in the bed-post.'

'Well, that's a lie!' Jessica exclaimed. 'You yourself, Ann, took the envelopes from the bed-post.'

'I know, and I thought I had them all then, but a few days ago it began to bother me that Mam should make a sort of will yet having nothing to leave, and I wondered if I had missed something. And so I came back. The bed-post was stuffed with pieces of newspaper, leaving room only at the top for Mam to put the package in. I did find a piece of paper, but there was only some poetry on it. Violet said she delved right down and made what she called her "discovery".'

'They're her words,' Jessica said. 'Knowing Violet, she could have written the letter herself.'

'She did find something else,' Ann said quietly. 'A photograph. She gave it to me, saying, "Let *dear* Kitty see it, tell her to take a good look at her mother's lover, because that's all he was".'

Kitty felt sick at having a beautiful love dirtied by someone as wicked as her sister. Ann held the photograph out to Kitty and she took it. She saw a tall, fair-haired man with an attractive, sensitive face. Then tears blurred any further impression of him.

Jessica said gently, 'Kitty love, it may not be your father. You know what your Violet is, she'd go to any lengths to make you believe she has a letter. The photograph could be one of a stranger.'

'I think it *is* my father,' Kitty said in a low voice. 'It's uncanny, but this is exactly as I pictured him.'

'I'm still prepared to argue,' Jessica said. 'Would your mother leave something so precious out of the package she left for you?'

There was a long silence after this, then Kitty sighed. 'Well, if there was no bigamous marriage it simply means I go back to being illegitimate and you four, Ann, are the legitimate ones. You can tell our Violet it's not bothering me one little bit. I'm only too pleased that Mother had some happiness and this beautiful love in her life. Nothing can alter that. So ... let's change the subject. I came to tell you that I'll be leaving the Earles in four days' time to start a new job.'

It was talking about this that helped Kitty over the doubts about her birth. Although she had said it didn't worry her, she wanted so much for her mother to have been married to Richard. She wanted their union to have been blessed, their honeymoon to have been a real one.

When Kitty got up half an hour later to leave, Ann said she would keep in touch, would let her know if there were any further moves from Violet.

Fortunately for Kitty there was so much to do during the next two days that there was no time to brood over recent happenings. Mrs Helder told her they would be travelling by carriage to Crescent House and this, Kitty felt, was something to look forward to.

On the morning they were leaving, she wore her best coat and hat. She had stitched a black armband on her coat, but Mrs Bramley thought she should have been wearing full mourning for her mother; anything less was being disrespectful to the dead. But she added, in a grudging way, 'I suppose you have to wear what you're told and I must admit you look a proper little lady.'

'And a very bonny one,' said Mr Walton, which was high praise indeed coming from him. 'Don't forget to write to Mrs Bramley and let her know how you are getting on in your new position. We wish you luck.'

There was only time to say a quick goodbye to the rest of the staff, give Ivy a brief hug and a whispered 'Hope you can get a job near to me,' before she was being urged upstairs by Mr Walton so as not to keep Mrs Helder waiting. Mrs Bramley called, a quiver in her voice, 'Be a good girl,' then seconds later Kitty was in the carriage.

When the carriage moved away she felt a sudden pang. She had been happy here. What was this new life to hold for her?

Any uncertainty Kitty felt about the change at that moment was dispelled by the luxury of the carriage. The morning was bitterly cold, but her hands were tucked into a fur muff – a pre-Christmas present from Mrs Helder – while there was a fur rug

236

over her knees and a foot-warmer.

Mrs Helder asked her once if she was comfortable, then afterwards was silent, no doubt also wondering about the change in her life. She had good friends, according to what Mrs Bramley had said the night before, but the only relatives were an estranged brother and his family. When Kitty asked if Mrs Helder had had children, Cook told her one daughter who unhappily had died when she was eight years old. 'A real tragedy,' she said. 'They doted on her. She showed me a miniature of the child – had a look of you, Kitty, that's probably why she's so taken with you. She's a good person is Mrs Helder; you do right by her and she'll do right by you.'

The big houses were now beginning to thin out and soon they came to groups of cottages, to farms; they met carts and men pushing barrows, and once a new-fangled motor car came chugging towards them. One of the horses neighed in fright. Mrs Helder must have gone to sleep, for she made no move.

Kitty found herself thinking of Luke. Twice in her letters she had asked about Louise, but he had never answered her questions. Perhaps he had avoided answering her purposely, knowing she was a little jealous.

Eventually Kitty began to doze. She had lain awake for ages the night before, and had been wide awake at four o'clock that morning, unable to go to sleep again.

It was a change in the air that roused her; they were climbing and it was becoming perceptibly colder. Mr Walton had mentioned that they would be going over the fells. 'Bleak land', he had called it. They were travelling the fells now. It was open land with rock formations, scrub, large patches of heather. A rabbit suddenly popped up, its whiskers twitching at the approach of the carriage; then it scampered away and was lost in a burrow. Pieces of dead bracken rolled over and over, carried along by the wind.

At the highest point the wind had a keening sound, it buffeted the carriage. Mrs Helder roused. 'Where are we?'

'On the fells, ma'am. Isn't it beautiful, so wild, so clean and fresh?'

Mrs Helder gave a wry smile. 'Beautiful to the young perhaps, Kitty, but to the older people it spells discomfort. I like the warmth, the hot sun of Spain, of Italy.' She settled back into her seat again and closed her eyes and Kitty thought she was probably dreaming of the wonderful places she had visited with her husband. It set Kitty thinking of her parents – something she had tried to avoid doing, not wanting to accept Violet's accusations.

When she had returned to Stratton House after seeing Ann and Jessica, she had studied the photograph of the man she felt sure was her father and found herself building him up in her mind as a man who would love passionately – being possessive in that love, wanting her mother with him every moment. But a caring man, sensitive to her every mood, looking after her if she felt unwell. A generous man who would want to give her the earth, but as her mother had suggested, who would not be a bulwark in a crisis.

Kitty did not want to think of her father as having any flaw, yet the common sense she had been taught at the farm told her that possessiveness could cause unhappiness. When she had been possessive of the kitten, Punty, and would never let it out of her sight, Harriet had told her gently that she must let it go free – a cat wanted to roam on its own. Eventually she had stopped grabbing hold of it every time it appeared and hugging it to death. In time Punty had been absorbed into the farming life and like the other cats on the farm had roamed and hunted. There had been a succession of kittens, but Punty remained in Kitty's mind as her favourite.

They left the fell road, dropped gradually to wooded land, then came to fields, to clusters of cottages, travelled along high-hedged lanes. It was then that Mrs Helder roused again and said they would soon see the house. 'You might find it strange at first, Kitty,' she said. 'Kirk van Neilson, a great-uncle of Tyler, built it. He was a very eccentric man, but I love the house – it's so different.'

They were driving now through forest land and when they came out into the open the house lay before them. Kitty sat up, feeling oddly excited.

It was brick-built, shaped like a crescent moon and had circular windows. At closer quarters Kitty felt awed by it. The massive front door of natural wood followed the deep inward curve of the house, and was covered with carvings. At either end of the house were two figures, a man and a woman, with evergreens planted in their oversized tub heads.

'It's like something from a fairy tale,' Kitty said in a whisper. As she spoke a woman in a black dress and white apron came out – quite an ordinary woman, Kitty was pleased to see. She bobbed a curtsy, introduced herself to Mrs Helder as Mrs Parker the housekeeper, explained that a boy had been sent to let Mr van Neilson know of their arrival then asked if the ladies would follow her.

They went into a half-circular hall – the walls and floor of unpolished oak – with a stone fireplace to the right and a staircase leading from the centre. The only furnishings were wooden settles at each side of the fireplace and a large tapestry above it.

They followed the housekeeper up a short flight of stairs and through a doorway that led into a passage with a domed ceiling which had several doors on either side. At the second door the woman stopped, said that this was Mrs Helder's room and the next room was the one Kitty would occupy. There was not one straight wall in either of them, but here the furnishings were a little more lavish. In Mrs Helder's bedroom the floor was scattered with sheepskin rugs; there were two in Kitty's room. Bedcovers were of quilted velvet, both in blue, while there were wall-hangings in brocade and some in tapestry. Bedheads were beautifully carved, chairs with curved arms had cushions of gold velvet, washstands had carved panels, the porcelain jug and ewer were hand-painted with grasses and flowers.

'A naturalist,' Mrs Helder said, smiling at Kitty. 'I hope we won't find the mattresses filled with straw.' The housekeeper assured them that they were feather-beds.

Two girls brought hot water for them to wash and when they were ready the housekeeper took them to the sitting-room which was circular with two unusual features: a floor to ceiling curved window spanning half the room and, in the centre of the floor, under circles of glass, were different species of foliage and flowers. Kitty did not know which to examine first, the vista from the window or the foliage and flowers. The view won. Above the tops of trees fields stretched into the distance to where hills, purple-shaded, were topped with snow. She turned to Mrs Helder. 'Oh, ma'am, isn't this wonderful, truly beautiful.'

The old lady came over. 'Yes, Kitty it is. I felt sure you would be as impressed as I was when I first came to the house.' Seats and sofas were grouped round the circles of glass, and on small tables were balls of glass containing roses in water. Kitty looked up, her eyes full of wonder, asking how the roses and water had got inside as there were no openings.

'I have no idea, Kitty. Perhaps it's an invention of Tyler's. He's a very clever man.'

'Thank you, Marguerite,' said Tyler van Neilson from behind them in his deep, pleasant voice. Kitty turned swiftly to see him smiling at them. She had pictured him many times in her mind, but had forgotten just how attractive he was. He was buttoning up a black velvet jacket as though he had just donned it and his dark hair was ruffled. Kitty's heart began to beat a little faster at the warmth of his smile.

He came over, took Mrs Helder by the shoulders and kissed her on each cheek. 'Dear Marguerite, how good it is to see you again!' Then he addressed Kitty, 'And you too, Kitty, I'm so glad Mrs Helder persuaded you to come with her. Did you have a good journey? What do you think of the house?'

'It's ... all wonderful, sir. I don't know what to look at first. These bowls of roses, how did you—?'

'I shall explain later. Here is Mrs Parker with tea.' The woman came in, put the tray on a side table, poured tea and handed round cakes. Then she left. Kitty could not take her gaze away from Tyler, who looked so animated as he answered Mrs Helder's question as to whether the laboratory was completed.

Tyler said Yes, and the furnace had been lit. Tomorrow he would take them both to see it.

Then he asked Mrs Helder about the Earles and mutual friends and Kitty took the opportunity to study the flowers and plants under glass. Never had she seen anything so beautiful, it was a study of colour and design. In the centre circle were nasturtium flowers in scarlet and flame and gold. Surrounding this were other circles of alternating leaves and flowers: pink campions, yellow celandines. Kitty slid off the edge of the chair and, dropping to her knees, ran a finger-tip over the glass. Then aware of a sudden silence, she looked up to find Tyler smiling at her. 'The glass is tough, Kitty, one can walk over it.'

'Oh,' she said in a breathless way. 'It's all so interesting, exciting!'

'I knew you would find it so,' Tyler spoke quietly. 'My great-uncle who built the house also made the glass for the floor and did all the carvings. The house was left to my godmother, who in turn left it to me. She is responsible for the wall hangings.'

Kitty thought she would never forget that first evening, sitting down to dinner in the oddly shaped room with the soft glow of lamps, being treated by Mrs Helder and Tyler van Neilson as a special guest. When she first put on the new evening dress of cinnamon silk with its taffeta underskirt, she had felt strange, out of her element, but when she began to walk in it she found the rustle gave her a feeling of importance, gave her confidence.

It was all so wonderful. And tomorrow she would see the laboratory where, with luck, she would attempt to fashion her first piece of glass.

CHAPTER SEVENTEEN

There had been no sign of any Christmas decorations in the house, but the next morning at breakfast Mrs Parker came in to say that two workmen were putting up a tree in the hall. Did Mrs Helder want to dress it or did she want Mrs Parker and the girls to do it? Mrs Helder said she would see to it, with the help of Miss Harvey.

It would be something to do, she told Kitty. Tyler would not be showing them over the laboratory until the afternoon. Tyler did not come down for breakfast, nor apparently was he coming in for lunch. Kitty, ever impatient, hoped he would not keep her waiting another day to have her glass-blowing lesson.

The tree was a huge one, nearly touching the ceiling, and Kitty enjoyed trimming it with Mrs Helder, especially as the old lady talked about her childhood and how she had spent some of her Christmases with her family in a hunting lodge in Switzerland. The sleigh-rides were what she enjoyed the most, she said, then added, 'Ah, for the lovely days of childhood. I particularly remember the Christmas when I was given a baby doll, I sat hugging it to me during this sleigh-ride and I—'

The bauble that Kitty was about to hang on the tree slipped from her fingers and lay shattered on the floor in a myriad blue and silver fragments. She found herself trembling and gripped the top of the step-ladder.

'It's all right, Kitty,' Mrs Helder said gently. 'It's just a bauble, accidents happen.' Then after a pause she came over. 'What is it, Kitty, what's wrong? Was it something I said?'

Kitty told her it was nothing, but the old lady would not accept this. She made her get down from the ladder, saying, 'I want to know what is wrong, it's no use telling me it's nothing.

When you know me better, you'll find out I'm a very determined woman. Now, tell me please!'

Kitty stood with bowed head a moment then looked up. 'It was when you ... mentioned a ... baby doll. It has something to do with when I was small, but I don't know what. And, ma'am, even if it could be explained I don't think I want to know.'

'You ought to try to find out what it was, Kitty. If you close a door on something unpleasant, it becomes a burden that could warp your life. But if you wish,' Mrs Helder patted her arm, 'that is one more thing we shall discuss in the New Year.'

It was after lunch when Tyler came to take them to the furnace room. The glow of the fire was visible before they came to the clearing in the forest where the furnace room and laboratory had been built, and Kitty could hear the sound of the furnace.

There were three men in the furnace room, an elderly man, a younger one and a boy whom Tyler introduced as his 'team'. He then said to the old man, 'William, the ladies would like to see a bowl or a bottle being made.'

William touched his cap in acknowledgment then, picking up a long blow iron, he dipped the end into the molten glass. Kitty had thought of this as picking up a blob of glass, but now remembered it was called a 'gather'. The whole process came back to her and she watched each step, fascinated: the glowing piece being rolled over the thick metal table to shape it, the old man sitting in the low wooden chair and rolling the iron backwards and forwards over the long arm, the shape growing. When the glass began to cool it was held in the furnace to make it more malleable, where it glowed once more with shades of gold and orange and red.

The boy then played his part, bringing a small gather on a punty rod to attach to the bottom of the bubble. Then William put water on the neck and, with a smart tap on the blow iron, the bubble was transferred to the punty and the end opened. After reheating it, William returned to the chair and used a tool to widen the opening.

Kitty, who had always been snatched away by Violet before she could see the final processing, now watched the young man tap the bowl free and, with gloved hands, carry it to the annealing kiln.

'Well,' said Mrs Helder, 'how very interesting! I know Kitty would like to try.'

Tyler said so she should but first they would go into the laboratory. After the heat of the furnace room the laboratory struck a chill. Kitty's gaze went first to a shelf where there were some beautiful pieces of coloured glass, a bowl in red and gold, an amber-coloured jug, a vase in emerald green which was deeply cut and a goblet shaded in blue and pink.

'Oh, sir, these are lovely!' Kitty enthused. 'How is the colour put in?'

'All in good time, Kitty. First you must know the basic ingredients for making glass.' He picked up various jars, showing her the ingredients: lime, soda ash, sand, red lead; then explained how other ingredients were added to get colours: antimonyoxide, arsenic, manganese, dioxide in small quantities and this is where the experimentation began.

Tyler talked quickly, one moment about blending colours and then the next about scientific experiments. He had spoken at some length about the merits of Isaac Newton when Mrs Helder interrupted.

'Tyler dear, I know that Isaac Newton was a very clever man, but I think it might be wise to let Kitty have a greater knowledge of glass-making before embarking on the world of the great scientists.'

He bowed his head. 'You're quite right, Marguerite.' To Kitty he added, 'Come along and be initiated into the art of glass-blowing.'

Kitty felt surprisingly calm now that the time had come and when she was handed the blow iron with the gather, she had an odd feeling it was something she had done before. She rolled the glass on the marver with so much confidence it brought a murmur from William of, 'Well done, girl!'

But when Kitty sat on the chair and made to roll the rod with her right hand, Tyler shouted, 'Left hand, Kitty, left hand, the rod is hot at this end!'

Even this in no way ruffled her. She went on with the procedures with the confidence of an old hand and it was not only the heat of the furnace that flushed her cheeks but Tyler's astonishment as he watched the bowl she had made being lifted into the kiln.

'It's unbelievable for a first attempt!' he declared. 'A fluke, surely. Try another one, Kitty.'

She made four altogether, proving her expertise had been no fluke, but although Tyler praised her she had a feeling he was not too pleased. When she mentioned this later to Mrs Helder, the old lady laughed. 'You shattered the proud masculine image that all men have of themselves, my dear. In Tyler's eyes you are his protégé; he wanted to initiate you into the mysteries of glass-making, wanted to show you that only an expert could do it and you knocked his feet from under him when you produced such excellent work.'

'Oh dear,' Kitty said, 'he might no longer be interested in teaching me any more. And perhaps what I did do today *was* a fluke. But . . .' she paused, then went on, 'the strangest thing was that I felt as if I had been doing this work for a long time.'

'You probably had in another life. I believe in reincarnation. But there, that is another subject. You needn't have any fears that Tyler will have lost interest in you. He has a vast knowledge of glass-making and will want to impart this knowledge, want to impress you. And, my dear, don't think any the less of him for that. My husband was just as proud, but I adored him.'

Kitty did not see Tyler again until breakfast time on Christmas Eve, and then he did not stay long. He was going to visit a friend who had a laboratory and also was very much interested in optical glass. He said he might stay overnight, but promised to be back the next day in time to have Christmas dinner with them.

When he had gone, Mrs Helder raised her shoulders. 'That is, if he remembers! When Tyler gets together with a colleague to do experiments he's apt to forget what day it is, let alone mealtimes.'

'Optical glass is such a dull subject,' Kitty said.

'To us, perhaps, but a boon to mankind. Think what has been achieved. Take the medical world, where men have been able to study germs under a microscope, learn the cause of illnesses. With the coming of spectacles people with poor sight could get about, could read. And think what a boon telescopes must have been to men who went to sea. There are so many benefits, too numerous to mention. It's not something I would want to study, but I can understand men like Tyler becoming absorbed in the work. And now, Kitty, what are *we* going to study today?'

The day was cold with light flurries of snow and in the evening they sat over a roaring fire while Mrs Helder reminisced about her younger days. 'I was such a rebel,' the old lady said, 'the despair of my mother. I ran away to get married when I was sixteen.'

'You did? So did my mother.' The words were out before Kitty could stop herself. But once she had mentioned it she felt it would be a relief to talk about her parents. And she told the story, concluding with the letters found after her mother's death and the consequences.

Mrs Helder said, 'I'm so glad you've told me this, Kitty. Now I can understand many things about you that have puzzled me. I've seen you pensive, wistful, happy when you are going to visit your foster-parents – and at times I've seen fear lurking in your eyes. There are a great many things to be thought over; I shall go into it and we shall talk later. Perhaps after Christmas.' She leaned over and touched Kitty's hand, adding gently, 'But let me say one thing now. If your mother's second marriage is not valid, it will make no difference to me whatsoever.'

Kitty thanked her for being so understanding and the old lady said she had been deeply moved by her parents' story, their love for one another.

Carol-singers came later and when Kitty heard the sweet treble notes of a young boy, she felt a wave of homesickness sweep over her. She wanted to be back at the farm, going to midnight service with Harriet and Abel and Luke. But then she thought of all she had achieved since she had left and knew that if she did go back, it would not be to stay.

Kitty was getting ready to go to church with Mrs Helder the next morning when Tyler arrived back unexpectedly and told them they were not to go out. Fierce storms were on the way; a forester and a shepherd had told him and the warnings of these people were not to be ignored. Kitty agreed; Abel could always forecast a storm by the behaviour of the animals.

When Mrs Helder said she really would like to go to church and pointed out that there were still only flurries of snow, Tyler spoke firmly to her. 'I was told the storm would come up suddenly, perhaps at hurricane force. You might get to church, but you might not get back. I'm going out to check the woodpiles. I've brought men with me to make a covered path to the laboratory – if we are to be marooned for days, I must work.' Tyler left then and Mrs Helder looked at Kitty in dismay.

'Oh, dear, I'm not going to like this.'

An hour later the storm started. The wind came suddenly, blowing at gale force, driving clouds of snow into great whirlwinds. Mrs Helder and Kitty stood at the window watching. There was something terrifying yet awe-inspiring about the wildness. In another half-hour it was dark – it was like the end of the world, Mrs Helder said, shivering as she described the screaming of the wind as being like a thousand knife-waving dervishes. They left the window and came to the fire. Kitty lit all the lamps.

A short while later Tyler came striding in, snowflakes in his dark windblown hair and on his shoulders. He shook himself. 'It's magnificent, but frightening. I could hardly battle my way to the back door. We do have everything movable lashed down and the men have managed to erect a covered path to the laboratory. It is somewhat sheltered in the forest; it may hold.'

It was a strange day when it was impossible to settle to anything, not even to reading. Tyler was in and out, checking to see that everything was all right. He said once to Kitty, 'If we are marooned for several days I shall take you to the laboratory, perhaps you can have another try at glass-making.' Which had Kitty feeling in a seventh heaven and hoping the storm would continue.

The storm raged for five hours before dying down. By then there were drifts ten feet high. In the lull Mrs Helder relaxed and talked about escaping to the sun. She felt constantly chilled during cold weather, even though the house was warm. By early evening the wind blew up again, at times moaning and at others screaming in its fury.

They sat down to a traditional Christmas dinner of roast turkey and plum pudding. Tyler talked about engraving scenes on glass and showed Kitty an example of a winter scene, with towering snow-covered mountains and frozen lakes. Kitty was intrigued, but Mrs Helder scolded him for constantly talking about his work. He apologized and asked her amiably what she would like to discuss. She shrugged her shoulders. 'Oh, warmer climes – Spain, Italy, preferably Italy!'

Tyler laughed. 'So now I know why you are teaching Kitty Italian. You are planning a holiday. Well, that will have to be for the future. At the moment I would say we'll be lucky if we can get out of doors.'

Kitty only hoped that a path could be kept open to the laboratory.

After dinner Tyler handed her a parcel. 'Just a small Christmas gift,' he said. Kitty knew that Mrs Helder had been given a fur stole by Tyler, but had not expected anything herself. When she took off the wrapping she found a gossamer-fine cream shawl with traceries of gold and silver. She looked up. 'Oh, Mr van Neilson, sir, it's beautiful, so soft, so warm. Thank you very much.'

He got up. 'Here, let me put it on for you, it will keep out the draughts.' He draped it about her shoulders and when his fingers touched her throat she felt a pleasurable tremor go through her. 'I'm glad you like it, Kitty,' he said softly.

Kitty thought it was one of the happiest evenings she had ever spent. Tyler stayed with them and he and Mrs Helder talked about the various countries they had visited. Once he talked about Russian glass and Mrs Helder made no protest. She followed by speaking of a group of mountains in Italy called 'the Glass Mountains' because of their jagged peaks and went on to describe them.

When Kitty went to bed that night she lay awake for a long time, listening to the fury of the storm, yet not worrying about it. Every now and again she would draw the gossamer shawl on her pillow against her cheek, thinking how Tyler had looked at her. And although she knew that nothing could come of it, still it was lovely to dream about him.

During the night the storm roused her, its fury seeming to increase until it was in her head. In a state between waking and sleeping, she could see Violet on a snowy day chasing her up the street, threatening what she would do to her when she caught her. Then Kitty was in one of her nightmares, being chased up a mountain by giant baby dolls with ugly faces who reached out at her with talons. She kept slipping on the ice and when one of the dolls got the talons in her hair she wakened herself screaming with the pain.

When arms went around her, she moaned, 'Oh, please don't hurt me!'

'You're all right, Kitty darling, you're safe now.'

'Oh, Luke,' she whispered, 'I had one of my nightmares.'

She was lifted out of the bed, a cheek was laid against hers and then a blanket was being wrapped around her and a woman's voice said, 'Bring her into my room.'

Then Kitty knew it was not Luke who had called her darling, nor Aunt Harriet who had wrapped a blanket around her.

When, the next morning neither Tyler nor Mrs Helder mentioned the nightmare, Kitty wondered whether this was done purposely so as not to remind her of it, or whether Tyler holding her in his arms and calling her his darling had been an extension of the dream.

The storm had died down and after breakfast Tyler suggested that Kitty went with him to the laboratory before it started up again, as he had been told it would later. He would come back for her in twenty minutes.

Kitty was ready when Tyler came for her. He asked if she was well wrapped up and when she made to put on a scarf he took it from her, wrapped it twice round her throat, looped the end and then ran the back of his fingertips over her cheek and smiled.

'You look like a little girl who's going for her first sleigh-ride, half-fearful, half-joyful.'

'And this is how I feel, sir,' she said.

After Mrs Helder had warned Tyler not to keep Kitty too long, they left, stepping out at the back of the house into a dazzling world of white. Although it all looked so calm a capricious wind stung Kitty's cheeks. A path had been cleared from the back door across to the trees, the snow piled shoulder-high on either side. Against the wall of the house the snow had drifted to such a height that it hid every pile of logs and covered the ground-floor windows.

When they went into the forest there was a vault-like silence. A layer of white covered the rich dark loam, the exposed roots of trees and the branches of the fir trees, creating a scene that Kitty found movingly beautiful. Even the man-made buildings had acquired a beauty, the beehive-shaped laboratory looking like an igloo.

William and his 'team' had been there all night, food apparently having been sent to them from the house. He and Tyler talked about the storm, then Tyler said, 'Yes, well now, Kitty, you said you would like to know how a twist is put into the glass. William will show you how to make a candlestick, then you can try your hand at it.'

She made one that drew praise from both men and Tyler said, 'You must have an ancestor who was in this trade; it seems to come naturally to you.'

Kitty was suddenly still. Then, aware that Tyler was watching her, she told him she thought there was someone, a man who had produced delicate porcelain figures.

'That explains it,' he said. 'You have an inherited gift.' He added on a teasing note, 'Who knows, you may make a master glass-blower one day and be in competition with me, or . . . be my partner!'

William said, 'Storm's beginning to blow up again, sir, it might be wise to leave before it gets too bad.'

'You're right, William. I'll see you get food, no matter how bad the weather. Come along, Kitty.'

It was not too bad in the shelter of the trees, but once they reached the open Kitty gasped at the ferocity of the wind and would have come to a standstill had it not been for Tyler's strength. With an arm around her waist they reached the back door and once inside he slammed it and stood laughing. 'It's a demon, but we beat it! You run upstairs and get warm, I want to see Mrs Parker. Tell Marguerite I'll be with you both for lunch.'

Kitty passed on the message to Mrs Helder, told her about making the candlestick, about being praised by Thomas and the 'master' and about the strength of the wind. She held out her hands to the glowing fire. 'But it was lovely, invigorating.' Mrs Helder shuddered.

During the next few days the weather alternated between snow blizzards and calms when a weak sun made diamonds of snow particles, turning everything into a fairy-tale world. Every road was impassable and in this isolation Kitty grew close to Mrs Helder and Tyler.

Every now and then the old lady would 'escape' from the whiteness, taking Kitty with her across the sea to colour and warmth and music. She spoke of a home she once had, a beautiful villa on the outskirts of Rome, built on the slopes – a villa with a tall-columned portico, cool rooms with art treasures, mosaic floors. She described the stepped slopes of vines, the gardens, pink bougainvillea spilling over arches and trellis, the one-time Roman bath converted to a swimming pool with its blue and green mosaic floor and sides giving the water ever-changing colours.

Kitty 'strolled' with the old lady under colonnaded arches around the pool, basked on sun porches partly shaded by canopies of trailing greenery. On all these 'excursions' Mrs Helder and Kitty were alone. But in bed at night Kitty, in her imagination, would walk in the gardens with Tyler's arm around her, the moonlight touching flowers and greenery with silver.

At times her imagination would run riot and Tyler would draw her close, kiss her passionately and call her darling. But in these fantasies he never told her he loved her; it was always that he needed her, she inspired him in his work.

There were moments when Kitty would feel self-conscious about these fantasies, calling herself a fool – Tyler would never be kissing her passionately, they lived in different worlds. But then, deep down she would think of her parents and their beautiful love story, and would know that anything was possible in life.

After a week of being 'snowed under' a thaw set in, with the consequent drip-drip from eaves – a depressing sound to Kitty, who had enjoyed being cocooned in her world of white. During that week she had improved tremendously with her Italian, read poetry with Mrs Helder, made several glass bowls, three goblets and a jug, and been complimented by Tyler on her expertise. 'You should have been a man, Kitty,' he said to her one day.

And Kitty, with perhaps her first touch of coquetry, replied, 'I would rather be a girl, sir!'

He laughed. 'Oh, Kitty, you are delightful, such a joy to be with.'

Sober now, she asked, 'Are there no women master glass-blowers?'

Tyler nodded slowly. 'Yes, there are; I know personally of three in Germany and two in France. There are others but I can tell you this; men do not like working with women.'

'Why not? Mrs Helder said that there are now women

working in offices as secretaries and in other commercial ventures.'

Tyler said that might be so. There was also a body of 'suffragettes' who were fighting to get votes for women, but he did not agree with it. His tone was sharp, dismissive, and Kitty decided she must be careful about mentioning such a thing again, or Tyler might take it in his head to bar her from working with him.

CHAPTER EIGHTEEN

Once the thaw had really set in, streams were beginning to run again and roads opening up, Mrs Helder said one evening at dinner, 'Tyler, after all this enforced imprisonment I need my mind stretched.'

He looked at her in surprise. 'But Marguerite, I thought you said you enjoyed the quiet of the countryside?'

Mrs Helder nodded. 'I do, but I need variety. My mother once told me when I was young that I was a very confused person, because I told her I would like to go into a nunnery on condition that I could be freed every so often to have a social life.' Mrs Helder smiled. 'A wild one!'

Tyler laughed. 'I couldn't imagine you in the cloisters, Marguerite, not even for a few weeks. So how do you want to stretch your mind? Would a visit to London help? I am planning to go in about ten days' time. I have some business to attend to.'

'Oh, that will be splendid, Tyler! While you are conducting your business, Kitty and I can look around the shops. I noticed in *The Times* that a big new store called Selfridges will be opening soon. This year is also Harrods' Diamond Jubilee; they are going to have afternoon concerts to seat over a thousand people and also hold fashion shows, so we would be kept occupied.'

While Mrs Helder and Tyler discussed a date for leaving and a choice of hotels, Kitty sat looking from one to the other with a wide-eyed wonder. London? Mrs Bramley had once worked in London and told her about Buckingham Palace, the Houses of Parliament, the 'Bloody Tower', and how wonderful it all was.

But the London that Mrs Helder described later was totally different from that of Mrs Bramley. They would go to art galleries, to the theatre, look at fashions. Kitty must have some new clothes. She would pay for them . . . yes, yes, she insisted as Kitty tried to protest. They would be staying at the Savoy and she did not want Kitty to look like a poor relation. She would introduce her as her ward, so she must stop calling her 'ma'am' and stop calling Tyler 'sir'.

Kitty lived in a state of excitement at the proposed trip and when Mrs Helder took her rest in the afternoon she was so restless she asked Tyler's permission to go to the furnace room. 'I won't interrupt the men,' she said. 'I won't talk, I'll just watch.'

'Is that possible?' Tyler asked, smiling. 'You may go, but don't ask to make anything, the men are working on something special for me.'

Kitty promised and was away at once in case he changed his mind. She arrived at the furnace room breathless. Thomas touched his cap to her and Kitty explained her reason for being there, promising she would not get in the way. William, who had seemed to be rather a dour man, said, 'You won't be in our way, miss, and you can ask what you like. It's the only way you'll learn. That there is Thomas and the lad's name is Ben.'

With these few words the old man made Kitty a part of their team. Then he took her to a small room she had not been in before and showed her what they were making: goblets in shades of blue and green, with clear crystal ornamentation on the stems which William said were called prunts. 'Oh, they're beautiful!' Kitty cried. William said they were making more, she had better come and watch.

And so Kitty was initiated into the making of coloured goblets. There were two pots of melt in the furnace, a blue and a green. Thomas took a gather from each one and it was his expertise that blended the colours, with Thomas and Ben playing their parts. Kitty was intrigued that the same blending produced different shadings.

'Want to have a try?' William asked. 'What the eye don't see, it can't grieve over!'

Kitty felt she ought to refuse, but with the wilfulness of her childhood she said, 'Yes I would – just one.'

She was not quite so assured as she had been previously and made her first mistake when she allowed the blob to drop into an elongated shape. William immediately told her to throw it around the rod, then Ben was there with a wooden box under it with William instructing her to keep the glass rolling. The result was a pot-bellied bowl, the green predominating in feathery fronds, giving the impression of an underwater cavern. It was her best work yet and William's praise gave her a warm glow that was not from the heat of the furnace.

She watched them working and William talked about glass-making terms as he worked. Later he showed her different kinds of candlesticks, naming them all. He also showed her a variety of glasses, putting names to stems and bowls. Kitty repeated these in an effort to memorize them.

When at last she knew she must go, William told her he would keep her goblet in a 'safe' place for her. He winked and tapped the side of his nose, thereby establishing a rapport of secrecy between them. Kitty smiled and nodded.

She walked back to the house going over all she had learned – the reason for glass exploding, warping, temperatures of the furnace and annealing oven.

Tyler came in for dinner that evening and after mentioning various items of domestic affairs to Mrs Helder, he turned to Kitty.

'Oh, yes, how did you get on with William this afternoon, Kitty?'

'Very well, he's an excellent teacher. He can talk and work at the same time. I had no idea, for instance, that there were so many types of stems and bowls of glasses.' Kitty, wanting to show off a little, reeled them off: 'Incised twist, opaque and colour twist, single corkscrew and trumpet-shaped bowls, funnel, ogee, thistle, bucket—'

Tyler held up a hand, laughing, 'Enough! The variety of designs could go on for an hour.'

'Yes,' she said. 'I had just started. There are lovely names for goblets: bun-shaped, stirrup, three-necked, honeycomb moulded—'

'Kitty ...' Mrs Helder gave her a warning glance. 'You've been told ...'

Realizing she had gone too far, Kitty apologized to Tyler.

255

'It's just that it's all so exciting,' she said. 'I felt if I kept repeating the names I wouldn't forget. I'll have to say them in bed tonight.'

'It's a good place, Kitty. Incidentally, I don't want you to go there tomorrow. I shall be there with business friends.'

As it turned out, Kitty would not have wanted to go for the following morning she had two letters – one from Luke and one from her sister Ann. Luke's letter was in answer to hers telling them about her new life, the strange house and how they had been marooned by the storms. He said the storms had caused great inconvenience at the farm; he told her they were pleased she was settling down where she was and that he was glad she had such an interesting employer and was learning to make glass. He concluded by saying his mother had a heavy cold, but was improving. They all sent their love and asked her to write again soon. The letter was signed simply: 'Luke'.

Kitty had a feeling of being let down. It was not Luke's usual chatty letter and he had not sent his love separately.

She puzzled over this until she began to realize how much she had talked about Tyler in her letter. She had said what a wonderful man he was and how easy it was to talk to him. She had told Luke about the proposed trip to London, the new clothes. She had talked a lot about Tyler ... too much.

Kitty found herself trembling. Luke must have felt as she had done when she had seen him and Louise together. She must do something, write another letter and explain. No, that would make it worse.

And yet, the more she thought about the letter the more she realised that it was not his way to be cool with her. He would have teased her about Tyler, told her to beware of falling in love with her employer. Had Harriet been more ill than he had mentioned and had he been worried about her? Harriet had not enclosed a note, nor had Abel. She must know the truth; she would write again and beg for a quick reply.

Ann's letter was to tell her that Violet was indeed getting married. Not to a titled gentleman, as she had boasted, but to a wealthy man who was eighty and in his dotage – this according to Jessica. 'Violet told us herself he can't live very long,' Ann wrote, 'and when he dies she's going to travel the world. Good luck to her! I only hope it's the last we'll see of our *dear* sister!

Freddie and I are planning to get married as soon as possible. We've been promised a house to rent in Elm Street. None of us want to stay on in Mam's house, it has too many unhappy memories.'

Whenever Violet's name was mentioned, Kitty had a feeling of chill. She wondered how her sister would react if proof was given that *she* was illegitimate. Perhaps she still would not accept it.

Kitty saw no hope of getting to Ann's and Freddie's wedding. Apart from the cost of the rail fare, they could be in London then.

Although Kitty tried desperately to hide her worry, the discerning Mrs Helder was soon asking what was wrong. Kitty centred her problem on Harriet – was she more ill than Luke had mentioned? The old lady soothed her. Kitty was forgetting that farmers must have had a load of worry on their minds through storm damage. Luke most likely had to *make* time to write her a few lines.

By return post Luke confirmed this. He was so sorry he had upset Kitty; his mother *really* was much better and she was not to worry. Yes, there had been storm havoc, barn roofs ripped off by the gales. He and his father had worked like Trojans to get the repairs done. Both his mother and father would be writing to her later. 'Love, Luke', he ended.

The 'Love, Luke' settled Kitty. Now she could go to London with an easy mind. There were only three days before they left.

But the following morning the London visit was cancelled, Mrs Helder having received a telegram to say that her brother in Scotland was seriously ill and was asking to see her. Because of the circumstances, Kitty did her best to hide her disappointment about the trip.

Mrs Helder, distressed, said to Tyler, 'I must leave as soon as possible. My brother and I have been estranged for years and it would grieve me if we were not able to make our peace with one another. Will you accompany me, Tyler?'

He said, Yes, of course. If Kitty would start packing he would look up the times of the trains. He was at the door when Mrs Helder called him back. 'Will you look up the times of the Leicester trains too? Kitty's foster-mother has been ill and she's been worried about her. I think it would be sensible for her to go and see her rather than travel all the way to Scotland to a house of sickness – and misery, which is what my brother's house has always been.' To Kitty she added, 'Can you manage the journey on your own?'

'Oh, yes – yes, I can, Mrs Helder, ma'am. I travelled from Leicester up North.'

'Good,' Mrs Helder said, 'then that is settled.' Tyler came in at that moment to say there was a difference of only twenty minutes between their trains, so they could all travel to the station together.

But a delay on the way to the station caused by a flock of sheep blocking a narrow road left Kitty with only seconds to spare to board the train. Breathless, she called goodbyes from the lowered window. Mrs Helder promised to write and Tyler called to her to look after herself. Then the train was on the move. When it gathered speed, Kitty sank into her seat.

In spite of the luxury of travelling first class at Tyler's expense, and having a meal in the dining-car, the journey dragged. Kitty found herself going back over her life from the time when her mother came to take her away from the farm, and thought how many things had happened since then. She was so impatient to see them at the farm that the drive from Leicester station seemed to be the longest part of the journey.

But at last the lighted windows of the farm came into view and all her exhaustion vanished. It was Abel who came out as the carriage drew up and the next moment Kitty was out and shouting, 'Uncle Abel, Uncle Abel!'

'Kitty!' He stood staring at her in utter astonishment, then his strong arms went around her. 'What's brought *you* here? I though you were going to London.'

'We were, but ...' She explained what had happened, then looked towards the kitchen window. 'Where's Aunt Harriet? I thought she would have been the first one out at the sound of the carriage.'

After a short pause, Abel said, 'Harriet is in hospital, love. Now you're not to get upset. She had a fall and hurt her back, but she's on the mend. Luke's out at the moment, but he'll be here soon. Come on, let's get you a cup of tea and something to eat; I expect you'll be famished after that long journey.'

The cosiness of the kitchen, the sight of the blazing fire and the cat stretched out on the rug brought a lump to Kitty's throat. She was home, but it was not the same without Harriet bustling around. Abel, who was making tea, began to talk about the fall. 'She was on her way to her sister's when she slipped and fell. It was right outside the Cottage Hospital, so they took her in there. But she's improving and we're managing all right, managing fine.'

Abel's over-bright tone worried Kitty. She went to him.

'Uncle Abel, you're not trying to keep anything from me, are you? Aunt Harriet is going to be all right?'

Abel put the teapot on the table. 'Yes, she is, Kitty, but I must admit it was a worry at first when we found she couldn't walk. But she's improving, she was up and walking for a few minutes last night when I visited. Now, what can I get you to eat?'

The sound of footsteps outside had them both looking up. Kitty's heart began to race. Luke!

When he came in she stood, expectant, waiting for his shout of surprise, waiting to be lifted off her feet and swung around. But he stood staring at her.

'What are you doing here, Kitty?'

She looked in bewilderment from Luke to Abel. 'What's the matter, what's wrong? It's Aunt Harriet – isn't it?' Her voice rose. 'You lied to me, she's worse than what you told me!'

'No, Kitty,' Abel said quietly. 'I told you the truth. It's just that ... well, other things have happened. I'll leave Luke to tell you.' He went out.

Luke drew up two chairs. 'Sit down, Kitty.' He sat opposite to her, his expression sombre. 'You took me by surprise, seeing you standing there. I was going to write and tell you. It's about Louise – we're ... going to be married.'

Married? In the heat of the room Kitty felt a numbing cold steal over her, a coldness worse than any she had ever experienced before. 'When?'

'In two weeks' time – quietly.' There was a sorrow now in his eyes and Kitty realized then the reason for it. He *had* to marry Louise!

The man was usually blamed for getting a girl into trouble, but in this case Kitty blamed herself. She had gone away, Luke missed her, was lonely and now – he was faced with living with a girl he didn't love for the rest of his life.

259

But when Luke began talking about Louise, Kitty got her second shock. He did love her, they wanted the baby, they would be living with his parents, Louise would be a big help and Harriet was looking forward to having another grandchild.

Kitty sat looking at Luke's copper-coloured hair which had taken on warm russet tones in the lamplight, and ached so much she wondered why she was not crying.

'So you've never really loved me,' she said, the words ending on a sudden strangled sob.

'Oh, Kitty, don't, please!' Luke touched her hand. 'I do love you, but in a different way. You've always been someone special to me. It's difficult to explain, but even if I could I don't think I would want to. Love shouldn't have to be explained.'

She wanted to tell him he was weak, but she knew this wasn't true. It was his strength which had sustained her through her nightmares, had helped her to understand her mother's need when she had come to claim her. From the time she first came to the farm, he had always been there when she needed him, a bulwark.

Kitty began to cry then, hopelessly, helplessly and was unable to stop. She was aware of Abel putting a cup of tea in her hands and saying gently, 'Drink this, Kitty.' She could smell the brandy in it, Harriet's cure for all ills. But how could a teaspoonful of brandy cure her of what ailed her at this moment?

Then Abel was saying, 'Luke, go and fetch Mrs Webster, Kitty will have to be undressed and put to bed. Just say she got a shock hearing about Harriet.'

When the neighbour came, Kitty offered no resistance. She wanted to be in bed where she could nurse her wounds. Luke carried her upstairs and before he laid her down he put his cheek against hers. Then a woman's hands took over.

*

It was daylight when Kitty awoke. Although there was a tight knot of misery inside her, she made up her mind she would try to accept the situation if only for Harriet's and Abel's sake. She washed and dressed, went downstairs and found Louise clearing away the breakfast pots.

Louise looked up. 'Oh, Kitty, I was going to bring some

breakfast up to you. Luke said to let you lie in. I'll make you some now.'

Kitty resented the fact that Louise had taken over Harriet's role. She wanted to say, 'Don't bother,' but instead she congratulated Louise on her engagement to Luke. In spite of her resolution she could not keep the coldness from her voice, however.

'Thank you,' Louise said quietly. 'I would rather that things had been different, but it's done and there it is. I'll cook you some bacon and egg and make some tea. Then I'll have a cup with you. I want to know all the things the men like to eat. I know Luke likes steak and kidney puddings. I only hope he doesn't say they aren't exactly like the ones his mother makes.'

'Well, you know what to do if he does,' Kitty said, her tone still cold.

Louise gave a little giggle. 'Yes, he'll get the pudding over his head, basin and all!'

Suddenly they were both laughing together, the ice broken, and Kitty wondered how she could ever have hated this gentle girl with the infectious laugh.

Later Kitty walked across the fields to the little Cottage Hospital, where she was told that Harriet was expecting her. Abel had apparently called earlier to let them know. The nurse pointed out Harriet's room, then warned her not to stay too long because the doctor was expected soon.

Harriet was lying back on the pillows with her eyes closed. Her greying hair was neatly plaited and although there was a pallor to the weatherbeaten face there was still the remembered plumpness. Kitty felt a wave of love sweep over her as she crept forward; she had reached the bed when Harriet's lids flew open.

'Oh, Kitty!' she held out her arms. 'To think you had to come to all this trouble!' They were both tearful, Kitty trying desperately to assume a scolding air.

'And what have you been doing?' she demanded. 'Rushing all over the place as usual, I suppose?'

'No, I simply tripped and fell. The doctor said I've done something to my back, but he promised I'll soon be better. Oh, Kitty, I want to be home, I keep worrying about—'

261

'Then you can stop worrying, Louise is coping marvellously. She's a lovely girl.'

Harriet's eyes suddenly filled with tears again. 'I'm sorry, love, I know how you feel about Luke.'

'But it hasn't to be, Aunt Harriet, has it?' Kitty said softly. 'I'm glad it's Louise he's going to marry. You'll get on fine with her, she's so funny.' Kitty told her about the steak and kidney pudding, then they were both laughing.

Harriet then asked about Mrs Helder and Mr van Neilson and by that time the nurse was looking in to say the doctor was on his rounds. Kitty left with the promise to call again soon.

She was not looking forward to facing Luke after her hysterical outburst of the night before and was dismayed to find herself alone with him for the midday meal. Louise had prepared it, then told Kitty she would just slip over to see her aunt for half an hour. And as Luke said that Abel was busy with a job, Kitty served up the food.

To her relief, Luke's manner was as easy as if nothing had happened. He asked about his mother, chatted about farming affairs and then asked Kitty what her plans were. Would she be going back to the van Neilson house?

'Oh, yes,' she said. 'Mrs Helder will let me know when they'll be returning. It was all such a rush when she had word about her brother. I only hope she arrived in time to make up her quarrel with him. Apparently they fell out years ago. It made me realize how foolish it is to fall out with anyone. We never know what's going to happen from one day to the next – do we?'

'No, we don't,' Luke said quietly. 'I didn't know when I saw you last, Kitty, that Louise and I would be getting married. I'm sorry I sprang it on you so abruptly last night. It wasn't fair to you.'

'I had to be told. It's your life and Louise's.' She watched Luke as he helped himself to more vegetables, and realized he was not as much at ease as he tried to make out, a pulse beat in his throat. She said, 'Luke – you've always been honest with me and I'll be honest with you. It still hurts not to be able to think of myself as being Luke's girl any more, but—'

'You still are,' he said earnestly, 'always will be.'

Kitty forced herself to go on in a resolute way. 'I'm going to do my best not to show the way I feel for the sake of all of you.'

She gave a small smile. 'And I'll try not to feel a martyr.'

'Oh, Kitty ...' Luke laid his hand over hers, his dark eyes holding her gaze. 'I wish—' For a moment there was the closeness between them she had always known, then he drew his hand away and the magic was gone. Never again would there be any such intimate moments.

Kitty was not alone with Luke again until two nights later and then she spoke of her ambition to become a master glass-maker. He eyed her in astonishment. 'A master glass-maker? I knew you were interested in glass-making, but surely you're not serious about achieving anything so ambitious? It's not for a woman, anyway, it's a man's job.'

'Why should it be?'

'I think a woman's place is in the home. It seems to me that this van Neilson is turning your head with talk of glass.'

'Mr van Neilson,' she retorted, 'is conceited like you and thinks that women were put on this earth to run after men, do their bidding. Well, if I get half a chance I'll show you all that I can be a success in industry!'

'Do that, I'll be interested!'

Kitty went out, slamming the door.

Half an hour later the postman brought a letter from Mrs Helder saying that her brother had died the morning after they had arrived and that, praise be, they had made peace with one another. She would be returning home after the funeral. Perhaps Kitty could manage to travel back about the same time? She sent her love; no mention was made of Tyler.

During the next few days Kitty spent as much time with Harriet as she could, became good friends with Louise and ached every time she came face to face with Luke.

On the day before she was due to leave, Harriet was allowed home. They made a celebration of it but Kitty was not sure whether the gaiety was forced or whether the fault was hers that it seemed so.

She only knew that from now on nothing would ever be the same again. Louise would be married to Luke, share his bed; she would become a daughter to Harriet and Abel, bear their grandchild ...

Kitty brooded over these things so that by the next day when she was ready to leave she had convinced herself they would all be glad when she was gone. There were hugs and kisses, waving, cries of "Write soon, Kitty ... Try and come again ... Have a good journey ... We'll write to you ...'

Kitty was fighting back tears as she climbed on to the cart of the neighbouring farmer who was to take her to the station.

It was not until she was half an hour on her journey that she had an image in her mind of the waving group at the farm and knew how wrong she had been about their attitude. Oh, yes, they waved, but there had been the brightness of tears in Harriet's and Abel's eyes, sorrow behind Luke's smile and Louise, she realized now, had stood in the background as though she felt this was where she belonged.

The journey seemed endless and the only thing sustaining Kitty was the thought of seeing Mrs Helder and Tyler again. But when she arrived at Crescent House to find only Mrs Parker to welcome her, she felt as though she was completely alone in the world.

Mrs Parker, as though aware of this, said, 'You'll feel better after a good night's sleep, miss, and Mr van Neilson and Mrs Helder will be back tomorrow evening.'

To Kitty's surprise and joy they arrived the next morning, having travelled on the overnight sleeper. Mrs Helder, looking frail, gave Kitty a hug. 'I've missed you, Kitty dear, missed your warmth and loving care. In my brother's house they are a loveless people. But more about that later. I'm going to bed, I did not sleep a wink last night. Tyler did, he is brimming over with life. My brother left me some paintings and Tyler insisted that we bring them with us. There's only one I like because it reminds me of you. Here is Tyler now.'

He came striding into the room, swept off his hat and gave Kitty a kiss on each cheek. 'How good it is to see you, Kitty!' To Mrs Helder he added, 'I've left the paintings in the hall until you decide where you want them hung.'

She waved a hand, dismissing them. 'Hang them where you want to, Tyler. I'm going to bed. I feel I could sleep for a week!'

While Kitty was helping Mrs Helder to undress, the old lady talked about the strife she had encountered from her sister-in-law. 'In spite of the fact that she was the one who asked me to come,' she said, 'she accused me of coming to see what I would

264

get from the estate. A terribly unhappy woman, terrible family! It's so wonderful to get back here, Kitty. You must tell me all about your visit later. Meanwhile, don't let anyone disturb me.'

No sooner was Mrs Helder in bed than she was asleep. Kitty kissed her gently on the cheek, knowing how she felt. Crescent House was beginning to feel like home to her now.

When Kitty came back to the sitting-room, Tyler was propping up a huge painting on the mantelpiece. It showed a biblical crowd scene. Two smaller paintings stood on pedestals. He took her by the hand. 'Come and see the painting of you. It could be – don't you think? Mrs Helder calls it "the girl in green", I think of it as "the girl with the pensive look".'

Kitty did not see any resemblance to herself at all. The girl in the painting was really beautiful with big dark eyes, a flawless skin and a beautifully shaped mouth. She was wearing a green velvet riding-habit and the small perky hat had a cream feather curling round on to her cheek.

'Well, what do you think of it?' Tyler asked.

'I think that you and Mrs Helder are being very kind to me.' Kitty had just moved to the large painting when Mrs Parker came in to tell Tyler he had a visitor. He excused himself to Kitty, saying, 'Don't go away, I'll be back.'

When Tyler returned a few minutes later Kitty was still standing studying the picture. He came and stood beside her. 'Well, and what is it that holds you so absorbed?'

'It's the figures, they're so alive. On some of the smaller figures in the background eyes, nose and mouth are no more than brushstrokes, yet they have expression. See that man there – I feel he's appealing to me. And there's movement in the dresses of the women and in the long flowing robes of the men.'

Tyler eyed her thoughtfully for a moment, then said, 'Look, Kitty, I have to see someone now. I'll be back in time for lunch, we can discuss your impressions then. In the meantime, take a look at the landscape.'

Kitty studied the landscape, liked it but came back to the biblical painting. The colours were subdued, yet they impressed her, they were so beautifully blended. Many of the figures in the painting were dressed alike, yet each one was an individual. Then an odd thing happened – she began to relate the figures to glass, realizing for the first time that there was a movement in glass. Kitty became excited, wanting to talk about it tó Tyler and feeling impatient for his return.

Kitty hoped that Tyler would not become absorbed in something else and forget about lunch, but he did return and no sooner were they seated than he asked, 'Well now, Kitty, tell me more about your impressions of the painting.' He shook out his table napkin.

She told him about realizing there was movement in glass and he nodded. 'Yes, of course, therein lies the beauty. Go on.'

Kitty moistened her lips, beginning to feel little tremors of excitement running up and down her spine at his interest. She said: 'There was a tall girl, her hand on her hip, and I began to see a claret jug.' She laughed a little self-consciously. 'Perhaps I'm letting my imagination run away with me.'

'If there was no imagination, Kitty, there would be no art.'

'I saw the stopper as the girl's head,' she went on. 'There would be just indentations in it, a suggestion of features. The lower part of the jug would have folds in the glass to indicate the skirt, and I saw the curved arm of the girl as the handle. I would put a circle of glass in the curve.'

'Why? Why the circle?'

Kitty looked at him, puzzled. 'I don't know why, but it's how I see it.'

Tyler took a drink of his wine, then dabbed at his mouth with the napkin. 'There's a trend at present for symbolic art. Perhaps you see it as the circle of life, or as the close-knit circle of your family.'

Kitty felt startled. The girl had been part of what she had thought of as a family group, but the fact that Tyler had mentioned the close-knit circle of *her* family brought a resentment. She looked away. 'I don't think I would like this ... this symbolic stuff.'

Tyler said gently, 'This *stuff*, as you call it, Kitty, can be very beautiful. I've seen some. A friend of mine who has moved to this district recently has an excellent collection of glass from all over the world. When Mrs Helder recovers from the strain of the journey, I shall take you both. I promise you will be impressed.'

Tyler went on to talk about the origins of glass and the

development over the centuries and Kitty alternated between listening with total absorption, making exclamations such as, 'Imagine! Three thousand years old. Who would believe it?' and a wide-eyed wonder that articles of glass had been found in the tombs of Egyptian kings.

Tyler leaned forward suddenly after one of these comments and said smiling, 'You have so many changing expressions, Kitty, I'm sure you would be a delight to an artist. I remember the day you were trying to shave me when I was ill at the Earles' house. I can see you now, tongue between your teeth – your expression so earnest, so dedicated as you tipped my nose and tried to scrape the stubble from my upper lip. You were a wonderful nurse!'

There was a twinkle in his eyes and Kitty felt her colour rising. What else had he remembered? 'Any maid would have done the same,' she said.

'Oh, no, I can't think of a more enterprising young lady. I'm no mean weight, yet you managed not only to wash me but to change my nightshirt.'

Kitty's hand flew to her mouth. 'You were conscious! You let me think – oh, that was cheating, Mr van Neilson, it was a terrible thing to do!'

'I was only semi-conscious, Kitty,' he said softly. 'I was not even sure whether it was a part of my delirium. But I was clean, I was changed and you were the only one who attended to me. I think it was that day that I fell in love with you.'

He was speaking lightly, but Kitty's colour deepened. 'I'm sorry,' Tyler said, 'I'm embarrassing you. Let's change the subject, shall we? How did you enjoy your visit to the farm? Had your aunt recovered from her indisposition?'

Kitty told him about Harriet's fall then, looking beyond him, said, 'Luke is getting married.'

Tyler's eyebrows went up. 'Getting married? But I thought that you and he—'

'I'm ... very fond of my foster-brother and glad he's getting married. Louise is a lovely girl and I'm sure she'll make him a good wife.' Kitty was aware of the stiffness in her tone.

'So what in your opinion constitutes a good wife, Kitty?'

'Well, she ... she must love him, of course. And she must be ...'

'Obedient?' Tyler was smiling.

An imp of mischief stirred in Kitty. 'Not all the time, or life would be very dull. Think how awful it would be if you had a wife who said, "Yes, sir, no sir," and never showed any spirit. I think perhaps it might be this that could drive a man to another woman's arms.'

'Is that so? You seem to know an awful lot about marriage, *Miss* Leddenshaw.'

Kitty, who was beginning to feel she was saying far too much, ended lamely, 'It's just what I've been told.'

'And I think it's good advice. I also think you'll make a very good wife, Kitty. A man would certainly not be bored in your company. Perhaps you would put my name down on your list of possible suitors?'

Kitty, matching his banter, replied, 'You would, of course, be on the bottom of the list.'

He looked at her in surprise. 'Why? I'm a very personable fellow, I could offer you a good home, a life full of variety; we would travel, and ... more important still, I am in love with you.'

'But I'm not in your class,' Kitty said.

'Kitty, I'm not the slightest bit concerned about class, but if *you* are then let me tell you now you have more class in your little finger than some daughters of titled people I know. Think about it. And now, I must go.' He gave her a teasing smile. 'While we're waiting to get married, think up some more interesting ideas for glassware.'

Kitty sat for a long time after he had gone, not quite sure what to make of him. Most of the time he had been teasing, but at others his manner had seemed serious. The thought of being married to Tyler at that moment was not altogether unpleasing. He was attractive, she more than merely liked him and she might have a greater opportunity of becoming more proficient at glass-making. She was suddenly appalled at the trend of her thoughts; she was actually contemplating marriage for gain, something she had bitterly accused her sister Violet of doing. Kitty also realized that at the back of her mind was the effect an announcement of her marriage would have on Luke, and was deeply ashamed.

Mrs Helder decided to stay in bed for the rest of the day and

Kitty joined her for the evening meal in her room. The old lady asked about her stay at the farm and Kitty repeated what she had told Tyler.

'Well, in my opinion it's fate, Kitty. You were not meant to marry Luke. Do you know that Tyler is in love with you?'

Kitty looked up. 'He told me so at lunch-time, but I didn't take him seriously.'

'You should. He's been in love with you for quite a while. Actually he's been fighting against it – and don't take that unkindly. He was about to be married five years ago when the girl suddenly married someone else. It was a dreadful blow to his pride and also because the girl married someone with more money. Tyler was not so wealthy then as he is now.' After a pause Mrs Helder added softly, 'Nothing would give me more pleasure, Kitty, than to see you and Tyler ...'

Kitty got up and moved restlessly around the room. 'I like him, I like him very much, but if he were to ask me seriously to marry him now I would have to say no. I'm still in love with Luke, I think I always will be.'

'All I can say is – don't let that ruin your life. Many jilted people have had happy marriages with a second love. Pining for a man who has married someone else can be destructive. Think about it. When I have more energy, I shall speak to Tyler about our postponed London visit. You will enjoy his company, he's an excellent escort.'

But Mrs Helder developed a chill and was confined to her room and the only times they saw Tyler were when he looked in to see how the patient was. He apologized for not being able to stay very long, but he was so busy. He was full of high spirits about his project, which he still would not divulge, and his effervescence was just what Kitty needed.

When Mrs Helder was on the mend, Tyler asked permission to take Kitty to the friend who had the glass collection. 'Yes, of course,' the old lady said, 'the change will do her good. And don't hurry back; Mrs Parker will see to my needs.'

It was a lovely sunny afternoon with buds opening and field and hedgerow and trees showing a rich display of green. Kitty, who had spent a great deal of time in the sick-room, took in deep breaths. 'Oh, it's heavenly,' she said. 'What would we do without fresh air?'

Tyler laughed. 'I was going to say, die, but instead I'll tell you how very fetching you look. And I *mean* it, it's not idle flattery to woo you.'

Kitty gave a little giggle. 'To woo sounds funny.'

'Everything is funny and lovely today, Kitty,' he said softly, 'because you are with me. I've missed you being here.'

Kitty had missed him, but seeing a rabbit she changed the subject and drew his attention to it. 'All right,' he said in a resigned tone, 'I shall stop wooing you.'

Kitty felt good. At last she was able to put the thoughts of Luke soon being married behind her and look forward to enjoying being with Tyler and seeing the glass collection.

The house standing in parkland was most impressive and so was the owner Mr Freeman – a tall, aristocratic-looking man with silver-grey hair. He bowed low over Kitty's hand. 'I'm delighted to meet you, Miss Leddenshaw. Tyler has told me about your interest in glass. I shall show you my collection, but first my housekeeper has tea ready.'

The high-ceilinged room had the simple elegance that Kitty was beginning to associate with wealth and good taste. They sat at a table near the window that overlooked the parkland, and she thought how far she had come since she had left the poverty of her mother's home.

The men talked on sundry subjects, but although she took no part in the conversation she did not feel excluded.

Then Mr Freeman led the way to a room on the first floor and unlocked the door. He ushered them inside.

Kitty just stood spellbound, unable to believe such beauty could exist. To Tyler's smiling enquiry as to whether she was impressed, she said, 'I could cry. I never imagined such beauty, such colours; it's like entering Aladdin's cave.'

Mr Freeman took them to see displays of glass in cabinets, on tables, on shelves; to pedestals holding a single object. There were lustres in jewel colours with drops of carved crystal; narrow-necked vases with figures painted on the inside, which Mr Freeman said had meant many months of patient work by the artists; bowls with figures between double layers of glass; rare figures of coloured glass which had been manipulated over a flame; goblets deeply engraved with scenes from mythology.

The endless variety came from all countries – Germany,

Bohemia, Ireland, China, Japan, Italy – and some had decorations so fragile one wondered how they could be handled without breaking them. Kitty learned about lace glass, which did indeed look like lace, and lattice glass, the effect of both being achieved by using fine threads of glass. There were pieces in every colour: blue, green, amber, yellow, red, turquoise, purple, and in many cases two or three colours were blended.

Then they were standing in front of a strangely shaped object in amber striped with clouded white and grey. From the base it curved upwards, turned in loops, rose again, then returned to the base. Mr Freeman told her it was entitled 'Thoughts'. Kitty looked at Tyler and asked 'Symbolic Art?' and he nodded. She puzzled over it for a while, then her frown vanished.

'I know now what the artist means. You can be thinking of something when the mind wanders, but eventually you are brought back to your first thought.'

The two men exchanged smiling glances and Mr Freeman said, 'You are most discerning, Miss Leddenshaw.'

After that Kitty became aware of a change in their manner to her. At times there was almost a tenderness towards her, as if she were a well-loved child or grandchild they wanted to indulge. 'See this, Miss Leddenshaw,' from Mr Freeman, and from Tyler, 'I know you will appreciate this, Kitty ...'

She was surprised to learn that a piece of glass from the first century AD could be worth considerably less than another from a much later century, depending on quality and demand. She found it difficult to believe that an armorial goblet of the seventeenth century was worth twenty thousand pounds.

'Twenty thousand?' she exclaimed. 'My goodness, that's an enormous amount of money. Aren't you afraid of breaking it, Mr Freeman? I once broke a small jug belonging to Mr van Neilson and I was terribly upset.'

Mr Freeman smiled. 'Is that why you are walking with your hands behind your back, Miss Leddenshaw? This was something my father insisted I do after I had broken a bowl he treasured. Now I don't think about breakages. If I did, all pleasure in my collection would be gone.'

They were there for another hour, Mr Freeman explaining many methods of working with glass and decorating it. Then Tyler said, looking a little impatient, 'Kitty, I have some business to discuss with Mr Freeman which will take rather a long time. I'll see you to the carriage, you can tell Mrs Helder I will not be back until late.'

Kitty thanked Mr Freeman, saying how she appreciated his kindness and how much she had enjoyed seeing the collection. He bowed low over her hand once more and told her he hoped he would have the pleasure of her company again soon.

CHAPTER NINETEEN

Kitty returned to Crescent House feeling her mind was overflowing with knowledge. She described to Mrs Helder much of what she had seen, then said, 'It made me realize how little I know about glass-making. I'm really just on the threshold, but I'll go on learning. I'll get there – I'll go to any lengths to achieve my dream.'

'I hope it comes true,' Mrs Helder said gently. 'Not all dreams do.'

'I know. One didn't, but I feel sure this one will.'

Tyler did not come in until late afternoon on the following day. He looked brimming over with energy, his dark hair wind-blown and his eyes alight with excitement. He slapped his palms together and said:

'Well, ladies! I can tell you my good news at last. I'm going to build a glasshouse and houses for the workers. It will be a small community with a church, shops and recreation rooms for them.' When Mrs Helder asked where it was to be built, he said it would be near the river on account of transport.

Tyler stood with his back to the fire, rocking back and forth on his heels as he outlined the work. He had engaged a team of men to start building the following week and hoped the project would be completed by early autumn. Before then, he said, he hoped to find time to get married and have a honeymoon.

At Kitty's startled look, he smiled and said, 'Mrs Helder has something to say to you, Kitty. I'll be back in half an hour with champagne.'

'Well now,' Mrs Helder said when he had gone, 'no doubt you've guessed, Kitty, that Tyler wants to marry you. He spoke to me earlier. He is deeply in love with you.'

'But I don't want to be married, Mrs Helder,' Kitty protested. 'I want to learn the trade of glass-making.'

The old lady pursed her lips. 'You said minutes ago that you would go to any lengths to achieve your ambition. How much are you prepared to sacrifice? Would you be prepared to bargain with Tyler? A chance to learn the trade in return for marriage? Mind you, I'm not sure he would consider such a proposition, but he might. He doesn't want to lose you.'

Kitty's thoughts were in a turmoil. Would it be too big a price to pay? Would there *be* a sacrifice involved? Tyler had stirred emotions in her; they shared the same interests. On the other hand he would want someone to run his house, not to be working at glass-making. Kitty thought of Luke. Would it be fair to marry Tyler loving another man? But why should she go on thinking about Luke? The minute she had left the farm he had turned to Louise. Kitty looked up.

'If Mr van Neilson would agree to allow me to spend some time making glass, I would marry him. And I do promise, Mrs Helder, I would do my best to be a good wife to him.'

'I know you would, Kitty, otherwise I would not have suggested making a bargain with him. It could be a good marriage – you both need love and you both have a lot to give. Go and get changed, we shall be celebrating a betrothal as well as the beginning of a new project!'

Kitty had three evening dresses and chose one she had not worn before. It was deep blue velvet and she had thought it too dark, but when she tried it on she found it had a neckline a little more daring than the others. It emphasized the creaminess of her skin and the tight bodice gave emphasis to her small but firm breasts and tiny waist. With her hair up and a cerise velvet ribbon threaded through it, Kitty was pleased and a little excited with the result. She hurried to the sitting-room.

A little breathless she said, whirling around for Mrs Helder's inspection, 'Do I look all right?'

'You look stunningly beautiful,' said Tyler from the doorway. Colour rushed to Kitty's face and he added, 'And quite

274

enchanting when you blush. Ah, here is Mrs Parker with the champagne!'

Mrs Helder proposed a toast to Tyler for his success with his venture and he in turn toasted 'The two most beautiful ladies in my life!'

Kitty, who never had more than half a glass of wine with her meals, felt heady after two of champagne, and loved the feeling. 'This is delicious,' she said, 'isn't it? It gives you a tingly feeling and you love everyone.'

'Oh dear!' said Mrs Helder. Tyler took the glass from Kitty and said they would go into dinner, since drinking on an empty stomach could sometimes cause complications.

Mrs Helder allowed Kitty only one further half-glass of champagne, but in spite of having food Kitty felt she was in a rose-coloured world. When coffee and *petit fours* were brought in, Mrs Helder excused herself. No, Kitty was to stay, she herself was not yet ready for bed but would read for a while. Tyler saw her to her room then came back.

'Well, Kitty,' he said softly, 'you know I'm in love with you and want to marry you, so ... ?'

She looked down at her hands. 'You do know that I was in love with Luke? Still am ... I suppose.'

'You do like me?'

'Oh yes ...' She looked up. 'I like you very much, Mr van Neilson, but—'

Tyler touched her hand. 'Under the circumstances, Kitty, I don't expect any more at first, but love can grow. Please say yes.'

Now that the moment had come, she wondered if she dare bargain with him. After all, she was no more than a paid employee and he lord of the manor, as it were. And yet, it was the only way to achieve her ambition. She clasped her hands tightly.

'I will marry you, Mr van Neilson, on one condition.'

She saw him tense, his expression change and become cold. 'If your condition is that you sleep alone, then the arrangement is cancelled. I'm a virile man with demanding needs.'

Kitty felt a tremor of sensuousness. She attempted a smile. 'Nothing as drastic as that. I would like ... well, I want the opportunity to learn glass-making, to study it seriously.'

Tyler flung up his hands. 'Nothing drastic, she says! Kitty, I want a wife to run my home, to give me children, not a blower of glass!'

She began to laugh. Tyler's lips trembled. 'Well, that's what it amounts to, isn't it? You working in a glasshouse? It's an impossible situation. How could you be working if you were pregnant? You do want babies, don't you?'

The word 'babies' sent her inside crawling as always. 'I – like older children, but not babies.'

He stared at her for a moment, then gave a great shout of laughter. 'Kitty, can you tell me how you are going to have older children without them being babies? Do you think they come ready-made at varying ages?' His laughter suddenly died and now he was eyeing her in an anxious way. 'Kitty, you do know about – marriage and ... what it entails? A man and a woman sleeping together—'

'Yes, I do – one learns very early about life, living on a farm. From animals,' she added quickly, not wanting him to think her experience came from being tumbled in a haystack.

'Oh, yes, the condition ...' Tyler sighed. 'Very well, Kitty, I agree, but it must be for only part of the day. If I bring a business colleague home, I expect you to be there to dispense afternoon tea and conversation. You can work in the present furnace room. Thomas will teach you.'

Kitty felt as though she were bathed in a sudden radiance. 'Oh, thank you, Mr van Neilson, thank you a million times. You won't regret giving me this opportunity, I swear it.'

'Time will tell,' he said gruffly. 'And you must stop calling me "Mr van Neilson" now that we are ... betrothed, as they say. Well, not quite.' He brought a small box from his pocket and took out a ring which he held out. 'It belonged to my mother, she was small; I hope it will fit you, Kitty.'

Tyler came round and picked up her left hand. He slipped the ring on to her third finger – a large ruby surrounded by diamonds, set in chased gold.

It fitted perfectly. 'It's beautiful,' Kitty said softly. He drew her to her feet and put his arms around her. His kiss was gentle, but the fast beating of his heart told her of his restraint. Kitty tried to stifle a regret that it was not Luke's arms holding her.

They went to tell Mrs Helder their news and the old lady's

eyes were full of tears. 'There is nothing that could have made me happier,' she said. 'Have you fixed a date for the wedding?'

'Not yet, but the sooner the better. I would prefer it to be quiet, a register office wedding if Kitty is willing.' He turned to her. 'Are you, Kitty?'

It would have been different, she thought, if she had been marrying Luke. The wedding would have been in the little village church and she would have been in white, the organ playing as she walked down the aisle on Abel's arm . . . Suddenly realizing they were waiting for her answer, Kitty said, 'I don't mind, I don't want any fuss.'

At this Mrs Helder made a strong protest, pointing out that getting married at a register office was the procedure for couples *having* to be married. People would talk.

'Let them talk,' Tyler said. 'If we arrange a church wedding the banns would have to be called, the workmen would get to know and expect a day's celebration. Then half of them would have thick heads the next morning and would not come to work! Time is crucial. When the building work is completed, we can have a double celebration.'

Mrs Helder could do nothing but agree. She did insist, however, that Kitty be married in white. Tyler said he would leave them to discuss details and fix a date.

The date for the wedding was set for the first Monday in June and Kitty chose a simple style for her dress. She agreed at Mrs Helder's insistence to wear a veil, a short one to be circled by orange blossom. In a matter of a few days all the arrangements were completed. Mr Freeman and Mrs Helder would stand as witnesses; they would all travel together to Newcastle the evening before, as though going to a musical concert. They would stay at a hotel and the following day, after the wedding and small reception, Tyler and Kitty would leave for London.

When all this was settled, Mrs Helder said, 'Kitty, there is one thing you must know – the name to put on your wedding certificate. Your mother was living with the man Harvey when you were born. Did she have you registered in that name or in your father's name?'

Kitty said she had no idea; her birth certificate had not been amongst her mother's papers. Mrs Helder told her she would instruct her solicitor to write to Somerset House.

Ten days later Kitty learned that her birth had been registered in the name Catherine Tierne. 'I'm glad,' she said. 'Although I have no wish to meet my father's family, I did want my correct name.'

Mrs Helder eyed her thoughtfully. 'I know you told me once before that you had no wish to meet them, but if you have children they are bound to want to know about their grandparents. And haven't they a right to know them? I feel quite sure they could be traced.'

Kitty shook her head. 'They would know about their son's marriage, that he had left a widow, and possibly know about me, but they've done nothing to trace me. I feel I would be an embarrassment to them if I appeared one day. I think we'll just let sleeping dogs lie.'

Mrs Helder made no attempt to pursue it.

Although Tyler was determined not to have any fuss over the wedding, Kitty wrote to Harriet, inviting them all. After all, they were the people closest to her.

A loving, warm letter came by return. Harriet said how pleased they all were to hear of her forthcoming marriage. According to what she had heard from Mrs Helder when she called, Mr van Neilson was a responsible, caring and generous man. She added that they would have liked nothing better than to be with her on her wedding day, but unfortunately it was impossible. Although her back was improving there were certain jobs she was unable to do, such as milking. Louise was a big help but, poor girl, she was having terrible bouts of morning sickness. Harriet said she felt sure that Kitty would understand the problems and concluded: 'We shall be thinking of you, Kitty, on your big day and may the love of all of us wing to you. We also hope that your husband will know the same joy that you brought to us. We love you dearly, Kitty.'

A postscript said, 'I am sending you my pearl-backed prayer book for you to carry on the day.'

Kitty wept over the letter, feeling a terrible wave of home-sickness and wondering if she was doing the right thing marrying one man while having an ache inside her for another.

It did not help that over the next two weeks she hardly saw Tyler. If she could have gone to the furnace room it might have eased things, but Tyler had told her she was not to go in any part of the forest. Many of the workers were casual labourers, rough men who would have no hesitation in molesting a pretty young woman. It would be different when the glasshouse was open and there were regular workers: they followed the rules or lost their jobs.

Kitty had written to Ann to tell her about the wedding and also to Jessica. Ann's reply was full of her own life, of her little house and of Fred, who had 'a dreadful hacking cough'. A proper 'graveyard' cough, as they say, she said. Kitty gave a shiver. Talk of graveyards was not exactly the thing a prospective bride wanted to hear. Ann ended: 'We all send our love, have a happy day. Perhaps you'll get to see us sometime.' A postscript said, 'Haven't heard a thing about our Violet, nor do we want to!'

Jessica's was a warm letter too. She had been quite poorly for a few weeks, but was slowly recovering. How good it was to hear news of the wedding:

> You deserve great happiness, Kitty, [she wrote]. I think so often of you. I met Mrs Bramley one day a week ago and she was saying how you had wrapped yourself around all their hearts, 'Even Mr Walton's', she said with a laugh. He apparently often talks about you. Thank you, Kitty, for your invitation to visit you sometime when you get back from your honeymoon. It would be lovely. Something to look forward to.
>
> I send you lots of love, dear Kitty, and wish you both much happiness . . .

And so the days dragged on . . .

Sometimes Tyler would have his meals sent to him at the factory and at others come in very late. One evening when Mrs Helder had left her lorgnettes in the dining-room and Kitty had gone to fetch them, she was surprised to see Tyler standing at the window.

'Oh,' she said, 'I didn't know you had come in. Does Mrs Parker know? Do you need a meal?'

'I've ordered a light meal.' He came over to her and put a finger under her chin. 'I've missed you, Kitty.'

'How strange that I haven't noticed it,' she said pertly. 'But then how could I, when I haven't even glimpsed you for days?'

His dark eyes held hers. 'Why do you think I stayed away? I work hard with the men – it's the only way I can keep my mind from straying to thoughts of being married to you, of carrying you up to bed, of touching you . . . making you want me.'

His words, the caressing tones had ecstatic tremors running through her. His lips touched hers then moved sensuously, bringing a surge of emotion, a need in her that she did not quite understand. For a moment she responded, then drew away, saying breathlessly, 'Please don't, Mr van Neilson.'

'I thought you were enjoying it,' he teased.

'I was, but Aunt Harriet was nudging me, warning me not to let a man take liberties until we were married!'

'Damn Aunt Harriet!' Tyler said, half-laughing. Kitty reminded him that he had once thought her a sensible woman and he nodded. 'Yes, she is, she's taught you well, but I'm suffering on account of it. Incidentally, may I remind you to call me by my christian name? If you start calling me Mr van Neilson on our honeymoon, people might think you are my mistress.'

'It must be exciting to be a mistress,' Kitty said, looking at him from under her lashes.

'Hey! *You* are a temptress, Kitty Leddenshaw! If you don't stop looking at me like that, I shall be picking you up and carrying you off into the forest!' He made to grab her and she backed away – then, reaching the door, she opened it and called over her shoulder, 'You would have to catch me first!' and fled in the direction of Mrs Helder's room. Tyler came after her, but she managed to get that door opened and closed before he reached it. She stood leaning against it, giggling. Mrs Helder asked, 'And what have you been up to, Kitty?'

There was a tap on the door and Tyler asked permission to enter. At Mrs Helder's nod Kitty opened it. Tyler glanced at her then appealed to Mrs Helder, his eyes twinkling.

'What am I to do with her, Marguerite? She's teasing me unbearably.'

'Because she's falling in love with you,' Mrs Helder replied promptly.

Tyler and Kitty exchanged glances and both were silent. Was it possible, Kitty wondered? Could she really be falling in love with him? She only knew she wanted to feel his lips again on hers, wanted to be held in his arms, caressed. Slow colour mounted to her cheeks.

Mrs Helder said, 'Come and sit down, both of you. Tell me your plans for the future, Tyler. Have you decided where you are going for your honeymoon?'

'Italy is out of the question because of the time factor. It will have to be London, a long weekend. As for the future, I've decided to concentrate on producing optical glass.'

'Optical glass?' Kitty eyed him in dismay. 'Oh, how dull!'

'Dull? It's exciting, Kitty! I've been experimenting with it for a long time. There's a growing need for optical glass of all kinds for medical use, microscopes, for telescopes, binoculars—'

'But what about all those beautiful coloured goblets you were making?'

'I'll leave that side to you,' he said. Then he held up a hand. 'But I warn you, no mass producing.'

She smiled sweetly. 'Not for the moment.'

'Kitty,' he said sternly, 'you heard what I said.'

'Yes, Mr van Neilson,' Kitty bobbed a curtsy, '*Sir!*'

Tyler raised his shoulders with a despairing gesture. 'Marguerite, I'm going to have trouble with this girl. I can see I will have to take her in hand, start taming her.'

Mrs Helder laughed softly. 'You'll never tame Kitty, and you would never want to.'

'I think she would rather enjoy *my* method of taming,' he said, a deliciously wicked gleam in his eyes.

Kitty felt a little quiver of excitement. Life, it seemed, living with Tyler van Neilson was going to be interesting . . . *Very* interesting indeed.

CHAPTER TWENTY

On the day before Kitty and Tyler were due to be married, it seemed as if everything was destined to go wrong so as to prevent the wedding taking place. Mrs Helder fell over a rug and sprained her ankle; Tyler was informed that rival workers had come to the site and were trying to wreck the buildings and, half an hour after he had left to investigate, Mr Freeman – who was to stand as witness with Mrs Helder – was laid up at his shooting lodge after a fall from his horse.

Kitty said, 'That's it, then, the wedding will have to be postponed.'

Mrs Helder told her, No, everything had been arranged; they would wait and see what Tyler had to say when he returned.

When Tyler did come back, he said the ruffians who had invaded the site had been routed, most with broken heads, then added, 'We'll put men on guard in case they come back, but although it means we will still get married, Kitty, the honeymoon will have to be cancelled. I must be available if needed on the site.'

Kitty tried to get him to cancel the wedding too, but like Mrs Helder he insisted it take place. It had been arranged that the eldest daughter of Mrs Parker, together with a business colleague of Tyler's, would be witnesses. They would drive to town, change at a hotel and after the ceremony return for a wedding breakfast. Tyler had it all so cut and dried that Kitty thought he might be arranging a business meeting. No wonder Mrs Helder begged her the next morning to try to look a little bit happy. Kitty and Mrs Parker's daughter travelled in one carriage into town, Tyler and his friend in another. Kitty was sure she must be the most reluctant bride-to-be there had ever been.

And from the moment of leaving the hotel in her simple white silk wedding gown and veil, the whole thing had an air of unreality. She should have been driving to church accompanied by Abel, instead of being with a girl she hardly knew. Although the day was warm and sunny, she felt ice-cold.

Although there was always a feeling of chill going into a stone-built church, there was also an air of reverence. Going into the Register Office with its shabby furniture, dust motes hovering in a thin shaft of sunlight coming from a small window, gave Kitty the feeling that no matter what words were said during the ceremony she would not feel legally married. She gripped Harriet's pearl-backed prayer book as though to draw comfort from it.

But it was not until Tyler, looking handsome in grey, took her hand in his and she felt its warmth, the firmness of his grip, that she began to relax a little.

Yet even with the ceremony over and the ring on her finger, Kitty did not feel married. They drove back to the hotel to change again and then all travelled to Crescent House in one carriage – with the men talking business! There was no one waiting to throw confetti over bride and groom, no ceremony of carrying the bride over the threshold to draw attention to them. It was all so soul-less and Kitty could not help thinking how different it would have been had she married Luke . . . but Luke was married to someone else and it was time she stopped thinking about him.

Mrs Parker had made the wedding cake and prepared savouries and sweetmeats. Speeches were made, toasts given, the cake cut and champagne drunk. Mrs Helder gazed fondly at bride and groom, but Kitty had the feeling it was all happening to another couple and she was merely a guest. She tried to analyse why; certainly she had a great liking for Tyler, could at times feel she might be in love with him.

And then it came to her. It was because they would be spending the honeymoon in the house and Mrs Helder and the staff would know what was happening. Kitty's face burned at the thought. If only they could have gone to London, even if it was just to spend their wedding night there.

Tyler's present to her was a beautiful gold and diamond necklace, Mrs Helder's a trousseau of nightwear, including a white pure silk nightdress and negligée for her bridal night.

When they had finished with the meal and speeches, Kitty was wondering what would happen next when Tyler held out his hand to her and said, 'Run upstairs and change – we're going to have a one-night honeymoon!' When she asked where he said, 'Wait and see!'

Kitty felt different immediately; it was going to be all right. She looked longingly at all the clothes she had had made for the London honeymoon and it was with reluctance that she wore a plain loose coat and a small straw hat, to give the impression of simply going for an afternoon's drive.

They said their goodbyes. Mrs Helder gave Kitty a hug, saying, 'You'll be happy with Tyler, I know it. Do as he asks and you can have anything you want. He's so in love with you!' Kitty thought about Tyler and his friend talking business in the carriage after the ceremony, but she said nothing, just smiled.

Then they were away and as the carriages reached the end of the drive, Tyler told her they were going to spend the night at Mr Freeman's house. He and his staff were at his shooting lodge, and the housekeeper – who would be the only person there – had been sworn to secrecy about the wedding. It seemed to Kitty that there was an awful lot of secrecy involved just to prevent workmen celebrating the wedding for a day, or two at the worst. But if this was Tyler's way, so be it. She had agreed to marry him.

The carriage had turned right at the end of the drive and Kitty found herself thinking that this was yet another road opening up for her: the road to marriage. And with this thought Luke came into her mind again and she felt a small ache, but she put him firmly from her mind and concentrated on the countryside. It was the beginning of June when everything was still fresh and suddenly she felt glad she had been married at this time – it was more romantic now than later on when bloom would be off flowers and foliage.

She had eased herself on to the edge of her seat, wanting to take in everything to store for the future, when Tyler said softly, 'There couldn't possibly be a more virginal-looking bride than you, Kitty. It's as though you have stepped into the world for the first time and are filled with wonder at what you are seeing.'

Kitty felt suddenly shy. 'That's how I feel, but then it's the first time I've been married.'

'And the last, I hope,' said Tyler fervently. He drew her into the curve of his arm and she felt small tremors going through her at his closeness. She wondered what it would be like to lie in his arms – in bed – and was astonished at the response of her body. When they reached the house, the housekeeper came out and without a word picked up a valise in each hand and carried them inside. There she told them a cold collation had been prepared. In the meantime, she would show them to their room.

The bedroom, on the first floor, was large with tall windows overlooking parkland. There was a tester bed with rose-coloured velvet drapes and quilt. The carpet and curtains were a pale olive green and there was a day-bed and chairs covered with cream rose-budded brocade. A large Florentine mirror enchanted Kitty and she was fingering the intricate work surrounding it when Tyler came up behind her and put his arms around her.

She drew a quick breath at his touch again. 'It's beautiful, isn't it, such delicate work?'

'*You* are beautiful, my darling, and we have not come here to talk about the merits of mirrors.' He laid his cheek against hers and whispered, 'I have other things on my mind.' He began to pull pins from her hair and she drew away from him in a panic. 'Oh, please don't, Tyler. We . . . we haven't had our dinner yet!'

He nuzzled the back of her neck. 'Who wants food? I could eat *you*, gobble you up!'

Kitty was both alarmed and excited at the feelings he roused in her. 'Tyler, wait, it wouldn't seem right somehow to – to . . .'

'To make love to my wife?' he enquired. 'Any time is the right time.' His voice was ragged. 'You must learn that, Kitty. I want you and I want you *now*.'

She turned to face him. 'I shall never deny you, Tyler, I promised Mrs Helder I would make you a good wife. If you want to take me, then you shall.' She pulled the rest of the pins out of her hair, hesitated a moment and then started to unbutton the top of her dress.

He stayed her hand. 'No, Kitty, I don't want you like this. I want you to enjoy it too.' He gave a deep sigh. 'I've waited so long I suppose I can wait another hour or two.' He picked up a strand of her hair. 'But I don't think you realize how tantalizing you are, how seductive.' He let the strand of her hair fall. 'You'd better go and get changed.' He slapped her bottom. 'Off with you, before I start undressing you!'

They had a dressing-room each and Kitty started towards hers; then she paused, looked over her shoulder and said earnestly, 'I'm quite sure it will be better when it's dark.'

'Will you get out of my sight?' he yelled. Kitty fled. Once inside the dressing-room she stood with her back against the door, her heart pounding. Why was there all this turmoil inside her, this feeling that teased a part of her body, exciting her? It was almost an agony. A sweet agony.

Kitty thought back to the earthiness of her farming days. Cows always seemed so passive when being 'served'. Did they have similar emotion? Kitty suddenly smiled to herself, wondering what Tyler would say if he knew she was comparing herself with a cow.

She washed herself, brushed and pinned up her hair and then changed into the saffron-coloured silk dress which had become a favourite with her.

Kitty kept taking deep breaths to try to calm herself before going back into the bedroom. Tyler had spurned the idea of having a valet and when she went in he was dressed and giving a final brush to his thick dark hair. He was wearing brown, the collar of the jacket having a velvet facing. He looked so elegant, so distinguished Kitty felt a wave of love for him sweep over her.

He turned to face her. 'I guessed correctly, I was sure you would wear that particular dress. I like it.' He offered her his arm. 'Well, Mrs van Neilson, shall we go downstairs?'

'How strange to be called Mrs van Neilson. I still feel myself to be Kitty Leddenshaw.'

He gave her a wicked grin. 'You won't after tonight!' Kitty's cheeks flamed and she felt as though her blood had turned to fire.

When they went into the dining-room Kitty's gaze went immediately to the centrepiece on the table – a lamp in cut crystal, shaded from deep rose to palest pink.

'Oh, how exquisite!' she enthused. 'Such tiny intricate pieces.'

Tyler picked up a small card propped up at the base of the lamp and handed it to her. 'It's our wedding present from Mr Freeman. The lamp is one of his most treasured possessions.'

Kitty gazed at him wide-eyed. 'How can he bear to part with it?'

Tyler touched her cheek gently. 'Because he thinks you quite the most charming and unaffected young lady he has ever met. And so do I, my darling.'

Kitty felt deeply moved and was on the verge of tears when the housekeeper came in. Having served the meal, she left them saying that she would see them the following morning at breakfast.

'And that will be quite soon enough,' Tyler said after she had gone. 'Such a sour woman!' Kitty remarked that the poor housekeeper might have something in her life to be sour about and Tyler held up his hand. 'All right, I'll accept that. Let us talk about something else, our wedding present for instance.'

They discussed the work that had gone into the making of the lamp, then Tyler asked Kitty what she would like to specialize in if she mastered the art of glass-making. He was smiling at her in an indulgent way, which made her think he was never going to take her work seriously. 'Peacock glass,' she replied promptly.

His eyebrows went up. 'Oh, and what gave you that idea?'

She explained it was when Mr Freeman had shown them some pieces which had the sheen of a bird's wing and she had thought of the plumage of a peacock. 'I would make an oval bowl with a handle, like a basket, the lovely colours incorporated into the bowl part and two crossed tail feathers for the handle.'

Tyler told her that peacock colouring was not new but she could experiment; it was experimenting that had produced famous pieces. Kitty went on talking about Mr Freeman's collection and Tyler began to appear more and more astonished.

'What a memory you have, Kitty. I'm beginning to think I have a very clever young wife.'

'Thank you, sir,' she said, bobbing her head, making fun of it, but delighted at the same to have his praise.

'You're a very sweet person,' Tyler said, his expression now sober. 'I hope you will always stay that way, Kitty, and not get so wrapped up in making glass that you will have no time for me.'

There was a loneliness about him then that moved Kitty.

When they had talked about the wedding, she had asked about his family, if they would come to the ceremony. He said not, and added that he had no wish to discuss the subject. Now Kitty decided to broach the matter again. 'Please tell me about your family, I know nothing whatsoever about them.'

He made small pellets from pieces of bread on his plate, then looked up. 'My mother died when I was eleven years old. I adored her. My father married again six months later to a woman half his age. I hated her. All she was interested in was clothes, jewellery, entertaining – and my father, besotted by her, gave in to her every whim. He fully expected me to go into banking and when I told him I had made up my mind to learn glass-making, he was furious. I ran away when I was seventeen, leaving a note to say that I would kill myself if he tried to find me. I was lucky enough to be taken on at a glasshouse and luckier still when a master glass-blower took an interest in me. He actually took me into his family. It's a long story, Kitty, but I worked hard and became successful. What did help me was when I was left a legacy by a relative. I went to Italy to claim it. My father refused to see me.'

Tyler stared into space and there was grief in his eyes. 'Although I had no love for my father then, I had loved him once and it hurt. I set up my own business, made a success of it but then became restless. I travelled to many places, working in other people's glasshouses, exchanging ideas. Then I came to England on a visit to my aunt, Mrs Earle – and met you, Kitty . . .' Tyler reached out and covered her hand gently with his own. 'It was the best thing that ever happened to me!'

Tyler talked about his travels and the people he had met and touched on his broken love affair, talking as though it was something he had kept bottled up for years. There were times when he would fall silent, then Kitty – because she felt he needed to get everything out of his system, all the sadness – would prompt him again and off he would go on a new tack. Dusk fell and the night sky rolled in and then they were both silent.

Tyler's face was just a pale blur when he said softly, 'It's dark now, Kitty.'

'Yes, I know.' Her heart gave a little flutter. 'I'll go up, if you don't mind.'

He came round to her and gave her a chaste kiss. 'I'll take a stroll, follow you in a while.' He tilted her face towards him. 'Don't go to sleep.' Although he had tried to sound teasing, there was a catch in his voice.

'I won't, I promise.'

Soft lamplight greeted her as she opened the dining-room door. There was light all the way up and in the bedroom and dressing-rooms. Kitty turned the bedside lamps lower, then walked over to the open window. The night air was cool and there were all the rustlings of animals in the undergrowth. An owl hooted. The fragrance of cigar smoke drifted up. Slow footsteps crunched on the gravelled path beneath her. Kitty drew the curtains, her heart now beating madly. In a little while . . .

She tried to visualize herself in bed, Tyler coming in, going into his dressing-room to get undressed. What would he say, what would she say? Would they say anything? She was glad she knew what a man was like physically, and Tyler knew she knew, from the time when he was ill and she had managed to change his nightshirt. Oh, heavens, she thought, I'm standing here and haven't yet started to undress.

Kitty had told herself she would be perfectly calm, knowing what to expect, but now that the moment was near she found herself trembling. Buttons refused to be unfastened and in her haste she pulled one off.

She had always slept in cotton nightdresses and when she pulled the silk one over her head and it slid down her body she gave a shiver, partly on account of nerves but mostly from delight at feeling the softness of pure silk against her skin.

Although the day had been warm, the linen lace-trimmed sheets felt cold. Kitty lay propped up against the pillows, lowered herself further down the bed and then propped herself up again, not wanting to seem as though she was eager for what was to come. At that point she felt none of the ecstasy she had experienced earlier.

When Tyler came up he went straight into the dressing-room. She heard him washing, cleaning his teeth, moving around. When he came in, he was wearing a dark blue velvet dressing-gown. He stood at the bedside watching her.

'You look beautiful, Kitty.' He touched her nightdress.

'Would you take this off, darling?'

She looked at him, horrified. 'Remove my nightdress?'

'You'll enjoy your wedding night much better without it, my sweet. Shall I take it off for you?'

'No, no! Please turn out the lamps.' First one went out, then the other, and even though they were in darkness she burrowed under the bedclothes and struggled to get her nightdress off. She heard Tyler laughing softly at her antics. She drew herself up and lay still with her eyes closed for what was to happen next, which at the moment she thought of as an ordeal.

The bed-cover was being lifted and the next moment Tyler was lying beside her. The sudden warmth against her flesh made her start. He was naked too! The next moment tremors were running all over her. Who would have imagined that the touch of his flesh against hers could have been so pleasurable? Tyler put an arm under her shoulder and drew her to him. Soft lips explored hers, gently at first and then hungrily. She responded and Tyler groaned, 'Oh, Kitty, how I've wanted you!' She found her own breathing ragged as fingertips explored her body, causing her once to cry out, which excited Tyler even more. 'I've waited so long,' he whispered, 'I can't wait any longer.'

Although Kitty had known what to expect and was prepared for pain, she was not prepared for the demands of her own body at the penetration. She had never thought about the word fulfilment, yet knew it was something which should happen by the urgency of her own need, the throbbing that was both pain and sweetness.

Then it was over and she felt frustrated, denied. 'I'm sorry, Kitty,' Tyler said ruefully. 'Next time.' He rolled away from her, lay for a moment and then brought her close to him – kissing her cheek, her throat with gentle kisses. The throbbing in her died. 'You were wonderful, darling,' he whispered. 'Did I hurt you?'

'Yes,' she whispered, 'but I didn't mind, it was ... pleasurable too.' Kitty paused. 'Tyler, should something happen to me ... as it did to you?'

'It will, my sweet, I promise you. And before long.'

A thought suddenly struck her and she drew away from him. 'I won't have a baby, will I?'

'No, not yet, I took precautions – this is something we shall have to discuss later. But not right now. Not at *this* moment!' His hand cupped her breast, bringing an instant response in her.

It was a long and beautiful night and although she knew fulfilment only once, she enjoyed the love-play, every caress was a delight and she wondered why, according to Ivy, women hated having their husbands make love to them.

She awoke to bright sunlight in Tyler's arms. He kissed each eyelid. 'Beautiful, adorable Kitty! What a tragedy that I shall have to go to work soon.'

'It's a good job you do have to go,' she said, smiling. 'Otherwise I would be a worn-out wife.'

Before Tyler had a chance to answer this, there was a sharp rap on the door. Kitty drew away and pulled up the bed-cover, 'Oh, my goodness, if the housekeeper should see us like this!'

Tyler reminded her that they were married, then called out a blithe, 'Come in!' The housekeeper brought them morning tea, gave them a brief greeting and told them that breakfast would be ready whenever they wished. After Tyler had said they would like it in half an hour's time, she left as silently as she had come. Kitty collapsed under the sheet in giggles. There was some love-play between them then, but no more actual love-making as Tyler wanted to get back to the site.

'But this is our honeymoon,' she protested. Tyler kissed her and told her with one of his wicked grins that they would still be on honeymoon for the next three weeks at least.

When he left her at Crescent House to go straight to the site, Kitty had a bereft feeling and thought this was what it must be like when husbands went to sea. She went straight up to Mrs Helder's room, and hoped she did not look like a cat who has stolen the cream.

She knocked, opened the door and hesitated when she saw a girl brushing Mrs Helder's hair. It was not Mrs Parker's daughter. Then the girl turned and grinned and Kitty shouted, 'Ivy! What on earth are *you* doing here?' and ran to hug her.

It was Mrs Helder who explained. 'Ivy served me very well when you had to go to nurse your mother, Kitty. And knowing I would need another companion when you were married, I wrote to Mrs Earle. Ivy was released and here she is, a surprise for you!'

'Oh, yes, indeed! Ivy, you must tell me all your news.'

'And you must tell me yours,' she replied, with a cheeky laugh. 'But first I must finish putting up Mrs Helder's hair.'

Ivy looked different; she was wearing a simple grey dress with a white collar and her hair had been neatly trimmed. Her manner was different too, more in keeping with her role of companion. Ivy had once said she could be anything she wanted to be.

While Ivy was finishing getting Mrs Helder ready, Kitty raced to the furnace room to tell William she had permission to learn more about glass-making. William said Yes, the master had told him, but it would be convenient if she could come that afternoon since they had work to finish that morning. Kitty agreed and when she got back Mrs Helder was ready and sent the girls off to have a chat.

The first thing Ivy said when they were alone was, 'So you're married then? I couldn't believe it. Oh, I do know I don't have to tell anyone. Aren't you lucky? He's a lovely feller, is Mr van Neilson.' Ivy grinned. 'Wouldn't have minded marrying him meself. *Myself*,' she corrected herself. 'Not that I would have had a look in where you're concerned.' She gave Kitty an impulsive hug. 'Eee, but it's lovely to see you again, I didn't half miss you after you'd gone! Did you know that old Bramley's getting married to Pa Walton? His wife died.'

'Oh, I'm so glad,' Kitty said. 'Mrs Bramley did so much want to be married.'

Ivy went on to tell her that Miss Lavinia was married to her gamekeeper and expecting a baby, and although they were living in a one-up and one-down cottage, they were very happy.

'It's being in love,' Kitty said dreamily. 'I wouldn't mind where I was living as long as my husband was with me.'

Ivy eyed her thoughtfully. 'Thought you were gone on that Luke feller?'

'He's married,' Kitty said, and changed the conversation back to the Earles.

There was a time later that morning – as Mrs Helder and Ivy were talking together – when Kitty had a feeling of being shut out of the old lady's life. Then she realized this was inevitable. She was a married woman now, with responsibilities.

Nevertheless, she was pleased when Mrs Helder sent for her and Ivy was not in the room.

The old lady patted a chair and smiled. 'We must have a talk, Kitty. Happy?'

'Oh, yes, very. It was good of Mr Freeman to let us have his house for our honeymoon. Mrs Helder, I know you will want to pass the reins of the house to me, but I would rather that you were in charge, that you saw Mrs Parker about menus and such like. Tyler has given me permission to learn the glass-making trade.'

Mrs Helder searched her face. 'I don't think that is a good thing, Kitty. I have a feeling you will be storing up trouble for yourself. Tyler will come in expecting to find you at home and if you are not here, he'll feel aggrieved. A man wants to be the important one in the house.'

'He will be, I'll only be working for part of the day. He has agreed to it.'

The old lady gave her a wry smile. 'How could he refuse his new bride? But I would think it over if I were you. It won't make for a happy marriage.'

Kitty refused to believe this. She would prove it could work.

But even that very day there was some friction over the matter. Tyler came home when Kitty was at the furnace room and Ivy came to fetch her, saying that the 'Lord and Master' was home and demanding attention.

Kitty left at once, but was furious at being interrupted in the making of a bowl.

'You've got a taskmaster there all right,' Ivy said with relish. 'I wouldn't be surprised but he'll beat you and lock you up!'

'Just let him try!' Kitty retorted.

Tyler greeted her coldly: 'If you want Thomas to teach you the trade, you must have a specified time for working. I told you this morning that I would be in during the afternoon for a meal. And what happens? Mrs Parker has nothing prepared. My time is limited, I want to get back to the site.'

Kitty, sure that Tyler was being deliberately awkward, retorted, 'You told me you would not be in for lunch, but mentioned nothing about wanting a meal during the afternoon.'

'I told you, Kitty, when I brought you home this morning. It was the *last* thing I told you.' His expression was thunderous. 'This is a good start to being a housewife!'

A vague memory of Tyler having mentioned it made Kitty calm down. 'I'm sorry.' She went up to him. 'We were parting and it wasn't food that was on my mind.'

All his anger vanished. 'You tantalizing little wretch, you know exactly how to get round a man, don't you?' He drew her fiercely to him. 'I have a good mind to carry you upstairs.'

Kitty exulted in his mastery. 'Why don't you?'

He swept her up in his arms and was at the door, both of them laughing, when a knock brought Tyler to a halt and he set Kitty down. It was Mrs Parker to tell him the meal was ready. Tyler gave Kitty a wicked glance, then said, 'Thank you, Mrs Parker. I'll come in a moment.'

Kitty teased him, asking if food was more important to him than making love to his wife, whereupon he said that without food he wouldn't be able to make love. Then he knuckled her under the chin. 'I'll be back at nine o'clock and I shall expect you to be waiting for me.'

'In bed?' she asked with a saucy smile.

'Of course, where else?' He drew her to him again, kissed her passionately and then left, leaving her in an agony of desire.

After Kitty had composed herself, she sat down to think things over. It was their first quarrel and only a day after their wedding. Mrs Helder had warned her that Tyler must be the most important person in the house. She would have to avoid such an incident in the future, otherwise there would be no lessons in glass-making.

At that moment, Ivy knocked to see if everything was all right.

'Yes,' Kitty said, 'a storm in a teacup. Come on in. Tyler is a masterful man,' she mused, 'but a . . .'

'Loving one,' Ivy replied with a grin.

'Yes, he is,' Kitty said softly, and because the thoughts of the coming evening were sending tremors through her body again, she began to talk to Ivy about glass-making.

CHAPTER TWENTY-ONE

During the next few weeks it seemed to Kitty that Tyler was determined to keep her from the furnace room. No matter what time she arranged to go for a lesson with William, there would be something Tyler found for her to do – or for William to do. He would change mealtimes at the last minute and want her with him when he ate, or ask for her to be there with Mrs Helder when he entertained a business colleague.

It was only the nights that made up for Kitty's frustration, with Tyler teaching her the art of love-making and often bringing her to a frenzy of emotion. He taught her to make love to him and although she was embarrassed at first, she overcame her shyness and enjoyed the reversed role.

But there came a night when he told her there would be no more precautions – he wanted a child, a son, he said. Kitty panicked and begged him to wait a little longer, but he refused. She accused him then of thinking only of his own pleasure and would not even discuss why the thought of having a baby was so abhorrent to her.

It ended with Tyler storming out of the bedroom and sleeping elsewhere and Kitty crying herself to sleep.

Although she was determined not to let Mrs Helder know what had happened, it was impossible to disguise her reddened eyes, and later in the morning the old lady dismissed Ivy and asked Kitty point-blank what was wrong.

Kitty told her, but as with Tyler she refused to discuss the reason for not wanting babies. And when Mrs Helder insisted she talk about the problem Kitty shouted, 'I can't, I won't – and I don't care if I never see Tyler again!'

'Kitty, calm down!' Mrs Helder spoke gently. 'You're becoming hysterical. How can you expect a husband to be loving towards you when you can give him no explanation for not wanting children? How long are you intending to keep him waiting? I think it might be a good idea if I asked the doctor to call and have a word with you.'

'No, I don't want to talk to anyone! And if Tyler wants to stay away from me, then that's it.'

'Do you really mean, Kitty, that you would ruin a marriage because of your stubbornness over discussing a matter that's of the utmost importance to Tyler? Are you prepared for him to turn to another woman for solace? Because I can assure you that is what he will do. And who could blame him, with you behaving so unreasonably? Give him an explanation, that is all he asks!'

Kitty sat with hands tightly clasped and head bowed for several moments; then she looked up, her eyes brimming with tears.

'Oh, Mrs Helder, help me, *please!* I don't want to lose Tyler, I don't, I really don't.'

The old lady held out her arms and Kitty went into them, sobbing.

When she was calmer, they talked, but all Kitty could tell her was that it was deeply embedded in her mind that babies were filthy, obscene – she had no idea why. Older children did not affect her in this way, even toddlers.

Although Mrs Helder probed into her life and asked Kitty all sorts of questions – had her mother's husband interfered with her at any time, had she ever witnessed a miscarriage, seen a deformed baby being born – Kitty said she could link none of these things with her problem.

Mrs Helder waited a moment, then said earnestly, 'Kitty, if you turn your back on Tyler you will know great loneliness in your life, an emptiness. Without love, without someone to care, you are nothing. And think of Tyler's feelings; he lost his mother when young. He's been a lonely soul, seeking love. Then he found you . . . only, it seems, to lose you again. Don't decide anything now, think about it.'

Kitty did think about it, she thought of nothing else all day and by evening knew she wanted Tyler back at any cost. She told Mrs Helder about her decision after dinner, and when she was in bed that night Tyler returned to her.

Their reconciliation was sweet, poignant – Tyler telling her how unhappy he had been away from her – but although Kitty wanted him to make love to her, longed for it, she found she was not responding as she had done previously.

Tyler made excuses for her, she had been upset, said that in time everything would return to normal. But as the weeks went by, the restraint on Kitty's part remained and unhappily this caused upsets between them. And one evening when Kitty's stomach suddenly crawled at the thought of having a baby, she pushed Tyler away from her and said she was not in the mood for making love. Whereupon Tyler, his passion at a height, was so furious he left her and for the next three nights they slept apart and were coolly polite to one another when they met. Although Kitty grieved about the state they had reached, she found it impossible to give in.

She had managed to have some lessons in glass-making, but her heart was not in it and after making a number of mistakes she decided to give up thoughts of glass-making for the time being.

Then, to make matters worse, she had two letters that depressed her. One was from Abel to say that Harriet was a little poorly. Abel's 'little poorly' meant that Harriet was back in bed, which worried Kitty. Then in the other letter from Ann, there was news of Fred who had consumption. 'He looked awful,' Ann said. 'He's gone to stay with a relative in Alston to get some good air. I miss him so much. I hope it won't be long before he'll be home again. Hope you are well, Kitty . . .'

News of Fred made Kitty realize how foolishly she was behaving. If anything happened to Tyler, she would never forgive herself for making him so unhappy.

When he came in for dinner that night, she reached for his hand. He squeezed it and said softly, 'Oh, Kitty, why do we torture one another?'

Their reconciliation this time was wild, tempestuous, as though it was the last time they would be making love. In the early hours of the morning they lay drained, both vowing they would never be parted again, not for any reason.

The following afternoon Kitty made three goblets, her best work yet, which won high praise from William. 'The master'll have to be looking to his laurels if you go on at this rate,' he said.

Kitty laughed and warned him not to tell Tyler, which had the old man tapping the side of his nose, indicating that this was something else to be kept secret between them.

Kitty asked her usual spate of questions and he answered them patiently and in some cases demonstrated various processes. She had stayed later than usual and ran all the way back to the house, hoping Tyler was not already home.

She met Mrs Parker, who told her that the master was with Kitty's sister in the sitting-room. 'My *sister*?' Kitty exclaimed.

'Yes, ma'am, she's had a bereavement; she's in widow's weeds.'

Kitty's hand went to her mouth. Oh, God, no! Fred must have died. She ran upstairs, opened the sitting-room door and went in, then stood . . . frozen.

The black-clad figure whose hands Tyler was holding was not her sister Ann, but Violet.

Tyler turned. 'Oh, Kitty, I'm afraid we have some bad news for you. Your sister has lost her husband. She's in dire straits, as he left her penniless. So she came to us for help.'

'Penniless?' She eyed Violet coldly. 'I understood he was a very wealthy man.'

'I thought so too.' Her sister's voice was low, her lovely eyes misted with tears. Violet had never looked more beautiful, and Kitty had never hated her so much. And knew it was because of the sympathy she had roused in Tyler, who was standing gazing at her as though he longed to take her in his arms and comfort her.

'My husband led me to *believe* he was wealthy,' Violet went on, 'but when he died I was told that everything, including the house, would have to be sold to pay his debts.' She held out her hands with a helpless gesture. 'I didn't know what to do, or where to go. Ann refused to have me to stay with her, even temporarily.'

'I can understand that, and you're certainly not staying here,' Kitty retorted.

Tyler looked at her, shocked. 'Kitty! How can you say such a thing? Violet is your own sister. She's lost her husband and she's destitute.'

Kitty stood her ground. 'Knowing Violet, she will not be destitute or alone for long. You don't know her – don't know how she behaved to me when I was a child. But we are not going into that; I only know that she is not going to stay here.'

Violet said in a woebegone voice, 'I'll go, I don't want to come between husband and wife.' She took a few steps and Tyler caught hold of her arm.

'You will stay here as long as you wish, Mrs Grainger,' he declared. '*I am master in this house!*'

Kitty was about to retort that if Violet stayed then *she* would leave, but bit her tongue on the words, knowing that this was something Violet had probably been aiming for; she had once said she could get any man she wanted, married or not.

Tyler rang the bell for Mrs Parker and when she came asked if she would prepare a room for Mrs Grainger, who would be staying indefinitely. Kitty had to dig her nails into her palms to stop herself from railing at them both.

Violet then asked if she could tidy herself and Kitty could do nothing else but take her to their own room.

Once there, she rounded on Violet. 'Now listen to me, our Violet, you might think you're very clever in worming your way in here, but I'll get you out if it's the last thing I do.'

'You won't, you know.' The triumph on her sister's face had Kitty raising a hand to slap her; then she let it fall to her side, knowing this would be more ammunition for Violet in trying to alienate her from her husband.

Violet unpinned her hat and threw it on the bed. 'Why didn't you tell me you were married, Kitty dear? Not that you'll be together for very long. Already he's attracted to me, very attracted! In another few days he'll be eating out of my hand.'

It took every ounce of Kitty's willpower to be able to answer calmly, 'You really are very childish, Violet. I feel sorry for you.'

'Childish?' Violet, who had removed her coat, stood eyeing her own reflection in the long mirror. 'I don't think your husband would regard me as a child.'

Although the mourning dress was long-sleeved and buttoned up to the neck, Violet looked as seductive in the tight-fitting bodice as if she were wearing a flimsy diaphanous nightdress. Kitty turned away, tossing over her shoulder, 'Come to the sitting-room when you're ready, it's painful to listen to your pitiful conversation.'

When Kitty looked back, she was startled at the black hatred in her sister's eyes. She was on her way back to the sitting-room to tackle Tyler about his attitude when she met Ivy, who jerked her thumb over her shoulder.

'The master's with Mrs Helder. What's all this about your Violet going to stay here? I saw her when she came, spoke to her. She's a bad lot, that one, you can always tell by the eyes. Oh, she makes great play with them, but if you watch her when she doesn't know she's being watched, there's a slyness in them; she's weighing everything up. Calculating! That's the word I want. It's a good word, isn't it? I'm learning. What're you going to do about your sister?'

Kitty raised her shoulders in a gesture of despair. 'I just don't know, Ivy. Tyler is very impressed with her, won't hear of her leaving.'

Ivy grinned. 'Don't you worry, I'll think of something. We'll catch her out, let your husband know that Violet is no shrinking little flower.'

What astonished Kitty and upset her most was the fact that Mrs Helder appeared to be under Violet's spell. 'She really is a charming person,' the old lady said. 'And most intelligent. Judging by her conversation, one would think her widely travelled.'

'Oh, yes, she's clever,' Kitty said wryly. 'Very clever indeed. If I'm not careful, I shall be losing Tyler to her.'

Mrs Helder dismissed this as nonsense and Kitty felt sure the old lady was putting her remarks down to jealousy.

When Tyler came to bed that night, which was late, Kitty told him that they must a talk about Violet. He gave a weary sigh. 'Not now, Kitty, please, I've had a frantically busy day.'

'And I've had an upsetting one, and now I'm determined to have my say. Violet was cruel to me when I was a child and I intend to describe her treatment of me. I shall also tell you how she blackmailed our mother.'

Tyler listened without making any comments, but when Kitty had finished relating the facts he said quite blandly that he was on Violet's side: 'You were disobedient as a child, you had to be disciplined.'

'Disciplined?' Kitty exclaimed. 'Being thumped all over my body by her, having my flesh pinched between forefinger and thumb and later starved by her?'

'This happened years ago, Kitty.' Tyler spoke to her in an indulgent way, as though she were still a child. 'The whole thing has become exaggerated in your mind over the years. According to your own version, you were consistently disobedient in running away to the glassworks. Violet was left in charge of you and would have been responsible if any harm had come to you. As for blackmailing your mother, I find this quite ridiculous; your mother was a grown woman. No, Kitty, I refuse to listen to any more accusations against your sister. And you will treat her with respect while she is in this house, is that understood?'

Kitty looked at the stern face and felt despair. Already Violet's wickedness was working.

'I will tolerate her,' she said quietly, 'because I have no choice, but she will never get any respect from me because my sister is vile.' Kitty slid down in the bed. 'Good night, Tyler, just beware that she doesn't get you into her clutches, or you'll suffer.'

His answer was another weary sigh as he went into the dressing-room. And when he did come to bed, he made no attempt to draw her to him as he usually did; he kissed her briefly on the cheek and turned away from her, which was the worst rebuff Kitty could have had.

The following week Violet was the darling of the house, apart from Kitty and Ivy who went on hating her between them. Kitty thought she would not have been able to endure the situation had it not been for Ivy. Violet's manner at all times was subdued – the grieving widow who was to be pitied – yet somehow she gave the impression of sparkling in her conversation and as Ivy remarked, 'She's bloody unusual, to say the least.'

Kitty's final humiliation was when Tyler took Violet to the site, something he had denied her when she had asked to see it. And when they came back and she watched Tyler helping Violet down from the carriage, putting his arm around her to lead her to the front door, she felt she wanted to be miles away.

Her opportunity came the next morning, but not in a way she would have expected or wanted. A telegram came from Abel to say that Harriet was seriously ill – could Kitty come.

Tyler said right away that she must go as soon as possible and he would see about the trains. Kitty, catching a sly look in Violet's eyes, was aware of what might happen while she was away, but at that moment she didn't care – all she wanted was to be with Harriet.

Mrs Helder was very sweet and gentle with her and Tyler was more loving towards her than he had been all the previous week, but Kitty could not help wondering if he too was pleased she was going away. He said he would drive her to the station and Ivy whispered to her before they left, 'Don't worry, I'll keep an eye on the bitch!'

Tyler was tender to Kitty before she boarded the train, holding her close and telling her she must try not to worry, that Harriet might not be as ill as she expected. Men were inclined to exaggerate the illness of a loved one. Kitty wished he could have been more loving towards her during the past week. She had been so full of hurt at his attitude, but this was not the time to tell him.

'Take care of yourself, Tyler,' she said. 'Don't work too hard, and try to have regular meals.' She wanted to say, 'I love you,' but the words refused to come.

'I will, I promise. Come along, you must get aboard, Kitty.' He gave her a quick hug, then they parted. He waited until the train drew out, then turned quickly away and Kitty wondered if he was hurrying to get back to Violet. After that all her thoughts were on Harriet.

It was Luke who met her at Leicester and when Kitty saw the stricken look on his gaunt face, the grief in his eyes, a coldness crept over her.

'Aunt Harriet's gone, hasn't she?' she whispered. Luke nodded, then they were in one another's arms, clinging wordlessly together, their tears mingling.

Luke took her into the empty waiting-room and there told her how his mother had collapsed suddenly the night before and had died at ten o'clock that morning without regaining consciousness.

'I grieve so for Dad,' Luke said. 'He's broken up, can't believe that Mother's gone. But then none of us can. Life revolved around her; she was our mainstay, always there to heal our wounds, offer advice, to scold us when we needed it.'

'And to love us all,' Kitty said. 'Oh, Luke, if only I could have seen her, talked to her before she died.'

Luke took her hands in his. 'I'm sure it will help you, Kitty, if

I tell you she talked about you all day yesterday. She kept going over the funny little things you said and did as a child. She also talked about the boys – not about them being killed in the war, but when they were children too, about all the scrapes we all used to get into. She laughed a lot and I feel sure she died happy. It's our one consolation.'

After a moment's pause, Luke added, 'There's something else you must know, Kitty. Louise lost the baby three weeks ago. Don't mention it unless she does.'

'No, I won't. Oh, Luke, I am sorry!' Kitty laid a hand on his arm. 'I know how much you wanted it.'

'Yes. I think we had better go.' He sounded choked.

Although Abel's grief was almost a tangible thing, he kept his back straight, planned their future and talked about Harriet to Kitty, repeating what Luke had told her.

Louise, pale and obviously not too well, helped Kitty cope with all the people who called to offer condolences; they made endless cups of tea and shared the work. When Kitty protested to Louise that she was doing too much, she said, 'I have to be doing something. There was the baby, as Luke would tell you, then Harriet ... Mind you, perhaps it was best about the baby, it saved the gossip. I think losing Harriet was the greater shock. I had grown so fond of her—'

Kitty put her arms around her. 'I know, I know . . .'

Not long after this Abel told her that a niece of his, a strong sturdy girl, was coming to live in.

When the funeral was over and all the mourners gone, Kitty looked around the kitchen and thought how she would never see Harriet bustling around again, never see her kindly, plump face or be wrapped in the warmth of her love. Grief overwhelmed her and she got up and went outside. Luke followed her. 'Let's walk, Kitty.'

They walked to the top of the rise and Kitty wondered how many times they had done this in times of stress. The last time had been when Harriet was ill and Luke had told her he was going to marry Louise. And now Kitty herself was married and in danger, it seemed, of losing her husband.

Turning to Luke, she said piteously, 'Oh, Luke, hold me a moment.' She cried against his shoulders, his strong arms holding her close, wishing she had never left the farm, wishing

303

Harriet was still alive and Luke not married to Louise. Then, feeling guilty at such thoughts, she drew away.

'I'm all right now, Luke.' The day had been warm, but the night breeze was cool. She gave a little shiver and Luke took off his jacket and draped it around her shoulders.

'Would you like to walk, Kitty, or go back?' She told him she would prefer to walk.

The faint dampness in the air brought out the scent of newly scythed grass, which made for more nostalgia: halcyon days of haymaking, riding on the wagon, going with Harriet to take the men their midday meal, the jugs of cool home-made lemonade, beer or tea.

They had walked in silence for a way when Luke said suddenly, 'Kitty, in all the talks we've had since you came, you've never once mentioned your husband. What's wrong?'

They stopped at a fence and Kitty gripped it. 'It's a long story, Luke, and begins before I came to the farm. There's some of it you know and some you don't.'

'Tell me, Kitty, and start at the beginning.'

And so she told him about Violet's cruelties to her, their mother's bigamous first marriage and then her legal marriage to Richard Tierne, ending up with Violet appearing at the house and Tyler's insistence that she stay as long as she wished.

'I don't see what else he could do under the circumstances,' Luke said in reasonable tones. 'She is your sister and she is homeless. You couldn't possibly turn her out.'

'I could! She's evil, I don't think you've been listening to what I've told you.'

'I've been listening, Kitty, but I'm asking myself why your sister behaves in the way she does. She must have known since she was young that she was a bastard and you the legal daughter. It's gone deep with her. Also she was put in charge of you, an unruly disobedient child, when she longed to go out to work and earn some money.'

Kitty stared at him. 'I can't believe I'm hearing aright. You're like the rest of them in the house, making excuses for her. What do you want me to do? Say "Poor Violet, of course you must stay, you can make love to my husband any time you want, help yourself!"'

'Oh, Kitty . . .' There was a smile in Luke's voice, something

304

she had not heard since she arrived. 'You're getting yourself all worked up for something you imagine. All right, your sister is beautiful and your husband is attracted towards her, but that doesn't say he's going to take her to his bed.'

'He probably has,' she retorted.

'If he has, and I said *if*, what are you going to do about it? Walk out? No, of course not – you're a fighter, always have been.'

Kitty sighed. 'You don't know Violet. She's just so wicked. If she sets her mind on having a man, she'll get him. She's like a leech, sucking away at his will-power.'

Luke cupped her face between his palms. 'Do you know what I think? I think you're so in love with your husband that you're exaggerating the whole thing.'

Kitty drew away from him in despair. It was no use, he would never understand. Only Ivy, who had seen the really seamy side of life understood Violet's kind of person.

She turned away. 'We had better go back.'

They walked in silence until they reached the yard, then Luke stopped and turned Kitty to face him. 'I just want to say one thing, love. Try to get rid of the hatred you have for your sister. Hate is such a destroyer. I want you to stay the way we've always known you – yes, a rebel, but a very lovable one. We all want only your happiness.'

There was no mistaking the love in Luke's voice and Kitty could have burst into tears again. She said quietly, 'I'll try, but I'm not promising anything.' They went back to the house.

Three days later she returned to Leicester. She had sent Tyler a loving letter, saying how much she had missed him, how lovely it would be to get back for it was lonely sleeping alone. And she found herself longing to see him. When the train drew in at the platform she looked eagerly for him, and felt a swift disappointment when she saw Mrs Helder and Ivy waiting for her. They greeted her warmly and Mrs Helder told her that Tyler had been called away on urgent business but she was not to worry – he would be back later that evening.

Kitty drew a quick breath. 'And Violet, is she still with us?'

'Not at the moment.' Mrs Helder's lips tightened visibly. 'She's staying with people she knows in Leicester – has been there since you left. It was my suggestion. Men are vulnerable,

305

especially when their wives are away, with a woman like your sister around. She has very, let us say – persuasive ways. I thought myself quite adept at weighing up people, but I was mistaken with your sister. I doubt whether she will stay on with her friends, but she will be there this evening anyway.'

During the drive to Crescent House they talked about Harriet, the shock of her sudden death. Mrs Helder said, 'Her poor husband, such a nice man, he must be so distraught. I met him the day I came to the farm with Mrs Earle.'

Kitty said, 'I think I shall always remember the day of the funeral and Abel going into church. His boots squeaked. Normally, I would have wanted to laugh, but there was something so touching about it. He had travelled all the way into Leicester to buy them specially. It was as though he were paying a tribute to Aunt Harriet, who had always seen he was spick and span to go to church on Sunday mornings. It's Uncle Abel I feel the most sorry for; he wept when I left.' Kitty had to swallow hard to get rid of the lump in her throat. Luke had Louise . . . and she would have Tyler later.

But Tyler did not come home that evening and doubts crowded into Kitty's mind that filled her with dread. Had he succumbed to her sister's witch-like influence and was he sleeping with her?

Tomorrow she would know.

CHAPTER TWENTY-TWO

All the next morning and into the afternoon, Kitty waited and watched for her husband's return . . . And worked herself up into a state at one time, feeling sure that he and Violet had gone away together.

During the afternoon when Mrs Helder was resting and Ivy had gone to the village to get something for Mrs Parker, there was the sound of a carriage coming up the drive. Kitty ran to the window of the sitting-room that overlooked the drive and watched, holding her breath.

It was not Tyler who stepped out but Violet, beautiful in black velvet, her skirt trailing the gravel. Kitty released her breath slowly, feeling a mixture of disappointment and relief. At least she would have Violet on her own, to tell her she would have to leave.

Violet swept into the sitting-room and said, as she began to draw off her gloves, 'I heard you were back. I couldn't wait to get out of the house of that pompous—'

'You had better return there,' Kitty said firmly, 'because no matter what Tyler says, you will not be staying here. This is my home too.'

Violet looked her up and down, a sneer on her lips. 'My *dear* little sister, you can save your breath. Tyler could not do without me. You were a fool to go away. He's a passionate man.'

Kitty forced herself to say calmly, 'You can stop trying to stir up muddy waters. Tyler would not demean himself by sleeping with you.'

Violet plucked the second glove from her hand and threw it on to a chair. 'Where do you think he was last night? Not in *your* bed! Oh, we had quite a long talk about you. He told me you had an aversion to babies!'

Kitty felt the colour draining from her face. She whispered, 'I don't believe it was Tyler who told you.'

'Who else knows?' Violet moved closer and now her expression changed, became vicious. 'I'm glad you hate babies, glad, glad! Do you remember Mam giving you a doll one Christmas? *You* – only one for *you*, not one for me or Mary, or Ann or Agnes. And do you remember that *dear* Jessica made a christening robe for it, a bonnet and a shawl? It was your very own little baby, you said, you christened it Angela. Purity!' Violet gave a shrill laugh. 'I soon took the purity from it.'

Kitty's whole body was trembling, because now remembrance was beginning to return. 'Stop it,' she pleaded.

'No, I won't stop – not until you've heard every little detail of what happened to your *beautiful* baby. Can you remember what I did with it?' Violet thrust her face close to Kitty's. 'Shall I tell you where I put it?' She drew back. 'In the privy, that's where, in all the filth! Then I brought it out and dangled it in front of you. I can still see the horror on your face. And there's more...' Violet's voice had dropped to a vicious whisper.

'And what did I do then? I wiped the filth across your mouth!' Her voice rose again. 'You were sick, oh how you were sick! And how I enjoyed watching you. I was sure then that it would put you off wanting babies for ever, for wanting a man to make love to you. And I was right. But *I* wouldn't mind having a baby. Your *husband's* baby! And I could be pregnant right now. Does that make you happy?'

Kitty felt as though every vestige of blood was draining from her body. The room began to spin round, then blackness engulfed her.

When she awoke she was in bed and was conscious of people in the room talking in whispers. The room was bathed in a soft pink glow from the bedside lamps. She tried to move and heard someone say, 'She's coming round.' There was a strange smell in the room and she recognized it as sal volatile. Had she been given some? But why?

'Kitty, are you feeling better?' It was Tyler's voice and a great feeling of revulsion came over her. 'Get away from me,' she whispered. 'You're filthy, filthy!'

There was some consternation at this and when she began to moan and could hear herself continue moaning, she was given a pill.

It was daylight when she awoke next and Ivy was there holding her hand. 'It's all right, Kitty, love, I'm going to stay with you. No one will harm you.'

Kitty lost track of time; it could have been days or weeks that went by, but she made no effort to ask. People came and went, but they were like wraiths in a dream. The only one who had any reality was Ivy, who became her lifeline. Whenever she roused fully it was to see Ivy sitting there, solid and reliable.

Eventually there came a time when she wanted to tell Ivy what had happened. She described it in a dispassionate way, adding that of course no one would believe it had happened.

'I know it did,' Ivy said. 'I came back in time to overhear the last part of your sister's rantings before you collapsed. But she's gone now and she'll never come back. Now you've got to concentrate on getting well. We'll talk some more another time.'

Recuperation was slow, but even when Kitty was up she refused to see Tyler. To every plea from Ivy, from Mrs Helder, she would give a stock answer: 'He slept with my sister, told her how I felt about babies,' and all their efforts to refute this only brought a parrot-like repetition.

But there came a day when Ivy got mad with her. 'All right,' she said, 'you've had a rough time, you've been ill, you've been looked after, fussed, spoon-fed, but now your spoiling days are over. You've got to "get down to the pudden". You must talk to your husband – and don't say no, no, to me. He must have a chance to put his side of it; he has a right to that, everybody has a right to have their say.'

When Kitty shook her head and tried to get up, Ivy pushed her back in the chair. 'If you don't give him a chance, I'm finished with you. I'll leave! I'm not wasting my time on someone who behaves like a stupid spoiled brat.'

The strong tactics worked. Kitty panicked. 'I'll see him, I will, I promise. Don't leave me, Ivy, *please!*'

'I won't, as long as you're fair to your husband and listen to what he has to say.' Kitty agreed, and so Tyler came in to see her.

He made no attempt to touch her, and in fact stood well apart from her. There was nothing pleading about his manner. He stood tall and straight and spoke firmly.

'Kitty, I admit I did tell Violet how you felt about babies – but only because, being your sister, I thought she might know the reason. I never slept with her; I never even kissed her.'

Kitty searched his face. 'Would you swear that on the Bible?'

'No, you will have to take my word. You must trust me if we are to have any married life together.'

Kitty was a long time in replying. When she did, she was quite calm. 'I'll take your word, Tyler, but don't ask me to sleep with you yet. Another week, two weeks perhaps.'

'Very well, Kitty. Two weeks. I'll be away during that time. When I come back . . .' He turned and left without even a backward glance, leaving Kitty feeling oddly piqued.

She said to Ivy, 'He didn't exactly behave like a loving husband, did he?'

Ivy groaned. 'Oh, gawd, what did you want him to do? The man's been sleeping on his own for weeks. You're not only expecting the moon but the sun and stars an' all. Come on, we're going to take a walk; the doctor said you had to start having some fresh air.'

Although it was just the beginning of August, there was an autumnal chill in the air. Ivy threw a shawl around Kitty's shoulders. 'We'll walk to that beehive place in the woods. I met the old foreman the other day. William, isn't it? I told him I'd never seen glass being made and he said I could call whenever I wanted.'

Kitty stopped. 'I don't want to go.'

'All right, you stay here, have a walk amongst the trees. I won't be long.' She walked away briskly, twigs snapping under her feet. Kitty hesitated a moment, then followed slowly. She felt she was being manipulated; she could imagine Tyler saying, 'Take her to William. Get her making glass, it will take her mind off all that has happened.' She didn't want to make glass, she didn't want to do anything. She was still sick in her mind – why couldn't they understand what she had gone through?

Yet when Kitty caught the bright glow of the furnace through the trees, heard its gentle roar, a faint excitement stirred in her.

William touched his cap to her when she went in. 'Good to see you around again, ma'am. I was just telling the young lady here, we're going to make paperweights – perhaps you'd like to watch. Have a seat, ma'am.' He motioned her to a piece of log on legs, and when she was seated, laid out three paperweights beside her to study. They all had flower designs made from tiny pieces of coloured glass, which William said was known as *millefiori*.

Ivy, who had been eyeing everything around her, came and sat beside Kitty as William, Thomas and young Ben began to work. They used five colours: green, blue, purple, red and amber. Gathers of some colours were taken separately and with the help of Thomas and Ben, these were stretched in a fine line the length of the furnace room. Then gathers were taken of several colours together and the process repeated. When the strips were cool they were cut into tiny pieces and the pattern assembled by William into pots, which were then put into the annealing oven. Later these would be sealed by a cover of glass.

Ivy was brimming over with delight, while Kitty was quietly excited, feeling it might be good to get started again. Their stay was short, she was feeling tired. William suggested to Kitty that she work out some of her own designs and come the next day to make a paperweight. Ivy too, if she wanted to try her hand, he said.

Ivy laughed, saying she was a dab hand with a scrubbing brush but couldn't even draw a daisy. Kitty noticed that Thomas never took his eyes off Ivy.

When they got back to the house, Ivy having talked all the way about glass-making, they went to Mrs Helder's room. Kitty had seldom seen the old lady recently, had been just vaguely aware that she came to see her when she was ill. Now she realized why. Mrs Helder had aged and looked terribly frail, yet her voice was still strong when she greeted Kitty. 'Oh, my dear, how lovely to see you and looking so well! I'm sorry if I seem to have neglected you, but my old legs are letting me down. Come and tell me what you've both been doing.'

Talking to Mrs Helder made Kitty aware what a remote world she had been living in. The big glasshouse and the cottages that were being built had never once crossed her mind until Mrs Helder told her they would be finished in a few weeks' time. Then there would be a big celebration and Kitty, being Mrs van Neilson, would be expected to be by her husband's side.

Aware that the old lady was hanging on her answer, Kitty said quietly, 'Yes, of course,' and was rewarded by a pleased smile.

That afternoon Kitty sat drawing, experimenting with designs, and found it intriguing. She drew several flower patterns and then went on to geometrical designs, followed by a country scene and finally a drawing of a peacock in full plumage. She was pleased with the peacock, feeling it would be more of a challenge if she could capture the iridescence of the feathers.

It was this design that interested William the next day. Kitty had gone alone, Ivy having to stay with Mrs Helder who was not at all well. 'We'll do some experimenting later,' he said, 'but first let us try these three designs.' He had chosen the country scene, a starburst and one with no set form, but which he thought could be effective.

They were all successful, the country scene being the most difficult but the one which had interested William. The pieces for this were so fine that Kitty knew it was only his expertise that made it possible. There was a cornfield with poppies, a stone church, trees and a pond.

'You have a gift, ma'am,' William said, 'that extra something which makes for fine pieces. You could go far, if you wished. Tomorrow we'll start experimenting with the peacock.'

When Kitty asked if he could spare the time, for he must have other work on hand, William said, 'Mr van Neilson told us we were to give you our time, ma'am; he'll be pleased with your efforts.'

Kitty had determinedly put Tyler from her mind, not wanting to think about him, knowing she would have to sleep with him when he returned. It was not that she still felt her earlier strong aversion to him, more her lack of emotion at the thought of having him make love to her.

During the next few days Kitty, by her own experimenting, managed to get the sheen on the peacock's plumage. She was delighted and hurried home to tell Mrs Helder and Ivy. When she went into the house, Mrs Parker handed her a letter; it was from Abel and Kitty started to read it as she went upstairs, then she stopped and held on to the banister. Louise had had another miscarriage. They were all very upset, but Louise was young, there would be other babies . . .

It was the word 'babies' that made Kitty feel weak. Would she ever get over this? What if she became pregnant? How could she possibly cope? She made an effort to pull herself together. She must try not to think about it. So she put the letter back in the envelope without reading any more.

When she went into Mrs Helder's room, the old lady eyed her in alarm. 'Kitty, how pale you are, has something happened?' She was alone at that moment and Kitty told her about Louise, then said in a stricken voice: 'What shall I do if I have a baby? I won't want it!'

Mrs Helder soothed her. 'You won't have one until you want one, Kitty. Tyler promised me this.'

Kity felt a surge of relief and was able to talk about her experiment. Later she read the last part of Abel's letter.

They were coping, he said, and his niece, who was a big, cheerful woman, helped tremendously. Louise had got over the miscarriage quite well. They were missing Harriet terribly, but life had to go on.

Abel concluded, 'We hope you're getting better, Kitty love. Mrs Helder told us you had been ill, but were on the road to recovery. Come and see us when you can, we all send our love...'

Kitty shed a few tears and wept for all of them, for dear Abel who was trying to put a brave face on the loss of Harriet, who would have loved another grandchild but was filled with concern about Louise. And for Luke, who loved Louise and would have made a wonderful father...

She kept the letter out to be answered.

But it was several days before she penned a reply to Abel because she got caught up in her experiments. She did designs of bowls, jugs, decanters, wine-glasses, goblets at every opportunity, and had tried out several of her designs by the time Tyler came home. Kitty was in the sitting-room alone when he came in. She had felt brimming over with life that afternoon and on seeing him, felt a surge of pleasure.

'Why, Tyler, I thought you were expected tomorrow?'

'I came a day early,' he said softly, coming to her. 'I couldn't wait any longer.' His voice, his eyes, held passion. 'Are you going to hold me to my promise of two weeks, Kitty?'

'No,' she said, and when he held out his arms she went into them, not yet being able to match his passion but nevertheless wanting him. It was a start – perhaps by this evening . . .

Unfortunately there was no fulfilment for Kitty that night, nor on subsequent nights, but Tyler was happy and full of love and at the moment that was the most important thing.

Then came the day of the opening of the glasshouse, and of what to Kitty seemed a small village on its own. There were neat little whitewashed cottages, with gardens attached, a church, school, small shops.

Workers and their families were milling about, all in their Sunday best. The hats and caps of the men were doffed to Kitty as she walked around with Tyler, and the women and young children bobbed curtsies to her. When she stopped to talk to some of the women, they all told her what a godsend this was to them – some of their menfolk had been out of work for weeks, some for months. Mr van Neilson had been so good to them, giving them money for food, clothes and some furniture. He had also given money to the women to make food for the party they were having that afternoon. Everyone had been working hard.

It was a mellow September day with no breeze. Trestle tables were laid with snow-white cloths and filled plates were being brought to the table. There were meat pies, sliced ham, beef, cakes . . . lemonade for the children to drink and beer for the rest of the people

Tyler said things might get rough later, but they would leave before then. Several of Tyler's business colleagues came and one of them made a short speech, introducing Tyler and Kitty. Then Tyler made a speech, quite a stirring one, in which he said that there was a good opportunity to make a success of the venture. He had decided that every worker would get a share in the profits, but only those he stressed, who *did* work. There was no place for shirkers.

There were cheers at this.

Tyler then told them that there would be a firework display later, also music and dancing. He wanted everyone to enjoy themselves, but reminded them he would expect every worker to report for work on Monday morning, pointing out that they did have all day Sunday to get over the celebrations!

There was a burst of laughter at this and three cheers were raised to the gaffer and his wife.

Ivy arived later in the company of Thomas looking quite demure in a pale blue cashmere dress and a hat trimmed with daisies. She said she had not wanted to leave Mrs Helder, but had left Mrs Parker's two daughters in charge and would not stay late.

Kitty and Tyler left when the men started getting rowdy and the stronger of the wives began taking them in hand. There was still the firework display to come, but Kitty watched this later from the top floor of Crescent House.

Tyler came in with champagne. 'Shall we have a little celebration on our own, Kitty?' he said gently. 'I feel we've overcome a lot of difficulties in our marriage.'

'Yes, we have,' Kitty answered quietly, 'but you have done especially well, Tyler, in your project. I just know it will be a success. Not that I'm interested in optical glass, but judging by what I heard today from the remarks of various people, there is a big demand for it in other countries as well as here.'

Tyler poured the champagne and handed Kitty a glass. 'To a long and happy marriage, Mrs van Neilson!' They touched glasses and their gaze met and held, Tyler's eyes dark with a longing that Kitty did not feel at that moment. 'A long and happy marriage,' she said, and hoped that this evening would bring fulfilment for both of them.

She had two glasses of champagne and watched the coloured lights exploding in the sky, merging into a beautiful blur.

When she began to giggle and her words became slurred, Tyler took the glass from her and sweeping her up in his arms, carried her to bed. She felt thrilled, excited, but when it came to the actual act of love she had to pretend her enjoyment and felt unhappy at having to cheat on something so important to Tyler.

And as the months went by, it was no different. She never once reached a peak with him. Their love-making was less frequent – not because of any complaint he had to make about Kitty, but simply because he worked late many nights at the glasshouse, experimenting with new ideas. Sometimes he would work right through one night, continue working the next day and evening, then drop into an exhausted sleep and sleep for many hours.

Kitty' own time was taken up with experimenting with

315

William. They attempted a peacock bowl, but although approaching what they wanted it was not yet to the complete satisfaction of either of them.

'We'll get it right one of these days,' William said, 'and then we'll make them to sell.' Although selling was not important to Kitty, she knew it would get Tyler to accept her as a professional, which he had not done until then, still treating her in an indulgent way – it was something to keep her occupied.

But they were happy, both doing work they were absorbed in. Mrs Helder had picked up during recent months and although not yet her former self, showed more strength and was able to take an interest in what was happening. She was especially pleased that Ivy had a young man. Thomas was courting her and Ivy pronounced him a 'decent feller, not one of those who has his hand down my neck and up my skirts all the time'.

Kitty said, laughing, 'Oh, Ivy, you are funny, what would I do without you? Sometimes I get so wrapped up in my work I think I have no time for fun any more.'

'Well, at least you don't have anything to be miserable about, do you?' And Kitty had to agree.

And that was how her life was during the following months – no exciting highlights, but no unpleasant incidents. The news from the farm was good; the harvest had been excellent; Louise was fit and well again; Abel and Luke were well and able to cope with the loss of Harriet. News from her sisters was also good. Ann's husband Fred had been cured of the consumption and Agnes and Mary were both courting. 'Nice chaps, both of them', Ann had written, 'with decent jobs.' A postscript added 'No news of Violet, I hope she's dropped dead!'

But Violet turned out to be very much alive and Kitty had dreadful proof of this in March on a bitterly cold evening when she was waiting for Tyler, who had promised to be in for dinner.

She had gone into the sitting-room and was talking to Mrs Helder and Ivy when Mrs Parker, after knocking, burst in greatly agitated. She said to Kitty, 'Oh, Mrs van Neilson, ma'am, can you come down to the kitchen? Someone's left a baby on the doorstep!'

Kitty stood motionless, feeling as if insects were crawling all over her body. She mouthed, 'Baby?' but no sound came.

Mrs Helder asked, 'Whose baby?' and Mrs Parker said, 'I

don't know, ma'am. There's an envelope pinned to its shawl. It was only by chance I heard it crying. I didn't want to bring the little thing away from the fire.'

The wind screamed around the house and Kitty felt it was a thousand devils trying to get at her. Ivy came over and caught hold of her arm. 'Come on, let's go and see what the letter says.'

'I know whose baby it is,' Kitty whispered. 'It's Violet's.' She restrained herself from adding, 'and Tyler's.'

Mrs Parker's eldest daughter was sitting by the fire nursing the baby. 'It's a boy,' she said, 'a lovely little thing no more than two or three weeks old. Healthy – and hungry, just look at him!' Kitty felt as though her feet were chained to the floor and it was Ivy who gave her a push. Her heart was pounding as she forced herself to go forward and take a look.

The baby's fist was tucked in his mouth and he was sucking avidly on it. He had a mop of black hair and a red face that was suddenly screwed up, ready to yell. Kitty wanted to back away, but was held there. The cry when it came was full of indignation.

'Oh, poor little thing!' Ivy said and took the baby in her arms. 'He's hungry, bless him.'

Mrs Parker came with some sugar in a clean rag and put it to the baby's lips. 'It'll keep him going until we can get a wet-nurse. There's a woman who was widowed three months before her baby was born. It lived two months, then died. She's longing for a child to care for; I know she'll be glad to come and live in.'

Kitty wanted to say, 'Take it to her,' but she couldn't. There was something about the tiny thing that was tugging at her. Mrs Parker handed her the envelope, saying, 'Who could leave a baby on a doorstep on a night like this? The mother must have been desperate.'

'Or evil,' Kitty said as she tore the envelope open. On a sheet of paper were the words, 'I'm sure you'll agree he's the image of Tyler! Love or hate this child, but give him a good home. I nearly kept him myself.' It was unsigned. Kitty folded the paper. 'I know who the mother is; we'll keep him until we decide what to do. Can you arrange to get this woman you mention, Mrs Parker? The coachman will collect her.'

Kitty went out and back to the sitting-room, where without a word she handed Mrs Helder the letter. She was trembling so much she had to sit down. The old lady scanned the note then said, 'Oh, Kitty, it could be any man's child. You know the type of person your sister is. She wants revenge on you and this is her way. And Tyler did deny having slept with her.'

Kitty's lips felt stiff. 'But I would never know if he was telling the truth, would I? It will always be there between us. Violet certainly knows how to twist the knife.'

Ivy, who had come in at that moment, said, 'Someone ought to strangle her, I wish I could get my hands on her! I haven't seen the note, but I can guess what's in it. It mightn't even be her baby, she's bad enough to pull this trick on you. I certainly wouldn't let it rest there until you make enquiries.'

Kitty shook her head. 'I don't want to be involved in any way with the child. Foster-parents will have to be found.' She turned away. 'I'm going to my room, I don't want anything to eat. Food would choke me.'

Five minutes later Tyler came to her. 'I know what a shock this must have been to you, Kitty, and I can only repeat that I have never slept with your sister. What we must discuss is the welfare of this child.'

'We shall get rid of him, of course,' Kitty said coldly. 'Find foster-parents. You couldn't expect me to bring him up, after what our Violet did to me!'

'No, but I would like to keep the boy.'

Kitty stared at him accusingly. 'It's obvious why! You're his father, why won't you admit it?'

Tyler's hands clenched. 'Kitty, I will say for the last time that I did not sleep with your sister. There are two reasons why I want to keep him: I want a son and I do have the means of giving him a good start in life. He deserves this chance, rather than being discarded like some chattel because of what his mother is. I will give him love and I hope that in time, you can bring yourself to show him the love and care that your foster-parents gave to you. In the meantime, a nurse will be engaged.'

Tyler stood for a moment and Kitty saw a look of appeal in his eyes, but she turned away from him and he went out.

That was the start of their occupying separate rooms, and of Kitty living in a house where a baby was the centre of doting females. She never saw the baby, and no one talked to her about him, but sometimes she would hear Ivy telling Mrs Helder of his progress.

'Fourteen pounds he is!' she exclaimed one day. 'Mrs Parker had him on the scales. He's a lusty male demanding food one minute and the next wrapping himself round your heart with his smile. He's beautiful, I could eat him.'

Tyler came in for meals, was polite to Kitty, asked about her progress in her glass-making, told her about his own progress and never once mentioned the child. She ached for love, but would not give in. Her salvation was her work.

Then on a sunny day in June, Kitty caught her first glimpse of the child since the night he had been left on the doorstep. She was on her way to the furnace room and had opened the wicket gate to go into the forest when she heard the hiccuping cry of a child. She looked around, but could see no one. The hiccuping became a wail and she realized it came from the trees ahead. A worker's child? She closed the gate and walked amongst the trees. The wail had now become a howling and she was getting agitated when she saw in a small clearing ahead a cot and small arms flailing. Again Kitty looked around her. Where was the mother? Surely it was not another abandoned baby? With her heart pounding she went to the cot and stood looking at the child, whose face was screwed up as though in pain. Then she knew this was Tyler's baby, not because of any resemblance to him but because of a remembrance of seeing the boy on that dreadful night.

'Hush,' she said softly. The leaves of the tree above made dappled patterns on his face. He was crying piteously now, his legs drawn up. Oh, where was the nurse who was supposed to be in charge. The baby's hands were twisting and turning on dimpled wrists, as big tears rolled down his cheeks. Kitty couldn't bear it any longer; she picked him up and held him against her shoulder, stroking his back. 'There, there . . .'

He nuzzled his damp face against her neck and Kitty felt a surge of emotion sweep over her. She went on soothing him and gradually the howling became a hiccuping cry again. Then it tailed off altogether. Now she cradled the child. He blinked away a tear and a slow smile spread over his plump little face then he pushed a fist playfully against her mouth; she kissed it and he gave a gurgling laugh.

There was a rug under the tree and Kitty sat down on it and hugged the child to her. How could she have blamed him for his mother's sins? She was holding him so tightly he began to rebel and she laughed at his grunts and attempts to get free. 'Oh, I love you, love you!' she said.

'Well, thank goodness for that!' said a voice from behind her. It was Ivy. 'We've thought of all ways of getting you two together; we knew you would love him when you did meet. This was Mrs Helder's idea.'

Ivy dropped to her knees beside Kitty. 'She's grieved about you and Tyler. You're daft, you know, Kitty – you're wasting your life when you could be together, a lovely little family. Your husband wants to adopt him properly, have him christened. We call him Johnnie, but it's just a nickname really. How about it?'

The baby was tugging at a gold brooch Kitty had pinned at the neck of her dress and was getting cross because he was unable to get it free. 'Hey, young Richard,' she teased, 'you behave yourself. I see I'm going to have trouble keeping you in hand.'

Ivy grinned. 'So he's not only named, but the story looks like having a happy ending.'

'Named?' Kitty queried, then realized she had given him her father's name. 'I hope it does have a happy ending,' she said smiling. 'I'll talk to Tyler this evening.'

It was late when she went to his room. He was in his dressing-gown and had been reading. When she knocked and went in he jumped up, the book slipping to the floor. 'Kitty! What's wrong?'

'A lot has been wrong, Tyler, which I hope to put right,' she said quietly. 'I held our son today and he won me over.'

Tyler's expression was a mixture of hope and uncertainty. 'Are you sure, Kitty? You'll have no regrets, no thoughts that I might be his—'

'None whatsoever,' she said firmly. Tyler gave a shout of exultation and sweeping her up in his arms, strode to the room they had shared. Kitty thrilled to his mastery, realizing just how much she had missed it.

At first their love-making was as wild and tempestuous as on their earlier reconciliation, but when the throbbing in Kitty's body was beginning to reach the point which she thought of as a step beyond supreme ecstasy, an image of Luke suddenly intruded. The image was so vivid she could almost feel his presence. Kitty dug her nails into Tyler's back and he, taking it as uncontrolled passion, reached fulfilment. When he rolled away he drew her to him and whispered, 'The best yet, my darling, the best ever!'

Several nights of love-making followed, but when Kitty found she was pregnant she had a feeling it was on this night that she had conceived. And when, nine months later, she was delivered of a baby daughter with copper-coloured hair and what seemed to be Luke's eyes, she was alarmed. Was it possible that by conjuring up another man's image rather than that of one's husband during lovemaking, the child could inherit this person's characteristics?

Tyler was delighted with his new daughter and intrigued over the copper-coloured hair, saying that as far as he knew no one in his family had this colouring. Kitty suggested the baby might be a 'Tierne' and this was accepted. They decided on the name Julietta, after Tyler's mother. Mrs Helder was delighted to be asked to be godmother; Mr Freeman was to stand as god-father.

Julietta turned out to be a quiet, dreaming girl, a contrast to the robust Richard who was in and out of scrapes. Although Tyler was the one who disciplined him, Richard adored him and would follow him whenever the chance came.

Kitty loved both children equally, but was irked that so many women in the house shared them. Martha, who had come as wet-nurse to Richard the night he was found, had stayed and was now nanny to both children. And it was to Martha that Richard ran if he was in trouble. Eventually there came a time when Kitty longed to go back to glass-making, but when she suggested this to Tyler he said definitely not – she was now a mother and wife and had responsibilities. Kitty did point out that she was not allowed responsibilities, since Martha had the main say about the children's welfare.

At this Tyler became angry. 'It's up to you, Kitty, to assert yourself as their mother and I don't want to hear any more about your doing glass-making.'

Kitty was fuming and decided that the Women's Suffrage

Movement certainly had a good case. Not that she wanted to join them, but she agreed that women had a right to be accepted in business as men's equals.

Determined not to be beaten, Kitty brought this up several times, which caused quarrels and a coolness between them. They still made love, but for Kitty it was a duty and she was quite sure that for Tyler it was only a need. His side of the business had flourished right from the beginning, but there came a time when he was inundated with orders for optical and medical glass – many for foreign countries – and although he would invariably keep dinner appointments, there were other times when Kitty hardly saw him.

And it was then she decided she would go to the furnace room during the afternoons when the children were resting. Both Mrs Helder and Ivy, when told, tried to dissuade her but Kitty was adamant.

'I need to be occupied, need to create something.'

Ivy teased her, saying she had created a bonny little lass as ever was. Create a few more like her and she wouldn't need to go glass-making!

Mrs Helder said, 'I understand your need, Kitty, but be prepared to face the consequences when Tyler finds out – and he will.'

Kitty said she would risk it.

And so she went to work with William, Thomas and Ben, who accepted her return as though there had never been a break. During her pregnancy Kitty had read a great deal, including many of Tyler's books, and was surprised to realize just how much she had absorbed. This helped her when she came back to glass-making and she astonished herself by the standard of work she turned out, especially her peacock glass. Thomas said the master ought to see it and Kitty begged him not to say anything – not yet, not until she had made more.

She knew there would come a time when she had to tell Tyler, but it came sooner than she expected. Mr Freeman often dined with them and in turn they dined at his house. One evening when they were having dinner with him, and after a discussion about the unrest in the world, they got on to their usual topic of glass – this time optical glass – and Tyler said he felt he would like to enlarge his laboratory for further experiments.

Kitty asked, 'Is this necessary? After all, Otto Schott made excellent melt samples in a primitive basement and won Abbe's praise.'

There was a sudden silence and because of Tyler's and Mr Freeman's surprised gaze on her, Kitty flushed. 'I'm sorry,' she said. 'I'm really not experienced enough to pass such an opinion, it was just something I read which impressed me.'

'And *you* impress me, Mrs van Neilson,' Mr Freeman said. 'You always have done so with your knowledge of current affairs; it's such a delight to talk to an intelligent woman. Most times when I am invited out, I find myself seated next to a lady who prattles on about her social life, whom she's met and about her luck in finding an excellent cook. Do go on – what else do you know about Schott's life?'

Kitty glanced at Tyler and when he gave her a brief nod, she told of what she had read, concluding, 'And I understand that his work has remained the very essense of glass manufacture today.'

Mr Freeman nodded, 'So it has,' and then went on to talk about just how much Schott had achieved. Until he was approached, it had been difficult to make a thermometer with the right temperature. Berlin had asked for his help.

From there the talk progressed to Abbe deeding the Carl Zeiss works to the foundation in 1891 and Kitty, who had read for increased knowledge, now found herself becoming more and more interested in optical glass and was able for the first time to understand Tyler's dedication to it.

Then right out of the blue, Mr Freeman asked Kitty if she had done anything further about her idea for peacock glass. After a slight pause she replied, 'Yes, I have, but my husband doesn't know about it.' She smiled. 'We shall have to discuss it on the way home. Did you get the Egyptian bowl you hoped to buy, Mr Freeman?'

Kitty knew it was taking Tyler all his time to keep his temper under control and was not surprised when he exploded once they were in the carriage on their way home. How dare she make such a statement in front of Mr Freeman? It was as bad as being told he had been cuckolded.

'Nonsense!' Kitty said. 'Mr Freeman is an understanding man. I would have told you eventually, he was simply the means of bringing it out sooner. And you should be pleased I was able to talk about experimenting. I would not have been reading about it had I not been pregnant.'

'And how is your *reading* knowledge going to help me?'

Kitty turned to him and said quietly, 'I don't know yet, but I think there is a purpose for everything we do. It's no use you being angry, Tyler – just be pleased that I do have something else to talk about in company other than my social life and domestic affairs.'

'Humph,' he said, but his anger had died and that evening when they made love Kitty felt there was more feeling in it.

CHAPTER TWENTY-THREE

During the next few years Kitty had the feeling of being completely detached from her family. She hardly saw Tyler; if he was not abroad, he was at the glasshouse. When she sold her first batch of peacock glass he said, 'Oh, how interesting for you, Kitty. Did I tell you we would be entertaining two professors from France next week?'

At times Kitty even felt the children did not belong to her. Mrs Helder, who seemed to have taken on a new lease of life since the birth of Julietta, was never happier than when having the child with her. Richard was Ivy's favourite and she would enter into his boyish escapades, but Tyler was still the boy's god.

Yet in spite of feeling detached from her family, Kitty still felt close to the farm. There were times when she longed to see Abel and Luke, especially Luke. It was mostly Louise who wrote to Kitty and she had said in her last letter that she had a feeling she might be pregnant, but there had been several false alarms. Both she and Luke were longing for a child. That day Kitty looked at Julietta sitting on the lawn with a doll in her arms, day-dreaming, and felt guilty that she had allowed her life to be dedicated more to the world of glass than to her children. She made excuses to herself for this: it would have been wrong to make a great fuss of Julietta when she thought of her as 'Luke's' child; as for Richard, she still thought of him, deep down, as having Violet for a mother. Nothing had been heard of Violet since that night. All her sisters were married now and each had a child. Ann was always wanting to know when Kitty was coming to see them and Jessica asked the same thing; she wrote about every two months and Kitty always replied by return. Kitty did wish she could see Jessica, she had been such a good friend.

Although Kitty was always interested in her work, there were times when she felt she was living in a backwater. A visit to Italy remained a dream and she had not yet even visited London. She needed something different to happen.

Something did happen, but it was not what she would have wished. On a beautiful day in June, Tyler burst in and announced that the Archduke Ferdinand of Austria had been assassinated by a Serbian and that the Archduke's morganatic wife had also been shot dead.

'This will mean war,' he said. 'It's been boiling up to it.'

Kitty went cold, remembering the Boer War when Abel and Harriet lost three sons. 'But surely England won't be involved?' she said.

Tyler told her it was possible and events proved it. Austria demanded such heavy compensation from Serbia that Serbia refused to pay. And from then on the ripples in the pond began to widen in ever-increasing circles. Austria, supported by Russia, declared war; Russia joined in on the side of Serbia; France, the sworn ally of Russia, became involved and two days later England declared war on Germany to uphold her written obligation to support Belgium now overrun by Germany.

When Tyler said he was going to enlist, Kitty panicked. Surely it was unnecessary, there were plenty of younger men who could go? Tyler said that they would want men of all ages and there was a light of adventure in his eyes which she had seen in the eyes of all men she had known who had volunteered during the Boer War.

Talk of war was on everybody's lips. Ivy, who was still being courted by Thomas but had refused to marry him, said, 'Perhaps I am daft not to get married. If Thomas volunteers and gets killed, I'm going to regret it. Better to be a widow than to die a spinster.'

Kitty knew this was not so callous as it sounded. Ivy had told her once that although she was fond of Thomas, very fond indeed, it would not be fair to marry him because she was not in love with him.

Men all over the country were rushing to volunteer and many of the younger ones left the glasshouse, this at a time when a spate of orders was being received for lenses, microscopes, field-glasses, telescopes for the Navy . . . Tyler, still determined to enlist, said women would have to be trained to replace the men. Claude Freeman had offered to take over the management and Tyler suggested that Kitty could assist. This was her opportunity. Kitty was furious that Tyler had been against the Suffrage Movement until *he* wanted to be free to go to war. When she accused him of being selfish, he accused her of having no loyalty towards her country. She should be pleased and proud that her husband wanted to enlist, he said. Relationships became strained between them.

In September the battle of the Marne began and people were shocked at the high casualty list that was published every day. In December a Zeppelin dropped bombs on the East Coast and later at Dover, and those who had been convinced the war would be over by Christmas were beginning to change their minds.

It was after the bombing on Dover that Tyler went to enlist. He returned in the uniform of a Captain some weeks later, with two days to spend at home before being shipped to France.

Kitty, who thought she had talked him out of volunteering, felt in a state of numbness for those two days, especially as Tyler gave her instructions about carrying on the business should anything happen to him.

'You're capable, Kitty, you'll be able to cope.'

She stared at him. 'How can you talk in such a cold-blooded way?'

'I have to, Kitty, don't you see? If I allowed myself to be emotional, I wouldn't want to go. But it's something I have to do. *Please* try to understand.'

But Kitty refused to understand. It was firmly fixed in her mind that all he wanted to do was to be free of responsibilities. She had heard men talking and laughing about how good it would be to be 'free of the missus and kids' for a bit.

Tyler made love to her on their last night, but Kitty was unresponsive and the next morning they parted without any show of emotion. It was Mrs Helder who wept. Julietta was too young to understand what it was all about and to Richard it was a glorious thing for his daddy to be a soldier; he strutted about with a wooden gun and sword.

It was not until the early months of 1915 when the Germans started to use flame-throwers setting soldiers alight and later to drop poison gas, blinding and killing men, that Kitty began to realize the full horror of war. Then she was ashamed of the way she had treated Tyler.

He was 'somewhere' in France, and his letters said very little. He asked about the business, about how she was managing and about the children; he sent his love, but mentioned nothing about himself apart from the fact that he was well.

She began to write him more loving letters, as well as telling him how they had managed to employ some older, experienced men and were training women and girls who were proving to be surprisingly adaptable. She concluded, 'I send you all my love, Tyler darling, and kisses and hugs from the children. Pray God this war will soon be over and He will send you safely home to us.'

Kitty had written to the farm telling them about Tyler joining up, and Louise wrote back to say that Luke was wanting to enlist but as she was pregnant he felt he must stay and see their child born. 'Whether he will change his mind or not,' she said, 'I don't know. I would have thought he would have had enough of war to last him a lifetime fighting against the Boers. But I suppose it's something inbred in men to fight for their country – and of course for all the people they hold dear. Would we want it any other way? Luke is looking extremely well at the moment and much younger than his years. Abel is beginning to age lately, but he still works as hard. He's such a good man. He still grieves over Harriet, I know, but never makes heavy weather of it. I have a great love for him.'

Kitty was surprised to feel a twinge of jealousy. Was it because of Louise having Luke's baby, or speaking of her love for Abel? She knew she was being childish, but she wanted to be the important one in Abel's and Luke's lives.

News of the war became worse and worse. Lord Kitchener sent out a personal appeal to British manhood to form 'New Armies', and this produced over a million recruits. Thomas was one of those to respond and Ivy then decided they would get married. Twenty-four hours later, Thomas left for the battlefield and Ivy, dry-eyed, said, 'I love that feller, I really do, I wonder why I didn't realize it before.'

The months went by and the casualty list of soldiers and naval men kept rising. When Kitty was without a letter from Tyler for a long spell, she would be in a fever of suspense. Had he been wounded, killed? Then a letter would come and she felt she could breathe again.

In January of the following year Kitty had a letter from Abel to say that Louise had died giving birth to a son; the baby had died a few hours afterwards.

Kitty sat, shocked, hating herself that she had been jealous of Louise. She thought of Luke, of Abel – two men bereft – and made up her mind she must go to them. She had been helping with the accounts at the glasshouse, but when she told Claude Freeman her news he said of course she must go, they would manage.

Ivy helped her to pack and Mrs Helder assured her the children would be all right; she was not to worry on that score, but stay as long as she wished. Julietta gave her a hug and a wet kiss, while Richard wriggled away from her embrace, saying that Ben was going to show him how to fly a kite.

There had been little work done at the furnace room recently. When they did produce anything, it was at Kitty's insistence. But at this moment, making glass was the last thing in her mind.

Abel's brother met her at Leicester station in his new motor car. 'It's a sad day, Kitty,' he said. 'I'm glad you've come. Both Abel and Luke need you. I don't know what's going to happen. I reckon Luke will join up. But that would mean Abel having to manage on his own and – well – I don't know . . . we'll have to see how things turn out. The news of the war is bad enough. Five more men from the village have been killed, three taken prisoner and another ten wounded.'

There had been a light fall of snow and in the purity of the country side Kitty found it hard to imagine the wholesale slaughter on a battlefield.

Both Abel and Luke had a grey, defeated look. They each held Kitty wordlessly for a moment, then Luke said, 'Thanks for coming, Kitty, it does help.'

Abel had delayed writing to Kitty and the funeral was to be the next day. With visitors coming in all the time and Abel's brother and his wife staying at the farm, there was no time for private talk with Abel or Luke. 'Afterwards,' Luke said.

The most tragic moments for Kitty were when she saw the tiny white coffin next to that of Louise and when Luke broke down for the first time at the graveside. It was she who led him away. 'Why?' he asked, on a sob, and Kitty had no answer.

That evening while people were still there, Luke got up, held out his hand to Kitty and said, 'Let's walk.'

It was a bright moonlight night with a cold wind that put a frost on the layer of snow. As usual, they made for the top of the rise. Luke said, unexpectedly, 'Do you remember the first dance dress you had, Kitty? It was white. There was a dance in somebody's barn. It was a night like this. You were so happy, so was I. We waltzed and we danced a polka. Mother and Dad danced too; they were like young lovers.' Luke's voice suddenly broke again. 'Oh, Kitty, forgive me, I'm trying to think desperately of all the happiness and forget that Louise . . . I blame myself for her death.'

'You can't, Luke, you mustn't! We aren't the ones who decide our fate.'

'Louise had had *three* miscarriages, Kitty, and although the doctor told her she was well enough to have another child I ought not to have allowed it.'

'She *wanted* a baby, Luke, she was *longing* for one. You couldn't have denied her that right. Your aunt told me she was overjoyed she had given you a son. That must be some compensation to you.'

Luke made no reply and Kitty guessed he was unable to speak. His grief was almost a tangible thing.

When Luke was calmer they walked on and he talked about his future. He wanted to enlist, he said, but could not leave his father to cope alone. There was also the fact that the country needed all the farm produce it could get. Luke then asked Kitty about her husband, about her children. She told him that Tyler was in France and was about to tell him about Julietta resembling Luke himself, but stopped herself in time and began to talk about Richard; Luke knew he was a foundling they had adopted, but did not know he was Violet's child. She made news of the children brief and told him about having women employed in the glasshouse.

There was a short silence, then Kitty stopped abruptly and turned to him.

'Luke, why don't you and Uncle Abel come and stay with us, even if it's just for a few days? It would help you get over the worst and you have plenty of neighbours and relatives who would see to the farm.'

'It's kind of you to offer, Kitty, and it's tempting . . . but I don't know. I don't think Dad would leave. We can ask him.'

But Abel when asked, shook his head. 'I couldn't leave here, Kitty love, I'm too set in my ways. The drive to market is about as much travelling as I want to do. But Luke can go, I'd be pleased for him to. I can get help, I'll be all right.'

Luke promised he would think about it, but it was not until the day Kitty was leaving that he said he would take her up on her offer. He would welcome the change and would like to meet her children. It would give him a couple of weeks to sort things out.

Kitty saw a difference in him then; he had lost the dreadful despairing look and seemed to see some future ahead without Louise. Abel looked better too and had talked the night before to some of his farmer friends. It made the parting easier for all of them and on the journey home Kitty had almost a joyous feeling. For the first time she would have Luke all to herself. She would show him around, take him to the furnace room, show him her work, take him for walks. She let her thoughts carry her further. Deep down she knew she wanted Luke to make love to her, just once, to satisfy a need that had been with her for so long – and with Luke too, she was sure. Was it so wrong? Although Kitty did have a feeling of guilt at such thoughts, she pushed it to the back of her mind; it would only be that once, no more.

When Kitty arrived home Mrs Helder said, 'The children tried so desperately to keep awake to see you, but sleep overtook them.'

Ivy laughed. 'Young Richard was like a tetchy old man while you've been away, wanting to know ten times a day when you would be back.'

Kitty felt moved by this and would have gone upstairs to take a peep at them had not Mrs Helder handed her a letter from Tyler, saying it had come the day before. Kitty tore it open; she had not heard from him for three weeks.

Tyler wrote that he was going to get leave, he couldn't wait to come home and see them all. It would be wonderful to enjoy the peace of the countryside. This was the first time he had mentioned the war. Last week when Kitty met a man from the village who had come home wounded, he had said the worst thing was the constant thunder of guns. Tyler said what a godsend Kitty's letters were, and that he was pleased to know all was going well at the glasshouse. He added a little touch of humour in saying that perhaps he had been wrong about the cause of the suffragettes, for he had an excellent woman driver! He concluded: 'I can't wait to hold you in my arms, my darling. Kiss the children for me, tell them I'll be with them soon. Love to Marguerite and kindest regards to Ivy and the Parkers.'

Kitty would not let herself think about Luke's visit then. She told Mrs Helder and Ivy all the tragic news from the farm and by then she was ready to drop into bed where she fell into an exhausted sleep. She awoke late and could hear the shouts of the children outside, so she got up, dressed, ran downstairs and went straight into the garden. It was Julietta she saw first – standing facing her, a few feet away, her whole concentration in the ball she was throwing into the air. And Kitty felt a sudden shock when she looked at the delicately boned face of her daughter and realized she was not like Luke at all. Her hair was darker than Luke's and she had Tyler's eyes. Then Julietta, seeing her, ran to her with arms held out, her face beaming. 'Mama! I've been good, very good.'

Kitty hugged her. Then Richard was yelling and running towards her. 'Mama, Mama, you're back!' He flung his arms around her legs. 'Why did you stay away so long? Come and see me fly my kite.'

For the next few minutes Kitty could hardly speak for the lump in her throat. She watched the red paper kite twisting and turning and when it came to earth Richard dropped the string and came running back to her. 'Ben's going to make a bigger one, Julietta can have that one.' Kitty was on her knees and he leaned against her, was silent for a moment and then said:

'I didn't let that lady take me away yesterday, Mama. I told her that my Daddy had gone to war and I had to stay and look after you.'

Kitty felt that all the colour was draining from her face. She forced herself to ask calmly, 'What lady, Richard?'

'The one who came yesterday. She wanted me to go with her; she started to drag me away and I kicked her. Then Mrs Parker came out and got hold of me and sent me to find Grandmother. I don't know any more after that. Oh! There's Ben, he's got me a bigger kite!' Richard was away, with Julietta toddling after him shouting, 'Ben, Ben . . .'

Kitty got up and walked, as though in a nightmare, into the house. And there she met Mrs Parker in the hall.

'Who was the woman who came yesterday, Mrs Parker, and tried to take Richard away?'

'Your sister, ma'am, the one who came in widow's weeds about six years ago. Mrs Helder said you were not to be told until you were settled back home again. I sent the lady packing, ma'am – if you would care to come into the kitchen, I'll tell you about it.'

Kitty felt as though her legs would hardly hold her. Violet! After all these years. Would she ever be free of her torment?

Mrs Parker pulled up a chair, poured Kitty a cup of tea and handed it to her. 'I've just made it, ma'am.'

After Kitty had taken a drink she said, 'I feel a little better, Mrs Parker. Tell me what happened.'

'Well, ma'am, I saw this lady yesterday morning trying to drag Master Richard away. He was shouting and saying he couldn't go, he had to look after you. I ran to her and asked her what she thought she was doing. She told me that Richard was her son and she wanted him back. I got the lad away from her and told him to go straight to Mrs Helder and stay there, and he ran off. She was hopping mad, told me to stop interfering or else – I told her I had every right to interfere when she was trying to steal the child of my employers. Then she went quiet, sort of horribly quiet. She said the boy was her flesh and blood, that she was married now, she wanted him and was going to have him and no one would stop her.'

Kitty's heart, which had steadied, began a quick beating again.

'And what did you say to that, Mrs Parker?'

'I told her she must be out of her mind. I said I had been with you during the nine months you had carried the baby and I had seen it being born!'

Kitty felt laughter trembling in her stomach. Who would have thought the expressionless housekeeper capable of such a thing?

'You didn't, Mrs Parker!' she said.

Mrs Parker gave a quick nod. 'I did! She said all right, so what happened to the baby she had left on the doorstep? I said, "Oh, *that* one." My sister and her husband adopted it, they had wanted a baby for years. I told her they had emigrated to Australia and I had letters to prove it.'

'Did your sister adopt a child?' Kitty asked.

'No, I haven't got a sister, but she wasn't to know that, was she? And to stop her causing any more trouble, I told her that if she ever tried to find them I would go to court and tell the judge how she had left her baby to freeze to death on a doorstep. That fixed her! I don't think you'll have any more trouble with her, ma'am.'

Kitty began to laugh. 'Oh, Mrs Parker, you're wonderful!' She gave the housekeeper a hug. 'What an imagination you've got, you should be writing books!'

Mrs Parker's sallow cheeks flushed at the praise. 'Well, it's like this, ma'am; you and the master have been good to me and my girls, I felt it was the least I could do.' Then after a pause she added, a slow smile spreading over her face, 'To be truthful, ma'am, I rather enjoyed it – lightened things up a bit.'

Kitty said softly, 'My husband and I will be eternally grateful to you, Mrs Parker. My sister has been a thorn in my flesh since I was a child. I don't think we'll be bothered by her any more.'

When Kitty went up to see Mrs Helder, the old lady said, 'I couldn't tell you about it, not after your long journey. Mrs Parker behaved wonderfully. Thank goodness she was there!'

'Yes, indeed, we never know what people are capable of, do we? Do we know ourselves?'

Mrs Helder looked thoughtful. 'I think we learn a little more about ourselves, Kitty, each time we have a crisis in our lives.'

Kitty found herself agreeing with this. She felt she had gone through a crisis this morning, that the loyalty of a member of her staff had made her aware of a flaw in herself. Her husband was away fighting for his country and she had been looking forward to sleeping with Luke! Something that Luke might never have contemplated. It was all in her mind, what she *wanted* to think, just as she had convinced herself that Julietta resembled Luke. She must stop him from coming, make some excuse.

As it turned out, it was Luke who made the move. He wrote to say that much as he would have liked to visit Kitty's home and meet the children, he felt he could not leave his father: 'he puts a brave face on it, Kitty, but he's heartbroken. He was very fond of Louise and still mourns Mother. Perhaps in the future, when this wretched war is over and we can all meet . . .' There was more, but it was the first part of the letter that was important.

This strengthened Kitty. From now on she would give more time to her children, but she would still make glass – it was necessary to keep her mind occupied.

Ivy had word from Thomas to say he would be coming home on leave and she was full of joy, titivating herself up. 'He's lovely and funny,' she said, 'when you get to know him. He can have me screaming with laughter!'

But it was a different Thomas who came on leave from the man who had left for the front. He had left, like all of them, with an eagerness to share in the adventure . . . and returned sombre-faced, with saddened eyes. He said, 'I'll only say this about the war, then I don't want it mentioned again. It's hell, it's horror, it's mutilation and mud. Even when I sleep, I can hear the pounding of the bombardment in my head.'

'Right,' Ivy replied. 'I don't want to hear talk of it either, we're going to have the honeymoon we never had. I've saved up for it. We'll go to Newcastle, get board and lodgings for a few days, go to the music hall, laugh our heads off at the comics, yell all the choruses of the songs – and don't say no, we're *going* to do it! It's what you need, what we *both* need!'

Ivy suddenly flung her arms about Thomas and burst into tears. Kitty felt choked; she wanted Tyler home, but there had been no more word since the letter saying he was hoping for leave. Mrs Helder kept saying that no news was good news, that letters went astray in war-time and ships carrying mail could have been sunk. If anything had happened to Tyler, she would have heard from the War Office.

But it only needed Richard to ask plaintively why *his* daddy was not home on leave for Kitty to have to fight back tears. Fortunately, Richard became absorbed in flying a kite, so absorbed that nothing else was of any importance. Julietta was his slave, fetching and carrying for him – that is, until the day when he told her to go and play by herself. She did so and when after a while he began to give her orders again to bring him this and that, she told him to do it himself.

Kitty laughed. Ivy said, 'Good for her! She's got a will of her own.' Julietta stayed apart from Richard until one day he grudgingly asked her to help him to untangle the string of his kite. She gave in then, but, said Mrs Helder, with the air of a duchess conferring an honour on one of her minions.

Both children were a delight to everyone in the house and Kitty longed for the war to be over so that Tyler would not miss all their early years and development.

When Kitty was not with the children, she divided her days between doing the accounts at the glasshouse and working in the furnace room. For two weeks she turned out some excellent work, then she became suddenly restless. There were nights when she would wake herself up moaning, without knowing why – there had been no dreams. But one night she had a nightmare when a huge glass bubble exploded and as fragments flew all over the place she could see Tyler's face, distorted, blood streaming from wounds.

She woke Ivy with her screaming and Ivy held her. 'It's all right, Kitty, you've had a bad dream.'

'It's Tyler,' Kitty whispered. 'Something's happened to him, I know it.'

The following morning, there was word from the War Office to say he was missing.

Kitty, dry-eyed, handed the message to Mrs Helder. 'They might just as well have added "believed killed" . . .'

The old lady looked up. 'No, Kitty, it's more likely Tyler has been taken prisoner. You mustn't give up hope, you mustn't! You have the children to think about.'

'Yes,' she said, 'I have the children to think about.'

For the next few days Kitty went about doing everything mechanically; she played with the children, did jobs, ate. There was no pain then, nothing. Then one evening when the children were ready for bed and Kitty lifted Julietta on to her lap to tell her a story, Richard came over and stood leaning against her knee. Normally he sat on the other side of the room, playing with toys, not wanting to be associated with 'baby' stories.

Kitty said, 'Well, shall we begin our story? Tonight it's about—'

Richard put a finger on her lips and asked, 'Mama, do you love us?'

The question startled Kitty out of her apathy. 'Why, yes, Richard, of course I do. I love you both very much, why do you ask?'

'I don't know,' he said, his tone piteous. He moved away and crossing the room, sat in a corner with such a desolation about him that it made Kitty catch her breath. What had she done? Had she been so wrapped up in her own grief that she had shut her children out? Julietta was too young to understand atmosphere, but Richard was old enough to be aware of it. She had underestimated his intelligence, his sensitivity.

Julietta's lids were drooping, so Kitty took her to bed and then came back to Richard. She held out a hand to him. 'Come and sit down, darling. I have something to tell you about Daddy.'

Kitty tried to simplify the situation, giving half-truths instead of destroying his father's image. She explained, 'Daddy has been involved in a great deal of fighting. There are many, many places where fighting is taking place, with thousands of men involved. This causes confusion. Sometimes it seems that men are missing, then they will turn up again. This, I think, is what has happened to Daddy. He's lost at the moment, but we must go on hoping and praying that he'll be home with us soon.'

'Oh, Daddy won't get lost,' Richard said. 'He's too clever for that. He could kill all the enemy soldiers on his own . . . couldn't he?'

The uncertainty in his voice told Kitty that the seeds had been sown. Perhaps in time he could come to accept that although all men who went to war were not heroes, they were all brave men.

That night in bed Kitty wept, releasing the rest of her tension. And afterwards she told herself she could at least hope; there were many women who were denied that solace.

But in spite of this the next few weeks were not easy; there were times when depression would swamp her, and it was only by convincing herself that Tyler would appear one day that lifted her spirits. After all, some prisoners of war were being exchanged between England and Germany.

But the weeks, the months went by and the news became

more and more depressing. Nobody talked any longer of the war soon being over. But worse was still to come. The battle of the Somme raged for five months, entire battalions of men being slaughtered. Young boys, many of them lying about their ages, rushed to enlist. A journalist described these men and boys as 'cannon fodder'. There were few homes that were not mourning some relative.

One day when Kitty went to the furnace room, Ben told her he had lost two brothers and three cousins, word of their deaths all arriving on the same day. Kitty felt anger growing in her until it consumed her. 'All people who start wars,' she declared, 'should face one another on a battlefield and fight to the death.'

That day she made a tortured glass figure of a boy – the body embedded with shards of broken grey glass. William said quietly, 'Destroy it, ma'am, or it'll destroy you.'

Kitty hesitated, then she raised it above her hand ready to let it crash to the ground but Ben stayed her hand.

'No, don't, ma'am. Keep it to remind people of the horrors of war. I didn't want to go, I was frightened. But now I'm going to enlist. I'm going to take the place of one of my brothers – this war has to be won. Make more figures like this, let more people see them.'

Kitty looked at Ben's round, smooth face. Yesterday he had seemed the boy he was; today he was an adult.

'Oh, Ben,' she said despairingly and turned away, her hope dying.

Kitty did make more figures – boys' distorted figures, none of them whole. William kept begging her to stop, to destroy what she had made, for they would warp her mind, but she went on in a feverish way.

Then one day when Kitty looked at the twisted figure of an eyeless, bloodstained soldier she had made, she shuddered, realizing she had lost all sense of beauty. So she made the figure of a young girl, her skirt swirling, her head up, a joyousness in her, and this took all the anger out of her.

There were still soldiers coming home to their wives, to parents; there were young people falling in love. There was beauty in a sunrise, in a sunset, in a field of waving corn. If one lost beauty, life would not be worth living.

338

As though reading her mind, there was a letter from Luke the following day:

> Dad and I were talking about you last night, Kitty, when we walked to the top field, remembering how enchanted you were when you first came to us with the animals, a leaf, a flower. We have two little boys living with us now, their father was killed on the Somme and their mother died a week later. They're from Newcastle. They're lovely little fellows, a bit bewildered at first, but finding the pleasure of the countryside. No one wants them, so Dad is aiming to adopt them; his niece Nellie dotes on them. They've given both of us a new lease of life.

There was more about neighbours and friends, then Luke concluded, 'I hope you hear soon about your husband, Kitty, I know your courage will sustain you. Write soon. Love from both of us.'

From that day Kitty spent more time at the glasshouse, where they were working at full pitch to help the war effort. Sometimes on the way back she would call at the furnace house and talk to Wiliam, work a little.

On a late August evening she left, feeling utterly weary and for once unable to appreciate the lovely sunset. What was her life to be in future? Making glass, without enthusiasm?

When she came out into the clearing she saw a figure outlined against the sunset, but was unable to make out who it was. She shielded her eyes, could see that it was a man, a man who limped. As he came nearer she saw he was a stranger, with stubble on his chin. A vagrant? He was wearing odd clothes.

He was close now and Kitty stopped, and her heart became a wild thing. Tyler . . . ?

A smile spread over the gaunt face, then he was limping quickly towards her. He threw down his stick and they were in one another's arms, weeping.

The first words they spoke were, 'Oh, Tyler . . .' and 'Oh, Kitty!' Then they were laughing through their tears, rocking to and fro.

'Tyler, what happened, where were you?'

'I was taken prisoner. I tried to escape twice, but was caught. I couldn't believe it when I heard we were to be repatriated.'

'You were limping, were you wounded?'

'In the leg. There's still some shrapnel in it, but I have both arms and oh, my sweet Kitty, am I going to hold you tight! I'll hug you to death.'

'What a lovely way to die, Tyler,' she said laughing, her voice breaking. 'I can't believe you're here. Have you been home, have you seen the children?'

'No, I wanted to get tidied up, shaved and changed first. I thought William might be able to help me out and then – there you were!'

Tyler cupped her cheeks between his palms, his eyes searching her face. 'Your image, my darling, was all that kept me going.' He drew her fiercely to him. 'I never want to let you out of my sight again.' They kissed passionately, Tyler's stubble chafing Kitty's face, but it was sweet pain.

He drew away. 'Tell me, how are the children? How is Marguerite, Ivy? And what about William, Thomas and Ben?'

'Our son tries hard to be boss but he's met his match in his small sister. Marguerite is very well. She – oh, Tyler, I'll tell you about everyone later! I want at this moment for the two of us to enjoy this lovely quiet!'

They went back into the forest, their arms around one another's waists, the only sounds being the cheeping of birds settling to roost.

And it seemed to Kitty then as though the long parting from Tyler had never been. Another Yesterday's Road was behind them.